T0085988

ALSO BY KATEE ROBERT

Dark Olympus
Neon Gods
Electric Idol

WICKED BEAUTY

KATEE ROBERT

sourcebooks
casablanca

Published by Sourcebooks Casablanca, an imprint of Sourcebooks
P.O. Box 4410, Naperville, Illinois 60567–4410
(630) 961-3900
sourcebooks.com

Cataloging-in-Publication Data is on file with the Library of Congress.

Printed and bound in the United States of America.
LSC 10

To everyone who prefers happily ever afters to tragedies.

THE RULING FAMILIES OF
Olympus

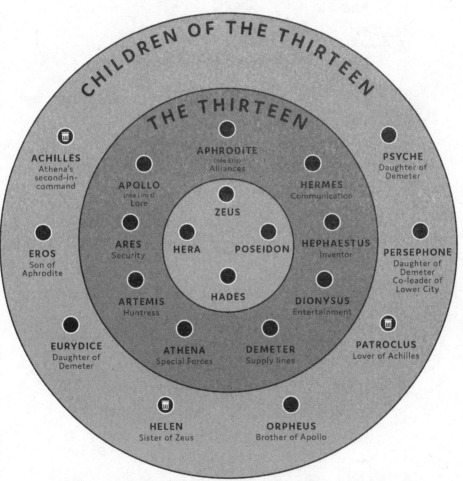

CHILDREN OF THE THIRTEEN

THE THIRTEEN

ZEUS

HERA **POSEIDON**

HADES

APHRODITE
(née Eris)
Alliances

APOLLO
(née Linus)
Lore

HERMES
Communication

ARES
Security

HEPHAESTUS
Inventor

ARTEMIS
Huntress

DIONYSUS
Entertainment

ATHENA
Special Forces

DEMETER
Supply lines

ACHILLES
Athena's
second-in-
command

PSYCHE
Daughter of
Demeter

EROS
Son of
Aphrodite

PERSEPHONE
Daughter of
Demeter
Co-leader of
Lower City

EURYDICE
Daughter of
Demeter

PATROCLUS
Lover of Achilles

HELEN
Sister of Zeus

ORPHEUS
Brother of Apollo

THE INNER CIRCLE
HADES: Leader of Lower City
HERA: (née Callisto) Spouse of ruling Zeus, protector of women
POSEIDON: Leader of Port to Outside World, Import/Export
ZEUS: (née Perseus) Leader of Upper City and the Thirteen

Olympus

upper city

University

HEPHAESTUS

POSEIDON

DEMETER

Agriculture District

Shipping Yard

ARTEMIS

EROS

APOLLO

ATHENA

APHRODITE

Dodona Tower

Hellebore Bridge

ARES

ZEUS

Upper Warehouse District

DIONYSUS

Cypress Bridge

Winter Market

HERMES

RIVER STYX

Juniper Bridge

HADES

Summer Market

lower city

JULIETTE

Lower Warehouse District

HELEN

"I AM SO FUCKING LATE," I MUTTER UNDER MY BREATH. THE hallways of Dodona Tower are blessedly empty, but that only makes the clock ticking down inside my head worse. Tonight is the night everything changes. The night when I stop being a pawn in other people's games and finally gain the agency I've craved ever since I was a little girl.

And I can't believe I'm fucking *late*.

I pick up my pace, barely managing to resist the urge to run. Showing up out of breath and flustered to an Olympus party is even worse than showing up late. Appearances matter. It's been a long time since Olympus experienced anything resembling traditional warfare, but every day, little battles are fought and won using the most mundane things.

A carefully designed dress.

A sweet word hiding a poisonous sting.

A marriage.

I duck into the elevator that will take me up to the ballroom floor and barely resist the urge to bounce on my toes with impatience. Normally, I wouldn't give a damn about any of this. I make petty rebellions an art form.

Tonight is different.

Tonight, my brother Perseus—Zeus, now—is making an announcement that will change everything.

Less than a week ago, Ares passed away. It was hardly unexpected—the man was old as dirt and had been knocking on the doors to the underworld for three months—but it's opened up an opportunity that's usually only seen once a generation. Of the Thirteen, Ares alone is open to absolutely anyone. A person's history, connections, finances don't matter. You don't even have to be Olympian.

You simply have to win.

Three trials, all designed to cull the wheat from the chaff, and the last person standing steps up to become Ares. One of the thirteen people who create the ruling body in Olympus. Each handles a specific part of keeping the city running smoothly, but more importantly to me, no one can compel any of them to take an action they don't want to.

Not even Zeus can force the hand of another member of the Thirteen—or at least that's the theory. My father never paid attention to those sorts of niceties, and I doubt my brother will now that he's inherited the title. It doesn't matter. If I'm Ares, I'm no longer daughter to one Zeus, sister to another, a spoiled princess with no real value beyond her pretty face and family connections.

Becoming Ares will set me free.

The elevator doors open, and I hurry in the direction of the ballroom. The long hallway has changed since the last party, the dour, dark drapes that hung floor to ceiling on either side of the doors replaced with an airy white fabric that has silver threaded through it. It's still not welcoming, but it's significantly less oppressive.

I'm curious who made *that* design call, because Perseus sure as fuck didn't. Since he stepped up as Zeus after our father's death, the only thing my oldest brother cares about is running his business and ruling Olympus with an iron fist.

Or at least trying to.

"Helen."

I stop short, but recognition brings a relieved smile to my face. "Eros. What are you doing out here lurking in the shadows?"

He steps forward and holds up a tiny jeweled bag. "Psyche forgot her purse." He should look ridiculous holding the purse, especially considering the violence those hands have done, but Eros has a habit of moving through life as if he's untouchable. No one would dare say a word and he knows it.

"What a good husband you are." I take the last few steps and press a quick kiss to each of his cheeks. I haven't seen him much in the last couple months, but he looks good. Eros is one of the most gorgeous people in Olympus—which is saying something—a white guy with curly blond hair and a face to make painters weep at its perfection. "Marriage suits you."

"More and more every day." His gaze sharpens. "You've pulled out all the stops tonight."

"Do you like the dress?" I smooth my hands down my gown. It's a custom piece, the golden fabric molded to my body from shoulders to hips before flaring out the slightest bit. It's heavy with a subtle pattern that's designed to catch the light with every move. A deep V dips between my breasts, and the shoulders have been shaped into sharp points that give the slightest impression of military bearing. "It's a showstopper, as my mother would have said."

I ignore the twinge in my chest at the thought, just as I always do when my mind tries to linger on the woman who died far too young. She's been gone fifteen years, having suffered a *mysterious* fall when I was fifteen. Mysterious. Right. As if all of Olympus didn't suspect that my father was behind it.

As if I didn't know it for certain.

Pushing *this* thought away is second nature. It doesn't matter what sins my father committed. He's dead and gone, just like my mother. I hope he's been suffering in the pits of Tartarus since he drew his last breath. When I think of his death, all I feel is relief. He died before he could marry me off to secure some bullshit alliance, before he could cause even more of the pain he seemed to enjoy inflicting so much.

No, I don't miss my father at all.

"She'd be proud of you."

"Maybe." I glance over his shoulder at the doors. "Maybe she'd be furious over what I'm about to do." Rock the boat? Fuck, I'm about to tip the boat right over.

Eros doesn't miss a beat. His brows rise and he shakes his head, looking rueful. "So it's Ares for you. I should have known. You've been missing a lot of parties lately. Training?"

"Yes." I brace myself for his disbelief. We might be friends, but we're friends by Olympus standards. I trust Eros not to slide a knife between my ribs. He trusts me not to cause him undue trouble in the press. We hang out on a regular basis at events and parties and occasionally trade favors. I don't trust him with my deepest secrets. It's nothing personal. I don't trust *anyone* with that part of me.

On the other hand, everyone in Olympus will know my plans very shortly.

I square my shoulders. "I'm going to compete to become the next Ares."

"Damn." He whistles under his breath. "You've got your work cut out for you."

He's not telling me he thinks he can't do it, but I wilt a little all the same. I didn't *really* expect enthusiastic support, but being constantly underestimated never fails to sting. "Yes, well, I'd better get in there."

"Hold on." He surveys me. "Your hair is a little lopsided."

"*What?*" I lift my hand and touch my head. I can't tell without a mirror. Damn it, I'm going to be even later, but it's still better than walking into that room out of sorts.

I start to turn in the direction of the bathroom back toward the elevators, but Eros catches my shoulder. "I got it." He opens Psyche's purse and digs around for a few seconds, pulling out an even smaller bag. Inside, there is a bunch of bobby pins. Eros huffs out a laugh at my incredulous expression. "Don't look so surprised. If you had a purse, you'd have bobby pins stashed, too. Now, hold still and let me fix your shit."

Shock roots me in place as he carefully fixes my hair, securing it with half a dozen bobby pins. He leans back and nods. "Better."

"Eros." I gently touch my hair again. "Since when do you do hair?"

He shrugs. "I can't do more than damage control, but it saves Psyche some trouble when we're out if I can help like this."

Gods, he's so in love it makes me sick. I'm happy for him. Truly, I am. But I can't help the jealousy that curls through me. It's not about Eros—he's more brother to me than anything else—but at the intimacy and trust he shares with his wife. The one time I thought I might have that, it blew up in my face, and I still wear the emotional scars from the fallout.

I manage a smile, though. "Thanks."

"Knock 'em dead, Helen." His grin is sharp enough to cut. "I'll be rooting for you."

I drag in a slow breath and turn for the door. Since I'm late, I might as well make an entrance. I straighten my spine and push both doors open with more force than necessary. People scatter as I step into the room. I pause, letting them look at me and taking them in at the same time.

This room has changed since Perseus inherited the title of Zeus. Oh, the space is still functionally the same. Shining white marble floors that I can barely see beneath the crowd, an arching ceiling that gives the impression of the ballroom being even larger than it is, the massive windows and glass doors that lead out to the balcony on the other side of the room. But it still feels different. The walls used to be cream, but now they're a cool gray. A subtle change, but it makes a difference.

Most notably, the larger-than-life portraits of the Thirteen that line the walls have different frames. Gone are the thick gold frames that my father favored, replaced by finely crafted black. I would have to get closer to verify, but each looks like they might be custom, unique to each member of the Thirteen.

Perseus didn't make these changes, either. I'm certain of it. Our father might have been obsessive about his image, but my brother doesn't give a fuck. Even when he should.

I start through the crowd, holding my head high.

Normally, I can identify every single person who attends a Dodona Tower party. Information is everything, and I learned from a very young age that it's the only weapon I'm allowed. Some people meet my gaze, others stare at my body in a way that makes my skin crawl, and still others all but turn their backs on me. No surprises there. Being a Kasios in Olympus might have its perks, but it means being born into generations-old grudges and politicking. I grew up learning who could be trusted—no one—and who would actually shove me into traffic if given half a chance—more people than is comforting.

But this party isn't a regular one, and tonight is not a regular night. Nearly half the faces are new to me, people who have arrived from the outskirts around Olympus or been ferried into the city by Poseidon for this special occasion. I don't stop moving to memorize faces. Not everyone here will be nominating themselves as champions; plenty of them are just like the majority of the people here from Olympus. Hangers-on. They don't matter.

I don't pick up my pace, moving at a steady stalk that forces people to get out of my way. The crowd parts for me just like I know it will, whispers following in my wake. I'm making a scene, and while half of them love me for it, the rest resent me.

Everyone has pulled out all the stops tonight. In one corner, my sister Eris—Aphrodite, as of three months ago—is laughing at something with Hermes and Dionysus. My chest gives a pang. I would like nothing more than to be with them now, just like I am at every other party. My sister and my friends are what makes living in Olympus bearable, but the last few months have driven home the new differences between us. It wasn't so noticeable when Eris was still Eris, but now that she's also one of the Thirteen...

I'm getting left behind. Being sister to Zeus and Aphrodite, friend to Hermes and Dionysus? It doesn't mean shit. I'm still a piece to be moved around on someone else's board.

Becoming Ares is my only opportunity to change that.

I catch sight of the Dimitriou clan in the opposite corner, Demeter with three of her four daughters, as well as Hades, husband to Persephone. Like everyone else, they're dressed to perfection. The fact that Hades and Persephone are here only spotlights the importance of what's to come. Every member of the Thirteen is present to stand witness to the ceremonial announcement of the tournament to replace Ares. Eros appears at his wife's side, and the way her face lights up at the sight of him... I turn away.

The throne is my destination.

Well, the pair of thrones—two more changes our shift in leadership has caused. Gone is the gaudy gold monstrosity our father used to love, replaced with a steel sculpture that's attractive but oh so cold. Kind of like Perseus himself.

The second throne is a daintier version of his. Callisto Dimitriou sits on it, a beautiful white woman with long dark hair dressed in an elegant black gown. She's staring at everyone gathered below her as if she'd like to shove each one of us through the huge glass doors that have been opened to let in the balmy June evening air. I doubt she'd stop there, though. More likely, she'd love to see us tossed right over the balcony.

Why my brother chose *her* to be his wife, to become Hera, is a mystery to everyone in Olympus. They certainly don't seem to like each other. Their marriage reeks of Demeter's meddling, but no matter how I dig or pry, I've never been able to find a proper answer. I suppose it doesn't matter *why* Perseus married her, only that he did.

I drop into a quick curtsy that *almost* manages to be polite. "Zeus. Hera."

My brother leans forward and narrows a cold look in my direction. While Eris and I take after our mother's coloring, Perseus is all our father. Blond hair, blue eyes, pale skin, and a ruggedly attractive face. If he put any effort behind it at all, he'd be good-looking enough to charm the whole room. Unfortunately, my brother never excelled at that type of skill the same way the rest of my family does.

Not Hercules. He was as bad at playing the game as Perseus.

I shove the thought away. There's no use thinking about Hercules, either. He's gone, and as far as most of Olympus is concerned, he might as well be dead. No, that's not right. People talk about the dead. They pretend Hercules never existed in the first place. I miss him nearly as much as I miss my mother.

"You're late." Perseus doesn't lift his voice, but he doesn't have to. The people nearest us have gone quiet, tense with the possibility of seeing Kasios family drama play out. I can't resent them for that. I've given them plenty of fodder for gossip over my thirty years.

"Sorry." I even mean it. "Time got away from me." The temptation to overprepare isn't usually one I fall victim to, but there's nothing usual about this situation.

Perseus shakes his head slightly, his gaze tracking the rest of the room. "I'm making the announcement soon. Don't wander off."

I bristle, but there's no point in taking it personally. Perseus talks to everyone as though they're a small child or a dog; he has since we were little. I might understand that it's just the way he is, but his preferred method of communication is already breeding resentment among Olympus's elite.

That's not my problem, though. Not tonight. I give him a bright smile. "Of course, dear brother. I wouldn't dream of it." After the announcement, people will have a chance to put their names forward to become champions, which will enter them into the tournament for Ares's title. The window to put a name forward doesn't technically close until dawn, but from what I understand, it's rare for there to be latecomers, so I want to make sure I'm on hand to get my name in before anyone can think to stop me.

I turn to study the room, though I can feel my brother watching me. Probably worried I'm going to embarrass him further. Another night, I might even see that as a challenge, but right now, I have my eyes on the prize. I will not be diverted.

After tonight, everyone will know that I'm a force to be reckoned with.

It doesn't take long for the rest of the Thirteen to drift over, taking up positions on either side of my brother and Callisto—Hera. She looks bored with this whole process, but she's the only one. A current of excitement surges through the room. I know Perseus just wants stability for Olympus, but this fanfare will be more than that for the city. It will give them something to cheer for, an event to raise civilian morale—something that has wavered recently.

The Thirteen might rule Olympus, but ultimately they are only a handful of people. Without the support of the greater population, that power is in name only. There has only been an uprising once in our history, a few generations back after a war between the Thirteen decimated the city, but it was brutal enough for us to know we never want it to happen again.

Things work best when the current members of the Thirteen play the celebrity game. When someone takes over a new title, they decide how they want to craft their image and run with it. Some—like Demeter, the last Aphrodite, Hermes, and Dionysus—go hard, using public opinion to further their respective goals. Poseidon and Hades have never played the game, though. Hades by virtue of no one on this side of the river knowing he existed until recently. Poseidon because he garners enough goodwill by being one of the few who can come and go across the barrier that surrounds Olympus freely, which means he imports anything industry in the city can't create for itself.

A bunch of new members of the Thirteen in a short time means uncertainty, and in uncertain times, anything is possible. Even revolution.

My brother will do anything to ensure that doesn't happen.

The crowd presses closer, and I angle myself away from the

front of it, shifting close to where Dionysus stands. He's a white man about my age with short dark hair and a truly impressive mustache that he's grown out just enough to curve it up at either side of his mouth. It should look ridiculous, but it's Dionysus. He makes ridiculous an artistic statement, from his peppy attitude to his brightly colored suit. He grins at me. "Ready for this?"

My stomach is twisted into half a million knots, but I smile back. "Of course. There's bound to be drama, and you know how I love that." *I* will be the drama shortly.

A light over Perseus brightens as the camera crew takes up positions across from him. This event will be broadcast to the greater city, which means the impressions champions make, starting now, are vital. Ares doesn't technically need civilian support to do their job, but being popular with the citizens helps smooth the way.

My brother straightens to his feet. He doesn't have the commanding presence our father did, but he *does* have the ability to make it seem like he's looking right into a person's soul. He uses that now, his icy gaze shifting over the people gathered before landing on me. Something flares there, something I don't recognize, but he moves on before I can identify it.

"You all know why we're here." He doesn't raise his voice, but he doesn't have to. My siblings and I were trained to speak in public from a very young age. To be perfect symbols of our perfect family line. "We're here to honor the passing of Ares. He served the title for nearly sixty years, and he's gone far too soon." Nice words. Meaningless words. The last Ares was, quite frankly, a dick.

Perseus turns to the other part of the room. "Tonight, we begin the process of finding our next Ares. Tradition states that three trials will be issued, the first of which you'll know in two days' time. The winner of the three challenges will become the next Ares." A weighted pause. Again, that strange look passes over his face.

It's the only warning I get.

Perseus looks at me, something akin to sympathy in his blue eyes as he seals my fate. "And marry my sister Helen."

ACHILLES

"TOLD YOU SO," PATROCLUS MURMURS.

I don't have to look at him to know what he's thinking. I *always* know what he's thinking. Namely, too damn much. At least the fawning groupies that descended the moment we walked through the door earlier have dispersed now that the show is underway. It's a relief; I can turn the charm on when it suits me, but this shit is exhausting.

The last Ares never worried about playing to the public. He was a right old bastard, and he didn't care if everyone knew it. I don't know if he started out that way when he took the title, but by the end, everyone hated him. Even his own people.

It's not how Athena operates, and I learned everything of value I know from her. Better to use honey than vinegar, better to get someone to do what you want with a little manipulation than by bashing them over the head with whatever weapon is closest at hand. Ares could have used a few of her lessons, but he was the type of guy who put himself on a path and didn't deviate.

Things are going to change when I'm in charge.

Zeus is still talking, spinning a whole lot of bullshit about tradition. Olympus is up to its tits in tradition. It's their excuse for everything, a line of reasoning that conveniently takes the responsibility from the people actually doing the actions.

"Yeah," I mutter. "You don't need to say it, though. I was already hearing the I-told-you-so loud and clear." Patroclus had been *sure* the title would come with a wife. It's been a long time since this title passed over, so I had my doubts, but one of Patroclus's many skills is gathering all the available information and running scenarios until he finds the most likely one. It makes him irritating as fuck to be around sometimes, but he's brilliant.

I glance around the room. No one seems particularly surprised by the announcement, so either they did their research like Patroclus or they have excellent poker faces.

He moves closer, pressing his shoulder to mine. He's frowning, that big brain of his working overtime. "I didn't expect it to be Helen, though. I didn't expect Aphrodite to choose *her*."

"Yeah." Even though I know better, my gaze tracks to the white woman standing in an empty circle, as if the people around her inched away to avoid being associated with what happens next. I can only see her profile, but it's enough.

To call Helen beautiful is the understatement of the century. She's *flawless*, the kind of perfect that only comes around once a generation. Her whole family is full of attractive bastards, but she's on another level entirely. She's also a reckless party girl whose exploits are constantly splashed across the gossip sites. She doesn't follow the same rules as the rest of us. She's never gone hungry or had to fight for anything.

The woman is a princess in a tower, and what's a princess good for except bait?

She shifts, the subtlest squaring of her shoulders. When she turns to face the room, she looks happy...as long as one doesn't stare into her amber eyes. They're as cold as Zeus's. She gives the room a little finger wave. "Lucky you."

A scattering of laughs. Neither I nor Patroclus make a sound. I glance at him. He's a few inches taller than me and built naturally leaner. Tonight, he's wearing the glasses I like so much and a suit that I can't help wanting to rumple. The man is always so fucking put together. Nothing fazes him, because before he takes action, he's already run half a dozen scenarios. Surprising him is damn near impossible.

Still. "You sure about this?" I murmur. He may have expected a wife to be offered as part of the tradition, but Helen complicates things. Might as well get into bed with a snake and pray it doesn't sink its fangs into you. It will bite. That's what snakes do. The woman is loyal to her family and her family alone. Being married to her means every interaction, both in and outside our home, will be a battlefield. She's a Kasios. She can't be trusted.

"This is the only way."

He's right. I don't know why I'm even questioning it. This is what I've wanted since I was old enough to realize the only thing people in Olympus respect is power. Getting a taste of it as I climbed the ranks beneath Athena? Yeah, I'm willing to sacrifice a whole lot to get that title. "Then we move forward with the plan."

He glances at me, handsome face completely calm, and gives a subtle nod. Patroclus never wanted to lead, let alone claim a spot as one of the Thirteen, but he's going to put his name forward so he can help *me* win it. This was the plan from the moment I decided on Ares. The first two trials are designed to whittle down the champions until only five remain for the final one. Alliances aren't unheard of, but I'm not willing to wager my success on the unknown. Which is where Patroclus comes in. He'll provide any assistance necessary to ensure I reach the final trial. I'm reasonably certain I could do it on my own, but he insisted.

Truth be told, I didn't protest that hard. Patroclus has been at my side since we met at eighteen. We've hit every major milestone since then as a pair. It would feel wrong to compete and win the title of Ares without him watching my back.

Still. "If you're sure."

"I'm sure. Stop trying to give me an out. I'm competing. End of story." He turns back to study the crowd. "I have files on every single possible champion from Olympus. You're the best. With me at your side, your win is all but guaranteed."

My win. Becoming Ares. Marrying Helen. Patroclus and I have an unconventional relationship, at least according to some, but I keep waiting for the idea of me being married to someone else to bother him. It sure as fuck would bother *me* if he married someone else. But he's as unruffled as always. It drives me up the wall. "Marrying Helen Kasios is going to be a giant pain in the ass."

He gives me another of those censoring looks. "Ares."

As if he needs to remind me. I'd marry a literal fucking harpy if it meant becoming one of the Thirteen. Unfortunately, Helen Kasios isn't far off from that. She's a spoiled brat who's always gotten her way, and even through her lying smile, I can see she's furious about this development. She'll make whoever wins this thing regret it, probably for the rest of their lives. That's not even getting into the fact that any information she gleans from me will be fed right back to Zeus.

It's a smart play on his part. Worthy of a plan Patroclus would put together. Ultimately, though, it doesn't matter. I will become Ares. I'll deal with all the other shit once the title is mine.

Movement on my other side makes me glance over. Paris. He's a lean white dude who obviously spends a shit ton of money on his appearance. It's there in the smoothness of his skin, in how perfectly styled his blond hair is. Too bad money can't buy a good personality; Paris is a fucking asshole. All the good-person genes in his family went to his older brother, Hector.

Hector, I like and respect.

Paris is looking at Helen like she's a piece of meat he can't wait to consume. I don't make a habit of paying too much attention to the gossip sites, but Paris and Helen's breakup was nasty enough to make headlines for weeks. Now the little shit is practically rubbing his hands together with glee.

He glances at me and grins. "Sorry, man, but she's mine. She can't say no if I become Ares and marry her."

Hector steps forward on his brother's other side and slaps him upside the back of his head with a familiarity that says he's done it enough times for it to have become muscle memory. "Don't be crude." He nods at me. "Achilles."

"Hector." He used to head one of Ares's squads, but after he got married and had a baby, he ended up transferring to work for another of the Thirteen, Apollo. I haven't seen Hector much in the years since, but he was a formidable fighter when I knew him. "How's the kid?"

"She takes after her mother." He gives a small smile. "I thank the gods every day that she didn't get my ugly mug."

Hector is good-looking in a rugged sort of way with his sandy-blond hair and kind eyes, but he's right; he won't be winning any beauty contests anytime soon. I grin at him, completely ignoring Paris. "Surely you're not going to fight? You already have a wife. I thought you were halfway to retired at this point."

He shrugs. "Family."

I nod as if I have any idea what he's talking about. My only family is Patroclus and the squad we run together. My parents are mysteries. Apparently they didn't want a kid, so they followed the old tradition of leaving the baby—me—on the temple steps. I grew up in one of the orphanages that's run in Hera's name, but I don't think an actual Hera has set foot in them since before I was born. At eighteen, I got a choice of working for Ares, Poseidon, or Demeter. Really, it wasn't much of a choice at all. I was a grunt for Ares for a few years before Athena plucked me out of obscurity and showed me what greatness can be.

I was always destined for this.

"Now, it's time for those who would be Ares to step forward."

Zeus steps back and motions to the tall Black woman at his side. She's wearing a suit instead of a gown, the pale gray setting off her warm brown skin, her black hair cut short on the sides with the curls longer on the top. Athena.

She surveys the room as if measuring every person's weaknesses. Knowing her, that's exactly what she's done. "Once you put your name forward, the only way out is elimination or resignation. While these trials aren't meant to be to the death... accidents happen. Be willing to sacrifice it all."

Paris ducks from under Hector's hand and moves forward. "I'm Paris Chloros. I will sacrifice it all."

I can't help it. I glance at Helen to see her reaction. Her pale skin has gone a little green as she glares at her ex. Paris winks at her as if he can't see the murder in her eyes. If he wins Ares, I don't like his chances of surviving the wedding night.

It won't be a problem, because Paris isn't even a contender. The bigger worry is Hector, who steps forward and repeats the traditional phrase. Ajax—another of the former Ares commanders and someone I consider a friend—is next. Then a Black woman with locs pulled back from her scarred face. Her name is Atalanta, and she's light enough on her feet that I already know she'll be quick as fuck.

Person after person comes forward in an endless stream. I note the ones Patroclus expected and the ones he didn't. None of them matter. There are a few actual contenders but mostly they're people from the elite families that move in the extended circles of the Thirteen. They'll attempt the tournament because they can't afford to ignore a chance to take the title, but they aren't true threats.

A wave of murmurs rises behind me, and I glance over my

shoulder as two men stalk through the crowd, people practically scrambling over one another to get out of their way. They have similar coloring—medium-brown skin, dark-red hair, dark eyes—and are both even larger than I am. "Big bastards," I murmur.

The taller of the two gives me a look that's eerily empty as they pass by. The entire room has gone silent, probably sensing the same thing I do—these are true predators in our midst. Even more importantly, they're *strangers*.

The shorter of the two steps forward first with a showy bow. "I'm Theseus Vitalis, and I'm willing to sacrifice it all."

Athena raises a brow. "New in town?"

"It's within the parameters of the competition."

"I'm aware of the rules." She glances at the taller one. "And you?"

"I'm the Minotaur." His voice sounds like someone hacked open his vocal cords and then poured burning embers into the wound.

Athena gives him a sharp look. "That's your name?"

"It serves its purpose." He pauses barely long enough for her to nod before continuing. "I will sacrifice it all."

"Dangerous," Patroclus murmurs.

"Yeah." I wait for them to move to the side before Patroclus and I step forward. I can't help looking at Helen again as Patroclus speaks the words to become a champion. She's doing a shit job of masking her expression, and I hate the sympathy that I feel in response. She obviously didn't choose this. Fuck, she obviously didn't know about it before Zeus made his announcement. This woman is nothing to me, but when I win the title Ares—and I *will* win—I'll ensure she's not mistreated. After the wedding, I don't care what she does or who she fucks around with as long as she stays away from me and Patroclus. It's a better deal than she'll get from anyone else.

Then it's my turn to speak, and I shove all thoughts of Helen effortlessly away. "I'm Achilles Kallis, and I'm willing to sacrifice it all."

Athena doesn't smile, but approval warms her dark eyes. It's about as effusive as she gets, and it makes me feel a little strange in response. I'm not someone who needs outside approval for validation, but I respect the fuck out of Athena, and her opinion matters to me.

She waits several long moments, but no one else steps forward. She lifts her voice to be heard in every corner of the room. "The deadline for putting your name forward is dawn. Best of luck."

The lights brighten slowly, signaling the end of the pageantry. The party will go on for hours, but our reason to be here is over. I turn to Patroclus. "Let's go."

For a second, it seems like he might argue, but finally he nods and turns with me for the door. People get out of our way. I've been to these kinds of parties a handful of times in the years since I was promoted to Athena's second-in-command, but she prefers to keep her people out of the viper's nest. Her words, not mine. I don't see the big deal, but then I'm not one to be swayed by a pretty face or prettier words. I know my fate.

I hold the door open for Patroclus, and we exit into the long hallway leading to the elevator down. He's got *that* look on his face, and I inwardly roll my eyes. "Tell me you're not worried about that golden princess."

"I feel bad for her." He shrugs, completely unashamed of his bleeding heart. "It can't be that comfortable being so close to so many members of the Thirteen. Her life was never her own, not even from birth."

This time, I can't stop myself from rolling my eyes. "Right. Poor little princess, born into the richest family in the city, having everything she could ever dream of at the tips of her fingers. She's never had to fight for a single thing in her life. Not like me. Not like you."

"That's not entirely true, at least for me. If things had fallen out differently, I'd be Aphrodite's son."

"It's different."

"If you say so." Another shrug. "I don't have the same ambition you do, Achilles. Working for Athena is just a job for me. It always has been."

I love the man, but sometimes I really don't understand him. If you're not fighting for something, you're going to get used as a stepping-stone for the people who are. Patroclus is one of the most brilliant people I know, but he's too soft. Without me to watch his back, he would have been fucked over dozens of times since we met each other as teenagers.

Then again, without me in his life, I don't think he'd be in Athena's special forces. With his love of knowledge and research, he might have gravitated to Apollo's businesses the same way Hector did.

Something like guilt slaps me in the face, but I shove it away.

When I'm Ares, Patroclus will be free to do whatever he damn well pleases. With that much power at my disposal, that many resources, he won't have to work at all if he doesn't want to.

I sling an arm around his shoulders and press a quick kiss to his temple. "Don't worry so much. When I'm Ares, I'll take care of both of us." I grin. "Fuck, I'll take care of Helen, too, if that will make you feel better." Even if she is a spoiled brat.

HELEN

"ARE YOU *FUCKING* KIDDING ME?" I DIG MY FINGERS INTO the fabric of my dress. It's do that or punch my brother in his infuriatingly square jaw. No matter how satisfying it would be, I can't risk injuring my hand. Not if I want to be Ares. Except how the fuck can I be Ares when Patroclus named me Ares's *wife*? "You made me a prize to be won! Married off to a stranger! Without even talking to me."

I managed to hold it together until the party wrapped up and a small group of us ended up in Perseus's office—me, Perseus, Eris, and Callisto. Me, Zeus, Aphrodite, and Hera. Perseus sits behind his large desk, looking bored with my theatrics. Eris has one hip perched on the desk and is smiling in a way I really don't like. I love my siblings. I do. But I can never forget that they're focused on power and ambition before all else. They always have been, even before they became members of the Thirteen. It's how we were raised, after all.

The only exception was Hercules, and look what happened to him.

Callisto stands in front of the floor-to-ceiling windows, seeming to be totally checked out of the conversation. Or argument, more accurately.

Eris examines her nails. "It's tradition for a wife to be part of Ares taking the title."

Somehow, in all my preparation, I missed that little detail. I was so focused on what the trials could be that I never bothered to look into the rest. The last Ares had several wives over the course of his time holding the title. It never occurred to me that one of them was the result of him gaining the title itself. "That's no excuse. You could have chosen someone else. You should have chosen *anyone* else. Why did it have to be me?"

Perseus steeples his hands before his mouth. "Because you're a Kasios."

I flinch. I didn't ask to be born into this family. I didn't ask for the consequences I've lived with my entire life. "So I'm going to be punished for having our father's blood in my veins?"

"Stop being dramatic, Helen."

I *hate* how patronizing he sounds right now. "No, fuck you. You don't know what it's like—"

He pushes slowly to his feet, cutting me off. "I don't know what it's like to... What exactly? Sacrifice in the name of the Thirteen? Marry a stranger for the sake of a greater good?" He doesn't look at Callisto. "I'm not asking anything of you that I haven't already done myself."

"I didn't ask for this," I finally manage.

"Don't be a child. You're not special. None of us asked for this." He turns for the door. "You were always going to be married off in a power match. You know this."

Honestly, it's a minor miracle that I've avoided it to this point. My father thought to break me before offering me up as a pawn to someone else, which is the only reason I haven't had a ring shoved on my finger and been carted down the aisle. But I didn't expect it from *Perseus*.

Silly me.

Of course my brother would never let a little thing like my happiness get in the way of his bottom line. Our father taught him too well. He taught all of us too well. Even Zeus, with his petty cruelty, protected Olympus in his own way. No one could protect Olympus from *him*, but at least we didn't have to worry about outside enemies with him on the throne. "But—"

"The Thirteen are too fractured, and with the changeovers, that's causing unrest. I will bring them all to heel, one by one, no matter what it takes. *You* will do your part by influencing Ares to my side. Exactly like you were taught to."

The side effect of being destined for a political marriage? It wouldn't stop being political the moment I said "I do." I will be walking a tightrope between my spouse and my family, and gods know my family might not be perfect, but they still have my loyalty. No matter how much it kills me to do what's required. Which means there's only one answer available to me. "I understand."

"Good." He turns and pins me with a cold look. "You will be there tomorrow during the opening ceremony, and you will sit next to Athena in a pretty dress and inspire the candidates to greatness. They need to put on a show for the ages, and I need your help doing it. It's your duty, Helen. You haven't forgotten the price of the life we live, have you?"

Shame lances me and it's everything I can do not to bow my shoulders. No matter how awful it's been growing up as one of Zeus's children, the fact remains that when it came to having my material needs met, I wanted for nothing. The best schools, the best clothing, a home in the upper city, moving through the circles of the rich and powerful. All of it was because of the family I was born into.

But, as my brother likes to remind me, there is a price to be paid.

Perseus is right in a way; he's not asking me for anything he's not willing to do himself. He married one of Demeter's daughters, after all. No matter my bitching, even I can recognize that alliance as valuable, even if I don't fully understand why it had to be *Callisto*. Of all of us, he's most aware of the horrifying legacy we carry in our blood, of the sins our father committed while he was Zeus. Perseus is already going out of his way to ensure he follows a different path. He might aggravate me in the extreme, but I can respect that about him.

But...

I don't *want* this responsibility. I didn't choose this.

It doesn't matter. I lift my chin, blinking past the burning in my eyes. I am a Kasios and Kasioses don't cry. "I'll do my duty." What are my other options? Run? The idea is laughable. The only way out of Olympus is at Poseidon's hand, and there's no way he'll help me. He doesn't like me, but more than that, he knows how valuable I am to this whole plan. Helping me means alienating Zeus, Aphrodite, and the next Ares, all in one single action. Probably Demeter, too, though that one isn't guaranteed. Perseus is too measured to do anything so reckless.

"Do I need to put one of Athena's people on you?"

I draw myself up. "Absolutely not."

"Fine. Don't make me regret this decision." He nods and then he's gone, leaving me alone with Eris.

Eris pushes off the desk. She's wearing a slinky gunmetal-silver gown and has her long dark hair pulled back in a complicated series of twists. "I know this isn't ideal, but he's right. A new Ares means we're introducing a wild card into the Thirteen. We need you to pave the way to secure a new Zeus-Ares alliance."

I love my sister. A lot. But that doesn't change the fact that like everyone else in my family, she's out for Olympus first, herself second, and everyone else dead last. Family might rank higher than the greater Olympian population, but not by much. She loves me. She's just not one to let that get in the way of decisive action—and stirring the pot every chance she gets. "You could have chosen someone else. Anyone else."

She shrugs, a small smile pulling at the edges of her lips. "You'll come out on top, Helen. You always do."

I tilt my head back and stare at the ceiling. "That was quite the backhanded compliment." My voice is high and tight. I have too much control to throw a fit over this turn of events, but I want nothing more than to throw something at my sister's smug face. "I'm very angry at you right now."

"You'll get over it. It's dog-eat-dog in this city, especially among the Thirteen. You know that."

"Yeah, well, I *would* have secured an airtight Zeus-Ares alliance if you'd let *me* become the next Ares."

She jolts like I've surprised her. "You can't really mean you considered stepping forward as a candidate. I thought you gave up that ridiculousness when we were still children."

It shouldn't hurt so much that my sister doesn't take me seriously. Of everyone, I'd think she'd realize my ambitions go more than skin deep. Apparently I was wrong. "I never gave it up."

She gives a tight smile. "Honey, I know you mean well, but look at the champions. Achilles, Hector, Atalanta, those two strangers. They're huge and they practically sweat violence. That's not even getting into the other thirty-odd people who put their names forward. You're..." She hesitates. "You're capable, but you're no warrior, Helen. There's no way you could win."

Somehow, this is worse than the fact she hadn't taken my ambitions seriously. She honestly doesn't think I could do it. My chest tries to close, and only years of practice keep me from buckling. "I *would* have won."

"I guess we'll never know now." Eris presses her lips together, looking almost apologetic in a way she wasn't when she effectively sold me in marriage without asking first. "I'm sorry, Helen. Truly, I am. But you know how it goes. Olympus comes first. Sometimes that demands sacrifice."

"Keep telling yourself that. You're not sacrificing a single damn thing." I'm so angry, I'm shaking. The temptation to let the rage out here, when it's just family in this room, is almost too strong to ignore. It's been many years since I brawled with Eris; the last time was when we were teenagers. It would feel so damn good to let off some of this horrible feeling inside me. The betrayal lies thick on my tongue, threatening to choke out everything else.

"Don't make that face. It's going to give you wrinkles. This will work out, Helen. Trust us." She turns and strides out of the office. Eris always did like to leave arguments unfinished.

It's so damn naive of me to believe my siblings would treat me differently than my father intended to. Helen Kasios, princess of Olympus, destined to marry someone who will bring more power to her family—as if they need it. "*Damn it.*" I force my hands to unclench the folds of my dress. "I wanted the title so fucking bad."

"Why not do it anyway?" Callisto's voice comes from the shadows, low and almost seductive.

I jolt and spin around, my heart racing. I'd completely forgotten she was in the room with us. She melts out of the shadows near the window where she'd been standing, near invisible. In her black dress with her dark hair, she looks like some creature of the night who wandered into this office by accident. I still can't believe my brother married *her*. I understand wanting to settle Demeter and her significant power firmly on his side, but surely Eurydice would have been a better choice. She's so much sweeter; marrying her would mean a much less tumultuous life.

Then again, Olympus would eat Eurydice alive if she became Hera.

"I can't do it anyway. That's not how things work."

"Isn't it?" Callisto examines her nails. "I'm a fan of asking for forgiveness instead of permission. That's what your brother did, after all. Why not give him a taste of his own medicine?"

I stare. "You're trying to cause trouble."

"Olympus is nothing but trouble." Something dangerous shifts through her tone. She's not entirely wrong, but that doesn't mean she's right, either. Her mother, Demeter, won the title and brought her daughters into the city proper a little over ten years ago. In that time, Callisto has made her derision of everything connected with the Thirteen known. Before she married my brother, she didn't show up for parties. She didn't play the game. She was always willing to step to the line and fight, no matter the opponent.

Now that she's officially become Hera, I don't know what to make of her.

I cross my arms over my chest and try to calm my racing heart. No matter how dangerous she seems, she's just a woman, and I've been playing this game longer than she's been in the city proper. I inject some false cheer into my voice. "It's really sweet that you're trying to be a supportive sister-in-law, but I am not about to become a pawn in whatever game you and my brother have going on."

Callisto gives me a long look, her hazel eyes downright predatory. "This has nothing to do with your brother."

"Lovely. Now I have some snake oil I'd love to sell you. It's great for the skin. Practically a fountain of youth."

Her lips curve. "Regardless of my motivations, we're talking about *you*. Is there some rule that says you can't be both prize and champion?"

I consider her. Despite my better instincts, I'm thinking her words through. "I'd have to check, but probably not. They don't have a rule against it because I doubt it would have occurred to anyone to even attempt it." I hate to lend any strength to Eris's doubt in me, but... "You've seen the people who stepped forward. That's a lot to combat."

Callisto shrugs. "If you were planning on making an attempt for Ares, you already intended to fight them and come out on top."

She's not wrong, but it still sounds like a trap. It's just...I'm not sure I care. If I compete and win, I knock out two birds with one stone. I become Ares and successfully dodge being married to someone I don't know. Despite myself, I picture Paris's smarmy face leering at me as he stepped forward earlier. *Or being married to* that *man.* I dodged that fate once and I'm determined to do it again.

Still, one thing doesn't add up. I carefully wrap up my growing excitement and inject coolness into my tone. "Again, what do you have to gain from suggesting I do this?"

Another shrug. "Maybe I have a thing against people being forced into marriages they didn't choose. Maybe I want to live vicariously through you because I would have competed to be Ares if I weren't already Hera. Maybe I want to stick it to my lovely husband in any way I can. My reasonings really don't matter, do they?" Again, that predator's smile. "You want to compete, Helen? Do it. All those fuckers who think you're just a pretty prize to be won? Prove them wrong."

It feels like she fired an arrow right into the very heart of me. I can't trust this woman, sister-in-law or no. But...that doesn't mean her idea is without merit. "You really hate my brother, don't you?"

"I hate all of the Thirteen."

"*You* are one of the Thirteen." Even if Hera has become a weakened title since my father became Zeus. Over the course of his three wives—three Heras—he stripped the title of what influence it had until it became nothing more than an empty term for Zeus's spouse.

"Yes. I am."

The door opens and Perseus steps back into the room. His gaze jumps from me to his wife and back again. "There you are."

Her smile is downright poisonous. "Just having some girl talk with Helen."

He doesn't comment on that, which is just as well. "It's time to leave, Hera."

"Of course, Zeus." The words seem polite enough, but fury lurks in their edges. She turns to me. "Congratulations on your pending nuptials, Helen. I'm sure you'll make a lovely piece of arm candy for the next Ares."

I watch her stalk across the room toward my brother, and the small hairs at the back of my neck rise. This woman is more predator than most of the Thirteen, and I can't shake the feeling that Perseus is going to greatly regret marrying her. For his part, he turns easily and places his hand at the small of her back. Always worried about appearances, my brother, even when no one else is here to witness the lie except me.

I follow them out of the office, and we take the elevator down to the parking garage. Only when we've walked well out of hearing range of the guard near the door does Perseus speak. "Do not, under any circumstances, take action to endanger this process. Promise me, Helen."

Damn him for throwing this curveball at me and then demanding I promise good behavior. Damn his wife for using clever words to poke holes in my already shaky determination to do what my family asks of me. I shake my head slowly. "You know, you really do take after our father."

He flinches, a barely perceptible movement that instantly has guilt surging through me. It was a low blow, and I did it intentionally to hurt him. I never mean to be a bitch, but sometimes the thorns inside me squeeze too tightly and horrible things burst from my lips. Words meant to strike to the very heart of a person.

Perseus nudges Callisto toward his SUV, and I wonder again that he touches her so easily, as if he's not worried about losing a hand. Surely he sees the sharp look she sends in his direction every time he gets too close?

He waits for her to climb into the passenger seat before turning to me. "I deserved that, but it changes nothing. Promise me, Helen."

"I promise," I lie without hesitation. I don't even feel guilty while doing it. It's practically a love language in our family.

He searches my face, the cold thawing for the barest instant. "Whoever becomes Ares will treat you well. I'll ensure it."

I laugh bitterly. "*How?* Are you going to set up surveillance to ensure my spouse doesn't abuse me? Please."

"Yes."

He's...not joking. I stare. "And then what, Perseus? What will you do if you sentenced me to be married to a monster?"

"It won't come to that. You're too savvy, and most of the champions recognize that harming you would alienate a good portion of the Thirteen."

Surely my ambitious, ruthless brother can't be this naive. "Most, but not all."

"The unknowns won't win, Helen."

No, they won't. Because I'm going to. The resolution takes root in my chest, steadying me. *I'm going to be Ares.* Still, I can't help pressing. I don't know what I'm looking for. Reassurance. Comfort. Something. I'm a fool. "What if one of the unknowns wins? What if *Paris* wins?"

"They won't harm you. If they do?" My brother turns for the SUV. "I'll make you a widow."

PATROCLUS

I LEAVE ACHILLES ASLEEP IN OUR APARTMENT AND MAKE my way to Athena's headquarters on foot. She likes to keep a low profile, occupying an older building in the northeast part of the upper city, just south of the docks and near the coast. It's far enough from Zeus's glittering city center that the buildings have more character, deviating from the steel and glass and concrete look that the blocks surrounding Dodona Tower favor.

There's not long until the deadline closes to put forth a name as champion. I expect most of the major players have already shown their faces, but I don't like being surprised. Dawn is a few hours off, and if anyone is going to be a late addition, they'll do it now, under the cover of darkness.

Historically, the three trials are more physical in nature, but the advantage of a surprise contender cannot be overstated. In order to ensure Achilles wins, I have to consider all variables and plan around them. Which is why I'm *here* instead of in the warm bed beside him.

Trees line this street at regular intervals, tall oaks that create a pleasant coolness in the early summer heat, even at this hour. I step into the shadows offered by one with a clear view of the entrance to Athena's building and settle in to wait.

I hear the person before I see them. Heels clicking sharply against the sidewalk, quick and pointed enough to convey a deep anger. I slide deeper into the shadows and angle myself to look for the source.

Surprise flares when I recognize the golden dress, glimmering in the streetlights. I can't see Helen's face clearly from here, but the determination in the set of her shoulders speaks for itself. She'd do the same thing when we were kids on the playground, throw back her shoulders before charging into a confrontation.

The stakes were so much lower then.

I half convince myself it's a coincidence that she's on *this* street, moving in *this* direction, until she yanks open the door to Athena's building and strides inside.

I'm good at strategy. I might even be the best in Olympus. I theorized Helen would be picked as the bride of the next Ares before it was announced because the data supported that outcome. I knew Paris and Hector would step forward for the same reason. I even projected that there would be a few non-Olympians in the bunch, though I haven't had a chance to dig into the few who showed up.

I did not anticipate *this*.

Helen means to compete for the title of Ares? The very idea is ludicrous, though as I mentally flip through the histories I read on the subject, I don't think there is any rule against it. It's simply never been done before. There is no precedent.

What happens if she dies in one of the trials? Champions get killed from time to time, though it's the exception rather than the rule. Zeus is hardly going to be able to switch out spouses as prizes on a whim. Even if he could and the Thirteen, the public, and the champions would stand for it... The very idea is laughable. Who can compare to Helen Kasios when it comes to connections and beauty? No one.

It will be a disaster no matter which way I look at it.

I'm so busy thinking that I don't hear her exit. I don't even notice Helen until she's standing right in front of me, an arch in her perfect eyebrow. "You never used to be sneaky."

"The last time you saw me, I was eight. People change." Except, now that I'm thinking of it, Helen always was the first to act against type back then. A cute little girl in a spotless sundress...who had no problem bloodying bullies' noses and making them cry.

"Some people change." She shrugged. "Either way, spying is beneath you, Patroclus."

We might have been friends as kids, at least until my mothers moved our family out of the city center when I was in third grade, but I haven't seen much of Helen since then. In hindsight, she was a cute kid, but she's always been a goddess to me. She's the one who befriended my awkward younger self and stopped the other kids from teasing me about my glasses. I missed her after I moved away, but those memories faded as time went on.

As an adult, I feel her beauty like an assault. In the night, with only the streetlights kissing her high cheekbones and full lips, she looks downright otherworldly. I might have considered her a goddess back then, but she truly looks it now.

"I'm not spying," I manage. My words come out a little hoarse, but fuck, she surprised me. I glance at her feet and frown. "Where are your shoes?"

"I saw you lurking out here and wanted a word." She holds up heels that are high enough to make *my* feet hurt in sympathy. "I figured you would bolt if you heard me coming."

"I'm one of Athena's people. I would not *bolt* to avoid talking to you."

Her lips curve. "Guess people do change, after all."

My skin heats. "I'm surprised you remember me." I don't know why I say it. I honestly don't. She's *Helen Kasios*. She might have been kind to me when we were eight, but that was a long time ago.

Her smile disappears. "We were friends, Patroclus. Of course I didn't forget about you. I missed you after you were gone."

I can't read her tone. She sounds almost stung, but I must be imagining it. "What are you doing here?" I know the answer, but I want to hear her admit it.

"I thought you and I could have a little conversation."

"We have nothing to talk about." *Especially* if we're about to both be competitors for Ares. I have no intention of winning. It was never the goal when I put my name forward. But by watching Achilles's back, I can ensure he makes it to the final round and wins. The best-case scenario, of course, is that we're the two last standing and then I'll step down, but in looking at the competitors, I'm not certain I'll last that long. My strength is in strategy, but I lack a fundamental trait that Achilles and several of the other competitors have—a drive that propels them beyond what normal people can accomplish.

Frankly, I don't like Helen's odds, either. But being taken under Athena's wing and learning from her brilliant mind means I know better than to take *anything* in Olympus at face value. Helen seems like a party girl who flits from event to event, a beautiful bird in a gilded cage. I can't afford to assume that's the truth.

I bet she still has a wicked right hook.

"Patroclus." She says my name slowly, almost as if she's tasting it. "You're the only one who knows I've put my name in as a contender—aside from Athena, of course. I'd say we have more than a few things to talk about."

Easy enough to catch her meaning. "You want me to keep it to myself."

"Yes. At least until it's announced in the opening ceremony tomorrow."

I'm already shaking my head. "No. We might have been friends once, but that was a long time ago. I don't wish you ill, but you're not my priority in this tournament. Achilles is."

She tilts her head to the side, and once again, her sheer beauty steals my breath. I love Achilles—I have since I was a teenager—but there's something about Helen that hits me in a place logic can't touch. She's like some old-world queen who could inspire entire countries to go to war on her behalf.

She's *dangerous* now.

She laughs, low and sinful. "What Achilles doesn't know won't hurt him." The words *almost* sound like she's trying to seduce me.

It worries me how hard it is to take a step away from her. My body fights my mind, which worries me even more. "I'm sorry, Helen, but I'm going to tell him." I clear my throat. "Is that all?"

"Actually, one other thing." She motions at my shoulder. "Would you mind?"

"Go ahead." I hold perfectly still as she braces herself on my shoulder and slips on one shoe and then the other. Strange to realize how small she is. The last time she touched me like this, leaning on me to slip on her shoes, she was taller than I was. She's got to be at least six inches shorter than my six three now; probably closer to nine because even with the ridiculous heels, she still has to look up to meet my gaze. Beyond that, she's built lean enough that I would call her breakable.

"What are you thinking, entering this tournament?" I don't mean to ask the question. What the fuck am I supposed to do with this strange surge of protectiveness? She's not a kid in need of protection. Fuck, Helen *never* needed my protection. Ultimately, it doesn't matter why she's doing what she's doing. The only thing that matters is how she's complicated the possible scenarios moving forward. Her presence will affect things, and I have to consider how.

She tests the second heel and then straightens, running her hand absently down my chest. I feel the touch like a brand. For her part, Helen seems almost unaware of the effect she has on me. She glances down the street, her expression unreadable. "Are you happy, Patroclus? You're not an accountant the way you wanted to be back then." She snorts and shakes her head. "What eight-year-old wants to be an accountant?"

Fondness rises inside me, even as I try to fight it. Nothing good will come from revisiting this strange connection with Helen that I'd all but forgotten about until now. "And you're not a pirate. Are *you* happy?"

Instead of answering, she fires back, "Do you ever get tired of standing in Achilles's shadow?"

"No," I answer instantly. "He's too brash, too impulsive. He needs someone to anchor him." Without me at his back, gods know where he would have ended up. Achilles is brilliant in his own way, but his priorities can be extremely skewed to the point where he doesn't see—or care about—the full picture. He takes in what he feels is enough information to act and then *acts*. His drive and momentum are both terrifying and aggravating by equal measures.

"What about what *you* need?"

Logically, I know she's not talking about me, not really. Still, I answer honestly. "I have everything I need." It's almost the truth. I truly *am* happy with what I have with Achilles. It's not a traditional relationship by any means; we don't bother to put labels on things and we're not exclusive, though I don't partake in others' charms as often as Achilles does. I love him. He loves me. We're both getting our needs met, at least for now. If I harbor a secret fear that someday I won't be enough for him? Well, that's no one's business but my own.

I'm not about to confess as much to Helen, shared history or no.

"Lucky you," she murmurs. For someone who's been moving through the upper circles of Olympian politics, she's got a terrible poker face. Or maybe the shadows are tricking me into seeing vulnerability where there is none.

"You seem to have everything you need." I know better than to make assumptions. Achilles thinks he has Helen and her ilk figured out, but even if my mothers withdrew from the petty politics when I was in grade school, I still recognize that very few in the upper city are entirely honest about what they need and what they want. Doing so with the wrong people hands them a weapon perfectly designed to hurt you.

"Do I?" Helen pats my chest and takes a careful step back. "Well, I guess it's true, then, since you say so."

"Helen." I don't mean to say her name like that, low and stern.

She smiles, the expression more of sadness than joy. "Not everyone is as lucky as you are, Patroclus. Loving mothers who sacrificed their ambitions to give you a safe space to grow up in. A boyfriend who's Athena's second-in-command. A promising career within her special forces."

"You seem to know a lot about me."

She glances away and then back at me. "I might have checked up on you occasionally over the years. I guess you didn't do the same."

I don't like the sad look on her face. I'm not the one who should be trying to lift it, though. Really, the thing I *should* be doing is getting out of this conversation as quickly as possible. Helen is too savvy to give me ammunition to use against her, and I can't say the same about myself. Not when I'm reacting so strangely to her. "I didn't have to check up on you. You're in the headlines all the time."

"I am, aren't I?" She laughs a little, a tiny sound of amusement that's gone far too soon. "I'm really going to give them something to talk about this time."

"You won't win." I don't say it to be cruel, but she flinches all the same. Still, I press on. "You might even die. It's not too late. If you ask Athena to strike your name from the list, she will. No one has to know you entered in the first place."

Helen gives me a bittersweet smile that makes my chest ache in response. "Some things are worth even the risk of death. Good luck, Patroclus. You have your hands full with that golden jackass." She turns and strides back the way she came.

I don't mean to move. I have a plan, after all, and that plan involves holding this position until dawn to ensure I know the identities of any champions who want to keep their identities secret until the opening ceremony. Or at least going back to Achilles and reporting this new development. But my body makes the decision for me, one step turning into two, turning into a jog that brings me even with Helen. "I'll walk you to your car."

"That's not necessary."

Despite my longer legs, I have to concentrate to keep up with her quick pace. "The streets are safe enough in this neighborhood, but you're Helen Kasios. Surely you realize you're in more danger being out alone without a security detail than the average person."

She gives me a strange look. "Isn't it in your best interest to let a champion be eliminated before the tournament even starts?"

"No." The word comes out too forcefully, but there's no walking it back now. I make an effort to shrug the tightness out of my shoulders. "I don't know what it's like moving in the circles you do, but I don't believe in acceptable losses. Not if they're avoidable."

"How precious of you." She's still watching me like I'm a strange new creature she's never seen before. When she speaks again, her voice is almost gentle. "Patroclus, it's really okay. If anyone is silly enough to jump me, I can take care of myself." She holds up a tiny fist. "Once upon a time, I took care of you, too."

I smile despite myself. "You were a terror on the playground."

"Like I said." She drops her fist. "I don't need you to watch out for me."

Maybe she doesn't. She must be able to if she's confident enough to enter the tournament. I can't make myself leave her side, though. Not until she's safe. "All the same. Consider it paying you back for punching Menalaus's nose after he broke my glasses."

She sighs. "I should have expected that being irritatingly stubborn is the one thing that hasn't changed. You'd have to be to share Achilles's bed. Very well. Tag along if it will make you feel better."

It strikes me that this Helen is a bit different from the one plastered across the gossip sites. The changes are subtle, but I make a habit of filing away every interaction with powerful people who move among the Thirteen. They're dangerous in their own ways, and it pays to never be caught flat-footed.

The version she plays in public is bubbly in an almost aggressive way. She lights up every room she walks into, stands too close, and laughs too loudly for polite company. It's as if she forces her mark into every space she occupies, dares people to ignore her.

This Helen still stands too close, but she's more subdued. She's *sad*. Almost vulnerable. It makes me feel strange to notice that she's more complicated than I first expected. "You didn't know about the marriage, did you?"

Instead of answering, she goes on the offensive. "Are you and

Achilles in a relationship? Or are you just friends who sometimes fuck?"

I miss a step. "That's none of your business."

"Neither is whether or not I knew about the marriage before-hand." We stop at the corner, and she pulls out a phone in a glitter-ing case. Everything about Helen seems to glitter. It's unnerving, reminding me of the various animals whose bright coloring signals their poisonous defenses. She flips it around to show me the screen. "My ride will arrive in a few minutes. You've done your duty. You can go now."

I plant my feet. "I'll stay until they get here."

"Fine." Helen plants her hands on her hips, which makes it impossible not to notice how well the dress fits her body. It's a piece of art, the cut seeming to defy physics in a way I don't completely understand. Surely there is some tape or contraption involved to keep her breasts from escaping?

Her low laugh has me jerking my gaze back to her face. Gods, I was staring at her chest. My skin heats, and I'm grateful for the shadows. Hopefully they're hiding my blush. "Sorry."

"It's really a shame you and Achilles are none of my business. You're very handsome, and I'm feeling a special kind of reckless." She steps close. Not quite enough to touch, but it's a near thing. Helen stares up into my face. "Want to get into some trouble with me, Patroclus? You can tell Achilles about it later in...extreme... detail."

I can see how that would go all too clearly. If she were anyone else, if this were any other situation, Achilles would get off on that. Usually, the situation is reversed. He'll have some fun and tell me about it while he's fucking me or I'm going down on him, though he always peppers me with questions when someone catches my eye enough to pursue a single night of fun. It's been a long time since I indulged, and in different circumstances, he'd be delighted by my uncharacteristic impulsiveness.

This, though?

This feels too much like a betrayal for reasons I don't particularly want to look into. I finally shake my head. "No. Under other circumstances, but…" I hate the disappointment that shades her features, hate it so much I catch her hand and lift it, turning to press a kiss to her wrist. "I'm sorry."

"Your loss." But she makes no move to put more distance between us or break our contact.

The moment spins out, as fine as gossamer and filled with possibility. Saying no is the right thing to do. I'm already reacting too strongly to Helen without a physical component involved. I have many strengths, but sex can occasionally muddy the waters, dull my normally sharp mind. I can't afford for that to happen now, when Achilles is poised to take everything he's worked and sacrificed so much for. I certainly can't do so with *this* woman, who is in direct opposition to that goal.

If Achilles wins, he'll marry her.

The thought brings a flare of heat so intense, I lean toward Helen without intending to. We'd planned for the marriage to be in name only, but…what if it wasn't?

She tilts her head back and licks her lips, her gaze on my mouth. "Patroclus."

Gods, the way this woman says my name, low and breathy

with a hint of question that makes me want to pull her close and kiss her until the only thing she can level that impressive focus on is *me*.

What the fuck is happening to me?

A horn honks, jarring us out of the moment. Helen takes a large step back and pulls her hand out of my grasp. "Another time, maybe." Her grin goes downright wicked. "I changed my mind. Don't keep this between us. I'm sure Achilles will be *thrilled* to know he's going to face me in all three trials."

If her competence is half as strong as her arrogance, she might actually have a shot. I stand there and watch her climb into the back seat of her ride. The taillights disappear quickly down the street, turning back toward the city center.

There's no doubt about it.

This situation just got even more complicated.

ACHILLES

I WAKE UP THE MOMENT PATROCLUS SLIPS INTO BED. HE'S trying to be quiet, but as stealthy as he is, I've never been that heavy of a sleeper. Not as a child, and sure as fuck not when I became a soldier. I roll over and hook an arm around his waist, pulling him to me, his back to my chest. I bury my face in the nape of his neck. He smells like summer night...and perfume.

I open my eyes. It's still dark. The clock reads 3:00 a.m. "You're back early."

"Yeah." He's so tense, he's like a block of concrete. Something happened. Something he doesn't want to talk about.

Yeah, that's not going to work for me. "Patroclus." I press him down onto the mattress and prop my head on my hand. "Talk."

I can't see his expression clearly in the shadows, but I don't have to. I know this man as well as I know myself. I can practically feel the guilt coming off him in waves, even if it doesn't make a damn bit of sense. Nothing he could have done tonight should spawn *guilt*. That's not how we work.

Finally, he drags in a breath. "Helen Kasios put her name forward as a champion."

"*What?*"

"Yeah."

I shake my head. "What the fuck is she thinking? She's going to get hurt, and that will piss off Zeus and Aphrodite and make things more difficult for the new Ares." For *me*.

"I used to know her."

That shocks me enough that I sit up. "What are you talking about? You don't know Helen Kasios."

"I used to." He says it like a confession. "We went to school together when we were kids, before my family moved away from the city center. We were…friends."

He's never once mentioned her in all the time I've known him. I know I should see that as proof that she's no one to him, but all I can focus on is that there are parts of Patroclus that I don't recognize. I scrub my hand over my face. "So you knew Helen Kasios once upon a time and she put her name forward as a champion." That's not enough to spawn this guilty reaction in him. "What else happened?"

"She…" He clears his throat. "I'm pretty sure she propositioned me."

People come on to Patroclus all the time. He's sexy, he's got a soldier's body, and he's smart as fuck. Anyone who talks to him for ten seconds knows he's a catch. Most of the time, he doesn't even register that he's being hit on. When he *does*, he politely disengages. It's rare for someone to interest him enough to allow himself to be seduced, and even rarer for him to act like this afterward. I'm pretty sure it's never happened before.

I don't like it.

I sure as fuck don't like how it makes me feel.

"How?" I don't mean to ask the question. The single word lands like a gauntlet thrown between us, too heavy for three little letters.

Patroclus tenses. "What?"

I'm already moving, climbing out of bed and motioning impatiently at him. "Show me how."

"Achilles..." He reluctantly follows and moves to stand in front of me. He's naked and half-erect and that shouldn't piss me off, but nothing about this situation is like it *should* be. Patroclus sighs. "Why are you doing this?"

"I want to know." I sound like an asshole, but I can't stop myself. I've seen Helen Kasios. Fuck, I've talked to her a few times, though her aggressively bubbly personality grates. She's easily the most beautiful person in Olympus. The kind of beautiful that would make a person forget themselves and act against their own best interests. The kind of beautiful that can spark wars and doom relationships.

I won't let her doom mine. I don't give a fuck if she's turned her eye on Patroclus. She can't have him. He's mine.

Patroclus sighs again. "Nothing good will come of this."

"Since when do we keep things from each other?"

"Nothing happened, Achilles. I don't understand why you're jealous."

Jealousy. That's what this feeling is. I hate it. I want to kill it with fire. Emotions aren't as easy to conquer as physical challenges, though. I step closer to Patroclus, close enough that

I can feel the heat coming off his body. "Did she stand close to you like this?"

He curses. "Fine. We'll do this." Patroclus takes my hand and places it on his shoulder. "She leaned on me to put her shoes back on."

Put her shoes back on?

I don't have a chance to voice the question, because he tightens his grip on my wrist and drags it down my chest. "And then she did this. That was literally it. You're being ridiculous."

His defensiveness tells me more than his protests do. Patroclus doesn't *get* defensive. "You wanted to fuck her." He sputters, which is answer enough. I drag my knuckles over his stomach and wrap my fist around his hard cock. Hard for me? Hard for her? The lack of confirmation makes something ugly snap inside me. I stroke him roughly. "She's gorgeous."

"You say that like everyone in Olympus doesn't already know it." His breathing goes choppy as I keep stroking him. "Achilles, let's go to bed."

I pause. "Patroclus." I don't have to say anything else. He knows me just as well as I know him. He knows what I want.

He digs his hands into my hair and presses his forehead to mine. "This won't make you happy."

"It might."

Patroclus huffs out a laugh, though he sounds pained. "Fine. Yes, I wanted to fuck her. If she wasn't destined to be *your wife*, I might have taken her up on her offer."

My wife.

I had no intention of doing anything about the wife aspect of winning the title, and I still don't. But in that moment, it's impossible not to let my imagination run with how a wedding night might look with Helen Kasios. Spoiled brat, yes, but I'm not immune to her. I don't think anyone alive is. She'd be fire in the bedroom. I don't know how I know, but I'm suddenly sure of it.

Patroclus kisses me. Or maybe I kiss him. It doesn't matter. We stumble back toward the bed. His hands are in my hair, stroking down my back, grabbing my ass and hauling me harder against him. There's no denying the source of this frenzy, and we both know it.

He drops to his knees and I barely get a chance to reach for him before his mouth closes around my cock. "*Fuck.*" Sometimes when he goes down on me, he's a little fucking tease, tormenting me with the slow slide of his mouth and his clever tongue until I lose my patience and haul him to the bed to fuck him.

That's not how he sucks my cock tonight. He pulls me deep, until his lips meet my base. I stare down at him for a long moment, but Patroclus has his eyes closed. He moves over me with a determination that has my balls tightening. Like he wants to escape something. Like he's trying to prove something.

"You're sucking me off like you're apologizing for something." I tilt my head back and close my eyes. "You're forgiven, Patroclus." He's right. He didn't do anything wrong. I don't know why I'm reacting like this, but I recognize that it's bullshit. His moan in response to my words confirms it. This man loves me as much as I love him. He'll fight to keep from endangering us.

I believe that. I do.

Most of the time.

This time, I don't topple him to the bed. I let him pay a penance he doesn't deserve because I know it will make him feel better. Every pull on my cock deflates my jealousy. It doesn't matter that Patroclus wants Helen. Fuck, *I* want Helen. What matters is that he's here, with me.

I tighten my grip on his hair. "I'm close."

His only response is to reach down and cup my balls. He knows what I like, what will get me off the hardest. I curse and come so intensely, my knees buckle. Patroclus doesn't stop sucking me. Not even when I have to catch myself on the edge of the bed to keep from hitting the floor. Only then does he release my cock and press a kiss to my hip. "I'm sorry."

"You have nothing to be sorry for."

"It doesn't feel like that."

I sink onto the floor next to him and lean against the bed. "I was out of line."

"Maybe a little."

"Definitely." Even with the orgasm blunting my thoughts, the jealousy lingers. There are thousands of people in Olympus who Patroclus could fuck and I wouldn't think twice about it. Helen? She's a different story. "I'm sorry, too." I hold up my hand. "Spit."

"Fuck, Achilles..." He obeys, though. He always does. Patroclus spits into my hand and watches with *that* look on his face as I wrap my fist around his cock and stroke him lazily. He always reacts like this, as if he can't believe he's here, that I'm touching him like this. We've been partners for a decade, ever since our friendship turned to fumbling hands and messy kisses when we were twenty.

"I'll make it up to you."

"Oh yeah?" His lips curve. More importantly, the tension lingering in his shoulders dissipates. He leans against the bed, leaning his head back to expose his throat.

"Yeah." I waste no time pressing an open-mouth kiss there as I jack him. It feels good to have him in my hand, to have him pulling me up for a rough kiss. I could finish him like this. I have so many times before. It's not enough.

I break our kiss, ignoring his sound of protest as I drag my mouth down his chest and stomach to take him into my mouth. The tremors in his thighs confirm it won't take long to get him off, which is just fine with me. I'm not any more interested in teasing tonight than he was. I suck him down hard, working him with lips, tongue, and that little edge of teeth he likes sometimes.

"Holy *fuck*, Achilles. I—" He doesn't get a chance to finish, at least not verbally. He comes in my mouth, and I moan as I drink him down. I don't stop there. Fuck, I don't stop until he tugs my hair, pulling me off his cock. "Damn."

I press a quick kiss to his lips. "See. Nothing to worry about."

"I never said there was anything to worry about." There's a smile in his voice now. "But I've apologized and you've very effectively staked your claim."

"Yeah." I grin, completely unrepentant. "Now, bed."

"Bed," he agrees.

We brush our teeth and do some minimal cleanup before climbing back into bed. This time, when I pull him back against me, he's relaxed and sleepy. He's still Patroclus, though. I think the only thing that will shut off that big brain of his completely is fucking him damn near into a coma. A single orgasm barely slows him down.

I'm not remotely surprised when he runs his fingers over my forearm and says, "I tried to talk her out of competing."

"I bet you did." I tug him closer. "I take it that went over well."

"Not even a little bit." He sighs. "It's going to complicate things."

I tighten my grip on him as if I can keep him by my side with sheer strength. "It doesn't complicate anything we don't want it to. I don't give a fuck if she came on to you. She's off-limits."

"I know." His tone goes dry. "I was talking about the tournament. Having the prize compete for the title is...messy."

"Oh. Right." I close my eyes. "Whatever happens, we'll figure it out."

"Always so confident." He brings my hand up and kisses my wrist. "But you're right. This won't be enough of a hiccup to ultimately affect things. No matter what else is true of Helen, she's not a warrior. She doesn't have a chance against you."

Damn straight.

Not in the arena. And not with my man.

HELEN

I'M SO NERVOUS, I FEEL LIKE I'M GOING TO PUKE. NO MATTER how I acted with Patroclus last night—and I refuse to think about *that* self-destructive behavior too closely—the fact remains that I'm having second thoughts about the intelligence of my decision. It seemed like a good idea when I was riding a wave of fury and indignation, spurred on by Callisto's tempting words. Even Athena didn't blink when I showed up at her office and put my name forward.

In the cold light of day, doubt creeps in.

Even though the announcement of the tournament was televised, this is the official opening ceremony. It's held where the rest of the tournament will be—in the arena next to the barracks. I pace back and forth between the concrete walls. I can hear the murmur of the audience creeping in from the arched doorway leading to the arena floor itself. I'm sure my brother and sister will be with Athena in the box seats specifically for announcers and the like. The other candidates will come in through the arch opposite mine, so this entrance is blessedly empty.

Once I step out and declare myself a champion, there's no going back.

I move to the arch and peer out. This building is a traditional arena format, the flat oval in the middle deceptively small compared to the tiered seating rising around it. I've seen it converted to a stage for concerts and even an ice rink sometimes in the winter. Right now, it's covered in sand with a line of thirty-six short podiums that are obviously for the champions to stand on.

The last Ares had a thing for the arena, and he put on regular events and tournaments showing off his people's expertise. They're great entertainment; when I was little, my favorite thing was watching his soldiers stage mock battles or one-on-one fights. Seeing those powerful people at the height of martial competence woke something in me.

Maybe that was when I started down this path, though it's been rocky from the start. My father had strong opinions about the kinds of activities his daughters should participate in. Any kind of martial arts was right out. Eris chose ballet, which proves she's an asshole with a masochistic streak. I'm not much better, though, because I chose gymnastics. I competed when I was in high school, but I was never going to be one of the greats. Still, it served its purpose in keeping me in peak physical condition. I kept up a good portion of the training even after I graduated, which means my upper body strength is deceptively good for my frame, and my endurance is top notch.

Both helped when I took up mixed martial arts. Six months is nowhere near long enough to come close to mastering it, but between my physical skills and the basics, I can manage. I hope.

Right now, it's all theory. I have an idea of what the trials will be since they seem to follow a similar format each time the title of Ares switches over, but there are too many variables. Besides, guessing at what the trials may be is all well and good, but the true wild cards are the champions themselves.

The lights dim and a roar goes up from the crowd. I lean a little farther out and follow the spotlight to where my brother and Athena stand in the box. He's wearing a suit that's, naturally, perfectly tailored and the exact right shade of gray to play up his lighter coloring. She's wearing a three-piece suit as well, deep maroon and with shoulders sharp enough to cut.

If Perseus is bothered by my absence, no one unfamiliar with him would be able to tell, but I know him well enough to see evidence of his displeasure in the way his eyes have gone ice cold. If my public mask is being aggressively bubbly, Perseus's is the exact opposite. The more he's feeling, the less he shows. Right now, his expression might as well have been carved from stone. He's *furious*.

Callisto stands at Perseus's shoulder and Eris at Athena's, both wearing black dresses. The perfect unified foursome. The box seats circling the arena all belong to the various members of the Thirteen, but none of them are currently being spotlit on the giant screens strategically positioned around the area.

My brother holds up a hand and the arena instantly quiets. "The trials begin the day after tomorrow. Tonight is for you to get to know your champions." He glances at Athena. "But first, let's show our support for the woman running this whole enterprise. Athena." He politely claps as the arena goes wild.

Athena is one of the members of the Thirteen who usually avoids the public eye. As the commander of Olympus's special forces, she prefers to do her work in the shadows without showing her hand.

Her reluctance to preen and pose for the cameras has created a cultlike following among Olympus residents. There are entire message boards devoted to people who want her to step on them or who write fanfic about all the Thirteen, but her in particular. She prefers to pretend they don't exist, but the side effect is that her popularity is among the highest of the Thirteen.

She flicks out a hand, her expression even. Immediately, the crowd's cheering cuts off as if something hit a dial. Impressive. She might not do the public thing often, but she's certainly got the presence and command for it. Athena sweeps a look across the arena. "Shall we begin? Good. Our first champion is Paris Chloros."

I flinch, my stomach twisting as I watch my ex walk out of the entrance opposite me and wave to the crowd as he heads for the short podium on the far right. Overhead, the screen flashes clips of him from various gossip sites, and I feel a little sick when I notice how many of them feature me as well. The pit in my stomach only gets worse at how *happy* I look in those videos. Some of it was a lie—dealing with the paparazzi means learning to project the image you want them to run with—but I really *was* happy with Paris...until I realized that my nice-guy boyfriend was an even bigger liar than I was.

Paris provided this video; I know because I was asked to provide the same thing for my entrance. What the fuck is he trying to prove? Surely this isn't all a bid to get me back? I shake my head. No, with Paris, this is more likely some kind of pissing contest, reminding everyone that I was his before I was the next Ares's wife. I shudder. There's a reason I broke things off with him, and I'll commit truly outstanding acts of violence before I let him near me again.

Out of everyone in Olympus, he's the one person I thought I could trust. The one I confessed my doubts and fears to. Instead of providing a soft place to land, he sharpened those same doubts and fears and shot them right into the heart of me, all with a smile on his handsome face.

By the time I ended things with him and managed to make the breakup stick, he'd brutalized my instincts and ruined most of my close friendships. I hadn't even realized he was isolating me until the relationship ended and I was left standing alone.

"Our second champion is Hector Chloros."

I smile despite myself as Hector moves easily across the sand to the second platform. All the good genes in that family went to the elder brother, a fact proven by his video. Ninety percent of it is of him and his wife, Andromache, and their daughter. It would be a strange choice if he were actually here to win, but this video feels like a declaration of a different sort. He's obviously acting as support to Paris.

That's going to be a problem.

It stands to reason that alliances are a possibility, but I'd been so focused on getting around my family to accomplish this that I hadn't thought much farther than getting into the tournament and competing in the trials. Now that I'm thinking about it, though...

I have three sets of allies to worry about who are significantly more dangerous than the rest of the champions. Hector and Paris. The two strangers who arrived together. And Achilles and Patroclus. Ajax will likely fall in with either Hector or Achilles, based on his history with them. Possibly even Atalanta, which would make a fourth pair to deal with. Each of those champions is a challenge on their own. Together? Things just got significantly more complicated.

"Fuck," I murmur. Maybe I can approach Atalanta before Ajax or the others get a chance and see if she'd be willing to work together to get past the first two trials. I won't have much time to work my charm, and I don't really know her at all, but surely the bond of sisterhood is enough to work in my favor.

I grimace. *Not likely.*

While I was waffling, Athena has run through a good number of the champions. They file in, one after another. Some slump alone with their shoulders bowed, obviously not here because they want to be. Others strut and wave at the crowd. I know most of them on sight, but it's clear that after Paris and Hector, Athena is saving the true contenders for last.

Sure enough, Ajax and Atalanta were announced next. Then comes the Minotaur—seriously, what kind of name is that—and Theseus. They look even bigger when lined up with the others. Hector and Ajax are no joke, but these two have several inches and quite a few pounds of muscle on both. Which means they positively tower over everyone else. Hopefully that means they'll be slow and we can knock them out in the first trial.

"Patroclus Fotos."

My attention drags back to the entrance as Patroclus walks through. The others have all dressed to impress, but he's wearing jeans and a white T-shirt. He looks like he wants to be anywhere but here, which is somehow endearing. I can't help comparing him to the boy I knew once upon a time, sweet and quiet and positively nerdy. He doesn't look the same, but he's familiar despite that. Not to mention the man is *hot* now. No one is going to look at him and decide he's an easy mark, not with those broad shoulders and big hands. And he's so damn smart, too. I could practically see his impressive brain whirling and spinning out from being so close to me. My personal taste these days leans more toward pretty and vapid, but I can't deny that I loved ruffling his feathers.

I want to do it again.

I want to ruffle them *a whole lot.*

"Achilles Kallis."

Despite myself, my breath catches at the sight of Achilles in a deep-blue suit. He's so damn attractive and he knows it, stalking across the sand with an intent that feels almost violent. Why is that so sexy? He's exactly the kind of person I would have gone for in the past, the exact kind of person who would have seen my proximity to Zeus as a tool to be used to their benefit. Paris certainly did. I can practically *feel* Achilles's intent and ambition. The others are dangerous, but he wants this more than anyone.

Except me.

Once the cheers die down, a small smile pulls at Athena's mouth. "And our final champion. Helen Kasios."

Chaos breaks loose as I smooth my hand over my short golden dress and stride down the walkway to the arena floor. Ultimately, it doesn't matter what the greater Olympus population thinks of any of the individual champions, because the victor is the one who becomes Ares. With all that said, only a fool wouldn't start to curry favor from the very beginning. Achilles obviously has considered this, but he doesn't have the kind of practice I do with manipulating public opinion.

I wink and blow a kiss at the camera pointed in my direction that's feeding video to the large screens overhead. The chaos morphs into cheers. Perfect. I wave and head across the sand to my podium. Walking gracefully across sand in heels is harder than it looks, but I practically live in six-inch stilettos; I make it look easy.

Achilles moves before I reach the podium, jumping down and closing the distance between us. I tense but manage to keep my smile in place. Is he really going to try to stop me?

The asshole grins and offers his hand. "Fancy seeing you here, princess."

I speak through gritted teeth. "You really don't think I need help stepping up twelve inches, do you?"

His charming smile doesn't slip. "Everyone loves a gentleman."

Oh yeah, Achilles knows exactly how to play the game. I'd find it impressive that an orphan soldier had a better public persona than some children of the Thirteen I know, but I'm too irritated to give him any credit. With one move, he's put me right back into damsel territory. I can't ignore his hand or I'll look like an asshole, which is something I can't afford this early in the game.

I set my hand in his, a secret part of me thrilled by how he seems to dwarf me, even when I step up onto the podium and am technically taller than he is. He holds my hand a beat too long, his gaze coasting over me in a way that feels appreciative without being gross. "You know, last night I thought having you as a wife was just a side effect of getting the title I want."

"You won't have me as your wife," I hiss.

"Oh yeah, I really will." His grin widens, his dark eyes lighting up with something I could almost believe is desire. "You won't win this, princess. Better to get some egg on your face now and keep those pretty features intact. Being married to me won't be so bad. Trust me."

I glare. "Take your hand off me."

He releases me easily, turning that winning smile on the crowd as he jumps back onto his podium. I swear I can hear people actually swooning in the stands, which only makes my blood pressure rise. Maybe that's the reason I forget myself and look up to the box seat where my brother stands. I can feel his glare from here, even if he's not on any of the screens. I have to fight back a shiver.

It's too late to go back. Not even Zeus himself can remove a champion once they've been announced. After this point, we'll all be housed in a secondary location and cut off from everyone else in the city. It's intended to avoid any meddling or attempts to cheat, but for me, it means that my siblings won't be able to show up unannounced and try to convince me to back out. The only member of the Thirteen who can come and go freely from the champions' quarters is Athena.

Athena waves an arm in our direction. "Greet your champions, Olympus."

The cheers and screams are loud enough that I swear I feel

the arena vibrate. It's overwhelming in the extreme. Up until this point, my interactions with the general public have been through a carefully curated filter. I'm a public figure with a public persona and am often featured on MuseWatch, our resident gossip site. But I've never done anything like this. Even my gymnastics meets were with closed audiences, a stipulation my father put on me if I wanted to compete. It certainly didn't earn me friends among my teammates and competitors.

I hope you can see this now, Father. In Tartarus or whatever hole the universe decided to shove you into. I hope it's dark and horrible and you're suffering greatly.

Things happen quickly after that. Several people dressed in Athena's special forces uniform—black shirt, black pants, a swooping owl on the right shoulder—appear and usher us off the podiums and toward the entrance where the other champions came in. This time, Achilles doesn't attempt to offer me a hand down, which is good because I don't like my odds at keeping control of my expression.

The champions are led through a series of concrete hallways, through a locker room, and out into a waiting room with a single exit. The tallest of the soldiers guides us to a line of vans with blacked-out windows.

I lift my brows. "Isn't this a bit much?"

In response, they open the door and give me an unreadable look. "It's your choice."

It's really not a choice at all. Failing to follow protocol now means I'm eliminated before the trials even begin. I sigh and climb into the back of the second van. It doesn't occur to me until far too late that I should have watched where everyone else was going and chosen accordingly. By that time, Paris is already climbing into my van and sitting next to me, too close. Hector follows, a resigned expression on his handsome face. Atalanta rounds out our foursome, her locs pulled back from her scarred face.

Paris leans close, his features so perfect that I have the sudden desire to break his nose and give him some character. Not that I minded his pretty face when we were dating. It's what tricked me into going out with him in the first place. He gives a small smile that has goose bumps raising across my skin. "Helen, what are you doing?"

"I'm not sure what you mean, Paris." No matter how hard I try to control my tone, my words are strained by his proximity.

His smile widens, his eyes sympathetic. "I get that you weren't happy about being the designated prize, but this is one step too far, don't you think? You're going to embarrass yourself and, more importantly, your family."

I can't help tensing. "Excuse me?"

"Don't get me wrong. You look sexy as fuck in that little golden dress. Like a princess." He makes a sympathetic noise. "But you can't honestly expect to get past even the first trial. Honey, you're too delicate for that."

Delicate.

Just another word for *weak*.

I turn my face from him. "It's not your business, Paris. Worry about yourself."

He laughs. "I really look forward to being your husband, Helen. It will give us the fresh start we need."

I think I hear Hector sigh over the roaring in my ears, but I can't be sure. That's the thing about Paris; to anyone who doesn't know him, his charming, confident tone seems totally reasonable. Even his words aren't overtly horrible. He used to keep that same patient look on his face when he'd burrow under my skin until I turned into a shrieking monster during our fights. He made me feel *crazy*, and that sensation is all too quick to rise again whenever I'm forced to interact with him.

"Let's get one thing straight, Paris." I keep my tone sweet and light, even though I feel like screaming. "If you win Ares and think that means you get a single marital privilege, you won't live past the first time you touch me without my permission."

He smiles, completely undaunted. I can't believe I used to find his persistence sexy. It took me longer than I want to admit to realize there's a fine line between a welcome pursuit and straight-up stalking. Paris has a nasty habit of only hearing what he wants. Obviously our time apart has not cured him of that habit. "When we're married, I'll have plenty of time to seduce you. You liked what we did together before, Helen. You will again."

This time, Atalanta snorts. She crosses one long leg over the other and leans back against the wall of the van. "Take a hint, pretty boy. She's about crawling out of her skin to get away from you right now."

She's right, but I hate that I'm being so transparent. I usually have a better poker face than this. I lift my chin. "I'm more than capable of defending myself."

Atalanta gives a careless smile. "Maybe, but I'm going to marry you when I become Ares. I'd be a poor wife if I didn't defend you against scum like this."

"No one needs to defend Helen from me." Paris leans in, crowding me. All I can smell is his cologne and my stomach lurches in response.

Atalanta's smile goes sharp. "Touch her without her consent and that's assault. Assault will get you eliminated."

Paris sits back with a muttered curse, but I can't appreciate the new space. My stomach drops out. I don't know how I didn't consider this in all my scrambling to put this plan into action. By entering as a champion, I've inserted myself into a group of people who fully intend to marry me. I'm the chum to their sharks, tossed into the water to drive them into a frenzy with my proximity.

Shit.

ACHILLES

I SUSPECT THEY'RE TRANSFERRING THE CHAMPIONS OUT OF the city proper, just like Patroclus predicted, and we're proven correct when the doors open to reveal several large buildings surrounded by trees. In the distance, I can hear the soft sound of the ocean, confirming that we're on the coast just north of the agriculture district. If we kept moving west, we'd hit the farmland Demeter oversees.

Ajax huffs out a breath as he hauls his big body out of the van. He hasn't stopped talking since we sat down, which is pure Ajax. That doesn't mean I don't want to gag him to get some peace and quiet. He whistles under his breath as he takes in the area. "Tall walls."

I follow his gaze. Sure enough, I can just see walls that have to be ten feet tall cutting through the trees. They'll encompass the entire property, serving to provide both safety and privacy to the champions. There will be interviews and shit at some point, likely after the second challenge when the weaker champions have been eliminated and there are only a few left. The thought makes my shoulders tense. I can fake it, and fake it well, when I need to, but there's a reason Athena doesn't put me on missions where I have to tiptoe around sensitive personalities.

I'm a human wrecking ball. Patroclus is the political one. He always knows the right step to take, the right thing to say.

Patroclus...and the person walking toward us right now. Bellerophon is tall with warm brown skin and a head of thick black curls. They rank higher than me in the shooting range but lower than me in hand-to-hand combat. I can pin them nine times out of ten, but they're squirrelly despite their long limbs.

They're also a friend, not that that matters right now.

Bellerophon stops in front of our ragtag group. "Ground rules." Their voice is smooth and deep. "You will be assigned individual rooms in the three available dorms. Fraternize if you want, but do not try to harm any of your fellow champions. Doing so results in an instant disqualification. Trying to leave this property without prior authorization will result in an instant disqualification." They meet each of our gazes in turn. "Do we have an understanding?"

There are various grunts and muttered assents in response, which seem to satisfy Bellerophon. "Each room has a schedule for mealtimes and open gym times, as well as a map of the common area. If you need something for your training that we don't have on hand, we'll see about getting it. First trial is the day after tomorrow, so you'll be expected to keep yourself entertained in the meantime without becoming a pain in my ass." They turn and head for the front door. "Let's get you to your assigned rooms."

They point at the two people at their back. "You, take the right third. You, the middle. Everyone on the left, come with me." They sweep their hand to encompass me, Patroclus, Helen, and another six people.

It's highly absurd to have a bunch of large warriors following Bellerophon like little ducklings. Well. A bunch of warriors...and Helen Kasios.

Even being warned ahead of time by Patroclus, it was still a shock to see her show up like that. I thought for sure she'd get cold feet and back out. What's a pampered princess going to be able to do against *these* competitors? She's not like Atalanta. *Atalanta* is one of Artemis's people. The woman is a scrapper and she's fiercely competitive. She's not one to underestimate.

Helen?

That's a different story altogether.

"Stop glaring," Patroclus murmurs.

I turn my glare at him instead. We're not exclusive by any means; we never have been. What we have works for us and I'm not exactly eager to change it... But I can't help my mixed feelings about how close he came to saying yes to Helen last night. He's not one to be ruled by his emotions and baser lusts, and he almost threw caution to the wind and acted against both our best interests to get a chance to take her to bed. That makes her dangerous in a way that has nothing to do with combat.

"Stop staring at Helen's ass," I mutter right back.

He lifts his brows, his silent censure making me even snarlier. Patroclus holds the door open for me and follows me into the dim interior of the dorm. I barely notice the expensive furnishings and the tasteful color scheme. All I can see is the golden sway of Helen's hips and ass as she walks in front of us. Surely she's putting a little more swing in each step to torment me in revenge for that little stunt I pulled with the podium.

I'm not going to apologize for it. I saw an opportunity and I took it. Simple as that. There's really nothing else to say.

"Achilles, control yourself."

Normally, I embrace Patroclus's calming effect. Right now, I kind of want to shove him into a room and fuck him until *I'm* all he can think of, instead of a certain spoiled princess. Gods, I'm fucked in the head over this. I thought last night would be the worst of it, when shock tangled up with jealousy and made my head spin. Apparently I was wrong. I should be concentrating on what comes next and mentally preparing, but all I can think about is those two together.

It would be quite the sight. Fuck, if she was anyone else, I'd make a case for Patroclus and her allowing me to watch...maybe to participate a bit, too. But she isn't anyone else.

She's Helen Kasios.

Precious princess of Olympus.

Sister to both Zeus and Aphrodite. Future wife of the next Ares.

Fucking her is out of the question. Getting near her at all is out of the question, a fact that complicates the current situation because someone is going to knock her out of the competition, which means there will be bad blood between her and whoever that may be. It can't be me. Fuck, it can't be Patroclus, either, because he's a permanent fixture in my life and will be even after

I become Ares. Creating animosity between her and either of us is a terrible idea.

She's put every single champion in a truly shitty position, and she doesn't seem to care. Which just lines up with what I know about her. Selfish, pampered princess. She decided she didn't want to be the prize, so she threw a tantrum and entered the competition herself, despite being outmatched and outgunned. She has no fucking chance of winning. Frankly, it pisses me off.

She pisses me off.

"Stop glaring," Patroclus repeats.

"No one here to see it."

Bellerophon turns down a series of halls to one that has three offshoots. They point to the first one. "Three people in here. Room choice is up to you, but don't get precious about it." We all wait for those three to peel off and head down the short hall to the pair of doors on either side and then walk to the second hallway. "Three more."

It happens so quickly. They peel off and then there's just three of us left. Me. Patroclus. *Helen.* Fuck.

"Last three."

Helen doesn't look at any of us, marching down the hallway. I hate how gorgeous she is. Her short golden dress seems designed to catch every ray of light, molding to her athletic body and giving a truly excellent view of her round ass. If I remember correctly, she used to be a gymnast or some shit like that. Looking at her body, I believe it.

A day ago, I'd have said my attraction to her isn't a bad thing.

I plan to marry the woman, after all. Attraction is near enough to liking someone that we could have made something work.

Now I'm not so sure.

Helen glances over her shoulder, lifting her brows when I jerk my gaze to her face. "This one's mine." She opens the middle door and steps inside, closing it with a click that feels final. Did she choose that room so she'd share a wall with both of us? I highly doubt it. No matter how pretty her smile, she's obviously not that savvy if she's here in the first place.

Bellerophon crosses their arms over their chest. "Is this rooming arrangement going to be a problem?"

"No," I answer quickly. Too quickly.

They give me a long look. "I wasn't aware you have history with Helen."

"I don't. *We* don't." I don't give a fuck if Patroclus used to be sandbox playmates with her. That was a long time ago and it's ancient history now. He feels no loyalty to *her*. "This is fine."

"It *is* fine." Patroclus shakes his head. "The room arrangements change nothing."

That's the problem; my man had a plan and nowhere in that plan did it include us competing against Helen herself. Knowing Patroclus, he needs some quiet time to get his thoughts in order and figure out an updated strategy. He thinks best when I'm not "hovering" as he calls it.

I nod. "I'll be over in a bit."

"Achilles." He holds my gaze. "Don't do anything impulsive."

I laugh and put on my most charming smile. "Me? Impulsive? Never."

"Uh-huh." Patroclus shakes his head and walks to the door on the right, disappearing through it.

Once he's gone, I turn to Bellerophon. "Athena around?"

"No." They prop their hands on their hips. "Even if she were, she doesn't answer to you and she has her own reasons for allowing Helen to participate. It's too late to do anything about it but move forward. Keep your eye on the ball, Achilles. We're all rooting for you."

Of course they were. Having me as Ares would create a new peace between Ares and Athena that hasn't existed in decades. By the nature of the two titles' responsibilities, as often as they work together, they're also competing for the same resources. Ares holds the security forces that most of the Thirteen utilize and Athena heads up the special forces. Both answer directly to Zeus, and the last Zeus liked to play them against each other. This one promises to rule with a more even hand, but having one of Athena's former people as Ares would smooth the way even more.

"I'll get it done." I nudge their shoulder. "I'm the best, after all."

"Yeah, yeah." They snort. "Get some rest and try to stay out of trouble." Bellerophon hesitates. "And keep an extra eye on the Minotaur and Theseus. They seem like trouble."

"I think so, too." We don't get a lot of outsiders in Olympus by nature of the difficulty to pass in and out of the city. A barrier wraps the city and surrounding area, large enough to encompass the farmland Demeter oversees and ensure the people are fed. I've never gotten a solid answer on why Poseidon and a select few of his people are able to pass back and forth freely. Patroclus has his theories and it has to do with bloodlines, but that shit is above my pay grade. For better or worse, Olympus is where I was born and it's where I will make my mark. I couldn't give a shit about the rest of the world outside it.

I eye the door Helen disappeared through. I need to have a conversation with the little princess. The glance I shoot at Patroclus's door isn't *quite* guilty, but I can't help feeling it as I lightly rap on Helen's door. He told me to behave, and I'm pretty damn sure he wouldn't approve of the conversation I'm about to have.

If there's even a chance I can get Helen to resign as champion, I should try. It's better for everyone if she's not competing—even her. Patroclus would agree with that reasoning... Probably.

Helen opens the door but doesn't move out of the way. She also doesn't seem surprised to see me. "Achilles."

"We should talk." There. That's nice and neutral.

She considers me for a long moment before finally stepping back and holding open the door. "You should know, if you try something, I will make you regret it."

I'm careful not to brush against her smaller body as I step into the room. I'm a big guy, and I'm not ashamed to say I've used my size to intimidate people in the past. It was part of my job, after all, but that's not what I'm here for right now. Even knowing that, my mouth gets away from me. "What are you going to do, princess? Stomp on my foot with one of those spike heels? That won't slow down any warrior who's worth a damn."

"Hmm." Helen shuts the door and leans against it, considering me. It almost looks as if she's measuring me up as an opponent.

"Spike heels can do plenty of damage against other parts of your body." She gives my hips a pointed look.

That surprises a laugh out of me. "I'd like to see you try it."

"Don't tempt me with a good time."

This interaction isn't going at all like I expected. The precious princess of Olympus should have swooned at the first hint of a threat, no matter how veiled. This woman looks like she's all too willing to follow through on *her* threat and sink one of those impressive heels into my fleshy bits.

I shift closer to her despite myself. "You think you can take me."

"Baby, I know I can." Helen meets me halfway, planting her feet and almost daring me to close the last bit of distance between us. She looks me up and down, and I don't think I imagine the lick of heat in her amber eyes. "The bigger they are, the harder they fall."

"As if I couldn't squash you with one arm tied behind my back." What the fuck am I doing? Threatening this woman? It's not even that she's a woman. I don't believe in that stereotypical bullshit about considering women noncombatants when they are obviously more than capable of being dangerous enemies. Anyone who underestimates Athena barely lives long enough to regret it.

I just didn't expect to find an enemy in *this* woman. If that's even what she is. *Enemy* feels like a strong word, but what else do I call her? She wants to snatch away the thing I desire most in this world, the title I've spent my entire life chasing. *Enemy* is the only label that does her justice.

Helen licks her lips. "Prove it."

I plant one hand on the door next to her head. The new position has me leaning down over her, and even as a voice that sounds a whole lot like Patroclus whispers that this is a mistake, that we promised to stay away from her, I can't seem to trigger my brakes. "You're not going to win this tournament, princess. You're not going to become the next Ares. Fuck, you're probably not going to get past the first trial. This little rebellion of yours is cute but ultimately meaningless. Your fate is to stand up on that podium and greet your new spouse when they emerge victorious." I grin. "Greet *me* when I step forward as the new Ares."

If I wasn't watching her so closely, I would miss the way she flinches the tiniest bit. Something like guilt tries to clamp around my chest, but I ignore it. There's more at stake than this woman's feelings. "Leave. Go back to your fancy penthouse and pretty dresses. You're going to get hurt if you stay here."

Helen leans back against the door, easing another inch of distance between us, though her hair brushes my thumb and I have the most ridiculous urge to move my hand a little closer to make it happen again. She lifts her chin, somehow managing to look down her nose at me despite being far shorter. "Are *you* going to hurt me, Achilles?"

"I don't want to." It's the truth. I take no joy in smashing opponents clearly physically weaker than me. I also can't afford to be precious about my honor right now, not with the stakes so high. "But yeah, I will."

She narrows those pretty eyes. "And Patroclus. Do you think *he'll* hurt me?"

No need to be a genius to read between *those* lines. I lean down until I'm right in her face, being a total dick about our size differences. "Leave him alone, princess. I don't give a fuck if you used to know him. You don't anymore. He's not like us. He feels too fucking much, and you'll break his soft damn heart if you brush against him carelessly." Fuck, I didn't mean to say that, either. I straighten. "I mean it, Helen. Leave him the fuck alone."

She gives me a slow smile that has alarm bells ringing through my head. "He told you about last night, didn't he?"

"What's that have to do with anything?"

"Achilles." She shakes her head like I'm a child who's disappointed her. "Baby, you sound *jealous*. If your relationship—your *non*-exclusive relationship—with Patroclus is so strong, who cares if I fuck him until he forgets his name?" Her expression goes almost contemplative. "Maybe I'll fuck him until he forgets *your* name. That would be quite the trick."

"Stay the fuck away from him, Helen."

She presses a hand to my chest, pushing until I retreat a step and then another. Helen uses the new distance to open the door. "This was a nice chat, Achilles. We should do it again sometime."

A clear dismissal, and one without a promise to stay away from Patroclus *or* resign from the tournament. I might laugh if I weren't so frustrated. She managed to run circles around me. She's also right; I'm fucking jealous of the fact she made a pass at Patroclus last night. More, she *got* to him and turned his head.

It's only when I've stepped into my room and shut the door

between me and the rest of the world that I can admit I don't know *who* I'm more jealous of.

Helen, for trying to sleep with Patroclus.

Or Patroclus for having the chance to take Olympus's precious princess to bed.

PATROCLUS

IT DOESN'T MATTER WHICH SCENARIO I RUN, THE RESULT IS always ambiguous. Helen Kasios entering the tournament has complicated things. The problem isn't that she's a formidable opponent—though I can't rule that out, no matter what assumptions Achilles insists on making. No, the issue is how her presence disrupts the other champions. Her being here might cause them to act in ways I can't anticipate, and *that* is doing a number on my head.

Paris's emotions are compromised when it comes to Helen because of their history. I can't decide if that means he'll try to help her to get in her good graces or go out of his way to ensure she's eliminated early.

Hector has obvious guilt about the way his brother has treated her, and that might cause him to help her if it outweighs his loyalty to Paris.

Even Achilles is acting slightly out of character, his temper shorter than normal ever since I gave him the rundown on what happened with Helen last night.

If I'm going to be perfectly honest, *my* reactions are off as a result of her presence as well. I can't stop examining my unexpected attraction to the woman from different angles, as if hyperfocusing on it will bring clarity. It would be easier if the only thing that drew me was her beauty. *That* would make logical sense. Unfortunately, it's…messier…than that. I feel a connection with her because of our history, ancient though it may be. I desire her now. Fuck, I respect her for entering the tournament and taking her fate into her own hands, even if it's complicated my life.

The bottom line is I feel drawn to her. It's not convenient and it's not logical, and the battling desires between wanting to follow my original plan and wanting to go knock on Helen's door to just be closer to her are making me want to crawl out of my skin.

I am not a man who is at war with himself. I run scenarios. I use logic and reason. Emotions play into it—I'm human, after all—but they don't rule me. My brain does.

Until now, when I can least afford to alter my course.

A knock on my door has my heartbeat speeding up, and I curse myself for the fledgling hope that it's her. It's not. Of course it's not. Helen has no reason to seek me out. We haven't spoken in more than twenty years aside from last night, and that was a conversation of circumstance. She'd been caught putting her name in as a champion and wanted to persuade me to silence. *She* probably hasn't given it another thought.

A second knock is in the brisk tempo I recognize as Achilles's preferred way of announcing he's about to enter a room. I bite back a sigh and open the door before he decides to knock it down. He nearly bowls me over entering the room. "That woman is a *menace*."

I stare. "You went to talk to Helen." Why am I surprised? Of course, the first chance he got, he immediately went back on his determination that we stay away from her. Achilles has his endgame in mind, and he won't take kindly to Helen throwing a wrench in the gears. Naturally, he decided to see if he could talk her into resigning. *If that's all it was...* I push the thought away. I have no reason to doubt him. "You should have asked me first. She's not going to change her mind."

"I thought I could talk her out of it."

I huff out a breath and head for the little kitchenette positioned in the corner of the living area of this suite. I'd have to walk through Achilles's room to be sure, but I'd wager the suites are all laid out the same. Main door into the living room with a small couch, television, and coffee table. Kitchenette tucked against the far wall with sink, mini fridge filled with snacks and a small selection of alcohol, and a microwave. Short hallway back to the bedroom and bathroom with its ridiculous shower and deep tub.

The couch is sturdy enough. I don't bother to be gentle when I sit. "Told you so."

"I don't need you to fucking manage me, Patroclus." But he follows me over and drops down beside me with a grunt. "She's going to get hurt."

"It's probable."

"You good with that?"

I give him the look that question deserves. He knows damn well I'm not good with it, but at least in this situation, I have to mimic Achilles's determination and drive. I can't afford to care about Helen. She's barely more than a stranger to me now, anyway. It's not *logical* to care about her, beautiful or no, history or no. "I highly doubt it will be serious. Even the new Ares will have to answer to Zeus, and no one wants to piss him off by seriously injuring his little sister."

Achilles catches my hesitation. "But?"

"But…" I really don't want to get into this, but it's been nagging me from the moment the champions put their names forward "But we don't have much information on the two non-Olympians. I can't completely rule them out as dangerous."

"Either way, we both need to stay away from Helen. She's off-limits." He gives me a long look. "Agreed?"

Some irrational part of me wants to push back, but that doesn't make sense. We don't have many ground rules, so when one of us requests something like this, it's important for the overall health of the relationship to respect that request. I can't remember the last time it happened. Maybe a few years ago when I asked Achilles not to pursue Cassandra. That time wasn't out of any jealousy, though. I just noticed the way Apollo looked at her—still looks at her, if the last event we attended is any indication. No one needs *Apollo* gunning for them.

I nod slowly. "I already agreed last night. Nothing's changed since then. Helen is off-limits."

"Good." Achilles stretches out his big body, kicking off his shoes and setting his feet on the coffee table. He catches my frown and laughs. "This isn't our place. Who cares if I have my feet on the table?"

"It's still rude."

"Relax, Patroclus." He nudges me with his elbow. "We're where we're supposed to be. It'll all work out."

I frown harder in response. "Don't pull that lazy god bullshit with me, Achilles. I know you're worried about this." He might put on the mask for other people, but he's not supposed to do it with *me*. "We need to—"

"We need to *relax*." He hooks a hand around the back of my neck and tows me down into a kiss. It's a little rough, a little sweet, and all Achilles. I'm tempted to keep arguing, but he's right. I'll go round and round in circles for days about this. Sometimes clicking off my brain is the right call, and we can't take any action until the first trial. So...

"Patroclus." He nips my bottom lip. "You're still thinking too hard."

"Sorry."

He laughs. "Good thing I know a trick or two to help with that." Achilles shifts, moving to kneel between my legs. The space really isn't big enough for both of us like this, but I don't say a single word as he undoes my jeans and jerks them down my hips. He gives me a devilish grin. "I love it when you look at me like that."

Gods only know what my face is doing, but moments like these feel almost too good to be real. This man, this powerhouse of a golden god, is mine, at least in part. Achilles was meant to be standing in front of a crowd of screaming people, to be the center of their attention, the one they adore and will tell stories about. He's larger than life, even when performing the normal activities that Athena requires of us.

It's even truer now, on his knees and wrapping a fist around my cock. I keep waiting for the day he realizes it and leaves me in the rearview. Achilles will always have his gaze on the stars. And me? My feet are firmly rooted in the earth. It seems inevitable that he'll move beyond me some day, so I try to cherish every moment we have, storing them up against the winter of my future without his shining warmth in it.

He dips down and takes my cock into his mouth, and my thoughts fade in the face of so much pleasure. We've been together for so long. We know exactly what touch, stroke, pressure the other requires to get off the hardest. Achilles isn't sprinting to that destination like last night, though. His mouth descends my length in a slow, wet slide that tells me he intends to take his time. He might be impulsive, but when Achilles sets his mind on a task, he's fearsome in the extreme.

Apparently he's set his mind on my pleasure tonight.

I sink my hands into his dark hair, not trying to guide, merely along for the ride. He teases me, alternating the deep strokes with long licks and flicks of his tongue. My legs start to shake all too soon and I yank on his hair. "Achilles!"

His slow smile makes my chest hurt. Times like these are damn near perfect. Too perfect. How can I not wait for the other shoe to drop? He wraps his fist around my cock and gives me a few slow strokes. "I'm going to take you to bed. Don't be quiet."

Understanding dawns slowly within the fog of my desire. I glance at the wall...the wall I share with Helen. "You want her to hear."

He shrugs, completely unrepentant. "I'm still feeling a little jealous."

The concept of *Achilles* jealous of anyone is almost beyond comprehension. Maybe I'm a selfish asshole, because I kind of like it. I tug on his hair again, more gently this time. "I won't try to be quiet, but whether things get loud depends on you."

He grins, just like I expected him to. "Challenge: accepted." He rises easily despite kneeling for so long and grabs my hand to tug me to my feet. We stumble down the hallway, kissing and rubbing on each other like a pair of fumbling teenagers, but the second we reach the bedroom, he's focused in on me again. Achilles knocks away my hands when I reach for the hem of my shirt. "Let me."

"Bossy."

"You like it." He pulls my shirt over my head and skims my pants the rest of the way down my legs. And then he's surging to his feet and taking my mouth again. This time, there is no gentleness, no sweetness. Achilles kisses me like a conquering warlord, and I am all too willing to cede to the demand of his tongue. He strips in between kisses as he backs me to the bed.

I try to move back so I can appreciate the view, but he's having none of it. He shoves down his pants and then he's on me again, bearing me down to the mattress and settling on top of me. I might be taller, but he's much larger, and moments like these really highlight the differences. He strokes his hands over my arms and down my sides. "I don't want to wait anymore."

"Impatient."

"For you? Always."

I arch up and kiss him. There are times when I want the slow buildup and the careful readying that being with a man Achilles's size sometimes requires, but tonight I'm just as impatient as he is. "Yes. I need you now. I don't want to wait."

He moves off me long enough to yank open the nightstand. I'm already blushing when he laughs because I know what he's going to say. I'm right. Achilles shakes his head. "We've been here twenty minutes and you already unpacked?"

"I don't like living out of a suitcase."

He fishes out the bottle of lube and gives me a searing look. "I know."

I watch, my heart in my throat, as he spreads lube onto his cock. Like the rest of Achilles's body, it's in perfect proportion... which means it's rather massive. Even after all this time, there's a moment of hesitation mixed in with my anticipation, the feeling reaching new heights as he begins to ease his cock into my ass. A rough moan slips free, and he sinks deeper in response. "I want to watch you come all over your stomach. I fucking love it when you lose control like that."

My ability to form words is rapidly disappearing. All that's left is desire. I arch up and kiss him. I need to be consumed entirely. There's no thought for anything else but taking more of him into more of me. Achilles seems to sense exactly what I crave because he thrusts fully into me and lets his body weight rest more firmly on mine, pressing me into the mattress as he kisses me like he needs me more than air to breathe.

I feel the same.

It's enough. It's *perfect*. We could stay forever like this, poised in this moment where lust and love meet.

But our desire won't be so easily sated. He starts to move first, tiny little thrusts that have me moaning and writhing for him. It's good, too fucking good. I try to last, to hold out, but I've never won a battle of wills against Achilles. Tonight won't be the moment I start.

I grip his hip, a rough moan slipping free. He grins. "More."

I'm helpless to do anything but obey. Every thrust drags another moan from my lips. It feels *so good* to have him fuck me like this, all his focus narrowed on me and me alone. Each thrust is rough and perfectly controlled, designed to curl my toes and short out what little thought remains in my head. By the time my body overrides my control and I come all over my stomach and chest, I'm chanting his name.

Achilles shifts back, propping himself up on his hands as he picks up his pace, chasing his own pleasure. He devours me with his dark gaze, a possessive stroke that I can almost feel over my face and down to where my seed marks my skin. "You're mine, Patroclus." He curses, his rhythm going irregular. "And I'm yours. Say it."

"I'm yours," I gasp out. I reach down to grab his hips, urging him deeper. "And you're mine."

At least for now.

HELEN

I DON'T TOUCH MYSELF TO THE SOUND OF ACHILLES fucking Patroclus...but it's a near thing.

The rhythmic thumping of his headboard, interspersed with low moans and Patroclus practically yelling Achilles's name, doesn't do much for my ability to sleep. I lie in my bed and try very hard not to picture those two going at it. They're both far too attractive for my frame of mind, and *I'm* far too attracted to both of them. If we weren't all competing for the same title, I might put a little more effort into seducing one or the other... or both.

By my logic, sleeping with one of them is good, so surely both of them in my bed would be a phenomenal night.

I roll over and punch my pillow. My desire for them might be real—and inconvenient—but it's just my recklessness talking. I spend so much of my life carving out the sensitive parts of myself so no one else can see them, touch them, *hurt* them. Is it any wonder that all the ugly bits bubble up and overwhelm me from time to time? That occasionally living in this skin is too much and I need an outlet?

There was a time when I chose more self-destructive methods than sex to relieve that pressure. I don't like to think about it now, but it wasn't like I had the tools to deal with living in Zeus's household in a healthy way. It wasn't until I started sneaking to therapy at twenty that I managed to curb the worst of my impulses. My therapist isn't thrilled about me using sex to appease that urge, but we have a compromise. I am always safe and always careful about who I sleep with, even when I'm doing things I know I shouldn't. It seems like an oxymoron but it works.

Sleeping with either Achilles or Patroclus—or both—is not safe *or* careful. Yes, I want them, though I also want to shove Achilles out a window. But Patroclus was right to turn me down the other night. Not to mention... Gods, I don't even know him anymore. Not really. And I sure as fuck don't know Achilles at all. They might be just as much monster as Paris is; I didn't see his true colors until it was far too late for an easy escape. Sex complicates things, even with the most emotionally unavailable person. Sex with two men who want the same thing I do, who will crush my dreams without a second thought?

Surely, I'm not that self-destructive.

Surely.

On the other side of the wall, the bed starts thumping again.

"Are you fucking serious?" There's no sleeping like this. I might as well not even try. If it were another situation, I might appreciate their stamina, but I'm tired and overwhelmed and listening to Patroclus get his back blown out is making me both crankier and green with envy.

I sigh and climb out of bed. Maybe the couch is more comfortable than it looks. We don't have overly long until the first trial, and I need sleep and to be mentally preparing. It should be easy. This is what I want, after all. But when I try to gather my thoughts about me, they scatter like marbles.

I'm just tired. That's all.

As I pad down the hall and step into the main living area, I half expect to find Hermes and Dionysus poking around. They like to play the part of stray cats, always showing up in your house when you least expect it. Except...I'm not home and even those two would hesitate to trespass on Athena's property during the Ares tournament.

Silly to miss them. Silly to miss my apartment and my carefully curated bedroom. Silly to have the faintest hurt that neither Perseus or Eris have come to check on me or yell at me or even acknowledge how thoroughly I've fucked up their plans. I don't know why I expected it. Our father taught us too well. When he was truly furious at me for one thing or another, he would stop acknowledging my existence. In hindsight, I should have taken that for the blessing it was, but I had even less self-control as a child. I would get louder, angrier, more dramatic, and he would simply ignore me as if I were really a ghost banging on the walls that no one could see or hear.

I shudder. I *hate* that my siblings are using Zeus's old tricks. They know how much it hurt when he'd do that, and they're doing it anyway... I shake my head. "Way to make yourself the center of everyone's universe, Helen. They're probably off doing important Thirteen things, and I'm too far down the list of priorities." I can't keep the bitterness out of my voice. At least I'm the only one to witness it.

I circle the living room. Times like these, when I'm feeling particularly isolated, I have the nearly overwhelming urge to call my little brother, Hercules. We weren't particularly close growing up. Even from a young age, he was too earnest, too pure, and it made him a target of our father's *firm instruction*. The rest of us distanced ourselves from him to avoid the same fate. In hindsight, the cowardice tastes foul on my tongue. Maybe if we'd tried to step in...

But the joke's on us elder siblings. Hercules got out. He's living in a happy little polyamorous relationship in Carver City, freer in his exile than he ever was within these city limits. Most people who live in Olympus are so focused on the city center that they never stop to think about how we're essentially rats trapped in a cage.

Ultimately, the barrier's existence doesn't matter. For better or worse, I have no intention of leaving Olympus.

I *am* glad Hercules got out, though. I'm glad he's happy. He's very careful to keep his lovers away from us, to shield them from the taint of this city and the Kasios family. Smart man. The rest of us are still dancing to the tune Olympus sets.

I won't call Hercules this time, just as I haven't called him any of the other times when loneliness and self-pity threatened to become overwhelming. The idea of his warm attitude is great in theory, but we have nothing to talk about, and an awkward sibling conversation where it becomes clear how distant we really are is worse than not talking to him at all.

I head back into the bedroom and glare at the wall where I can still hear Achilles and Patroclus fucking. "The couch it is." I drag the comforter off the bed and do my best to make the couch comfortable. It's obviously not meant for this type of thing, but just when I think I'll never get to sleep...I wake up to the morning light streaming through the window.

I sit up and rub my eyes. My back feels like it's got a permanent kink in it, but hopefully that will dispel once I'm up and moving. I stagger to the fridge and eye the schedule that's been put there. A quick glance at the clock on the microwave says I need to hurry if I want to make breakfast. Since I can't cook my way out of a paper bag, skipping a catered breakfast isn't an option. I need my strength, which means I need the calories.

A quick shower later, I pull my hair back into a simple braid and get dressed in running tights and a sports bra. After I eat a light breakfast, I'm going to find the gym and work myself hard enough to earn a nap this afternoon. Hopefully Achilles and Patroclus take tomorrow's trial as seriously as I do and don't plan to have another all-nighter. I grimace at the thought of another night on the couch.

Honestly, if they're going to be fucking like rabbits, maybe I'll request a room change and take Achilles's room so I don't need to share a wall with them. It was a silly power play to take the middle room, but I didn't think I'd come to regret it so quickly.

It's not hard to find the breakfast room. The three dorm buildings create a U-shape around the main area, which contains the breakfast room, a living room, and a massive gym. The space is obviously designed with a group in mind. The kitchen is huge and filled with industrial appliances. A dining room holds four tables with seating for all the champions and then some. Even the living room has groupings of couches around a massive television, though I doubt many people will take advantage of it.

I circle the long kitchen island, eyeing my options. I finally decide on some of the scrambled eggs from the buffet-style setup with salsa and avocado. A scoop of mixed fruit and a giant mug of coffee finish things up. The dining room table is empty except for the two non-Olympians. I almost sit near them to prove they don't unnerve me as much as they truly do, but the threat of indigestion is too strong to risk. Instead, I take a spot at the opposite end of the table.

It allows me a good view of the two men. I study them as I pick through my food. They're both attractive enough in a rough sort of way, but even I would hesitate to flirt if we met at a party. There's something dangerous about them, though I can't say explicitly what gives me that vibe. The short-haired one, Theseus, has a bold, crooked nose that would almost be too big for his face if not for his square jaw. The other, the Minotaur, has long hair that falls in a gentle wave to his shoulders. He obviously takes care of it, because it's thick and healthy looking, which is a feat in and of itself for some guys. The hair almost distracts from the scars: thin, faded white lines, so many that it looks like someone tried to cut his face right off. I shudder at the thought of what those wounds might have looked like fresh. Still, he's got nice, strong brows and surprisingly sensually shaped lips.

Both are dressed unassumingly today in shorts and T-shirts; obviously they intend to use the gym, too. The short sleeves give me glimpses of tattoos crawling up their arms, but I'm not close enough to get any details. Maybe they're organized crime?

They wouldn't be the first to attempt to infiltrate Olympus. The way the Thirteen are chosen means some outsiders are tempted to make a bid for power. The theory is that anyone could take over enough titles to wrest power away from Zeus, Poseidon, and Hades to run the city. It's why so many of the upper-city families flock to the Dodona Tower parties and indulge in arranged marriages with each other. Everything boils down to the power and politics and the alliances that hold the majority of the Thirteen who effectively rule Olympus. Or at least the upper city.

Sometimes people outside the city realize the same thing. It's hard to cross the barrier, but not impossible. My father used to talk about some old enemy making a coup attempt right around the time he inherited the title Zeus, but I never made a habit of listening closely to my father's old "war" stories since they were roughly 90 percent fiction.

Ultimately, it doesn't matter. These two men are opponents, and their motivations for joining the tournament don't change that. Even if one of them somehow managed to win this and become Ares, that's hardly the majority. They can't touch the legacy titles, and they have no chance of getting either Aphrodite or Demeter, albeit for very different reasons. I pity the fool who tries to take Athena's title. Ditto with Hermes.

There is the little-known rule about murder, but...

I shake my head. It's a little-known rule for a reason. Even if murdering one of the Thirteen would technically be a shortcut to bypass the normal path to claiming the title, no one is foolish enough to try it. The others would turn on them with a ferocity that would ensure they didn't survive their first day. It's in everyone's best interest to go about things the proper way.

Attempting a coup of Olympus is a fool's errand.

I finish my meal and sit back, intending to nurse my coffee for a bit and enjoy the view through the big windows along the wall behind the table. Footsteps are the only warning I get before another group of champions comes into the room.

Atalanta makes a beeline for the coffee, ignoring everyone. Hector winces a little when he sees me and steps between me and Paris, obviously trying to guide his brother toward the food and give me a chance to escape. I sigh and push to my feet. The moment of peace was nice while it lasted.

The sight of Achilles and Patroclus stops me short. Patroclus, the adorable creature that he is, seems to be blushing and is very pointedly not looking in my direction. Achilles, on the other hand, has a self-satisfied smirk on his face as he holds my gaze. Well, that answers that. They definitely knew I could hear them.

They *wanted* me to hear them.

Surely you don't think I'll blush and stammer like a teenager, you fools. Three can play this game. I set my cleared plate in the sink and make my way in their direction, putting a little swing in my step. Patroclus looks almost like he's trying to make a getaway, but Achilles throws an easy arm around his shoulders, holding him in place. Perfect.

I cup my coffee in two hands and smile sweetly at them. "Achilles?"

He gives me that easy grin that's a complete lie. "Yeah?"

"Next time you want to mark your territory, why not whip out your cock and pee on his foot instead? It would allow the rest of us to actually get some sleep." I ignore Patroclus's sputtering and lean forward, giving him wide eyes and an innocence I certainly don't feel. "Unless you meant that to be an invitation, in which case, use your words next time." I speak low enough that the conversation won't carry. This is just between us, after all.

His light-brown skin goes a little dusky. "I—"

"Have a nice day." I easily step around them and walk out of the room. It's only when I've rounded the corner that I permit a smile. There's truly nothing as satisfying as a dramatic exit. He made it *so easy*, too.

The feeling of petty victory fades with each step. I'm allowing myself to be distracted by those two, and that's unacceptable. It will be best if I keep away from the rest of the champions during this process. Something I should have remembered before I needled Patroclus and provoked Achilles.

The gym is exactly what I would expect from Athena. Filled with a solid mix of free weights and equipment that looks state of the art, all of it gleaming. I finish my coffee and consider my options. I want to work off some energy, but I don't want to overly tire myself out. A three-mile run will barely take the edge off, but I'll do a quick round of circuit training afterward and that should do the trick.

With that decided, I head back to my room to wash out the coffee cup and grab a bottle of water from the fridge. The gym is still blessedly empty when I get back there, and I waste no time putting in headphones and getting on the treadmill.

By the end of the first mile, my muscles unclench and I start to relax. Things haven't gone as planned, but that's okay. I've been adapting to the whims of others my entire life. Why should this be any different?

Sure, I didn't think Perseus would follow so literally in our father's footsteps. He told the truth when he said he's made sacrifices, too, but he's intentionally neglecting to remember that he *chose* his sacrifices. He didn't give me the opportunity to do the same. Instead, he made the decision for me and expects me to dance to his tune, a puppet on strings he commands.

And Eris? *She*, of all people, should realize that I understand the inner workings of Olympian politics. If they'd asked this of me instead of ambushing me with the announcement... I shake my head, wishing I could shake the thoughts clear as easily. Eris knew I'd argue and she'd have to convince me, so she jumped right over that conversation and went around me. I don't see *her* lining up to marry a stranger, but she was all too happy to throw me to those wolves.

Gods, my family really is the worst.

I turn up the pace on the treadmill. It's only three miles. I can go a little faster, a little harder. Anything to avoid thinking too closely about the fact that my brother and sister sat down and decided, together, that they were willing to sacrifice me for the goodwill of the next Ares. I don't care what reassurances Perseus mouthed; in that worst-case scenario, I would already be harmed. Vengeance isn't for the victims. It's to make the people around them feel better for not doing anything to stop it in the first place.

I am no victim.

Not anymore.

I was helpless in my father's house. My mother tried to help, but all she got for her trouble was a broken neck while my father moved on to another woman, another Hera. People used to *joke* about his Heras being interchangeable, toys shattered by an angry man and replaced just as easily. He would have done it again if he hadn't died. He already had his sights set on Persephone, a woman younger than *me*.

Perseus was the one to tell me the news of our father's death. I sat there and waited to feel anything at all. Sorrow. Guilt. Joy. *Something*. Instead, it simply felt like someone had lifted a great weight from my shoulders. The monster with the charming mask couldn't hurt or control me anymore.

I didn't expect my brother to step into the role of Zeus so completely. I didn't expect him to essentially put me on lockdown—for my safety, of course. To start dictating what was and wasn't acceptable Kasios behavior, just like our father used to.

To designate me a pawn to be sacrificed, *just like our father planned*.

I turn up the speed on the treadmill. This isn't helping. I'm still thinking too much. I can't outrun the skeletons rattling around inside my brain, but I *can* exhaust myself until they slumber. I have to. I can't fucking live like this. Not when I'm so close to freedom, not when distraction means failure.

A hand appears in my field of vision. I don't have time to

do more than flinch before Patroclus hits the stop button on the treadmill. The belt slows, and I yank my headphones out of my ears. "What the fuck is wrong with you?"

"That's enough, Helen."

I open my mouth to tell him where to shove his opinion, but the red numbers catch my attention. Seven miles, not three, and at a pace that I know better than to hold. Now that my momentum has been brought up short, the shakiness in my limbs registers. The sweat coating my body. How each breath saws painfully in and out of my lungs. I've run farther and faster, but this wasn't meant to be this kind of workout.

Weak. Reckless. Impulsive. I try to shove the words away, but they linger just out of reach, taunting me.

Patroclus doesn't move, his hand still on the stop button. I suspect to keep me from ignoring him and turning the damn thing back on. I swipe sweat from my forehead with my forearm. "I'm fine."

"You sure? Because you look like you went too hard and were going to keep running until your legs gave out." His gaze coasts over me. It's not sexual. He's looking at me like he's checking for injuries. There's absolutely no excuse for the shiver of awareness that goes through me in response. I blame the air conditioner against my sweaty skin for the way my nipples go tight and hard against the thin fabric of my sports bra.

"I'm fine," I repeat. It's not true this time any more than the last time I said it. I'm so far from fine, it's laughable, but what did I really expect? My siblings threw me under the bus; that's going to affect me, even if a small, dark part of me isn't surprised in the least. I'm not in the mood to try to explain that to Patroclus, though. He seems like a good guy, but he's *Achilles's* good guy. Just because we were childhood friends and he did a nice thing for me just now doesn't mean he signed up to have all my baggage dumped on him.

Still, I can't leave things so curtly. I hesitate. "Look, I'm not inviting you to meddle in the future, because I don't need a babysitter, but thanks for stopping me."

"No problem." He drags his hand through his short, dark hair. He's got a bit of a five-o'clock shadow going on, which gives him a roguish look that isn't great for my libido.

Not that anything else about Patroclus is roguish. Best I can tell his nice guy routine isn't a routine at all. *That* hasn't changed, at least. I could use that to my advantage, but I'm suddenly so damn tired that I can't think straight. He deserves better than to be the whip I pick up to flog myself with, which means I have to get out of here before I do something unforgivably foolish. "I'm going to go take a shower."

"Helen."

My stomach dips a little at the sternness in his tone. I stop short. "What?"

"Stretch." He nods at my legs as if he can see the little tremors shaking them. "You'll regret it later if you don't."

He's right. My needs war with one another, one demanding I retreat to my room until I feel a little less brittle, the other wanting to stay in this man's presence a little longer, to let him chase away the ghosts haunting me. Surely he doesn't actually care as much as he seems to. It has to be a mask like everyone else in Olympus wears. I don't know what purpose kindness would serve—possibly to have others underestimate him—but each of us chooses our own path to survival.

Still...

When was the last time someone tried to take care of me? Even in something as mundane as demanding I stretch after a vigorous workout? My chest goes tight. I can't remember. The last soft person in my life was my mother, and she's been dead fifteen years. How fucking pathetic is that?

Even knowing I should leave, the reckless urge rises in me, too strong to ignore. I smile up into his kind, dark eyes. "Will you help me stretch, Patroclus?"

ACHILLES

AJAX WAYLAYS ME BEFORE I MAKE IT INTO THE GYM. THE big man clamps a hand on my shoulder. He's got a few inches on me, putting him at damn near six five, and he's shaved the sides of his head to give him a Mohawk of curly black hair. Ajax's skin is a dark brown and he's got plenty of it on display because he's only wearing a pair of shorts and a muscle tank top that's more holes than fabric. He grins. "I was thinking."

"Dangerous of you."

Ajax laughs. "Yeah, yeah. We both know I prefer a big hammer to a political roundtable, but things change."

"You're going to suggest an alliance for the first trial." Patroclus predicted this. He's done his research and run his scenarios, though sometimes the way his mind works is downright spooky. This one, however, even I could have seen coming. Ajax, Patroclus, and I are known quantities. We've worked together in the past, so it makes sense to align ourselves in an effort to eliminate as many people as possible in the first trial. The alliance doesn't have to last longer than that to be worthwhile.

He laughs again and gives my shoulder a squeeze. "Yep. I'd say there are a few champions no one wants to see become Ares. No reason to make it easy for them to pick us off."

Interesting. I frown. "You're allied with others?"

"I get around." He drops his hand and shrugs. "What do you say?"

I say that Ajax is savvier than either of us gave him credit for. Still, it changes nothing for the first trial. There are a few champions I would like to see eliminated early, and Ajax as an ally makes that more likely to happen. But with that said, there's no reason to muddy the waters. I have Patroclus. He's all I need, and frankly, it would benefit us if Ajax is eliminated early.

I smile and shake my head. "Not this time, friend."

"Damn. I was hoping to get you on my side. Ah well, it was worth a shot." He clamps me on the shoulder one last time and ambles down the hall in the opposite direction I'm headed. "See you tomorrow, Achilles. Good luck."

"I don't need it."

His laughter trails behind him as he rounds the corner and disappears. I head for the gym. Patroclus will have some theories on who Ajax would have allied himself with; I'd put good money on Atalanta. Ajax worked with Hector for a few years, and I think they're on good terms, but Hector is a package deal with Paris, and no one wants to see Paris as the new Ares. None of us have had close contact with Atalanta, but her reputation precedes her. She's steady under pressure and is pretty fucking brilliant. Not as brilliant as Patroclus, but definitely more than me and Ajax.

The gym is a nice setup, but I expect nothing less from Athena.

She has her priorities in order, and she would have seen this room outfitted specifically to her directions like everything else in the house. Plenty of variety to fit the needs anyone could dream up.

I catch sight of the Minotaur on one of the benches, but he makes no move to lie back and pick up the bar with a truly outstanding number of weights piled on it. No, he's staring at something I can't see, his expression that of a hawk watching a particularly juicy mouse wander the field below it. That can't be good. I stride down the space between equipment and stop short when I see what he's looking at.

Patroclus...and Helen.

She's on her back on the mat taking up one corner of the room, one long leg stretched up over Patroclus's shoulder. He's on his knees, pressing her leg down toward her chest. Rationally, I realize it's a hamstring stretch and that they have all their clothes in place, but my brain sees the position and says *fucking*. Especially when he shifts forward and presses her leg another inch lower. They're close enough to kiss, and even from here I recognize the flush of his skin.

He's turned on. Really, really turned on.

Fury rises. I told them to stay away from each other, and it took all of ten minutes for her to have him on the floor, hot and bothered. Fuck, *he* knows better, too. Does no one listen to me when I talk? I clench my fists, fighting against the instinctive desire to stalk over there and rip him off her.

A snort has me looking at the Minotaur. He arches a scarred brow. "She's moving fast with that one."

I was just thinking the same thing, but that doesn't mean I like other people noticing. "Shut the fuck up."

He gives that snort again and leans back, easily picking up the bar and beginning to press it to his chest and up again. I watch for several repetitions before I turn back to Patroclus and Helen. She's switched legs, and it irritates me further that neither of them even noticed me standing here. That spurs me into motion, the possessive ugly thing inside me taking control. I stop a foot from them and snarl. "Get up."

Patroclus startles, which pisses me off more. He's damn near impossible to sneak up on because he's always thinking ten steps ahead, and yet he's so focused on *this* woman that it put his big brain on hold. He sits back and shifts his hips as if I can't tell that he's got a raging boner. I glare at him and then turn my attention to *her*. "Up."

Helen looks good. Damn it, I hate that she looks good. She's got on a pair of pants and a sports bra that cling to her sweaty skin, showing off her toned stomach and nice tits. She sits up slowly, her expression pure challenge. "He was helping me stretch."

"I can see *exactly* what he was doing." It would be bad enough to have been the one to catch them, but with the Minotaur watching, judging, fucking *laughing*, I can't get ahold of my anger. "You." I point at Patroclus. "Get your head on straight."

"Achilles—"

I ignore the exasperation in his tone and turn to Helen. "And you. Back to your fucking room, princess."

"Funny thing, that." She pushes to her feet, and I fucking *loathe* the way Patroclus watches her as if he's going to jump in and catch her if she stumbles. The Minotaur is right; she's working fast, and she's working on *my* man. Helen stretches her arms over her head, pure challenge in those amber eyes. "You're not the boss of me."

"Helen." Now Patroclus turns that exasperation in her direction, which is another indicator of how close they've gotten in such a short time. He might be soft, but he's very careful about who he extends his circle of protection to because of it. It usually takes ages for him to warm up to a new person. How the fuck did she manage it in just a few days? It can't be because she knew him before I did. It *can't*.

"I might not be the boss of you right now, but I'm going to be your husband, and you *will* stop acting like a spoiled little brat."

Patroclus sucks in a breath, and Helen's spine goes ramrod straight. "Say that again," she snarls.

I don't bother. Instead I grab her and toss her over my shoulder. Patroclus starts to move forward, but I hold up a hand. "I don't want to hear shit from you right now. Do your workout. We'll talk later." I don't give him a chance to respond. I just turn and haul a cursing Helen out of the gym and through the halls. After the briefest hesitation, I go through my door instead of hers.

I barely have a chance to set her on her feet before she swings on me. I dodge back, easily catching her fist. "Sloppy."

"I'll show you *sloppy*, you asshole." She aims a kick for my balls, and I turn my hips. The impact hits my thigh and she's put enough strength behind it to stagger me. She's quick, too, dancing back a step and snapping another kick at my face.

I catch her ankle and yank her off her feet, following her to the floor when she immediately tries to jump back up. She's scrappy; I'll give her that. She manages to elbow me in the face before I wrestle her to the floor and pin her wrists on either side of her head. "That's enough."

"Fuck you." She's so furious, she's vibrating, her amber eyes practically shooting lasers at me. "No wonder you want to be Ares. You're just like the last one: a fucking bully."

"Shut up."

But she doesn't. She snarls in my face and tries to throw me off her, like I don't outweigh her by a shit ton. And she keeps running that godsdamned mouth. "Poor little Achilles got his pride hurt because Patroclus was nice to me. Gods, you're pathetic."

"Shut *up*," I grind out.

"Make me!"

There is no excuse for what happens next. One moment I'm ready to haul her to her feet and kick her ass out my door. The next... I don't know who moves first. Maybe she arches up. Maybe I dip down. The end result is that I'm kissing Helen Kasios, precious princess of Olympus, the woman I fully intend to marry when I become Ares.

She tastes like victory.

I jerk back and stare down at her. She looks nearly as shocked as I feel, nearly as furious. This was a mistake. "I—"

"*Shut up.*" She arches up again, and this kiss sweeps away what little rational thought I have left. There is nothing soft in this. Maybe if there was, I'd figure out how to stop. I can't think, though. Not as we go to war with each other, a battle comprised of tongue and teeth and surprisingly sweet little moans she makes into my mouth.

Helen shifts beneath me, rubbing her calf up my leg. I release her wrists and hook a hand under her knee, fitting us more closely together. She runs her hands down my chest, and the only warning I get is a slight tensing of her body before she hooks her foot around my thigh and flips us. She lands astride my hips and, fuck, Helen has never been more beautiful than she is in this moment. She's a fucking mess, but she's *real*.

The frenzy rises between us, as if we both can sense that slowing down will let reality creep back in. I don't know what she's running from. I don't fucking care. I'm still so furious, I'm running on instinct alone, and I reach between us to grab the fabric of her pants and yank hard. It tears along the center seam, so I do it again, ripping the damn things in half.

Helen arches back and slaps me, the blow turning my face to the side. "These are my favorite running tights, you piece of shit."

"Bill me." I flip us again, using the change in position to settle between her thighs. She wrestles my shirt off and rakes her nails down my back, the pain making me thrust against her. We both moan, our air mingling in a furious exhale. I should gentle the kiss, should slow us down, but Helen dips her hands into my shorts and digs her nails into my ass. I thrust against her a second time and then a third, each one working my shorts lower on my hips until she shoves them the rest of the way down.

Fuck.

This is out of control.

I start to pull back, to try to insert some kind of reason, but she tilts her hips and then my cock is nudging against her entrance. We both freeze. She's so wet, so damn welcoming, that I slide a little inside just from the force of our harsh breathing. Helen gives a breathy little whimper. "More."

I should stop. I should tell her to wait, to slow down until we can talk about this. This wasn't what I intended when I hauled her in here. Fuck, I don't even know *what* I intended. I can't think past how good she feels, how wet she got from this fighting, how badly I want to sink the rest of the way into her.

"We shouldn't," I manage.

"You're right." But her nails prick my ass again, and I sink another inch into her. I can't see her face from this position, can't stop myself from turning my head and setting my teeth against the soft skin of her neck. She responds by arching up, taking me another inch deeper. She gasps. "I hate you."

"I hate you, too."

Helen shivers. "Then fuck me like you hate me, Achilles. Stop pussyfooting around and do it properly."

The last thread of my control frays and snaps. I jerk back, her moan of protest only spurring me on. I yank her pants the rest of the way off and then do the same to her bra. She tries to slap me again, but I grab her wrist and use the hold to flip her onto her stomach. She's already lifting her ass as I move between her thighs, and then I'm inside her again.

This time, I don't stop. I don't hesitate. I use my bigger body to bear her to the floor and pin her there as I fuck her roughly. She moves as much as I allow, lifting her hips to take me deeper, but it's not enough. I work my arms beneath her, clasping her throat with one and pressing the other between her thighs to stroke her clit. She's completely wrapped up in me, completely at my mercy.

Except it feels like I'm at *her* mercy when she starts speaking.

"Yes. Like that. Harder." She grabs my arms, her nails once again setting to my skin. I'll be wearing her marks for days, and the thought only spurs me on, making me rougher.

"You're a fucking menace." I find the touch she likes on her clit, the one that makes her flutter around my cock hard enough that I have to fight not to lose it. My orgasm is already threatening. She feels too fucking good. "Come around my cock like a good little princess."

"Make me," she gasps, pressing her throat harder against my palm. "Unless you're just as bad at this as you are at everything else." Another moan. "Maybe I should ask Patroclus for an assist."

"You *bitch*." I don't stop, don't slow down. I keep fucking her as she comes apart around me, her poisonous words fated to linger even after we're done.

Helen cries out as she orgasms, her body shaking sweetly even as her pussy clamps around me. I don't even try to hold out. I just keep thrusting into her until need overwhelms me, filling her up with me.

It's only when I roll off her and drop onto my back that reality starts setting in. I open my eyes and stare at the ceiling. "Fuck."

"Yes, we did that." She sits up.

"Are you okay? I…" I make myself look at her, make myself search her expression for any sign that we went too far.

Helen picks up her pants and frowns at them. "I'm fine." She glances at me, her face carefully blank. "You're not about to go soft on me, are you?" When I don't immediately reply, she sighs. "It was just sex, Achilles. You've had sex before, haven't you?"

"Not like this."

She hesitates. "Patroclus said you weren't exclusive—"

"We aren't." But I've also never been with anyone like *this*, so rough and out of control. I am always very fucking aware of how easy it would be to hurt my partners on accident, and as a result, I'm always leashed. Except with Patroclus; our history means we know each other's limits more thoroughly, and I still am careful not to cross his lines. Helen and I don't have that history, that trust. We don't even fucking like each other. I can't say that to her, though. It feels cruel, even if it's the truth. Instead, I focus on something small and mundane. "You can't wear those pants."

"Don't worry. I fully intend to bill you for them." She climbs slowly to her feet. There are faint rug burns on her knees, but fuck, she looks like a magnificent mess. It makes me want to...

I jerk upright. "We didn't use condoms."

"I know." Helen sighs again. "I'm on birth control. I've been tested recently enough that I can confidently say you're safe."

Somehow, that doesn't detract from the tightening in my chest. I can't believe I lost control so thoroughly as to forget a *condom*. "The only person I have unprotected sex with is Patroclus, but we're both tested regularly since we're not exclusive."

"Then there's nothing else to say." She turns for the door.

I'm on my feet before I decide to move. "Helen, wait."

Another of those sighs. Gods, the woman sounds so exasperated with me that I want to toss her to the floor again. This time, when we're finished, neither of us will have the breath left for *sighing*. Oblivious to the direction of my thoughts, she smooths back some of the hair that's escaped her braid. "Look, there's really nothing else to say. I lost control. You lost control. It ultimately doesn't change anything for either of us, so let's never speak of it again."

She's being remarkably coolheaded about this, and I don't understand how the fuck she's pulling if off when it's everything I can do not to yank her to me and kiss her again. I snatch my shirt off the floor and stalk to her. Helen rolls her eyes at me. "My door is—" I pull the shirt over her head and wait for her to get her arms through it. She gives me a bored look. "Are you happy now?"

"No." Somehow, this is even worse than her naked. Seeing her in my shirt... I already knew I was a territorial asshole, but I didn't expect to have those urges rising up with *this* woman. "No, I'm not fucking happy."

"Didn't think so." She turns and walks out of the room without another word.

I stare at the door for a long time. "Fuck. *Fuck*." There's no doubt about it. No matter how I try to spin this out—and I'm having a shitty time coming up with a reasonable explanation for why I fucked Helen Kasios on my floor like a godsdamned animal—there's only one conclusion to be had.

I just screwed up spectacularly.

11

PATROCLUS

I KNOW WHAT HAPPENED THE SECOND I SEE THE LOOK ON Achilles's face. He's so used to being in the right that when he knows he fucked up, he acts like a dog who chewed up my favorite pair of shoes. He walks through the door into my rooms with his shoulders bowed, and he won't meet my eyes. Considering where he just was and the familiar flush to his skin, I can take two guesses to figure out what he's done. He all but confirms it when he finally speaks. "I screwed up. I'm sorry."

No need to ask for clarification. The evidence is right there in the scratches on his forearm and the faint perspiration dampening the dark hair at his temples.

He had sex with Helen Kasios.

I drag in a slow breath, but it doesn't help because all I can smell is the faint scent of fucking still clinging to him. Achilles takes a step toward me, but I hold up my hand. "Go take a shower before you try to tell me you're sorry."

He curses and veers toward the hallway leading to the bedroom.

From the back, I can see more scratches peeking out at the neck of his T-shirt. My stomach twists. I have absolutely no logical reason to be upset about this. We're not exclusive. Achilles fully intends to win Ares and that means marrying Helen. Demanding that he not sleep with his wife is a ridiculous ask and unfair. I knew what I was signing up for when I fell in love with this man.

He was never meant to be only mine.

But all the logic in the world can't quell the awful feeling twisting in my stomach. Tighter and tighter, harsher and harsher. I don't mean to speak, but as he opens the bedroom door, the words slip free. "You hate Helen."

Achilles glances over his shoulder at me. "'Hate' might be a strong word." He has the grace to look ashamed, but there's still a relaxed line to his shoulders that speaks of good sex.

The thing in my stomach twists harder. Achilles and I have been together too long to have a relationship free of ups and downs and occasionally intense fights. This feels different. Everything about this feels different. He's occasionally selfish and impulsive; sometimes I'm selfish and distracted. Neither of us is ever cruel, but I don't know what to call this except cruel.

"Were you that angry that I was helping her stretch? That fucking *jealous*? What happened to us not doing jealousy, Achilles?" It's never been a problem before, but surely he understands this is different. Everything about his reactions to her are as outside our norm as *my* reactions to her. Achilles might play the golden fool sometimes, but he's too smart to pretend he doesn't understand why I'm upset.

His expression goes stony. "This is different."

"Yeah. Exactly. This is different. So why did you do it?" I rush on before he can answer. For once, my mouth is moving faster than my brain. "Is it because you're going to marry her? It'll be your ring on her finger, so she's just for you?" The words are out before I can call them back. I'm feeling sick enough that I don't *want* to call them back. "You said she was off-limits less than twelve hours ago."

He stares at a point over my right shoulder. A sure sign that I'm not going to like what comes out of his mouth next. He doesn't disappoint. "She's already getting to you."

"You fucked her. Anyone looking at the evidence would say she's getting to *you*."

He clenches his jaw. "She knows exactly what she's doing, too. She's trying to cause a rift between us."

I curse and turn away. I can't look at him right now, not when he's being so damn stubborn and misguided. Not when he's being a fucking hypocrite. "Stop blaming her for *your* actions. Did she tie you down and fuck you, Achilles?"

"No," he grinds out.

"Yeah, I didn't think so. It took the two of you to have sex, and I'm not in a relationship with Helen. I'm in one with you. *She* didn't put down a ground rule and then promptly break it in a jealous rage after we both agreed to it. *She* isn't putting all our goals and plans in jeopardy because of her impulsiveness. *She* isn't the problem."

"Patroclus."

I reluctantly turn to face him. Achilles looks angry, but that's no surprise. For as long as I've known him, he'd rather be angry than upset or regretful. It's an easier emotion for him. I thought we'd gotten past him doing that to *me*, though. I'd thought a lot of things up until we became champions. Now I'm not sure what the truth is. "I changed my mind about the shower. I need you to go."

He jerks like I reached out and struck him. "What?"

"Get out. I can't stand looking at you right now." It hurts too much. I suspected things with us would eventually reach some kind of conclusion, but not like this. Never like this. I thought we had more time. This isn't the end, not yet, but it's the first sign of it. I need time to process, and I can't do that with him near me.

For the first time since he walked through my door, he actually looks worried. "We need to talk about tomorrow." An excuse and we both know it.

"There's nothing to talk about."

"Ajax wants an alliance."

I shrug. "We predicted that. It doesn't mean anything has changed about *our* plans." It's even the truth. Nothing has changed. I will still follow Achilles into the underworld and damn myself in the process. It's always been that way with us. Maybe if I were a better person, a stronger person, I would cut ties now before things spiral fully out of control and he tosses my heart into a meat grinder. He would never harm me on purpose, but he's careless. He's always so fucking *careless* with other people.

I'm not a better person. I'm certainly not strong enough to walk away from him, no matter how painful the future is destined to be. I just...can't look at him right now. "Go."

He doesn't move. "I'm sorry."

"I don't believe you." If I let him, he'll hug me and promise never to do it again, but I can't stand the thought of him lying to me, even unintentionally. One of the things I love most about this man is that I never have to guess where I stand with him. He speaks his truth, even when it might be hurtful. A small price to pay for that clarity.

Right now, nothing feels clear. He might intend to never touch Helen again, but he never *intended* to touch her in the first place, and look where that's gotten us. "Go, Achilles. Please."

He finally nods and walks to the door. Achilles isn't one to run from a fight; it took years before he realized that trying to hash issues out all at once instead of giving me time to process is a surefire way to escalate things. It still feels fucking terrible to watch him walk out of my rooms and close the door softly behind him.

A premonition, a vision into our future.

Someday, Achilles will walk away from me, and that time, he'll never return.

I move to the door and flip the lock. I'm not in the mood for company right now, not that anyone is going to seek me out the night before the first trial. I pace around my living room, too agitated to sit down. Achilles didn't cheat on me. That's not what we're about. But it still feels like a betrayal. I can't parse out my feelings properly. There's anger and hurt, yes, but also a thread of guilt.

I can't guarantee I wouldn't have done the same damn thing if the opportunity came my way first.

There's something about Helen that gets all my wires crossed. It's not just that she's beautiful, though she is. It's not that once, a very long time ago, she saved me from a bully. It's not even the cunning mind she's given me glimpses of during our handful of conversations. It's the strange vulnerability that crept into her amber eyes the first night and then again when she was on the treadmill, obviously trying to outrun something in her head. The woman is a puzzle, and I know myself well enough to recognize that I am weak for a puzzle.

Most people act in ways I can anticipate, even if it's illogical. Humans are driven by basic urges, even when they're playing political games. Everyone wants something, and once I figure out what it is, it's easy enough to see ten, twenty, thirty steps ahead.

I can't figure out Helen's purpose for becoming a champion. She has power, influence, more money than most people can spend in a lifetime. She's savvy enough not to balk at a political marriage; she'll have been prepared to navigate it from the moment she became an adult. Is she just another power-hungry Kasios making a grab for a title? Or is this all a rebellious act to stick it to her brother? Neither of those answers feels quite right.

Helen being a puzzle aside, the physical attraction I feel for her is downright uncanny. I have no idea what Achilles saw when I had her on the floor, but I'm all too ready to admit that I was far closer than I needed to be, that my body had gotten the better of me even if neither of us commented on it. And the way she kept looking at my mouth...

I don't blame Achilles for having sex with her. The problem is I don't know what I'm supposed to feel. Jealousy. Anger. Hurt. Guilt. It's not a simple situation, and the fact that we're competing tomorrow in the first trial only muddies the waters further.

It doesn't matter. It *can't* matter.

When we started down this road, I decided to have Achilles in my life for as long as he'll have me, to support him and do everything in my power to ensure he realizes his dream of becoming Ares. Feeling hurt that he slept with Helen after declaring her off-limits changes nothing. I will still do what it takes tomorrow to get him through the first trial. Not that he'll need my help, but Achilles can have tunnel vision when it comes to his goals. If the factors change, he doesn't always notice. That's why I'm here.

I just...never expected to resent the role.

——————— .

The next morning brings no clarity. I duck into the main living space earlier than anyone else and grab food to take back to my room. I'm still not ready to face Achilles, and I don't even know what my reaction will be upon seeing Helen.

I was telling the truth yesterday. I don't blame her for what happened. She knows we have an open relationship. She has absolutely no reason to think she crossed any lines by having sex with Achilles.

My jealousy isn't logical and has no basis in fact. It's pure emotion, and I don't trust it not to surge the moment I see her. I'm not sure what I'll do if it does. She deserves to be more than the club Achilles and I bludgeon each other with, but I can't guarantee I won't do exactly that if given half a chance.

It's not a comfortable realization.

By the time Bellerophon comes to collect us, I'm filled to the brim with restless energy. The sensation only gets worse when I step through my door and find both Helen and Achilles already standing in the hallway. We were given no clothing guidelines, so I went with a pair of compression pants and a T-shirt. Clothing that's easy to move in but fitted enough that it's unlikely to catch on anything or provide a handhold for another champion. Achilles is wearing the gear we commissioned for him, a similar style to mine but with a black and silver pattern on it that's designed to catch the eye. He looks good, just like the handsome god he plays when he's required to deal with the public on Athena's behalf.

Helen...

Helen looks like the princess Achilles has named her. She's wearing tiny shorts that leave her long legs bare and a tank top that clings to her skin, both a black-gold that shines even in this low light. There's also glitter on her skin and in her slicked-back hair. She hasn't downplayed her beauty today. Smoky eyes and black lipstick should be too intense, but combined with the glitter, she appears otherworldly.

They look...like a couple.

Bellerophon clears their throat, and I realize I've been staring. "Let's go." They turn, leaving us to follow them down the hall in the direction of the exit.

Achilles tries to catch my eye, but I shake my head. I'm not in the mood to try to hash out anything, and even if I were, now's hardly the time. "Stick to the plan," I murmur.

He nods, but not like he's happy. That's fine. I'm not particularly happy at the moment, either. I glance at Helen again, but she seems lost in her own thoughts, her gaze a thousand miles away.

The other champions are already gathered by the time we make it out there, and everyone is quiet as we file into the vans—even Paris. I end up sitting between Achilles and Helen, which might make me laugh at the irony if I could draw the breath. My emotions are a messy tangle in my chest, so I do the only thing I can think of. The only thing that makes sense.

I focus on the trial ahead.

It will be physical—all the trials for Ares tend to be physical. It's also likely to be something timed rather than a trial that pits champions against champions. Historically, they save those for later, usually the last one. In the last four out of five Ares competitions, the first trial has been some kind of race. An easy way to cut out the majority of the champions in one sweep. That's what I'd put my money on.

But just because it's a race doesn't mean there won't be fighting. That's usually well within the parameters of the trial. People love a good show, after all, and blood sport is the oldest show of them all.

The van stops and the doors open. It's time. I move first, needing to get out of the enclosed space with these two. It doesn't matter that neither Helen or Achilles have so much as looked at each other or that the simmering connection between them might be all in my head. I need space. Unfortunately, space is the one thing I don't have access to and won't until the trial ends.

My nerves don't settle as the other champions file out. If anything, they get worse. There's always a moment like this before I go into conflict, a sickening lurch in my stomach where I'm suddenly aware that all the planning and strategizing in the world still isn't enough to fully prepare for reality. There will always be variables I can't account for.

The stakes have never been so high before, though.

Bellerophon clasps their hands behind their back and looks at our group. "The first trial begins shortly. You will have two minutes to study the area before the horn sounds. Once it does, you will have five minutes to complete the course. If you fall, you will be automatically eliminated." They barely wait for us to answer in the affirmative before spinning and heading down the long concrete hallway that we exited from the other day.

Even before I see the crowd, I can hear them. I can *feel* them in the vibrations of the concrete around me. It's disconcerting, but I push the feeling away. They're not here to see me, after all. Understanding that, embracing that, means I don't have to think overmuch about them. I'm not here to win. I'm only here as support.

Achilles falls into step beside me. "We good?"

"I'm still angry with you." Except that isn't quite right. There's anger, yes, but the overwhelming feeling is *loss*. This is the beginning of the end that I've feared ever since I fell for Achilles. He might not be gone yet, but the grief still takes root all the same.

He gives a jerky nod. "Okay." He doesn't tell me we'll talk later. It goes without saying that we will. Neither of us is the type to leave something festering for long, even if I can't see a way through this. It doesn't matter. The only thing I need to see clearly is the trial.

We step through the doorway, and my attention immediately lands on the course in front of us. It's a series of raised platforms interspersed with different obstacles. I've seen similar on television, but this one seems geared equally toward lower body as upper. There are three pathways from beginning to end, and I examine them in sequence, painfully aware of the large red clock ticking down the seconds to when we begin. "Shoes off."

Achilles doesn't question me. He simply obeys, yanking off his shoes and socks. "First route?"

I shake my head. "The jump from the end of that rope will be too tricky to time properly. The second looks faster, but that rope swing on the rail might get stalled out in the middle since it's so long. Go third." The climbing wall up won't be a problem, but descending might. Still, it's better than the other two. Fewer variables in play, even though it's technically the longest of the bunch, the course jutting out toward the crowd before doubling back to the finish. Each route has four obstacles of varying difficulty, and there's the time limit to consider. But surely it's not that simple?

Even as the thought crosses my mind, people in black file out from the entrance opposite us. They're all wearing Athena's uniform, and they have black masks pulled down over their faces. That creates an eerie image, and the crowd shrieks with glee at the sight of them. I sigh. "Of course it wouldn't be so easy as just getting through the course."

"Where's the fun in that?"

I take off my shoes and socks. Even though I should be focused entirely on the course, on the opponents filtering through it to key positions where they can most effectively stop the champions, I glance at Helen. She's got a look of concentration on her face, but she's staring at the first route. It's on the tip of my tongue to suggest the third, but I bite back the words. Helen isn't my priority. She *can't* be my priority.

Overhead, only thirty seconds remain. The lights flicker and then turn toward the boxed seats overhead. Athena stands there, watching us. I thought the crowd was loud before. It's nothing compared to when the spotlight shines on her. The entire arena shakes with the force of their sound.

She holds up a hand, a conductor to their fervor, and they go silent almost immediately. As the seconds tick down to zero, her amplified voice says, "The first trial begins...now."

HELEN

I DON'T HESITATE. I FLING MYSELF FORWARD, VEERING toward the left side of the course. Each of the routes available is gnarly, especially with the black-clothed opponents lying in wait, but this is my best bet. My upper body strength is great, but the taller champion's longer legs will give them an advantage on the climbing wall. I have to aim for the shortest route instead. Or, rather, the shortest route that actually makes sense. The middle one is tempting because it's basically a fancy rope swing, but I don't like the angle. It's a trap.

This whole fucking course is a trap.

One of the other champions, a guy I vaguely recognize from my father's parties, shoves me aside with a laugh and starts across the raised platforms. He barely makes it through three before one of Athena's people knocks him off. It's not even a fancy move. They literally shove him and he goes flying, landing on the padded ground with a sound I can't hear over the roar of the crowd.

"Helen."

I glance over to find Atalanta standing at my shoulder. She's fastened her locs back and is wearing a bodysuit of deep silver. She gives me a quick grin, the smile turning her scarred face from merely attractive into striking. "Temporary alliance to get through this?"

I should be able to do it on my own. The whole point of fighting for the title of Ares is so that everyone will be forced to take me seriously. But...I'm no fool. I give a jerky nod. "Through the first trial."

"Let's see what you can do." She hops up onto the first platform, and I follow quickly. She's quick, she's strong, and she's obviously well trained. Even seeing her coming, Athena's person barely has a chance to tense before Atalanta sweeps their legs out from beneath them and sends them tumbling off the platforms. Then it's a clear shot to the hanging rope ladder.

I fly over the column platforms in her wake. They're deceptively far apart, which forces me to slow down, but it's a small price to pay. I cross them quickly enough and land on the final one below the rope ladder. It sways and I look up in time to see another of Athena's people dropping down from above.

I lurch back, nearly losing my footing, but manage to course-correct at the last moment. They land in front of me and slowly raise to stand. The all-black uniform, complete with mask, sends a shiver through me. They're also quite a bit taller than me. That will work in my favor for once.

They lunge, obviously planning to shove me back off the platform. Instinct demands I scramble back, but I plant my feet and duck down just as they reach for me. From there, my muscle memory takes over. I grab their arm and use it as leverage to stand and send them flying past me… Right to the ground.

I don't wait to watch them land. I'm already scrambling up the ladder after Atalanta. I haul myself to the top of the ladder and loop a leg over, starting down the other side. The majority of the other champions seem to have chosen the third path, and I catch sight of one of Athena's people moving through a group of them, sending people flying left and right. Five champions eliminated by the time I descend the ladder.

My feet barely touch down on the next platform when I hear it. A loud whoop and a whizzing sound. I turn in time to see Ajax flying along the rope swing in the center route.

Atalanta shakes her head. "What a fool."

I frown, trying to judge the momentum. "He might make it." He's certainly tall enough to force physics to work to his benefit.

"He won't make it."

"Neither will we if we don't keep moving."

Atalanta and I turn as one to the next obstacle. A series of panels is suspended just close enough that a person could use their feet and hands to wedge themselves along without falling. In theory. The trickiest part is going to be sticking the initial landing and the dismount, which requires jumping from the panels, grabbing a rope, and swinging myself over to the platform. Time it wrong, and I'll be just as fucked as Ajax. At least I took off my shoes, so I don't have to worry about the soles of them slipping.

"At least there are no opponents on this one." There's no place for them to lie in wait. I look around. We're the only two left on this route. The rest of the champions are on the third, and it looks like most of Athena's people have followed them there. Good.

Atalanta rolls her shoulders. "I'll take the right one."

It's slightly wider, which would make it damn near impossible for me to move well. I glance at the taller woman. "Why help me?"

"I don't need to fuck with you in order to win." She shoots me a grin. "I'm currying favor with my future wife." Atalanta blows me a kiss and then jumps, landing with her feet and arms spread to keep her in place in a way that looks effortless. Only the slight shake of her leg muscles betrays her, but that doesn't stop her from moving forward.

Gods, what am I doing? Checking out her thighs when I'm supposed to be racing.

I shake my head, take a breath, and leap into the left path. The landing vibrates through me, and I slide a few precious inches down toward the empty space below. I grit my teeth and start forward.

As I inch along, I watch Ajax's momentum slow out of the corner of my eye. He stops a good twenty feet from the final platform and curses, swinging his body back and forth in an attempt to move closer to the platform. It won't work, but I have my own problems to worry about.

I'm achingly aware of the time ticking down as I move forward. This is so much harder than it looks. I'm in the best shape of my life, but it takes concentration to ensure at least two opposing limbs are pressing against the panels while still moving forward. I grit my teeth and keep going.

I have *not* come this far to fail now. I have too many

motherfuckers to prove wrong. My siblings. Paris. Achilles. Every single person in Olympus who thinks my value begins and ends with the family and face I was born with.

Atalanta is outpacing me, which tempts me to rush, but a single mistake means ruin. I concentrate on breathing as I move down the panel. *Step, press, step, press.* Over and over again. By the time I reach the end, my body is shaking. I eye the distance I'll have to cross to reach the rope and swing to the next platform. It looks like miles. I could make it easily if my muscles were still fresh, but I'm exhausted.

"I can do this," I mutter. It doesn't matter if I can or can't, because I don't have time to waffle. Every second clicking by pushes me closer to ruin, to the time running out or my body giving out.

I leap.

The second my feet leave the panels, I know I've misjudged. I hit the rope several feet lower than I planned, too close to the bottom. The rope swings, but I slide down a few more precarious inches, my legs flailing.

Fuck, fuck, fuck.

The platform is higher than I expected based on where I planned to grab the rope, and my momentum is less than anticipated. It doesn't matter. I have to jump. I release myself at the pinnacle of the swing and slam into the platform, only my upper body clearing it. My breath whooshes out of me, but I don't let myself freeze up. If I do, I fall.

I scramble for purchase against the flat surface, but I lose an inch, sliding back toward the floor. Back toward defeat. *No*, damn it. I have come too far. I'm not going to let a little thing like gravity beat me now. I force myself to go still, to *think*. If I can get a leg onto the platform...

A dark boot appears in my field of vision, and I look up in horror to find one of Athena's people standing over me. They raise their foot, obviously intending to kick me in the face. Oh fuck, this is going to hurt.

They never get a chance.

Atalanta appears behind them. At first I think she's simply going to shove them off the platform, but she's more of a showwoman than that. She hauls them around and delivers a devastating punch to their face. They go boneless and fall to the platform. Holy shit, she just knocked them out with a single hit.

She grins at the crowd and gives a cheery wave before focusing on me. She leans over, medium-brown skin shining with sweat, and offers me a hand. I shake my head. "I've got it."

"You really don't."

I hate that she might be right. My arms quiver, but I shake my head. "*I've got it.*"

She makes an impatient sound, her tone exasperated. "Stop wasting time and take my hand, or I'll leave you and you'll fall."

When she puts it like that, there really is no other choice. I slap my hand into hers and let her pull me up onto the platform. The crowd goes wild in response, the very arena seeming to shake. Atalanta gives me a quick grin, and then I'm in her arms. She doesn't give me a chance to react before she bends me back into a showy dip and gives me a quick kiss. She sets me on my feet and then she's gone, racing up the last obstacle, a thick knotted rope that we'll have to climb to reach the final platform.

There are three ropes, so I hurry to the one in the middle. My arms and legs protest violently at the thought of more, but I've worked through that kind of pain more times than I can count. Being a gymnast *hurts*, sure, but not more than growing up in my father's house. Really, I've been training for this moment my entire life.

I start up the rope, fighting against gravity and my own weakness as I ascend. I'm halfway up when the opponent Atalanta knocked out stumbles to their feet and looks up. I can't see their face through the black mask, but I *feel* our eyes meet. They start for my rope, staggering a little. "No," I whisper.

I did not come this far only to fail now.

I fight against my exhausted muscles, fight against gravity itself, to pull my body up another six inches. It won't be enough. They're too tall. They reach the bottom of the rope and jump, grabbing my ankle. The contact almost rips me right off the rope. I slide down a few inches with a shriek that the screams of the crowd swallow up. Another yank rips me clean off the rope.

The platform rushes up to meet me, and I land flat on my face. It hurts. *Fuck*, it hurts. But if I stay down, I'll be eliminated, and that isn't an option. I stagger to my feet, the arena spinning wildly around me. The crowd sounds like a feral beast baying for blood. They want to see me fail. *Everyone* wants to see me fail.

On the other side of the rope, Athena's person is climbing to their feet as well. They still don't look steady, but if they're anything like Achilles and Patroclus, that won't make them less dangerous. I'll only get one shot at this.

I don't stop to think about all the things that could go wrong. There's no time for that. I take two quick steps and leap, grabbing the rope. It's too heavy to swing much, but my momentum works in my favor. I straighten my legs just as my feet make contact with their chest. The impact nearly takes me off the rope again, but it sends them flying off the platform.

There's no time to savor my victory. I haven't won yet. Fuck, I haven't even passed the first challenge yet. A quick glance at the clock has panic seizing me. If I fall again, I won't get another chance.

Fear gives me strength. I haul myself up, hand over hand, with a speed I would have thought impossible. This time, no one assists me as I reach the final platform and scramble onto it. I look at the clock, barely daring to believe it. I did it. I'm here.

I passed the first trial.

You didn't do it on your own. You needed help, and everyone saw that you weren't strong enough.

The voice sounds horrifyingly like my father. I shudder, my chest going tight and throat trying to close. It doesn't matter that I needed help. I won't let it matter, even if it means I have to go above and beyond the next time.

All that matters is that I passed this trial, so there *will* be a next time.

I stretch my arms overhead and concentrate on breathing through the ache in my body. Easier to focus on that than the tumultuous emotions running riot inside me. I force myself to look around and take stock of those on the platform around me. Atalanta is nearby, looking barely winded. From the third route, there are ten people who passed the first trial, among them Hector, Paris, the two strangers...and Achilles and Patroclus.

Despite myself, my attention narrows on the latter two. Of course *they* made it. I doubt they needed help, either. Even more irritatingly, they both have a fine sheen of sweat on their skin and the sign of exertion only makes them both more attractive. A traitorous little zing jolts my body, and I force myself to look away.

Up to this point, I've done my best not to think about what happened yesterday. I can't believe things got so out of control. I never would have slept with Achilles if I wasn't already reeling from the events of the last couple of days. If he hadn't tossed me over his shoulder like I truly was some princess a conquering knight happened across and ripped from her safe tower. If he hadn't essentially offered himself as the perfect target. Someone to take all my ugly emotions out on without having to worry about the aftermath. I highly doubt I can do a single thing to hurt that man, either emotionally or physically.

He might not have been the safe choice of an outlet, but I can't deny that he was the perfect one all the same. He took my blows and let me provoke him to do exactly what we both wanted. To fuck me like he hated me. Except...it didn't entirely feel like that.

I know what it's like to have sex with someone who hates you. Paris proved that toward the end of our relationship. He hurt me on purpose. Never physically, of course. He's a *gentleman*. But he spilled poison into my ear when I was most vulnerable, when my barriers weren't as strong as normal.

Gods, Helen, if you're not going to do it right, you can leave and I'll do it myself.

Sorry that you didn't come, honey. You're so damn hard to please.

You keep acting like I'm *the problem. Have you ever thought that* you're *the only one with an issue in this relationship?*

Even when Achilles was tossing me around, even when he was growling at me, I still felt safe in a way I never felt with Paris. I didn't have to worry about being called a selfish bitch because I was after my own pleasure. Achilles simply took it as fact. More than that, he made sure it was good for me. That orgasm wasn't feigned, and he didn't leave it up to me to get myself off. He didn't act like it was a *chore* to make sure we both had a good time even while hate fucking, either.

After? Well, I can't think about after too much. I need to dislike Achilles. He's standing between me and what I want most in this world. I absolutely cannot afford to soften toward him.

Patroclus glances at me, and the second our eyes meet, guilt swarms me. Having sex with Achilles might or might not have been a mistake on its own, but I can't help feeling extra bad because Patroclus is involved. I went from flirting with him and coming on to *him* to sleeping with his boyfriend. It doesn't matter that they're in an open relationship. The way I went about things is shitty.

Now's not the time to think about this, though. Not when Athena is lifting her hands, once again calling for silence in the arena. "Congratulations to the champions who have passed the first trial. The second will begin in two days' time."

It's over.

It seems almost underwhelming to be led down the ladder at

the back of the platform and guided toward the exit. We were here less than ten minutes. Ten minutes to decide whether or not our dreams would be stopped short or allowed to continue. It makes me a little sick to my stomach to think about how close I came to elimination. If Atalanta hadn't helped me...

I could have done it on my own...I think.

As we're led back to the vans, I don't miss how Achilles and Patroclus seem determined to keep as far away from me as possible. I'm so busy looking at them, I don't realize Paris is beside me until he drops an arm around my shoulder. "That was quite the performance you put on, Helen." He uses my surprise to tug me close.

"Let me go, Paris," I say quietly. I have to speak quietly because if I start yelling, I might do something I'll regret, something that will get me eliminated from the tournament. He's not attacking me, for all that he's touching me without permission. I have no outward justification to so much as slap him. "Right now."

He, of course, ignores me. His arm probably doesn't appear tight from the others' point of view, but I can't get away from him without making a scene. "You would have fallen if Atalanta didn't step in. No matter what you look like—cute getup by the way, even if I prefer you in dresses—you're the same old Helen. You can't function without someone there to hold your hand and tell you what to do. It's okay, honey. I'm more than happy to give you a guiding hand."

His words sink deep into the raw spots I don't show anyone. How fucking naive had I been to confess my darkest fears to Paris? He's never missed a chance to sink the knife in deep and twist it.

He's wrong, though. My fears are wrong, too.

I'm not helpless. I don't need a savior. I *don't*. It takes everything I have to keep a quiver from my voice, to offer only calm even as panic flutters in my chest. "Get your hands off me or I'll remove them myself."

"Do it." He grins, every inch the charming prince. "I know how you like it rough. Daddy's little princess in public and my little slut in private." Words designed to hurt me, to turn something that I thought was a safe space dirty and unclean. I thought we were having fun and playing out fantasies I'd never admitted to anyone. Paris was simply adding more weapons to his arsenal.

My skin prickles and I have to concentrate in order not to drop my gaze. I will not back down from this man, will not let him undermine my confidence in myself, will *not* let him shame me for something he enjoyed just as much as I did. "Let go."

"You liked protesting then, too." He squeezes me tighter. "Keep going. I like it."

A chill skitters down my spine. This is the scariest thing about Paris. He never actually threatens, hardly ever yells. But his unrelenting determination to see the world his way regardless of evidence to the contrary? His nice-guy smiles even as he's calmly launching verbal assaults? It's terrifying.

The panic fluttering in my chest gets stronger, and a little tremor flickers through my tone when I speak. "You don't have the right to touch me." Attacking another champion is strictly forbidden and he knows it. He's using it against me. I try to duck out from beneath his arm, but he tightens his hold. I'm trapped. All the training and all the preparation and I'm held captive in the arms of a man who means me harm. I try to swallow past the way my throat closes. Not again. I will *not* do this with Paris again. I look around for help, but Achilles, Patroclus, and Atalanta have disappeared into the first van. Hector and the other four champions are nowhere to be seen, and Bellerophon is occupied arguing quietly with the Minotaur and Theseus. There's no one coming to save me.

Wait.

I don't need saving.

Godsdamn it, it took Paris all of a minute to slam me right back into the helpless skin I've worked so hard to escape. I am *not* helpless. I am more than capable of saving myself. I turn toward him until we're nearly chest to chest. "Paris?"

His gaze drops to my lips and his voice deepens. "Yeah?"

I grab his cock in an iron grip and squeeze. He makes a pained noise and tries to jerk back, but I have too good a hold. All he manages to do is hurt himself. My body hides what I'm doing from Bellerophon, which is just as well. This would *definitely* qualify as an attack. I twist my wrist a little, enjoying the way Paris goes a sickly green. "If you touch me again without my permission, I'll gut you."

"Bitch." His voice is a little too high. "You want to play rough? We'll play rough."

I ignore the wave of fear his words bring and twist harder. Hard enough that his knees buckle. "You will never, *ever*, play with me again, you bastard."

"You'll pay for this," he wheezes.

"No, I won't. Because you're not going to win. *I* am." I

release him and take a quick step back, putting some much-needed distance between us.

He straightens slowly. "Helen." Gone is the anger, quickly masked behind the charm. He's always been able to tuck away his negative emotions like that. At least until the rare occasions when they explode without warning. Paris winces a little and smiles as if I just did something clever. "Always so reckless. Always so willing to hurt yourself to hurt me."

"Shut up." I realize my mistake the second I say the words. I might as well wave a red flag in front of a bull. Paris loves nothing more than getting beneath my skin.

Sure enough, his smile widens. "Do you really think your brother is going to let someone like you become Ares? Your temper alone will bring down Olympus. You're not strategic; you never know when to fold or bend. You can't even pass a simple obstacle course without help, and you think you can direct Olympus's army? Don't make me laugh. You'll make us weak, easy to pick off for our enemies. Enemies like them." He nods at the van that the two non-Olympians have disappeared into. "If you really want what's good for the city, you'd step down now."

Even as I try to come up with a response, his words burrow deep and plant poisonous roots. I *am* impulsive and reckless. I have been my entire life. How many times have my father, my brother, accused me of the very same thing? If I weren't reckless and impulsive, I would never have had sex with Achilles last night. I wouldn't have made a pass at Patroclus. I wouldn't have done a lot of wild acts I've committed over the course of my life when the pressure beneath my skin becomes too much to bear.

I never would have dared attempt to become Ares.

I don't care. Paris is wrong. He has to be wrong, and I will not let him make me doubt myself. Not ever again. I swallow past the thickness in my throat. "Next time you touch me without permission, I'll cut off your arm and beat you to death with it."

"Temper, temper." He laughs and moves around me to climb into the nearest van.

I'd rather cut off my *own* arm than follow him, so I turn on my heel and head for the next one down the line. Bellerophon lifts their brows at me. "Problem?"

"Of course not." I can't quite manage a smile, so I duck around them and climb into the back of the van.

It's not until I'm sitting there between the two strangers that I pause long enough to wonder if I've made a mistake by picking this van. Then the doors shut, and it's too late. *Damn it.* I'm too raw to keep my shit together, practically vibrating out of my skin with feelings I don't know what to do with. I'm not up to sparring with either of these men, verbally or otherwise.

The one with shorter hair, Theseus, stretches out his big legs and gives me a long look. "Back where I'm from, women know their place."

Wow, he's not even going to try to soften me up, is he? Weirdly enough, that's almost a comfort. I don't have to be sweet and sunny and political in my response. I blink slowly at him. "That must be so nice for you. Where you come from, do they also offer unsolicited opinions to strangers?"

He smiles briefly, but it's not a happy look. "You're not a stranger, though, are you? You're the prize."

Thanks for reminding me. I glance at the Minotaur. He watches both of us with an empty look in his blue eyes. Creepy. I give them both a mock sympathetic look. "You don't stand a chance of winning, and *our* women know their place is equal to everyone else. Go home before you embarrass yourselves." I feel sorry for the women in question if he's telling the truth, but where could he possibly originate from? Mars?

Theseus shakes his head. "You're proof that Olympus is soft. You and your people have lived in the lap of luxury for so long, you've forgotten what it's like in the real world."

Cold slithers through me. "I suppose you're here to teach us the error of our ways. Lucky us."

"You have quite the mouth on you. We'll work on that."

The panic I experienced from that confrontation with Paris comes back—with interest. A single conversation with this man, and he's quickly competing with my ex for the person I least want to win. It's more than the threat he poses to me personally; it's the way he's calling Olympus *soft* as if he'll have an opportunity to change it. Maybe I was too hasty in writing off a coup attempt. We can*not* allow either of them to win. I shudder. "Thanks, but no thanks."

He leans forward, but the Minotaur grunts. Whatever the relationship between these two, that sound is enough to call Theseus off. He leans back and closes his eyes, effectively ending the conversation.

It's just as well. I feel a bit like cracked glass at the moment. One wrong move will shatter me completely. It doesn't make any sense. I passed the first trial; I should be ecstatic. I should be *celebrating*. Instead, I'm fighting the urge to cry.

What in the gods' names is wrong with me?

I don't have an answer by the time we arrive back at the dorms. I keep my gaze on the floor as we file back to our respective rooms. It's only when I close the door between me and the rest of the world that I start to shake. At least I held it together until this moment when I can break down alone.

Which is right around the moment I realize I'm not actually alone.

Hermes and Dionysus lounge on my couch. She's flipping through channels so quickly, there's no way she's registering each one. He's supine on the couch, his head in her lap while she idly sifts her fingers through his hair.

I should be happy to see them. They're my friends after all, and I was just thinking about how much I miss them last night when I was all alone and out of sorts. I sigh. I *should* stop using the word *should*. It doesn't matter that they're my friends, because they're my friends second. As with my siblings, for Hermes and Dionysus, being a member of the Thirteen comes first. "What are you two doing here?"

"Silly question. We came to see you, bestie." Hermes clicks off the television and angles her body to face me. Her hair bobs around her head in black ringlets, and she's wearing bright-pink lipstick that sets off her dark-brown skin and matches her jumpsuit and shoes. Her style is flawless, as always.

Dionysus lets out a faint snore. He's got on a graphic T-shirt from some band I've never heard of and a pair of faded jeans. His mustache is curled perfectly despite the nap, so he's either faking it or he just fell asleep.

It doesn't matter. I don't have the energy for this right now. "I need a shower and a meal before I do anything remotely entertaining." Not that I can leave the house or property while I'm a champion, but Hermes and Dionysus are more than capable of creating their own entertainment. Especially with the kinds of people the champions are comprised of.

"Oh fine, you caught me." Hermes rolls her eyes, though she's still smiling. Enjoying herself at my expense. No reason to take it personally; Hermes enjoys herself at *everyone's* expense. "I have a message for you from your brother."

Disappoint lashes me. Trust my brother to send Hermes in her official capacity instead of coming himself. I try to keep my feelings off my face. "How strange that he couldn't make the time to have a polite little sit-down with me. It's enough to make a sister doubt where she stands on his list of priorities." Kind of like when he makes plans to marry off said sister without consulting her first.

"You know how it is." She shrugs and starts braiding Dionysus's hair. It's short enough that she makes quick work of each braid, but they stand out straight from his head. "Zeus is busy being Zeus. Ruling Olympus, putting out fires, entertaining our out-of-town visitors." She gives a mischievous smile. "And being married to *that* Hera is a full-time job on its own."

I don't comment on the fact that Hera is the one who suggested I join the tournament in spite of me being the prize. If Hermes doesn't already know—and how could she?—I'm not about to be the one to tell her. I don't *think* she'd run right to my brother with the information, but she likes to keep people on their toes, so I can't guarantee it.

Besides, I'm certain Callisto's motivation was simply to stir the pot and cause trouble, even if she indirectly helped me in the process. If Perseus finds out his wife prodded me into this action, it will cause even more drama. No matter her reasons, Callisto did me a favor by snapping me out of my self-pity spiral. I won't out her. "No one twisted his arm and forced a ring on his finger." *Not like he's done to me.*

"You'd be surprised." She finishes another braid. "Will you hear the message?"

As if I have a choice. "Yes."

She clears her throat, and a startling approximation of my brother's deeper voice emerges from her lips. "You've had your fun. It's over now. Resign before the next trial."

I wait, but she seems to be finished. "That's it? Normally he likes to threaten some kind of consequence."

Hermes shrugs. "He's a little distracted. The Minotaur and Theseus didn't come to Olympus alone, and your brother has his hands full dealing with the leader of their little group, Minos."

Easy enough to read between the lines. Their leader is here, watching me make a fool of my brother and the rest of the Thirteen. It's undermining Zeus's authority and doing the exact thing he doesn't want—making us look weak. More like making *him* look weak.

Olympus needs a firm hand.

A sliver of regret goes through me. I might want to wring my brother's neck right now, but even I can admit he's likely doing the best he can in circumstances not of his own making. He hadn't thought to take over the title of Zeus for years yet, but our father's unexpected death changed the whole timeline. I *do* want Olympus safe and stable.

Maybe I should resign.

My stomach clenches at the thought, but I force myself to consider it. If I resign now... I shake my head. It won't help. The damage was already done the moment I put my name forward and defied my brother publicly. More, now that I'm directly competing with the Minotaur and Theseus, I can't afford to do anything but put on a good showing. I'm representing Olympus against their outsiders' interests. I'm representing *my brother*, even if he's furious about it.

I'm a Kasios, after all.

Humiliating me means humiliating him. Resigning now is weak, and it will make *him* appear weak. He's not thinking clearly or he'd have realized that on his own. I take a deep breath. "Backing out now won't change the fact that I participated in the first place. It won't suddenly make him look better."

"I don't know that Zeus is thinking clearly at the moment," Hermes says, mirroring my thoughts.

I suspect she's right, but I won't talk shit about my brother right now, not when he's in a precarious position and I'm partly to blame. Instead I laugh, loud and giddy and fake. "Sure. As if he's ever let emotions get the best of him even once in his life." Even as the lie flies free, guilt pricks. Perseus wasn't an effusive child, but he felt everything very deeply. Our father saw it as a flaw, a weakness to be exploited by future enemies, and spent most of our childhood carving that softness out of my brother, piece by piece.

Hermes considers me for a long moment, and I find myself

holding my breath. I might have been friends with her for years, but in this moment, we stand almost as equals: her one of the Thirteen, me a contender for being a member of the Thirteen as well. She finishes a braid and sits back. "Are you sure about this?"

"Please inform my brother that while I appreciate his *request*, I'm seeing this through."

"Will do." Hermes pats Dionysus's chest. "Time to go, love."

He opens his eyes, blinking at me. "Hey, Helen. When did you get here?"

"Hey." I manage a tired smile. "Have a nice nap?"

"Always do." He sits up and stretches. The little braids in his hair give him the look of a startled bird. "Good show on the obstacle course. We're rooting for you."

"Thanks." I don't know what else to say. These are my friends, but if—*when*—I win this tournament, the dynamic of our relationship will have to change. I'll be one of the Thirteen, too. I wave a tired hand at them. "Are you sticking around?"

"Nope." Hermes jumps to her feet. "The night is young, and we're off to have fun."

Dionysus takes my hands and presses a kiss to each of my cheeks. "She means we're off to get some of Minos's people drunk and see what information we can mine from them."

That pulls a laugh from me. "All in a day's work." I don't tell them to be careful. Despite outward appearances, both Dionysus and Hermes are more than capable of taking care of themselves. And each other. Beyond that, this is part of Dionysus's specialty. He might play the fool in public, but he didn't win his title by accident. He's got a cunning mind behind that ridiculous mustache.

I walk them out and lock the door behind them. Only then do my shoulders slump, weighed down by all the things both said and unsaid. No one believes I can pull this off. Not my enemies. Not my family. Not even my friends. No matter what words they mouth, they're all waiting for me to fail. They're *sure* of it.

I turn away from the door and plod down the hall with heavy steps. I need a shower and about eight hours of sleep.

Maybe the world will make sense in the morning.

ACHILLES

"STOP HOVERING."

I swallow my frustration and pace another lap around the living room. "I'm not hovering." I *am* hovering. I have been since we got back to the rooms. I want to blame it on all the adrenaline with no output. That trial was too damn short, even with the opponents causing snags along the way. If I'd just been able to work hard, to expel some more energy, maybe I'd be able to settle down now.

Patroclus sighs and sets down his e-reader. He's got glasses perched on the end of his nose, and he looks so adorably nerdy, I want to kiss him. Too bad trying would probably mean a black eye with how pissed he is right now. It's not often my man gets riled, but when he does, it takes a long time for him to work through it. I have no one but myself to blame for the current shitstorm.

He gives me a long look. "You're getting what you want. Why are you so upset?"

I hate it when he does this. Instead of admitting just how

furious he is, he turns it around and talks to me as if I'm the one being ridiculous. It's patronizing in the extreme, one of Patroclus's shittier habits. The fact that he's right only irritates me more. "I fucked up. Why don't you just like...yell? Throw something? Fuck, punch me if it will make you feel better."

"That's abuse."

I cross my arms over my chest. "Then *talk* to me. Stop icing me out." He's barely spoken six words to me since last night. I hate it when he does this; he's sitting in front of me, but he might as well be on another planet for all I can reach him. These kinds of fights don't happen often, but when they do, they drive home how different we are. It serves as a reminder that one day Patroclus will get tired of my shit and ice me out permanently.

Not this time.

Not yet.

Please, gods, not yet.

"I'm sorry. I said I'm fucking sorry. I've said it a dozen times. What else do you want from me?" It's not a fair ask, and we both know it, but I'm so frustrated, I want to shred something.

"Do you regret having sex with Helen?"

I start to say yes, but he'll know if I lie because I'm shit at it. I *hate* lying. I'd rather keep my mouth shut and say nothing at all than lie. Neither is an option under his intense look. "No." Gods help me but I don't hate her as much as I thought I would, and I can't blame the orgasm on that shift. She's nothing like I expected, and yet somehow also everything that I expected. I don't really get it, but I'm intrigued all the same.

And the sex was so fucking *good*. It was intense and a little terrifying, but I can't say I wouldn't do it again. When I become Ares and she becomes my wife, it's almost a certainty.

"Which means you will do it again." He considers me for a long moment. "And if I said I want to sleep with her..." Even as I try not to tense, I can feel my body locking up. Patroclus nods slowly. "Yeah, I thought so. You're a fucking hypocrite."

"I've been called worse." Worse has been true, too.

"I know." He picks up his e-reader again. "I am still angry with you. I can't just snap my fingers and get over it, even if you're not happy that I'm angry. It's not how emotions work."

There he goes being patronizing again. I exhale harshly. "I know how emotions work, Patroclus."

He doesn't look up. He just adjusts his glasses and leans back against the couch. "I need some time. I thought I'd made my peace with your pending nuptials, but I have to work through my side of it because it's significantly more real now that Helen is more than just a theory."

My stomach drops. *Is it happening? Is this the end?* It's come at me too fast, too out of left field. I swallow hard. "What does that mean?"

"I love you." He taps his e-reader, turning the page. "One fight doesn't change how I feel, and it doesn't change the plan. Just...give me time, Achilles."

That's the problem. If his impressive brain gets going on this tangled situation, he might decide that the end of this tournament is the end of our relationship. I know it's selfish as fuck to want to keep him even while I'm married to someone else. It's even more selfish now that I've had sex with Helen and there's a distinct possibility of it happening again no matter what protests I make. Most of all, it's damn near unforgivable that I can't stand the thought of him and Helen together without me in the picture. No matter which way I look at it, we're no longer speaking about a political marriage of convenience. Now it's messy. It's my fault, but there's no easy fix for this.

Damn it.

"I'll give you time, then." The words come out dull. I turn and walk out the door. I'm too restless to try to sleep yet—if I'll be able to sleep at all—so I head down the hall. Wandering the dark is something I used to do when I was a kid. Back then, I didn't sleep a lot. It was a game, a way to battle my deep fear of the dark. The monsters can't hurt what they can't see, hear, sense. It wasn't like the orphanage was bad or anything. I don't know if any of the last Zeus's Heras even bothered to mess with it, but the people in charge were nice enough. It wasn't like the movies say. No one was trying to touch me or abuse me or use me for experiments to summon a demon or some shit.

Still, no matter how Ms. Hebe tried to ensure we were being raised as well adjusted as possible, sometimes the nights were... rough. Wandering the place after dark helped. Movement has always helped me.

It's been a long time since I felt the compulsion, though. I don't worry about the shit I can't see anymore. I see what I need to, and I'm not the same scared little kid I was back then. I'm a warrior. There's nothing life can throw at me that I can't handle.

Or so I thought.

I've had Patroclus at my side since we were enlisted in Ares's security forces at eighteen. His moms thought it would be good for him, with the structure and physicality and all. I had a chip on my shoulder and something to prove. I know everyone thinks we're too different; they thought it back then, too. But even as teenagers, we just...clicked.

I don't know what I'd do without him. Even though part of me always thought eventually Patroclus would move on to someone who stressed him out less, most of me never believed it would happen. Now, the possibility is all too real.

It's late enough that the house is deserted, everyone in their beds and keeping out of trouble. Bellerophon or their people will have clocked my movement, even without me turning on the lights. They're too good to let people get into trouble after dark. I'm not interested in getting into trouble, though. I just want to expel some of this awful feeling churning in my gut.

I've fucked things up. I knew that the moment I came out of the haze of lust on the floor next to Helen. Even then, though, I half convinced myself that Patroclus would roll with this the same way he rolls with all my other bullshit. Wishful thinking.

I see the way he looks at her.

He's never looked at anyone like that...except for me.

I wish I could claim I slept with her solely because I wanted to and not because I was jealous of her and Patroclus. I wish I wasn't that big of an asshole to do something so selfish just to keep them away from each other. Even when he's fucked other people, it's been all in good fun or satisfying a curiosity. He's never watched someone walk across the room with a longing I can fucking *feel* even from a few feet away. He's only been in close contact with

Helen as an adult for a few days. How much stronger will that get in a week? In a few months after we're married?

If he falls in love with her...

Yeah, I'm an asshole. I want to have my cake and eat it, too, and it's not fucking fair. If I'd slowed down long enough to think about it, I'd like to pretend I would have made different choices. But then, I don't like lying, do I?

I huff out a breath and open the sliding glass door to the back patio. The heat of the day has cooled, and the night air feels good against my skin. It doesn't bring any clarity, though. This situation is so fucked up, and I'm to blame for a large slice of the pie. I know that, but it doesn't mean I'm comfortable stewing over the mess I made. I'm a creature of action. Why sit around and twiddle your thumbs when you can do something about it?

Too bad there's nothing to be done right now.

Patroclus doesn't want to see my face again tonight, and talking to Helen isn't going to change a single damn thing...

I hesitate. It might not change anything, but it's still true that I don't feel particularly good about how we left things yesterday. She seemed really unconcerned with the whole thing, but she's a Kasios; she'll have learned to lie from birth. *Fuck*. I should have remembered that. *Patroclus* would have remembered that, would have pushed for the truth instead of taking her at her word that sex was just sex and I wasn't too rough with her.

I glance up at the sky. It holds no answers, but I'm not going to be able to sleep now. Maybe she's still awake. We can talk or fight or whatever. Maybe she'll actually be honest with me for once, and at least *that* part of this clusterfuck will be resolved.

Action plan in place, I turn and walk back into the dorm. It's just as silent, just as dark this time, but I move faster, surer. I had the floor plan memorized the first night; it pays to know where the exits are, just in case. Working damn near ten years for Athena taught me that you never know when you might need one.

Back in our hallway, there's still a light shining from beneath Patroclus's door...but not Helen's. I almost turn for mine, but I haven't come this far to stop before I at least try to talk to her. I'm about to knock when I hear a thump on the other side.

There's absolutely no reason for the small hairs on the back of my neck to stand on end. This is one of Athena's buildings, and our people have secured it. We're the best. The champions are safer than Zeus himself. Helen probably just ran her shin into the coffee table or something.

All the rationalization in the world doesn't change my instincts screaming that something is wrong. I've been a soldier since I turned eighteen. At twenty-two, Athena herself took me under her wing and taught me to trust the very instincts she's spent years honing. I can't walk away until I'm sure I'm wrong.

I try the door, and the handle turns easily against my palm. What the fuck? Something is definitely wrong. The time for hesitation is gone. I shove through the door and into Helen's suite. The room is bathed in shadows, lit only by a single standing lamp next to the couch. That light is enough to catch sight of someone ducking into the door leading to Helen's bedroom.

Someone damn near six feet tall with broad shoulders.

Someone who is *not* Helen Kasios.

I'm moving before I fully process the stranger's presence, a

decade's worth of training and muscle memory kicking in. I rush
down the hall on silent feet and shove through the door in time to
see the figure standing over Helen's bed.

A flash of metal in the moonlight. I can't tell if it's a gun or a
knife, but it doesn't fucking matter. I'm not thinking anymore. I'm
reacting.

I throw myself at the attacker, wrapping one hand around
their wrist as I tackle them to the floor away from the bed. They
curse in a low voice and then the fight is on. They roll us, managing to come out on top. I've got a shitty grip on their wrist so I
can't force them to break their grasp on the weapon.

They jerk their arm down, breaking my grip, and scramble off
me to stand. With the black clothing and black mask, they almost
look like one of the opponents we faced today. All they're missing
is the owl on their shoulder. But this is *not* one of Athena's people.
I'd stake my life on it.

I barely get to my feet when they charge. This time, I'm ready.
Going unarmed against a knife-wielding opponent isn't exactly
the best-case scenario, but it's not outside my skill set. I dodge at
the last moment, sliding my body just far enough out of the way
to avoid the blade and grabbing their arm.

I'm so busy focusing on the knife that I don't see their fist until
they punch me in the face with it. It's a good punch, so good I see
stars for a half a second, which is all they need to kick my legs out
from beneath me. I land on the floor with them straddling me, the
knife still in their hand.

I react on pure instinct, getting my hands up around their wrist
and stopping the blade mere inches from my chest. Fuck, they're

strong. They lean down hard on the knife, putting all their weight behind it, and it descends another inch.

What a ridiculous fucking way to die. Saving Helen Kasios from a godsdamned assassin. When Patroclus finally joins me in the underworld, he'll never let me live it down.

A dull thump and the assassin goes limp on top of me. I'm so surprised, I shove them up before I realize what happened. Helen stands over us, a lamp in her hands and a fierce look on her face. I blink. She just…hit the attacker over the head. She saved me. Isn't that a kick in the pants?

She goes to bring the lamp down again, but I throw a hand out. "Wait!"

"Fuck off! They have a knife!"

"We need to question them." I grab the knife and toss it away. "We need to tie them up and go get Bellerophon."

She hesitates long enough that I belatedly realize I'm not talking to one of my subordinates. No matter how well she accounted for herself in the first trial, Helen is not trained in combat, and this is probably the first dangerous situation she's ever found herself in. *Fuck.*

"Helen." I try to keep my voice low and even, the way Patroclus would, as I shove the assassin to the floor and yank their arms behind them so I can keep them pinned even after they wake up. "Take a breath."

"I'm fine." Her unsteady tone makes a liar out of her. She's trying, though. I admire that despite myself.

"That was quick thinking with the lamp." I adjust my hold on the assassin's wrists. "Pretty sure you saved my life. Thanks."

"Just returning the favor," she says faintly. She gives herself a shake. "Bellerophon. Right. I'll call them."

I watch her as she staggers to the phone by the bed and picks it up. If she passes out or something, I'm not going to be able to do a damn thing about it without releasing the attacker, and that's not an option. But Helen manages to keep it together as she speaks into the phone, giving a quick rundown of what just happened. "Yes, please hurry." She hangs up and drops down to sit on the bed. Neither of us speak in the thirty seconds it takes Bellerophon and their people to all but bust down the door.

They rush into the bedroom and flip on the lights, already issuing orders. "Secure the attacker and transport them off the property, and do it *quietly*. Athena will want an update immediately." They turn to us. "Achilles and Helen, please wait a moment and then I'll speak with you in the living room."

I don't offer to help. They have things well in hand...except for the fact that there's a godsdamned *assassin* on the property. "How the fuck did this happen, Bellerophon? This place is supposed to be secure."

"I plan on figuring that out," they snap.

I move out of the way while their people slap zip ties on the attacker and haul them to their feet. They're a white dude with nondescript features, short dark hair, and narrow blue eyes. They blink blearily, taking in the room and everyone in it. I tense, ready for them to say some shit, but they only glare silently at us as Bellerophon's people haul them out of the room.

Bellerophon makes a face. "I have to call Athena. Give me two minutes."

"Yeah. No problem." I watch them leave and exhale slowly. Things happen fast in combat situations, but I'd come to Helen's door prepared for a tough conversation and ended up in a fight for my life. I glance at her. She's got that thousand-mile stare going on. *Shit.* I drop down onto the bed next to her. "You good?"

"No."

Her honesty surprises me. I would have thought she'd try to play it cool even though I can feel the bed vibrating with the force of her shaking. I twist to face her. She's gone even paler than normal. I'm pretty fucking sure I can hear her teeth chattering. "Helen—"

"I'll be okay in a minute." Even her voice sounds wrong, thready and weak. "Just…just give me a fucking minute."

"You just had a scare of a lifetime. No one's expecting you to waltz through an attempt on your life without, uh, having an emotional reaction. It's okay to fall apart."

"It's really not." She stiffens. "And I'm not falling apart. It's adrenaline letdown. I'm *fine.*"

Fuck, I'm terrible at this. I always, always say the wrong thing no matter how hard I try. Patroclus would know words that would put her at ease and reassure her. I'm better at action. With that in mind, I reach over, pick her up, and set her on my lap. She makes an angry hissing sound, but she doesn't immediately punch me in the face.

"You're safe." There. That's nice and neutral. When she doesn't try to move, I wrap my arms around her. Even precious princesses find hugs comforting, right?

Slowly, breath by breath, she relaxes against me. That, more than anything, tells me how fucked she is in the head right now. She should be fighting and clawing and running her mouth, but instead, she's shaking like a kitten. My chest gives an uncomfortable lurch, and I hug her a little tighter. "You're safe," I repeat.

"Funny, but waking up to someone trying to kill you doesn't exactly translate to *safe*." She rests her head against my shoulder. "I still don't like you. I think."

"I don't really like you, either. Much."

She exhales slowly. "I don't know why you're in my room right now, but thank you for being here. I..." A little shake rocks her body. "Just...thank you."

The door opens and Bellerophon walks back inside. They don't comment on my holding Helen, which is just as well. I don't know what I'd say in response. Instead, they assume an at-ease posture. "We're still not sure how they got in, but we should have answers by morning."

Another little shake from Helen. "Forgive me if that's not comforting."

If they don't know how this person got in, there's nothing to stop others from doing the same. The thought leaves me cold. I might not like Helen—much—but I don't want her dead. "You'll stay in my room."

She tenses. "That's not necessary."

"Yeah, I kind of think it is." I nod at Bellerophon, who's watching us with a carefully blank look on their face. "They're going to be occupied dealing with this and patrolling. Plus, I think you'd rather have me as a babysitter than some stranger."

"You're barely more than a stranger." But she makes no

move to get up. As much as I want to press, I've learned at least a little patience from being around Patroclus for so many years. Sometimes, the best way to win an argument is to sit down and shut up and let them see that you're being logical. I'm rarely the logical one, but it's been known to happen once in a blue moon. I *know* I'm right this time.

It takes Helen roughly thirty seconds to realize the same thing. "Fine. I'm willing to stay in your room."

The breath I release isn't in relief. It's really not. I sure as fuck wouldn't be losing sleep worrying about her if she hadn't agreed to this. I give her one last squeeze and set her on her feet. "Get your shit, princess. Time to switch rooms."

PATROCLUS

I'M STILL AT WAR WITH MYSELF WHEN SOMEONE KNOCKS on my door. I recognize Achilles's brisk impatience and bite back a sigh. I hate fighting at much as he does, but I can't just turn off my feelings because they're inconvenient. Obviously I don't want to be this twisted up when we need to be focused, but nothing about this situation with Helen is logical. Not my attraction to her. Not *Achilles's* attraction to her. Not either of our jealousy.

I don't understand it. I doubt I'll get the opportunity to even try now.

I open the door and stop short. Achilles, quite frankly, looks like shit. It's more than the exhaustion on his face. He looks like he just came to my room after being in a brawl. His shirt is torn, his hair is askew, and I'm nearly certain someone punched him in the face.

Dear gods, don't tell me he slept with Helen again.

I swallow hard, tasting bile and jealousy. "What happened to you?"

He blinks. "What?"

"You look..." I stop myself before I accuse him. It's not fair to jump to conclusions, even if *logically* it's impossible to divorce him showing up at my door looking like this from the last time he did, from what he confessed immediately upon my letting him into my room. I finally try for a neutral enough question. "Who punched you?"

"Who punched..." He touches the spot and winces. "I forgot they landed a strike. Sloppy of me."

My stomach drops. This isn't a confession. This is something else. I straighten. He only left my room an hour or two ago. What trouble could he have possibly gotten up to in that time? Obviously more than I could have anticipated. He wasn't brawling with the other champions; he's too focused on Ares to get baited into a fight, and even if he did, he would already have been dragged from the dorms. He wasn't with Helen, or he would still have that kicked-puppy guilty look on his face. "Achilles, what the fuck is going on?"

"Someone tried to kill Helen."

"*What?*"

"I was going to her room to apologize and caught them about to attack her. Bellerophon is getting answers."

Shock lances me. The words don't make any sense. Someone tried to *kill* Helen? And Achilles was there and... I close my eyes, take a deep breath, and force myself to focus. "Did you recognize them?"

"No." He shakes his head. "White guy, the sort of looks that are instantly forgettable. But they weren't one of Athena's, and they weren't on any list we have of problems."

Athena keeps an ongoing list of people who are considered dangerous in Olympus. Not the normal kind of danger that the Thirteen or the powerful families can bring. Her list is filled with people who are either loose cannons or willing to cross all sorts of lines with the right amount of money involved. If I'd had to take bets about the attacker's identity, it would be on that list.

That it's not... "That's going to be a problem." Unknowns can throw everything into a tailspin, especially during an event as important as this tournament.

"Yeah. I know." He shifts from foot to foot. "That's actually not why I'm here, though. She's freaked out and won't admit it, so she's staying in my room tonight."

It's already happening. He's already moving on with her.

I shut the irrational thought down. My fears don't make sense. His moving Helen into his room does. If we were trying to secure someone after an attack, this is exactly the proper protocol to follow. The fact that he had sex with her a little more than twenty-four hours ago is immaterial. Except it doesn't *feel* immaterial. "You'll both stay here," I find myself saying. "It will be easier to protect her if it's both of us."

Achilles studies my expression. For once, he's not jumping into action. I hate that we're moving so tentatively around each other, but I don't know how to fix it. I can't shut off my emotions any more than Achilles can shut off his ambitions. Maybe if we weren't all piled on top of one another from this tournament and stuck in this building, it would be easier to navigate the thorny situation. I don't know. All I know is that the thought of either Achilles or Helen in danger makes me break out in a cold sweat.

He finally exhales in a rush. "You sure?"

No, but I'm not about to let that stop me. "Yes."

For a moment, I think he might press me on my answer. I don't know what I'll say if he does. This situation is so damned messy. I probably should have anticipated it, but I'm quickly learning that some variables are beyond comprehension. "Then you come to us. We've already hauled all her shit in there, and she's unpacking now." He makes a face. "She's a lot like you when it comes to living out of a suitcase, apparently."

"Okay." It will give me some time to process, to get my head on straight. "I'll be over shortly." I wait for him to leave and then start the process of repacking. It gives my hands something to do, and my mind races ahead. I can't deal with thinking about Achilles and Helen and what he was doing in her room to stop that attacker. Apologizing, he said. Achilles doesn't lie, so that must be what it was. I hate the doubt that worms through me.

Better to focus on the larger problem at hand.

Who wants Helen dead?

Zeus and Aphrodite are her siblings. Hermes and Dionysus are her friends. Hades isn't the type to send an assassin, no matter what the greater population believes. Athena wouldn't do it, not during a public tournament where the champions are under her protection. I doubt she wants another Kasios at the table, but she has no reason to believe Helen will be victorious, not with Achilles in the mix.

The others? Harder to say. Artemis isn't above murder, though she's careful to keep her hands clean publicly. The same can be said of Apollo, though I wouldn't put money on him being a possibility. Hephaestus is a harder read. He's smart and strategic, and he might have looked ahead and decided not to take his chances with Helen becoming Ares. I don't think our new Hera has that kind of power, but her mother, Demeter, might. Poseidon rarely concerns himself with power plays and politics, so he won't be bothered one way or another.

And that's just the Thirteen.

There are dozens of powerful families who weigh the push and pull of Olympus politics and make moves behind the scenes. Paris and Hector belong to one of them. So do Atalanta and Ajax. So do I.

And then there are the non-Olympians. It doesn't seem logical that they would be behind this, though. If you're going to waste the resources on an assassin, why not take out one of the more dangerous competitors? Achilles or Hector or even me would be a smarter target. No matter how determined Helen is, when it comes to the combat trials, she'll be eliminated. She simply doesn't have the training or the strength to beat out all the major players.

By the time I have my things back in the suitcase to change rooms, I still have no answers. I can't even effectively narrow down potential candidates. It's not my job to. Not this time. Bellerophon and Athena will take care of it, starting with questioning the attacker. I have the utmost faith in them.

I'd rather be chasing this mystery than walking through Achilles's door, but there's no other option. No matter how messy my chest is right now, the fact remains that he needs me, and I won't hesitate to be there for him. We've done bodyguard duty more than a few times over the years, and it's best scheduled in pairs so someone is always awake with the client. As tonight proves, assassins don't usually stick to business hours. We can't discount the possibility of there being more in play, so vigilance has to start tonight.

I take a breath and open the door.

The first thing I see is Helen, wrapped up in a blanket on the couch. Every time I've interacted with her, even when she was obviously out of sorts on the treadmill, even when we were both children, she's seemed larger than life. That presence is nowhere in evidence now. It's so easy to forget how small she is. Athletic, yes, but she's barely five six, if that. Right now, with her huddled on the couch, she seems even smaller. If the attacker was my size, or Achilles's, she wouldn't have stood a chance.

The thought leaves me cold.

She looks up and blinks those amber eyes at me. She's paler than normal, her perfect features drawn and exhausted. Even her hair is a bit of a mess, the dark strands tangled with sleep. She still smiles when she sees me, a little movement that seems almost fragile. "Hey."

My heart starts racing, which is the most ridiculous response. I should be worried about her safety or her proximity to Achilles or *something*. Instead, I'm standing here, trying to pretend my palms aren't sweating because she's smiling like she's happy to see me.

I clear my throat. "Hey."

She pulls the blanket a little more firmly around her. "He roped you into this, too?"

"I offered to help." I set my suitcase down. Now that I'm here, I'm realizing I didn't need to repack things. I could have just popped over to the other room to change and get ready each day. That would be the *logical* thing to do, instead of spending time and energy repacking and unpacking to move across the hall. Another clear indication that I'm not thinking clearly. Damn it.

Achilles comes out of the bedroom. "Two ways in and out. The window in the bathroom opens, but it's not big enough for an adult to get through. The bedroom's going to be a problem, though. The window is practically a door, and the lock is bullshit. It's an access point we can't secure properly."

Which means one of us will have to be in there with her.

I hate how my stomach drops. I must have a masochistic streak, because volunteering to put myself in close proximity with these two already stings. I don't know what prompted Achilles to offer to have her stay with him instead of bringing in a pair of Bellerophon's people as bodyguards. Sometimes, I have no idea how that man's mind works. No, that's a lie. I know exactly what he was thinking. He probably decided we'd do a better job of things than anyone else. This was already complicated, and we just made it even more so.

It's too late to change our minds, though. "I'll take first watch."

For a second, I think he might argue, but he finally nods. "Works for me. The couch is comfortable enough."

"It's really not," Helen mutters.

He shrugs. "I've slept in worse places." Achilles studies her for a long moment. Does he realize how transparent his expression is? He keeps saying he doesn't like her, but he looks at her like she's this strange creature he doesn't understand and yet wants to keep safe. He's always had a desire to protect those who can't protect themselves, but this is different. Finally, he says, "You want to talk about it?"

"What's there to talk about?"

Another shrug. His casual body language doesn't match the intent look in his eyes. "Most people get shaken up after being attacked. Have some shit on their mind."

"I'm not most people."

I should say something, but it feels like they're having a moment I'm barely part of. My feet stay planted, and my mouth feels sealed shut.

"Yeah, you're right. You're not most people." Achilles nods, and his expression goes devastatingly gentle. "Go to bed, princess. You can get back to fighting everyone who looks at you sideways tomorrow."

Her smile firms up a little, losing the fragile element. "I don't fight everyone who looks at me sideways, Achilles. I just fight you."

"Guess I'm special, then."

"Guess you are."

I turn away, unable to bear witness to what feels like such an intimate moment. To be reminded of the future I'm destined for, to be perpetually on the outside looking in. Easier to busy myself hauling my suitcase into the bedroom and making quick work of unpacking it again. Staying in motion is usually Achilles's go-to, but I've never appreciated it as much as I do now. The rhythm of unpacking calms me, even if it doesn't soothe the ache in my chest.

I'm nearly done when Helen walks into the room. She's

obviously just come from the shower, her skin dewy and flushed, her hair wet and slicked back from her face. She's wrapped up in the blanket again, but I get a hint of a silky pajama strap over one smooth shoulder. I focus on her face, but there's no reprieve for me there. She's too fucking beautiful and somehow only seems to get more so every time we interact. It's not fair.

How am I supposed to keep my heart intact and my head on straight when she looks at me like *this*?

She sits carefully on the bed and offers me a tentative smile. "You really are type A, aren't you? Everything in its place."

"Yeah." No reason to deny it. It's the truth. Being organized makes me feel a modicum of control over a world where I will never be a big fish. Power isn't something I've craved for myself, not like Achilles has, but being close to him means his big moves make big waves sometimes. I've mostly learned to surf them, but occasionally the stress gets to me. Organizing soothes me the same way planning and strategizing does.

Helen looks a little better than she did in the living room. She's regained her color, and she's not huddling in on herself anymore. Still, I can't help asking, "Are you okay?"

"I'm getting there." She tucks her feet up under the blanket. She seems younger like this, more vulnerable. More like the girl I used to know. I don't know how to deal with it. I want to wrap her up and protect her, but I already know her well enough to realize that she won't accept it. It's honestly a little shocking that Achilles managed to get her to agree to staying in his suite. He probably steamrolled her when she was feeling off-center. He's good at that.

"You're safe here. We won't let anyone touch you."

"I'm getting that impression." Helen sighs and looks at me directly. "You're upset with me."

"Why would I be upset with you?" The words come out too quickly, too harshly.

Her smile goes a little sad, a little bittersweet. "Because I had angry sex with Achilles."

"We have an open relationship." Again, the right words. Again, the wrong tone.

"That's what I told myself, but it doesn't mean I was in the right." She huddles further under the blanket, but she doesn't drop my gaze. I respect that, even though I'd be able to think a lot clearer if she wasn't looking directly at me. "It wasn't like I set out to do it, but intentions don't really matter. Actions do. I'm sorry."

They both keep saying *sorry* as if that changes what happened, and I have a feeling that they'd both do it again if the circumstances lined up. And why not? They haven't done anything wrong or violated any agreement. I'm the fool who let my feelings get tangled up with a woman I barely know. I have never, not once, reacted to Achilles being with someone else the way I'm reacting to him being with Helen. It's a *me* problem, not a *them* problem.

The logic makes sense in my head.

What comes out of my mouth is something else entirely. "That's not going to stop you from doing it again."

She blinks. "I have no intention of fucking Achilles again."

"You had no intention of fucking him the first time."

"You've got me there." She fiddles with the edge of the blanket. It strikes me that this is the first time I've seen Helen fidget. "He's irritating, isn't he?"

I try not to bristle, but I can't help it. Fuck, I'm a mess right now. "He's a lot of things."

"Yeah." Her expression goes contemplative. "I don't want to hurt you, Patroclus. I never did. I'll try really, really hard not to fall on Achilles's cock again."

I shake my head and stalk to the window. Achilles is right; it's impossible to secure properly. It's large, and while it doesn't face the fence, it would be all too easy for someone to perch on the roof across from us and shoot her through the glass. I shut the curtains. "You'll be safe tonight. Hopefully we'll have some answers tomorrow."

"Why are you doing this?"

I turn to face her. "What?"

"This." She motions vaguely at the room. "I'm a big, glaring problem between you and Achilles, which is reason enough to want to put distance between me and both of you. But we're also competing for Ares. It's in your best interest to let the attacker scare me off. So why help me? It can't be because we were friends a lifetime ago. Why try to make me feel safe when it runs counter to your goals?"

That's a good damn question. If I were more ruthless, maybe I'd do exactly that. I don't want Helen hurt, but fear never killed anyone. That's the problem, though. I don't want her afraid, either. Achilles has always accused me of having too soft a heart, and it's never been more apparent than right now. Even though it fucking *hurts* to have both of them in the same space, to see their obvious connection, I can't hurt her to save my own feelings. "I'm not willing to stand by while people are terrorized just to reach my goals."

"That's naive, don't you think?"

I stare. She's not being snarky. She's asking a serious question. "There's always another way."

"Even if there's another way, sometimes it's easier to be the bad guy and save yourself the trouble in the future." She doesn't look away. "You're very smart. You must have played out all the scenarios. If I make it to the final trial, whoever eliminates me will earn my enmity forever. If it's you or Achilles, that will endanger your ability to act effectively as Ares. Surely you've considered this."

I have. I don't know why it's surprising that she has as well. She's more than proven herself to be as intelligent as she is ambitious. It's still strange to have my own thoughts mirrored back at me. I clear my throat. "There's always another way," I repeat.

"But—"

"Go to sleep, Helen. I'm sure Bellerophon will have information tomorrow."

For a second, she looks like she might argue with me, but she finally drops the blanket and crawls up to climb under the covers. Her black pajama set is... Holy fuck, I shouldn't be staring, but I can't stop. The sleep shorts are split up the sides to reveal tantalizing glimpses of her hips. And that tank top barely covers the essentials, riding up to reveal her toned stomach and pressing tightly enough to her breasts that they're in danger of escaping. She's not trying to be seductive, and yet seduction is there in every move she makes.

I jerk my gaze away. What the fuck am I doing? Ogling her

after she's just had a traumatic experience. Ogling her after she slept with Achilles. Ogling her when she's not for me, has *never been* for me.

"Patroclus?"

The tentativeness in her tone brings me back to myself. I give myself a shake and cautiously look at her. Thankfully, Helen is fully covered now, the blankets pulled up to her pointed chin. I breathe what I hope is a soundless sigh of relief. "Yeah?"

"The bed is huge and you're making me nervous standing there. Can you sit or lie down or something?"

I almost choose the chair by the window. I even take a step in that direction before my brain decides to provide all the reasons Helen might have suggested I take the bed, too. I discard the ridiculous ones—she intends to ambush me, or she intends to seduce me. The most likely motivation is because she's still scared out of her mind and my proximity would be a comfort.

I try not to look into the request. She's already proven herself to be intelligent and strategic. It's logical that she would believe one of Athena's people wouldn't want her dead, even a fellow champion. That's all.

Still... "Are you sure?"

She nods and reaches a pale arm out to pat the bed next to her. "Please."

I gingerly sit on the indicated spot and inch back to lean against the headboard. The bed is plenty big enough for both of us and probably Achilles too... I pause. No. Following *that* thought to its inevitable conclusion is a mistake. Even so, it surprises me when Helen scoots over until she's nearly pressed against me. I'm over the covers and she's under them, but I can feel the heat coming off her body. Or maybe that's the overactive imagination I seem to be developing on the spot.

I clear my throat, desperate to focus on anything but the fact that Helen Kasios and I are in a bed together. I am on *bodyguard* duty. The only thing I should be thinking about is keeping her safe, not how good she looks in her sexy little pajamas.

In desperation, I say the only thing I can think of. "Who would want you dead?"

"I can think of a few people." Did she inch closer? I can't be certain. I can't see her face properly in the deep shadows cast from the lamp behind the bed. "No one's really happy I'm participating in this tournament. We're also operating under some rather large assumptions that they wanted me dead instead of just scared enough to drop out."

I start to protest, but she's right. "*Are* you considering dropping out?"

"Fuck no. This is the only chance I have to be something other than a prize to be passed around as best suits my brother and future spouse. If I'm Ares, they *have* to take me seriously."

I know what Achilles thinks of Helen and her charmed life, but it strikes me that it would be awful not to have control of your own fate. Regardless of our origins, both Achilles and I have made our choices again and again without anyone forcing our hands. No one has tried to marry us off to secure some kind of alliance or refused to acknowledge anything about us beyond our looks. "I suppose a diamond cage is still a cage."

"Yes." The word is little more than a sigh. "Patroclus?"

"Mmm?"

The tiniest hesitation. When she speaks again, she sounds soft and tired and not at all the fiery woman I've dealt with up to this point. "I really didn't mean for things to get out of control with Achilles. I...like you. I've always liked you. I never would have hurt you on purpose. I just..." She gives a bitter laugh. "I get reckless when I'm hurting, and I was feeling vulnerable after... Well, if you hadn't stopped the treadmill, I probably would have run myself into the ground. It doesn't excuse what I did, but I truly am sorry."

I'm not sure what I'm supposed to say to that, but I get the feeling that Helen doesn't open up to anyone, so I can't leave this confession hanging. "I know you didn't mean to hurt me." Ridiculous that all I want to do is comfort her, hold her until that fragile shake in her voice disappears. I should be clinging to my anger, but it all feels like too much effort right now. I lean against the headboard and close my eyes. "It's okay, Helen. We're good."

"Oh. Good." Her voice goes faint, as if she's falling asleep. "The funny thing... I want to sleep with *you*. I don't even like Achilles. Mostly." She yawns. "But I would happily climb you like a tree."

Desire shoots through me, as intense as it is inappropriate. Knowing the attraction I feel is reciprocated... Does it even matter? Achilles should be my first priority. Even if I wasn't his first priority when he fucked Helen.

When was the last time I took something—someone—solely because I wanted to without worrying about how he'd feel about it? He is the selfish one, the brash one, the one with a heart he's all too happy to give to anyone who catches his fancy. Yes, he keeps part of himself for me and me alone, but even when I've indulged with other people, it's been about a moment's pleasure rather than chasing a connection.

I feel a connection with Helen. I don't know if it's lust or the potential for something more. Up until this moment, I had resigned myself to it remaining unexplored. But Achilles pulled that trigger first, didn't he? It's not as if he can blame me for making the exact same selfish choice he made...

I drag in a rough breath and guide my thoughts away from the brink. "Go to sleep, Helen. I'll watch over you tonight." And tomorrow?

Tomorrow, we'll see.

HELEN

I WAKE UP PRESSED AGAINST PATROCLUS, HIS LARGER BODY spooning me from the back. His very, *very* large cock is making itself known. *Good morning.* Instigator that I am, I roll my hips a little, rubbing along his length. His low groan in my ear is so very Patroclus that I smile without opening my eyes. I'm not sure when he ended up under the covers with me, but I'm not complaining.

This is…nice.

"Are you awake, Helen?"

I reach up to trail my fingers over his forearm where it bands across my ribs just under my breasts. "Yes."

"We should get up." But he holds me tighter, burying his face in the back of my neck. I think I feel the brush of his lips against my skin, but I can't be sure. He's right. We should get up and start the day and face the reality of what almost happened last night…

I don't want to. Not yet.

It's been so fucking long since I've woken up next to someone, and even longer since I've enjoyed the moment instead of going through the motions of getting them out of my apartment as quickly as possible. Maybe it's my history with Patroclus, maybe it the man he's become, but he makes me feel safe. He let me spew all that bullshit at him last night and didn't tell me to stop indulging in self-pity or being dramatic. He didn't call me *weak* for having messy emotions after being attacked. He just listened and then told me to go to sleep in that deliciously stern tone he adopts when he's got my best interests in mind.

My treacherous desires whisper that this is what it could be like if things were different, if we were different people in a different situation. If I let down my barriers a little and he wasn't already in love with a big golden dick. Achingly honest conversation that's somehow gentle despite the rawness. For the first time in my life, I haven't been watching my words and hiding behind doublespeak and carefully curated words. Both Achilles and Patroclus bring out different parts of me, and they're *honest* parts. I don't know how to deal with that, but this isn't the time or place for that sort of soul-searching, not with the stakes so sky-high.

Truthfully, I don't want to deal with anything right now... except the man trying not to thrust his hard cock against my ass.

Patroclus really is too polite.

That stops me for a moment. "Patroclus?"

"Yeah?"

I don't want to speak the words that might stop this, but I've already done this man wrong when he didn't deserve it. I can't do it again. I won't. I close my eyes. "I, uh, get reckless when I'm hurting or scared."

He goes still behind me. "Are you feeling reckless right now?"

"Yes." I can't help expanding the answer, giving him the truth he seems to ask for without saying a word. It's easier with my eyes closed. This hardly feels real. Can something that's mostly fantasy actually hurt me? *Don't answer that.* "But I meant what I said last night. I want you. That's not me being impulsive or reckless. That's the truth."

"Helen..." He curses against the back of my neck. "I should care that you might be using me to escape. It should bother me."

My chest goes tight, but I can't blame him if he pulls away. I've never really talked about this before outside therapy, and never with a person I'm aiming to seduce. It's so much easier to let my partners see what they want to see so I can get what I want—a few hours of pleasure where I don't have to think about anything but the next touch, the next kiss. This isn't a carefully orchestrated hookup, though. This is Patroclus. With him, in this moment, I can stop being selfish for once. "Do my reasons bother you?"

"Maybe they should." His arm goes tight around me, and he curses again. "I don't give a fuck what I *should* be doing or feeling. I want you too much. Let me touch you, Helen."

The relief his words bring makes me almost giddy. I sink back into him, letting his strength buoy me. Patroclus might be a brainiac, but his body is all soldier. I want to explore it at length. I inhale deeply, relishing the way the move drags the underside of my breasts against his forearm. "Touch me, Patroclus. Please. I need you to."

I expect him to do it all at once. I really should know better, even after spending so little time with him. Patroclus is a man with a plan, and that's never more evident than it is right now as he shifts his hand to press to my stomach. His thumb brushes the curve of one breast, a slow drag that has me shifting restlessly against him.

He moves to tug the thin strap of my pajama top over my shoulder, easing it down to free my breast. It's an almost teasing move, and it only feels more so as he traces the line of fabric, brushing my exposed breast to tug down the other strap, too. It takes a little more work since I'm lying on my side, but once again, he doesn't rush. It's a fucking *torment.* "Patroclus."

"I like the way you say my name." He cups one breast and then the other, trailing his fingers over my nipples. Not enough. Nowhere near enough.

I worry my bottom lip, but I can't keep silent. "More. Please."

"I like the way you say 'please,' too." His voice sounds rougher than normal, but he doesn't move faster as he trails his hand down the center of my stomach and teases the strings of my shorts. His touch isn't tentative, but he's sure as fuck not rushing. Not like I want him to. Each small tug against the strings creates an answering tug deep inside me. I press my lips together, determined not to beg. Not yet.

Finally, what feels like an eternity later, he dips beneath the band of my shorts. I expect him to move slowly in this the same way he has in everything else, but it's as if all his patience has been used up. Patroclus cups my pussy, his touch rough. We both exhale harshly at the contact.

I have no desire to be owned outside the bedroom, and not even *in* the bedroom most of the time. The power balance in my life is too precarious, too keen to tip to weigh against me. But right now? With Patroclus guiding us? I love it. I bite my bottom lip and whimper a little. I can't pretend it won't have consequences, but when have I ever let consequences get in the way of doing what I want?

It feels too good to stop.

Now that Patroclus has me where he wants me, he slows down again, gentling his touch as he explores me. He traces my opening with his middle finger, still cupping me almost possessively. He doesn't act a caveman and shout *mine*, but he's holding me like he owns me, like he's claiming me. It doesn't matter that we shouldn't. It's happening.

Achilles said that, too. That we *shouldn't*.

A voice inside me whispers that I'm being even more reckless than normal, that I'm playing with these two men's relationship just so I won't have to feel vulnerable, but it's too quiet in the face of my desire. Or maybe I'm really that selfish. Patroclus says he doesn't care, and that should be enough to spare me any unnecessary guilt.

It's not like I've been honest with partners in the past about the fact they're just a convenient escape.

It's not like they've cared enough to ask.

I meant what I said last night, what I said this morning. I've liked Patroclus since we were kids, have wanted him since I met him again as an adult, when he essentially gave me an itemized list of why we couldn't go home together the night before the trials started. I'm not sure I care if he's using me as a weapon to hurt Achilles. All that means is that we're both using each other for selfish purposes. I should just enjoy it instead of thinking so hard.

The whole point of indulging in this reckless behavior is that I'll *stop* thinking.

"Helen." He goes still.

"Yeah?"

"You're thinking very hard right now. Do you want to stop?"

I'm already shaking my head before he finishes speaking. "No. Absolutely not. Give me more."

For a moment, I think he might stop anyway. This isn't the impulsive wave that overtook me with Achilles. This is *intentional* and maybe that means it's a mistake. *I don't care. I still don't want to stop.*

Apparently Patroclus agrees, because he shifts behind me and wedges his other arm between me and the bed. The new position brings me even closer to him, gives me the sensation of being entirely wrapped up in this man. He palms one breast; it's less a stroke than him holding me to him, but I'm not complaining. Not when he's working two blunt fingers into my pussy in the process. Methodical. Patroclus is so damn methodical. It's sexier than I could have anticipated. It's more than that, though. He holds me like I'm something precious, something he's all too capable of shattering into a million pieces.

The difference between him and Achilles is stark, but they're similar in one aspect: no partner I've had in the past has touched me like either of them. I've never been cherished. I've also never been tossed around like an equal, my strength taken as a given instead of a fantasy. Neither of them treats me like I'm a princess to be coaxed into giving up my supposed virtue or a weak thing that a harsh word will leave crumpled and broken on the floor.

The entire time Achilles and I were fighting, I was an enemy to be conquered through mutual orgasms. I never expected it to be so sexy.

Patroclus is fucking me slowly with his fingers like this is the only chance he'll get, and he's determined to maximize it for all it's worth. He presses the heel of his hand to my clit. Not enough to give me the friction I need to get off. No, he's still teasing me. His mouth brushes the shell of my ear, his voice deeper than I've ever heard it. "You're not for me, Helen. You were never meant for me."

I can't decide if the words sting or just stoke the need between us hotter. Nothing sparks as fiery as something that's destined to be temporary. It makes me greedy, makes me want to soak up every second of this because I'll likely never get it again. I drag in a rough breath. "Then let's make it count."

He gives a choked laugh. "Yeah, we'll make it count." He shifts away and moves me easily despite the awkward position, pressing me down onto my back. It's so seamless, I'm still blinking in surprise as he slides down my body, taking the blankets with him. Patroclus pauses to worship my breasts with his mouth, but he's got a destination in mind and I'm not about to start complaining as he tugs off my shorts and settles between my legs. He presses a kiss to one thigh. "Achilles will get restless and come looking for us before too long."

Again, that lash of almost sting. I most certainly should *not* want to get caught with Patroclus's mouth all over my pussy, but the reckless wave inside me only gets stronger. What will Achilles do? I honestly can't focus enough to guess for certain. Start a fight or join in? Start a fight and *then* join in? The possibilities set me aflame. I won't pretend I hadn't considered sharing a bed with both of them. I have.

Still…I'm not so far gone that I can jump into this without a little clarification first. If I'm going to feel guilty about this later, I have to know how much guilt is truly mine to shoulder. I have enough already; I don't need to carry anyone else's. "Are you using me to prove a point?"

He's oh so serious. Even in this, with heat turning his dark gaze scorching and his breath ghosting against the most private part of me, Patroclus contemplates my words with the utmost severity. I like that about him. A lot. He doesn't just fire off an answer and intend to bullshit his way around it being false later. He actually *thinks* about it and then gives me honesty. How novel.

Finally he nods. "A little. Does that bother you?"

Yes. No. I don't know. I can't think properly. I drag in a breath, determined to match him honesty for honesty. "Maybe it will later, but I need you too much right now. Kiss me, Patroclus. If you need to prove a point, do it by making me come."

His slow smile has my whole body lighting up. Gods, this man is handsome. It's different from the perfect features Achilles is blessed with. I noticed Patroclus had grown into a good-looking man the first time I met him as an adult, but each time since, it's like that attractiveness has been compounded again and again. My heart gives a strange little lurch, but I ignore it, just like I ignore the inevitable consequences of doing this.

"I need you too much right now, too."

Then there are no more words. He leans down and drags

his tongue up my center. Slow. Methodical. Determined to learn every inch of me. He presses my thighs even wider apart and dips his tongue into me. First a tease, then a full thrust that has me moaning too loudly. I try to arch up, but he responds by shifting, banding one forearm over my lower stomach and using his shoulders to wedge my legs open even wider. I'm pinned and loving every moment of it.

Still, I'm not one to lie there passively and take whatever he wants to give me.

I dig my fingers into his short hair and tug, urging him up to my clit. He doesn't hesitate, following my unspoken instructions to give it the same thorough treatment he's given every other bit of my pussy. He tests out motions, his gaze on my face, until he finds the one that has me arching and moaning and writhing against him. "Yes, like that," I moan.

Pleasure builds in me, higher and higher. Patroclus never deviates. He doesn't speed up or slow down and shift the pressure the slightest bit. He winds me tighter and tighter and…

The bedroom door opens.

Achilles steps into the room and pulls the door shut behind him. We both freeze. I'm so fucking close, I could cry. I should have known this wouldn't last, that we'd get interrupted before things escalated enough to truly offer me a reprieve. I should have known this was a foolish, impulsive thing that would most certainly backfire in an aborted orgasm.

I should have known…a lot of things.

I tense, waiting for Patroclus to scramble away from me, to sputter out excuses, to fight or leave. He doesn't move. If anything, he tightens his grip on me, a silent command to stop trying to inch up the bed away from him. I freeze. Patroclus gives me a quick look as if testing my reaction. Whatever my face is doing, apparently it satisfies him. He turns his head just enough to look at Achilles. "You're interrupting."

Achilles's slow smile doesn't reach his dark eyes. "Yeah, I know." He stalks to the chair next to the bed and drops into it, stretching his big body out and taking up too much space. He waves a negligent hand in our direction. "Don't stop on my account."

Oh my gods.

I look down my body and meet Patroclus's gaze. I expected him to look ashamed or guilty. Maybe regretful. I sure as fuck didn't expect his desire to burn even hotter. He doesn't seem happy, but there's no doubt that Achilles's casual command sparks something in him.

Still, he is Patroclus, and because he's Patroclus, he hesitates. "Are you okay with this?"

I don't know. I feel like I'm free-falling. It's one thing to know I'm neck deep in a messy relationship and sinking deeper. It's entirely another to... I don't even know what's happening here. But my aborted orgasm beats just as strongly as my need to escape for a little while. Didn't part of me hope this would happen? Yes. I didn't expect it to happen like *this*, but it's not as if it was outside the realm of possibilities when I urged Patroclus to touch me, to make me come.

I glance at Achilles and, wow, his smile might not reach his dark eyes, but he's looking at us like we're a banquet laid out for his pleasure and he's not sure where he wants to start. I shiver. There's no taking back what I've done, and maybe that's an excuse, but I don't care. I don't want to stop. I want to charge forward and see what happens next. "I'm okay with it."

"If you change your mind—"

"For fuck's sake, she said she was good with it. Even I can see she's about to fucking come. Get on with it."

Patroclus turns his head to glare at Achilles. "Audiences should be seen, not heard."

"Said no one ever."

"Gentlemen." I wait for them both to look at me. I can't stop shaking. I'm about to come out of my skin with need, and they're bickering like an old married couple. "If you're going to argue, go do it in the living room and I'll finish myself off in peace."

Achilles snorts and Patroclus offers another of those little smiles I'm starting to like so much. He doesn't give me a chance to decide if I'm bluffing or not. He just dips down and resumes stroking my clit with his tongue in the exact same rhythm that had me dancing on the edge before we were interrupted. I whimper. "Oh fuck."

"Take off your top, princess. If you're going to put on a show, do it properly."

I don't even think. I just obey, wrestling my pajama top off while Patroclus works my pussy like we've been lovers for years instead of less than an hour. I manage to get the offending garment off and toss it at Achilles. He snatches it out of the air and sifts the silk top through his fingers almost contemplatively, but his gaze never leaves us.

Patroclus's gaze threatens to light me aflame. Later, I'm sure

I'll have some complicated feelings about playing the part of a pawn in a game between these two men. Right now, I'm too close to coming to care about anything but Patroclus's tongue working my clit. So close... So fucking close... I palm my breasts, pinching my nipples as he edges me closer and closer to orgasm. It felt so good before, but with Achilles watching...

There are no words.

I've never done anything like this before. Oh, I've been plenty experimental when it comes to sex, but only with a trusted handful of people over the years. Being Zeus's daughter means anyone caught in my bed would see horrific consequences. Olympus likes to pretend it's forward-thinking, but that so-called progressiveness doesn't include the purity culture that pervades the upper circles. As a result, I've never trusted someone enough to let them watch while I fuck. It would be all too easy for them to record while I was distracted and then...

Patroclus turns his head and nips my thigh. "Stop thinking so hard."

"Means you're not doing your job properly," Achilles rumbles. He stretches out his legs. "Two fingers."

I barely comprehend his words when Patroclus moves, releasing my thigh and pushing two blunt fingers into me. He shifts the angle a few times, searching...searching. He grins. "There." He flicks his fingertips against my G-spot. Holy shit, that was fast.

My whole body goes molten, the feeling only compounded by the fact that he's following Achilles's directive. I look over at the other man, but his gaze is on Patroclus, his eyes narrowed. "Now, her clit. Make her come, loud and messy."

Once again, Patroclus obeys immediately, moving back to my clit. The combination of him stroking my G-spot and licking my clit and... *"Fuck!"* I orgasm, back bowing and my heels digging into the mattress. Patroclus doesn't move, doesn't stop, just keeps going, driving my orgasm higher and...

"Don't stop," Achilles barks.

I cry out. It's almost a scream. The pressure builds and builds and then something gives inside me, and I squirt all over Patroclus's hand. Only then does he gentle his touch, easing me down until the only thing I'm able to do is stare at him and shake. He gives my pussy one last long, thorough kiss and lifts his head.

Achilles's low laugh draws our attention in his direction. His body language is perfectly relaxed, but the way his giant cock presses against his sweatpants gives lie to the image he's projecting. As I stare, he palms his cock roughly and grins. "That's a good start."

ACHILLES

I CAN'T DECIDE IF I'M MORE PISSED OFF OR TURNED ON. When I heard Helen's moan, I knew what I'd find the second I walked into the room. She and Patroclus fucking around, or just flat-out fucking. I walked through the door anyways. There's something selfish in that. If I were a better man, I would have let Patroclus have his moment with Helen without me involved.

I'm not a better man. I'm a selfish asshole.

Watching him eat her pussy... The way he responded to my commands...

We've never done anything like this before. I'm naturally bossy in bed, and we've shared partners in the past, but not like *this*. Not with me taking the lead so intensely and him following along without a word. Not with a woman both of us are drawn to in different ways. Helen is nothing like anyone we've shared in the past, and this situation is a first for us in so many ways.

I'm not ready for it to stop.

Patroclus leverages himself up to look at me. The entire bottom half of his face is wet with Helen, and fuck if that doesn't send a bolt of lust straight to my cock. I want to kiss him, to taste both of them mixed up on his tongue. Not now. If I cross that line, I'll be fucking her again before I leave that bed.

He shakes his head a little as if waking from a dream. "What?"

I make an effort to keep all the tension from my body. "You know you're not satisfied with one orgasm. You're so hard, you're about to come in your pants." I lean forward and prop my elbows on my knees. "Fuck her, Patroclus. You think that pussy tastes good? Feels good clamped around your fingers? It feels even better around your cock."

Helen makes a little writhing motion and turns her head to blink those big amber eyes at me. She's got a shell-shocked look on her face, but that doesn't stop her from running her mouth. "I'm right here."

"Yeah, you are." And what a fucking picture *she* makes. Hair all fucked up from sleep, her skin golden in the morning light, flushed from coming all over Patroclus's face. Her tits are even more perfect than I remember, and with this minuscule distance, I can appreciate the deceptive strength of her body. Every single muscle stood out when she came. I want to see it happen again. I think they want it, too.

There are a dozen reasons to stop this now, but I ignore every single one of them. "Don't pretend like you haven't been panting after Patroclus's cock since that first night. You think he eats pussy good? Let him focus all that attention on fucking you properly."

She gives another of those long blinks, and I can practically see her brain jumping back online. "You are such a dick."

"I've been called worse. By you."

"Yeah, guess so." Helen bites her bottom lip. "Patroclus?" A whole lot of subtext in that single word, and for once, I can read most of it. She wants this. She doesn't want to, is pretty sure she's going to regret it, but she wants it too much to be the one to stop us.

I can't speak to regrets. I don't fuck with them all that often. Once something's done, it's done, and there's no point to wish on stars that you can go back in time and redo things differently. You live with the consequences and move on, maybe learn a thing or two in the process. Maybe this shit is a mistake, maybe it's not, but if all three of us want it, why shouldn't we go for it?

For once, Patroclus isn't lost in thought. He's staring up her body like he wants to taste every inch of her, like he's finally found someone besides me who clicks off that impressive brain of his and leaves only instinct behind. He's still Patroclus, though, so he shakes his head and attempts to focus. To *reason*. "I want you, Helen. I don't want to stop. If you're good with this—"

"Yes."

I snort at how quickly she responds, and he gives a little laugh. "You sure?"

"Yes. This is…" Helen drags in a breath that makes her tits jiggle. "This is messy, but I think it's safe to say neither of you is going to use it against me?"

What the fuck is she talking about? Use *what* against her? I frown. "The only thing we're going to use against you is Patroclus's cock."

He understands, though. He always seems to be able to

make the jump even when I'm floundering behind him. Patroclus smooths a hand over her stomach. "You're right. This is messy. But what happens in this bedroom is between us. It goes as far as you want, but it won't affect what happens once we leave the bed."

That sounds like a whole lot of bullshit. He's already thinking of the future. She is, too. Fuck, even I am. "It's already messy." I can't keep the impatience out of my voice. "It was messy the moment we fucked, the second you came all over his face. It's not going to get messier." But I get what her fear is now. Someone has used sex against her in the past and left her bruised because of it. I try to soften my voice, but it still comes out in a rumble. "Helen." I wait for her to give me most of her attention. "Patroclus is right. What happens in this bedroom is just between us. It will *stay* just between us."

"Okay." Her smile is almost tentative...trusting. She clears her throat and looks away. "Look, guys, this is really hot, and I don't care if I'll regret it later. I don't want to stop."

That snags at me even as I tell myself it's none of my godsdamned business if Helen regrets this. She doesn't have to see things my way, to believe that the experience is worth the consequences. Not yet. I have plenty of time to convince them both. "You're going to be coming too hard to regret anything."

"Maybe." She shoots me a sharp look. "But we'll see how I feel when you two start fighting again."

"Don't worry about later." I slice my hand through the air, wishing I could cut off that inevitable future as easily. She's probably right, which is frustrating. This might be my selfish version of an apology, but ultimately it doesn't fix shit with me and Patroclus. I'm still not really sure *how* to fix shit between us. A worry for later, just like Helen's regrets. "This is now. You in?"

"Yes." Again, no hesitation. I might not really understand Helen, but I do appreciate that once she decides on a course, it doesn't seem like much deters her. We have that in common. I very carefully don't think about what else we might have in common.

"Patroclus?"

He hesitates, searching my expression. I don't know what for. I'm practically wrapping up Helen like a gift for him, even if this might not be the perfect scenario he imagined when he thought about what it would be like to seduce her. Honestly, though, he's probably considered this scenario, too. Patroclus knows I'm a human wrecking ball. Just like I know his mind is ten steps ahead of us right now and thinking too hard about potential outcomes and consequences.

I see the exact moment he discards all that and throws caution to the wind. He gives a short nod and turns back to drink in the sight of her laid out for him. "Yeah."

Relief and anticipation twine through me, but I refuse to show any of it. With these two and their determination to overthink any given situation to death, there was a decent chance one of them would have slammed on the brakes and stopped this before I was ready to end it. It takes me a few seconds to let that concern go and refocus.

They both said yes. We're in this. Time to have some fucking *fun*.

I inhale slowly, letting my plans spin out. I want them both to come hard, but I also want a damn good view. I snap my fingers. "Patroclus, on your back. Helen, on top."

I prefer to be in the middle of any sexy shit happening, but I can't deny how fucking hot this is. I might not be the one having sex, but they're acting out *my* commands. Patroclus stretches out on the mattress on his back, and Helen wastes no time moving to straddle his hips. She's a little shaky still, and he catches her thighs, holding her steady. They look at each other, and it's like I can *see* the connection between them.

It pisses me off and turns me on. I guess that's no surprise. Everything about this pisses me off and turns me on. Isn't that connection the reason I lost control and fucked Helen on the floor like an animal a single day after badgering Patroclus into promising to stay away from her? I can't erase what's obviously growing between them, but I'm starting to realize I *can* ensure I won't be left behind. "Rub on his cock, princess. Let him feel how wet he made you."

She plants her hands on Patroclus's chest and rolls her hips. My chair is angled just right to see everything. The way she drags her pussy over his cock, pressing its hard length down between them. It wouldn't take much for him to be inside her now. In fact... "Helen and I didn't use protection."

They go still. Patroclus looks at me, a line appearing between his brows. I speak before either of them have a chance to. "There's no reason for you two to use it, either. She's on birth control. You aren't with anyone else but me right now. All of us are tested regularly."

Helen shoots me a sharp look, her pretty lips thinning with irritation. "Speak for me again, and I'll gut you."

"Promises, promises." I shouldn't enjoy her threats so much. But the last time she threatened me, she ended up coming around my cock. Hard to complain with that kind of reward in mind. Except, no, right now isn't about only me. I drag in a breath. The room smells of sex with the promise of more.

The promise of more if I don't fuck this up and piss one of them off. I can do this. I can pump the brakes just enough to make sure everyone is on the same page. "Do you want to use a condom, princess?" I smile slowly, enjoying the way her gaze narrows in response. "Or do you want to ride Patroclus's cock bare and let him fill you up?"

She flushes a pretty pink and shifts her attention to the man between her thighs. "While I'm inclined to protest just to piss him off, I'm not one to cut off my nose to spite my face." She shivers a little, her rosy nipples peaked on her perfect tits. "I like the idea of you fucking me bare, Patroclus. I like it a lot. I'm okay going without a condom if you are."

"It's not a good idea."

I cannot count the number of times I've heard him say those exact same words in that exact same tone. It's a protest for the sake of protest. Patroclus wants this just as much as we do. More, even. There's a fine tremor in his hands where they grip her thighs. He's fighting for control, to be the rational, reasonable one.

Fuck that.

"We don't need a treatise on why it's a bad idea. A yes or no is good enough." I barely pause, barely give his impressive brain a chance to start chugging down the path that derails us. "She feels so good. Wet and tight. Tell me you don't want it."

He curses, and I know we have him. He confirms it a second later. "I want it."

Yeah, but *I* don't want extra room for claiming miscommunication or scooping up more regrets than necessary. "Use your words. Be explicit."

Patroclus strokes his hands up her thighs and then down to hook the backs of her knees. He jerks her a few inches up his stomach. "I want to fuck you bare. I want to fill you up."

Helen nods so fast, her hair falls in her face. "Yes. Yes, let's do it."

Satisfaction curls through me. They're doing what I want, and little feels better than that, especially because I know how bad they both want it, too. Just like I know they wouldn't have done this without my pushing for it. They're both too damn sensible. I make myself lean back in the chair and relax as much as I can manage. "You know what to do, princess."

Helen wraps a fist around Patroclus's cock, and *my* cock twitches in response. She strokes him slowly, her long fall of light-brown hair shielding her face from me. I want to tell her to pull it back, to show me everything, but I can't quite manage it. Maybe it's better not to see the way she looks at him. Bad enough to witness *his* expression as he watches her rise to notch his cock at her entrance. Patroclus is as shell-shocked as he was the first time we had sex, as if he's waiting for someone to pinch him and say it's all a joke, a trick, a sham.

He still looks at me like that sometimes.

I push the thought away and focus on watching Helen fight her way down Patroclus's cock. He's girthier than I am, and even though she just came hard enough to soak the bed, she's still got to work to take him. "He's spreading you so wide, princess. Feels good, doesn't it?"

"Yes," she gasps. Another inch of his cock disappears into her. The jealousy curdling my stomach only gets stronger. It's dual-sided, a room full of fun-house mirrors that reflect and amplify. I want to feel her clamp around me. I want to experience the almost pain of that first slow slide of his cock as he pushes into me. I want it all.

Patroclus shifts his grip to her hips. "Slow."

"No, not slow." I can't keep the bite out of my words. "Take him all."

"I'm trying, you asshole." She rolls her hips again, working herself down the last bit of him. The moment they're sealed together, all three of us exhale harshly. Helen's nails dent the skin on his chest, but she doesn't rake them over him the way she did with me. Instead, she's being so damn gentle, I want to shatter something.

"Ride him," I snap. "Make yourself come again."

This time, she doesn't snarl at me. She simply obeys, moving almost decadently slowly. It's sexy as fuck to watch the way her body rolls over him, but it's like an itch I can't quite scratch. It's too intimate, too sweet. The way they look at each other, I might as well not be in the room. The sensation only gets worse when Patroclus brushes her hair back and then arches up to kiss her, her face cradled gently in his hands.

Yeah, no, this isn't what I signed up for.

"That's about enough of that." They both freeze, and the guilt written across his expression is more of a slap in the face than anything else that's happened here. I swallow past the sudden ache in my chest. It's just sex, and I don't do regrets. I fucking *refuse* to. "Patroclus, sit on the edge of the bed. Princess, on his lap, facing me."

This time, they move slower. That causes the ache to get worse. Not even Helen's perfect tits are enough to combat the feeling of being immaterial. I'm a selfish prick. I like being the center of attention. And I'm...not right now.

Helen eases onto Patroclus's lap with her legs on the outside of his. If I enjoyed the view of him entering her before, it's a thousand times better now. His cock spreads her almost obscenely, and I palm myself roughly in response. This time, she doesn't have to fight as hard to take him. She leans back against his chest and slides one arm up to hook behind his neck. "Is this better, Achilles? Can't pretend you're not here when you're making us stare right at you." Her lips curve. "Is someone feeling insecure?"

"Shut up."

Patroclus cups her breasts, temporarily distracting both of us. She gasps at him pinching her nipples just shy of roughly. I enjoy the way her hips jolt in response, seeking pressure against her clit. He knows. Of course he knows. He always seems to divine what his partners need next. He wastes no time sliding one hand down between her thighs to stroke her clit. I can appreciate the fact that he keeps most of his hand up on her stomach, though, offering a clear view of them fucking.

What I can't tell is if he's trying to prove a point or not.

Both of them watch me as he winds her up stroke by stroke.

She's still doing that sexy slow roll, obviously not in a hurry to reach any destination. Helen's breath hitches. "Poor Achilles. Is this better? Now you can watch how much I'm enjoying Patroclus's cock." She whimpers when he switches up his touch against her clit. "You can see how much he's enjoying my pussy."

"Shut up." It's an even more terrible comeback this time because I'm just repeating myself, but I can barely speak through the lust coating the room, so intense it's like a stronger force of gravity against my skin. I dip my hand into my sweats and grip my cock. Somehow, that only makes it worse. Because I'm not really involved, even if I *am* right here.

Helen's gaze flicks to where my fist moves in my pants, and she licks her lips. I tense, waiting to see if she'll really toss the gauntlet at my feet. I should know better by now. If there's one thing Helen can be trusted to do, it's escalate the situation. She bites her bottom lip. "You want to shut me up? Get over here and do it properly."

I'm on my feet before I can think of all the reasons this is a shitty idea. If I wanted to stop, though, I'd ask Patroclus to give me a bullet-pointed list. I don't want to stop. "Sounds like you need a cock to choke on."

She arches an eyebrow, never missing a beat of fucking Patroclus. "Bold of you to assume I'll choke on *you*."

"Only one way to find out." I hardly sound like myself. I glance over her shoulder at Patroclus. He looks just as conflicted as I feel. We've shared partners in the past, yes, but we both know better than to lump Helen in with them. It was complicated enough with each of us fucking her on our own. Doing it together feels like a mark of intent that I'm not sure we can follow through on without crashing and burning.

Not just ruining what little tentative peace we have with Helen, either. If this blows up in our faces, it might very well fuck my and Patroclus's relationship beyond all repair.

We're barreling down a path of no return, and it's too damn late to stop. I've never had much in the way of brakes, always relying on his steadier hand and cooler head to stop us before we do shit we can't take back. With him balls deep in Helen's pussy, there's no appealing to the only god he worships. Logic has nothing on the lust bringing a sexy flush to his handsome face.

I step closer, letting Helen hook her fingers into the band of my sweats. She tugs them down just enough to free my cock and looks up at me. Fuck, she's sexy, and the fact she's riding Patroclus's cock right now only makes her sexier. She licks her lips again. "This doesn't mean I like you."

The words might sting if she weren't looking at me like she wants to consume me whole. I can't quite laugh. Not right now. "I think you like me just fine, princess."

Her smile goes downright mischievous. "Maybe I just really want to suck your cock."

Behind her, Patroclus curses. "Then stop talking and *do it*." He wraps a careful fist around her long hair and nudges her head forward. I half expect Helen to snarl at him, but she follows his guidance eagerly, letting him urge her forward until she can wrap her lips around the head of my cock.

For all my shit-talking, I only ease forward a little, giving her time and space to adjust to my length. Patroclus does something with his hand between her thighs that has her whimpering and taking me deeper. I hold perfectly still and watch her suck me down. It looks just as hot as it feels, her tongue working the underside of my cock even as her lips meet my base. "Someone taught the precious princess to deep throat," I murmur, voice rough with need.

Helen pushes against Patroclus's hold on her hair, and he lets her off my cock. She gives me an arch look. "Now that we've established I can take you, stop trying to pretend you have a noble streak and fuck my mouth like you mean it."

PATROCLUS

UP UNTIL THIS POINT, I'VE BEEN ACTING ON INSTINCT AND lust with little thought behind it. For the first time in my life, the draw of the forbidden is too much to ignore. I know I'll regret this entire experience later, but the spell cast by first Helen, and then Helen and Achilles, is too strong. It's only as Achilles sinks his fingers into her hair, gripping my hand in the process, and starts to fuck Helen's mouth that I wonder what *her* motivation is...and if we're taking advantage.

She said she gets restless and impulsive. She admitted as much to me last night and again this morning. She asked me if I was okay with it, and I'd been so out of my mind with need and hurt and jealousy that I said I didn't give a fuck. Yes, she's shown enthusiastic consent this whole time, but if the motivation for that is harmful, does that consent mean fuck all?

Godsdamn it, we *are* taking advantage.

"Get the fucking look off your face, Patroclus," Achilles snarls. "You can feel guilty later. Right now, you're going to stroke her clit until she comes. If you want to finish her before I come all over her tits, you'd better pick up the fucking pace."

I want to call him selfish. To agree with Helen's earlier statement about him being an asshole. I *should* do that and cut this thing off right now until we can have a conversation where someone isn't on the verge of orgasming or half-asleep or running from some internal demons only they can see.

I don't.

I lift my hand from Helen's clit. Achilles anticipates my need just like he so often seems to and leans down to take my fingers into his mouth. He growls a little as he licks the taste of her from my skin, but he doesn't pause in his relentless pace. I withdraw my wet fingers and resume stroking Helen's clit. She moans around Achilles's cock and tries to keep fucking me, but she's too damn distracted. Too trapped between us.

"Achilles," I grind out.

"Yeah. Down." He's already moving, shifting back and easing to his knees. I band an arm around her hips, and we follow. Of course we fucking follow him. Sometimes it feels like my whole life has been spent following Achilles, whether it damns me in the process or brings me untold amounts of bliss.

We move down to our knees beside the bed. The new position allows me to sink even deeper into Helen's tight pussy. I don't know if I believe in the afterlife, but this must be what it feels like. Hot, wet perfection. No wonder Achilles forgot himself and fucked her bare. It feels so good, it short-circuits something in my brain. My thoughts keep trying to reassert themselves, but then she'll clench around me, and they scatter like marbles.

I barely allowed myself to think about what it would be like to fuck Helen Kasios, but reality is so far beyond what I could have possibly imagined.

I don't mean to match my rhythm to Achilles's. No matter how conflicted my feelings about him are right now, he is my sun and I am helpless against the gravity he exerts. I work Helen's clit as we fuck her, and it doesn't take long before she's moaning and shaking. Still, I don't relent. I want to feel her come apart around me. I want to fill her up, just like Achilles commanded. So easy to put the responsibility on him, on his orders, rather than admit I want to experience what he did with her, want to make my own mark so I'm not left behind. This is only temporary, but at least I *have* this right now. It's more than I thought possible.

She sobs around his cock as she orgasms, and her pussy clamps on *my* cock so tightly, I lose control. I release her hair and pound into her. Too fast. Too fucking rough. It doesn't matter because she's arching back against me, spreading her thighs to take me deeper yet. "Helen, I—"

Achilles leans forward and captures my mouth. He kisses me like he owns me, like he owns *this*. I'm not sure he's wrong. Even when he was sitting on the chair watching us, his presence consumed the space. Neither of us could escape it. I don't think either of us wanted to. I sure as fuck don't want to now. I come with the mingled taste of him and Helen on my tongue.

He barely lets me finish before he's pushing us back. Rough. Achilles is too damn rough. But then, he knows I'm there to break Helen's fall. She lands on my chest, and it's the most natural thing in the world to wrap my arms around her. I hold her steady as he pulls out of her mouth and strokes his cock once, twice, a third time. Achilles curses as he comes across Helen's breasts in jerking spurts. She moans and arches her back as if she enjoys the sight.

Achilles braces one hand on the mattress behind us and drags a single finger through the mess on her chest, idly circling one nipple. "Next time..." He drags in a rough breath. "Next time, I want Patroclus to come all over your pussy and thighs, and then I'm going to fuck his come into you."

Helen makes that sexy little whimpering sound. "Making a lot of assumptions," she finally manages.

"Nah. I know what I want. And I know what Patroclus wants, even if he won't admit it." Achilles slumps down next to us, his ragged breathing joining ours. "I'm starting to know what you want, too."

A shudder of near fear goes through me. Achilles has that look on his face, the one like a hound that's caught a scent. I can count on one hand how many times I've seen him look like this in the twelve years I've known him. One, when we went through boot camp to become Ares's security forces. They tried to wash us out, didn't want an arrogant orphan and a nerd who'd rather have his head in a book. Achilles had already decided he'd get through whatever they threw at him, and he did, dragging me along with him.

The second time, when Athena poached him, and me with him. Within the first week training under her command, he dropped onto my bed one night and grinned. *I'm going to be her second-in-command within ten years.* It only took him six.

The third time, the final time, was when he decided becoming Ares was what he wanted.

Now, he's looking at her, at *us*, in the same way, and there's not enough air in the room. Helen doesn't know him well enough to understand what danger we're in, but she tenses up all the same. I let her push my arms away from her and sit up. "Well, that was fun—" She shoots to her feet.

Or she tries.

Achilles moves before I even realize her intent, putting an arm out in front of her. Helen bounces off it and lands back against my chest. "What the fuck?"

"Yeah, no, you're not doing that cut-and-run bullshit again, so sit there, let Patroclus cuddle you, and enjoy the afterglow."

As much as I like the weight of her on my lap, as much as I *do* want to put my arms around her and cuddle her close, he just crossed half a dozen lines. I take a deep breath, trying not to react to the scent of Helen and Achilles and sex in the air, and strive to be calm and reasonable. "Achilles, let her go. You can't just keep people where they don't want to be."

"Except I'm bigger than her, so that's exactly what I can do." He leans back and closes his eyes, but his apparent relaxation is a lie. I used to fall for it when we were teenagers, and as adults, I've played this game with him more times than I can count with pleasurable end results.

Helen didn't sign up for that sort of game, though. "Achilles."

He opens his eyes, and for the first time since he walked into the room and caught my tongue in her pussy, he looks absolutely furious. "No, you will *not* be talking to me like I'm being a dick. I often am, but not this time."

"I beg to differ," Helen snarls.

"Beg all you want. First time for everything. Who knows, you might even like it."

Even though I don't want to, I carefully set Helen down between us. The alternative is her vibrating with rage in my lap, and I'm only human. I won't be able to stop my body from reacting, just having orgasmed or not. Without her delicious weight against me, I can finally think a little clearly. "*Achilles.*"

"Don't say my name like that, *Patroclus*. She doesn't get to fuck us and take off without another word. She's not running away until we talk. Not this time."

Helen shoves her hair out of her face, but she doesn't try to stand up and leave this time. "You didn't bargain for a conversation, asshole. You only wanted to fuck my mouth and come all over my chest. Mission accomplished. There's nothing to talk about."

As much as I hate the way he's going about this, Achilles isn't wrong. No matter which way I look at this, what we just did complicated things beyond comprehension. I feel so damn tangled up, I can barely think straight, and Achilles still has that flinty look in his eyes that fills me with foreboding. Every other time, his goal has been a position or meeting an external challenge. I don't like to think of what he'll do if *people* are his goal.

Maybe I'm reading him wrong. I must be. It's sex clouding my thoughts. I rub my hands over my face and try to think. "It's safe to assume you're not going to resign from the tournament."

"Brilliant deduction, Sherlock," Helen snaps.

Achilles crosses his arms over his chest and settles back against the mattress. "Are you pissed because you just came harder than you ever have before and that hurt your pride, or is it something else?"

Helen makes a sound that has me fighting not to inch away from her. She's naked and smaller than I am. What harm can she do? Even as the thought crosses my mind, I shift my thigh so my cock isn't an easy target. She doesn't seem to notice, though. She's too focused on Achilles. "I don't know, what could *possibly* be upsetting to me? The fact that my siblings tossed me to the sharks without so much as a warning? Or maybe that my ex is competing in this fucking tournament solely to win me because he finally has external confirmation that I'm nothing more than a prize to be won? Oh, I know! I bet it's because I was *attacked* by someone with a *knife* last night. Ring any bells?"

Guilt hits, a blow that would take me off my feet if I wasn't already on my ass. "Shit, we shouldn't have done this."

"There he is," Achilles murmurs. "Right on schedule."

"Fuck you."

Helen twists to look at me. Her mouth is pink from the fucking Achilles gave her, and there are faint tear tracks on her face, but her look of concern is for *me*. She reaches a hand up and cups my face tentatively, as if expecting me to reject her. "It's not regrets. I'm pissed and out of sorts and all fucked up, but it's not regrets. That's not what this is about. You didn't take advantage."

Ironic that she's trying to reassure *me* when we sure as fuck *did* take advantage of her. Gods, we're two of the biggest pricks in Olympus. "You came into our room to stay safe, and we used that proximity to fuck you."

Helen arches a brow, suddenly looking more like herself.

"Please. I meant what I said last night. I fully intended on seducing you the first chance I got, and I already fucked *him*." She jerks her thumb over her shoulder at Achilles. "If anything, *I* took advantage of *you*."

"That's about enough of the useless blame game." Achilles stretches. "Here's what's going to happen—"

"Oh yes," Helen drawls. "Please enlighten us, fearless leader. As if you've ever had an original thought in that pretty head of yours. We all know the brains of this operation is Patroclus."

"Aw, princess, you think I'm pretty. I'm touched."

"Don't let it go to your head." She examines her fingernails, which I belatedly see are painted a matte color that matches her skin. "You came very fast, Achilles. Just like last time. Truly, it seems to be a trend, and I wouldn't be bragging about it."

Achilles opens one eye to glare at her. "I'd think after two stellar orgasms, you'd be in a better mood."

"It's not like *you*—"

"Holy fuck, will you two stop bickering like an old married couple?" The words come out too sharply, but everything feels too sharp right now. We're in this mess up to our necks, and there's no rewinding the clock to take it back. I can't think about the fact that someday Helen and Achilles *will* be an old married couple. "Helen, are you okay? Truly okay, and not just saying that to make us feel better?"

"No, I'm not okay." She flicks her hair over her shoulder. "But if you're asking if I'm about to sob with regret because I just had two outstanding orgasms and got railed by two sexy men... also no. Unlike *some* people, I can compartmentalize."

"Liar." Achilles says it almost fondly. "But the next time you're looking for a distraction, we're here and willing."

"How selfless of you."

"Nah. You're sexy as shit, and you know it." He finally opens his eyes and gives a lazy grin. "You're a whole lot more agreeable when you're choking on my cock. Let's be honest, though. You're downright *likable* when you're coming all messy and loud. Can't wait for round two—or three, if we're being honest."

"*Achilles.*" When he finally falls silent, it's everything I can do to gather my wits. If she says she's okay with what happened, then I have to take her at her word. But that means it's time to unpack the rest of the issues plaguing us. "Helen, he's right. We need to talk."

"We're talking right now."

I give her the look that statement deserves. Good gods, what have I gotten myself into? "If you're seeing this through, you'll be staying in our room until the tournament is over."

"So you can guard my *body*."

I try to ignore the barbs in those words. She's right, though. We're shitty bodyguards right now. Anyone could have walked into the suite while we were fucking, and while Achilles has excellent situational awareness, I can't guarantee he would have reacted quickly enough in the event of another attack. I sure as fuck wouldn't have. "He saved you last night."

"Yes, well, even a broken clock is right twice a day." She rises to her feet. Achilles shifts but Helen holds up her hand. "You're both right about us needing to talk, but I'm not having a serious conversation while covered in bodily fluids. I'm going to take a shower."

This time, neither of us stop her as she steps over Achilles's outstretched legs and walks into the bathroom. The door shutting sounds unnaturally loud in the sudden quiet. Achilles sighs and lets his head fall back against the bed. "Well, that was unexpected."

"Was it?" I don't disagree exactly, but something about Helen feels inevitable. This isn't forever, but I'm drawn to her in a way I don't understand. Maybe this was always going to happen, even if I didn't account for it. It makes me wonder what else I haven't accounted for. "Achilles..."

"Don't apologize." He doesn't look at me. "Don't you dare fucking apologize. I don't care if you fucked her because you wanted to hurt me or if things just got out of control. I'm the one who started this anyway. She was into it this morning, so you can take that off the list of things you feel guilty about."

"And you?"

He turns his head just enough to look at me. "What part of what just happened makes you think I wasn't into it?"

"That's not what I'm asking." But as he waits for me to elaborate, I can't quite find the words. I don't want to. If I ask him what he was thinking while he looked at her—at *us*—with that particular expression on his face, he'll answer me honestly. I know he will.

I'm not sure I'm ready to hear that answer.

"I swear to the fucking gods, if you say some dumb shit like this being a sign that we're on the way out with each other, I will take you onto the training mat and beat the piss out of you."

"You'll try," I snap.

"Yeah. You win nearly as often as I do." He smiles a little, though it fades far too fast. "I know shit is fucked up right now, but it won't always be like this. Once this tournament is over, things will go back to normal. Better than normal."

That's the thing. They wouldn't have gone back to normal, even if Helen wasn't in the picture and complicating things. Achilles and I might be relatively high up the power structure beneath Athena, but we're still just soldiers. At the end of this tournament, Achilles will become *Ares*. One of the thirteen most powerful people in Olympus. There is no going back to normal after that. He'll be thrust into the spotlight with Helen at his side as his wife. No matter how much he loves me, it doesn't change the fact that I will be shuffled back into the shadows.

The future had always held an element of dread for me because the moment he becomes Ares, I lose him. It might not happen with the snap of his fingers, but eventually he'll outpace me once and for all, and I'll be left behind.

That was before Helen.

Watching them move on *together*? Fuck, I can barely stand to think of it.

Saying as much to Achilles is just asking for a fight. He doesn't see things my way, is so certain he can power through and mold the future to *his* impressive will. It's not until he fails that he'll finally admit I was right, at least in this. He won't believe me that our eventually ending up on separate paths is all but inevitable. He'll try to fight for us, to hold us closer, and it will only hurt worse in the end.

Better to focus on the problem at hand. A simple mystery that must have a solution. "Helen won't back down, and whoever is trying to scare her off is only going to escalate."

He gives a nearly soundless sigh but doesn't try to haul me back to the original topic. "Next trial is going to take us from twelve to five. She'll get knocked out then."

I wish I had his confidence. Helen has surprised us again and again. The odds might be against her, but they have been from the start. "And if she's not?"

He shakes his head. "She will be. We just have to keep her cute little ass safe until that point, and then Zeus will sweep in and toss her in some ivory tower until the tournament is over."

I finally move, leveraging myself to my feet. I can't look at the bed, the chair, the floor. The memory of what we've done is imprinted over all of it. I can't believe things got so out of control, but this feels as inevitable as everything else surrounding this situation. "This can't happen again. You and me and her."

Achilles, the bastard, laughs. "Sure. Whatever you say."

He doesn't believe that any more than I do.

HELEN

IT TAKES ALL OF TWO MINUTES IN THE SHOWER FOR REALITY to catch up with me. I just had sex with Patroclus *and* Achilles. I lean my forehead against the cool tile of the shower wall and try very hard not to make a liar out of myself by regretting it. Truth be told, I *don't* regret the sex. It was outstanding and then when Achilles stopped giving orders and joined in...

I shiver.

Actually, *outstanding* doesn't begin to cover it.

But the fact remains that I just slept with Achilles *again*, and I don't like him. I think. Probably. Mostly.

I sigh. Okay, it's time to be honest, at least with myself. I might keep saying I don't like the big man, but it hasn't felt like the truth since... I'm actually not sure when things shifted so much, but the fact remains that they have. It's not even that Achilles is sexy as fuck—though he is. It's not even that he *saved* me last night.

I can't entirely discount a little hero worship because of it, though. The man basically broke down my door and fought my attacker, who had a fucking *knife*. Sure, Achilles is special forces and more than capable of handling a single person, but that is beside the point. He didn't have to do that. He could have turned away and left me to my fate and simplified his life. If I'm gone, so are a lot of complications in his future. He wouldn't be to blame, either, so it's not like my brother could do anything about it.

People die in this tournament. Bellerophon said it themselves. Sure, this wasn't during a trial, but Perseus's hands would be tied. At best, he could duke it out with Athena, but that would still spare Achilles the fallout. *He* didn't hold the knife, after all.

He did, however, hold me while I tried not to fall apart in the aftermath. That's the crux of it, the point where I tipped right out of hating him and into...something else. Anyone else would have used that moment of weakness to manipulate me. *Helen, honey, this just proves that you shouldn't be in this tournament. You should go back to your penthouse where it's safe and wait for someone else to be declared the winner. Someone stronger. Someone who wasn't helpless in the face of a single attacker.*

Achilles didn't use my fear as a weapon against me. He barely used words at all. He simply wrapped me up in his big body and held me until the shaking stopped. I didn't expect gentleness from him, though if he'd asked me if I wanted a hug, I would have told him to fuck off. That's the thing about Achilles; he seems more an "easier to ask for forgiveness than permission" kind of guy. He decided I needed to be held, so he picked me up and deposited me on his lap.

He never even posed the question of me resigning from the tournament. He simply took it as fact that I wouldn't. That I'd set myself on this path and he respected me enough to respect that choice. How novel.

Not to mention, I kind of *like* bickering with him. I'm so used to the veiled insults that a person doesn't feel until minutes or hours later that Achilles's blunt crassness is a relief. No matter how much he snarls, there's no real venom behind the words.

Damn it. I like the big jerk.

I push off the wall and duck back beneath the scalding spray of the water. Ultimately, my feelings don't change anything. Achilles wants what I want, which means we are opposing forces. Patroclus, too, because no matter how much he wants me, his heart belongs to that beautiful fool. My time with him—with them—was only ever going to be temporary.

I knew that going in. Honestly, it was a perk. I'm only able to give so much. It's not as if they'll want to keep fucking after I ruin Achilles's chance of realizing his dream. I'll probably never see them again once the tournament is over, aside from official business.

There's no reason at all for that knowledge to sting *now*.

Showering any longer would translate to hiding, so I shut off the water and take a few minutes to dry off, lotion up, and braid my hair back from my face. I stare at myself in the mirror. I look exactly like I always have. Too pretty, even when I attempt to downplay it, even when I'm tired and there are faint smudges beneath my eyes. The face of a woman people see as a prize, have always seen as a prize. They only care about the surface until what's underneath inconveniences them, and then they drop me like yesterday's trash. Or, worse, try to change *me*. Yeah, this face has brought me nothing but trouble.

Still, it's the only one I have.

I sigh, straighten my spine, and walk out of the bathroom. The first thing I notice is that someone—probably Patroclus—changed the sheets and made the bed. The memory of why that's necessary hits me hard enough to make every muscle in my body clench. Gods, that orgasm was good. The second one was even better, albeit in a different way. My entire body aches faintly from what the three of us did, and I'd be lying if I said I didn't want more.

I just can't be sure *why* I want more. To keep hiding from the uncomfortable reality that I am in over my head for real this time? Or simply because I'm in lust with two men I most certainly shouldn't be indulging with? Neither option is particularly flattering. Both will bite me in the ass before this is over.

Achilles is probably my strongest competitor, though the rest of the champions are no slouches. But he wants Ares nearly as bad as I do, and that gives him an edge I can't afford to ignore. Having sex with him... *Continuing* to have sex with him... It's a mistake.

Sleeping with Patroclus, his boyfriend, lover, partner? Whatever they call each other, it's like poking a bear with a sharpened stick. I'm making things complicated, and if somehow I fail and Achilles becomes Ares, that means he'll be my husband and both of them will be in close proximity with me for the rest of my life. Messy does not even begin to cover it.

I'm not sure I care. Not enough to stop.

I find the men sitting at the table by the kitchenette. Achilles is still wearing his gray sweatpants, and I can't help my physical response to seeing them and his bare chest. His body is unreal, and knowing how effectively he uses it for his partners' pleasure?

I shiver a little. Patroclus has pulled on a pair of shorts, but he's left off his shirt, too. This must be how they always are in the mornings: half-dressed and relaxed, easing into their day with a comfort I barely comprehend.

After I graduated from high school, the first thing I did was move out of my father's penthouse and into one of my own. Living with Zeus was hardly a comfortable, soothing environment, and my siblings and I all dealt with that in different ways. Usually by starting shit. Living alone was a huge adjustment, and I quickly became territorial enough that I rarely let people stay the night. Even—especially—romantic partners. I'm not a morning person, and that means I have a difficult time getting my public persona into place before noon.

The only time I let that practice slip was when I dated Paris, and he gave me cause to regret it. It only took a few days of waking up together for the comments to start. Initially they were innocent enough. *You look tired, Helen.* It didn't take long to graduate to full-on criticism. *Maybe you shouldn't leave the bedroom without makeup. What if you get photographed through the window? They're going to think you're sick.* It got to the point where I'd wake up an hour before him to put my face on and do my hair so he wouldn't have ammunition against me.

Paris, of course, just found other ways to pick me apart at the seams.

Best not to think too hard about the fact that I haven't even *thought* to keep that mask secure around these two men. Achilles is the first person outside of family who's experienced my bite, and Patroclus brings out something unforgivably soft in me that I'd completely forgotten existed. More, I haven't worn makeup except when we're going to be in front of a camera, and neither one of them has made a single comment. I'm not certain they even noticed.

The scent of coffee makes my mouth water, so I make a beeline for the counter. "I didn't realize we had a coffee maker in our rooms." I'm sure I would have seen it in mine if I had one, but I've been understandably distracted since arriving here.

"We don't. We requested one after we got here because Achilles is a bear without his morning caffeine." Patroclus holds up a mug, and I realize he's already got one in front of him. "Cream and sugar, right?"

I change course, heading toward the table and accepting the mug from him. How could he possibly have memorized my preferred way of drinking coffee? He wasn't even in the room when I made it yesterday morning. I consider him but decide it's a question for another day. I sip the coffee and offer a reluctant smile. "Perfect."

"Helen..."

The small pleasure of a perfect cup of coffee fades. "I know. Time to talk."

Patroclus glances at Achilles. Again, I'm struck by the intimacy of the moment. They've obviously known each other a long time because they're doing that couple thing where they have an entire conversation without speaking. I ignore the stab of jealousy. It's not that I want that with either of them, but I do want that level of comfort in a relationship.

Unfortunately, that means letting my guard down, and the last time *that* happened, I ended up with Paris.

I take another sip of my coffee. This is where they either let me down gently or try to hard-sell me on quitting. The former, I'll accept. The latter? Good luck with that. I take the third chair at the table. There were only two last night, so one of them must have brought this one in this morning. A tiny thoughtful gesture that I have no business feeling emotional over. Gods, I'm a mess.

"We should keep fucking."

Patroclus makes a choked noise and starts coughing, but I'm too busy blinking at Achilles. Surely he didn't say what I think he just said. "What?"

"It was fun. I want to do it again." He stares at me as if daring me to contradict him. "You want to do it again, too."

I'd be smart to argue. The sex was mind-blowing, to say the least. I was telling the truth when I said I compartmentalize well— *thanks, Father*—but even I can't be sure my heart won't revolt and get involved if I keep sleeping with both of them. Maybe I could hold out against Achilles, but...

I glance at Patroclus. He's a mottled red, but he seems to be breathing okay now. "He didn't discuss this with you first."

"No," he bites out. "He didn't."

Achilles shrugs and drinks his coffee. He puts on a good act like he doesn't give a shit, but there's a thread of tension in his shoulders that tells me he cares about the destination of this conversation more than he wants to admit. "I don't have to talk about it with him first. Patroclus will let guilt get in the way of doing what he wants, but what he wants is to bend you over the table and—"

"That's *enough*, Achilles." Patroclus sets his mug down hard enough to splash coffee onto the back of his hand. He doesn't seem to notice, though. He's too busy glaring at his lover. "It's like you never fucking think before you speak. We took advantage, and—"

That's about enough of that.

I know he doesn't mean it to sound like he thinks I'm weak, like I can't stand up for myself or make my own decisions, but I've had too many people ignore my own words because they wanted to control me. I don't think there's a drop of malice or manipulation behind this, but it doesn't change the fact that he's overriding *me* about my own thoughts and feelings. "Why don't you ask me?"

He stops short. "What?"

"Ask me," I repeat. He's being stubborn right now, and maybe another time I'll enjoy provoking him to get a reaction, but right now I have to draw my own line in the sand. Either he'll respect it and we can keep negotiating, or he won't and this ends now. When he doesn't immediately speak, I prod. "It's very easy. You say 'Helen, now that the afterglow has worn off, are you feeling any different about fucking us?' Now, you try."

Achilles snorts, and Patroclus glares. Finally, he says, "Helen, now that you've got some distance, I would like to apologize—"

"No."

"What?"

I shake my head, holding his gaze. "No, you don't get to apologize and pretend like I'm not an adult with agency. I was not drunk, drugged, or otherwise incapacitated. You both asked me several times if I wanted to continue, and I consented enthusiastically. Are you really going to try to argue that I'm not capable of making my own decisions simply because you want to flog yourself with guilt?"

Patroclus stares at me, mouth agape. Achilles, the ass, leans over to press a single finger to his jaw and close it. He grins. "It's not often someone leaves him speechless."

I wait, but Patroclus is still staring like I've grown a second head. I have no business feeling disappointment in his reaction. I thought he might be different from the others I've interacted with all my life, but apparently he's not. He formed beliefs about me before we even met again as adults, and he'd rather stick to those beliefs than actually get to know the real me.

The impulse rises to get up and walk away, to retreat somewhere that I don't have to navigate other people's feelings for a little while, but I shove it down. Either I want him to take me seriously, or I don't. If I do, then I have to deal with this like an adult, and adults don't flee conversations just because they make them uncomfortable. I try for a smile, but my voice is still too sharp to pass off as humor. "I mean, if you want to be flogged that badly, I'm sure I can scrounge up some latex and a whip. It's not really my cup of tea, but I'm willing to try anything once."

Achilles laughs again. "Told you so."

Finally, a small eternity later, Patroclus lifts his mug and sips. He's looking at me like he's never seen me before. No, that's not quite right. He's looking at me like I just gave him a new piece of information to chew on, and now he has to realign his assumptions. We'll see if it sticks.

When he finally speaks, he sounds almost normal. "Your point is taken."

"Thank you." I've been around the block too many times to believe him based solely on his words. Even for someone like Patroclus, words are easy enough to fake. Or that's what I tell myself. My brain is on board with the plan to leave a little distance between me and these men. My chest, though? It gives a strange little thump that has me pressing my palm to my sternum.

I turn to Achilles to distract myself. "As to your suggestion that we keep fucking, the answer is…it depends."

He gives me that lazy smile that has my body flushing with heat despite myself. He really is too handsome to be real. "What's it depend on, princess?"

On how badly I need to escape the thoughts circling my head.

Except that's not entirely true, is it? It may have started out that way, but things are both more and less complicated now. I liked what we did together. I want to do it again. I also realize it's a terrible idea, but I doubt that will be enough to stop me. I'm not a masochist, and there's plenty of pleasure to be had in my normal life—at least these days. No, there's something that draws me to both these men, a tug deep inside me that I don't know how to quantify or deny.

I haven't worn a mask with them since this tournament began. They've seen the real me, warts and all. No matter their motivations or how doomed this whole thing is, that's a heady feeling that I'm not willing to give up yet. I take a slow breath. "It depends on whether or not you're going to stop trying to convince me to quit." Just because Achilles didn't capitalize on my being off-center last night doesn't mean it won't keep coming up. I know him well enough by now to know he's just as stubborn as I am.

"No. Next question."

I blink. He didn't even hesitate. "What do you mean, *no*?"

"No. It's a small word, but you probably don't hear it often." Achilles rolls his head on his shoulders in a slow circle, making his neck pop. "You're going to get hurt if you don't quit, and you might be a pain in my ass, but that doesn't mean I want to watch one of the other champions crush you. Why?" He pins me with a surprisingly shrewd look. "Are you wavering so much in your goal that you think *I* can change your mind?"

"No, of course not." It's the truth. If anything, I'm more set than ever.

"Then what's the problem? It doesn't matter what I say...or do." He injects enough insinuation into the last word to sink an armada.

It's a fair point, even though I don't want to admit it. Something warm and unforgivable curls in my chest at the easy belief Achilles has in me. Both that I won't change my mind and that I won't allow myself to be convinced. Does he realize what a compliment that is? More, how *rare* it is for the people around me? "Fine," I say slowly. "Then I guess we should keep fucking."

"Great. We're decided." He turns his attention to Patroclus. "Do you want to argue in circles for a few more hours, or do you want to finish that coffee and make Helen ruin the bedsheets again? The next trial isn't until tomorrow morning, so we have plenty of time for fun before we need to sleep."

Patroclus shakes his head slowly. "Bellerophon will be here in ten minutes. Get your head out of the gutter."

"You know what they say about all work and no play,

Patroclus." I've never seen Achilles like this. The gorgeous warrior. The irritating asshole. The sexy dominant. But never the playful puppy. It's disconcerting in the extreme, especially when he catches my eye and *winks* at me. "Look at the princess. You hurt her feelings when you acted like fucking her was something to be guilty about."

The exasperation on Patroclus's face is really, really attractive. He glances at me and shrugs. "Sorry, Helen. He's being ridiculous."

It isn't even a question of playing along with Achilles. I simply do it. I give Patroclus a sexy pout. "He's right. My feelings are very, very hurt."

"See." Achilles nods sagely but his dark eyes are sparking with mirth. He's absolutely irresistible right now, and he knows it. "Do you want to guess what would make our princess feel better?"

"I'm sure you're about to tell me."

"Orgasms."

"Yes." I nod quickly. I'm not touching the *our princess* with a ten-foot pole. "Lots and lots of orgasms."

Patroclus gives another of those sexy exasperated sighs. "Gods save me, now there's two of you."

"You're acting like it's a bad thing." I'm still pouting and feeling a little ridiculous about how fun this is. The only people I play around with are Hermes, Dionysus, and Eros, and it's not sexual in the least with any of them. I didn't realize anything related to sex could be this *fun*. I nudge Patroclus's bare calf with my foot. "Double your pleasure, double your fun."

Achilles barks out a laugh. "Listen to her. She knows what she's about."

"Oh, for fuck's sake." A knock on the door has Patroclus rising. He points at us. "Behave while we get to the bottom of the *very serious* attack on Helen last night." He pauses. "If you manage that, we'll spend the rest of the day naked in bed."

"Deal," we say at the same time.

I can't help the lightness in my chest as I sit back and drink my coffee. Gods help me, but I'm enjoying my time with these two far more than I could have ever expected.

ACHILLES

THINGS GO SOUTH THE MOMENT BELLEROPHON ENTERS the room. They take up an at-ease stance, their dark gaze pinned just above the top of my head. That's not good. I've known Bellerophon for years, and the only time they get overly formal is when conveying bad news. They only confirm my suspicions when they say, "The attacker is no longer with us."

Beside me, Helen startles. "They're dead?"

"No." Bellerophon shakes their head. "They were picked up this morning and removed from our facility. It went up the chain of command, and there was nothing I could do about it. Unfortunately, my team wasn't able to get answers before that time. I'm sorry."

Patroclus leans forward and braces his arms on the table. I can already see his big brain kicking into gear. "Picked up by who?"

Their gaze flicks to Helen, and Bellerophon hesitates for so long, even I already guess the answer before they speak and confirm it. "By Zeus himself. You have to understand, there's nothing I could do about it. Not even Athena could step in at that point."

"Well, that's...something." Helen goes a bit green. "They were being held..."

"Here." Bellerophon resumes staring over my head. "There are several cells on the property in the event that we need to intervene with a confrontation between champions. We decided it would be prudent to keep the attacker there until Athena was able to retrieve them. Zeus came instead."

It's a token of our history that they give the information so freely. I doubt they'd do the same if anyone else was asking the questions. "That makes logistical sense to keep them here. Why are you asking, Helen?"

"No reason." She's got that look on her face, the one that says she's seeing things outside this room and thinking dark thoughts. For once, I don't need Patroclus to step in and make his strategic jumps to understand why she's upset. If the attacker was being held here, then that means her brother was on the property this morning and didn't bother to come check on her before he whisked the attacker away...ensuring no one would get any answers.

Sometimes, when I hang out with Patroclus's moms, I get a sick feeling in my stomach wondering about what my life would have been like if I had two loving parents instead of being dropped on the temple steps to be donated like a toy that no longer served its purpose. Polymele and Sthenele treated me as an honorary son from the moment they met me as an angry little fuck at eighteen.

If Patroclus had been the one attacked, his moms would have all but beaten down the door, would have challenged both Athena and Zeus to ensure he was okay. They wouldn't care who they pissed off or what the long-term consequences were, not until they reassured themselves with their own eyes that their son was healthy and whole.

Zeus would have gotten a report about Helen's health; Bellerophon is a rule follower and would have written it up as soon as the attacker was secured. Even knowing she wasn't physically harmed... What kind of brother doesn't even bother to stop by and see her? Especially since he's able to come and go from this place without consequences.

It's far more likely my parents—if they're still alive—have more in common with Helen's fucked-up family than with Patroclus's moms. Every time I get a reminder of it, the flicker of gratitude is something I hold close. It still feels shitty to be reminded of it while *Helen* is being hurt by her family's carelessness. "I'm sure he had a reason," I finally say. The words feel flat and wrong.

Helen doesn't smile, doesn't so much as look at me. She's holding herself so tightly, as if worried she'll shatter. I don't like that shit. I don't like it at all. "He always does." She sounds tired. No, beyond tired. She sounds the kind of exhausted that comes from fighting an uphill battle on a timeline numbered in years.

I have the strangest impulse to tell her that I'll take up both sword and shield for a little while, give her time to rest. I won't say it, though. Who the fuck am I to offer her that? She wouldn't trust it; she's too smart to, even if there are no strings attached.

Patroclus frowns. "But that doesn't make any sense. Why would he interfere with Athena's ability to get answers from the prisoner when his little sister is the one who was attacked? We need to know who the attacker was working for and how they got into the building. Even if a different champion was the target, it will make both Zeus and Athena look weak if this gets out."

"It won't get out. Not from me or my people." Bellerophon shifts from foot to foot, obviously uncomfortable with this conversation. They tend to prefer working behind the scenes where they don't have to interact with victims of any sort. Helen *isn't* a victim, but this is still a shitty piece of news to have to convey. They finally clear their throat. "Helen, I can put a pair of guards on you to ensure your safety."

"That won't be necessary." I push slowly to my feet. "With all due respect, Bellerophon—"

They roll their eyes, relaxing for the first time since they stepped into the room. "I don't know why you start like that when you're about to say something disrespectful."

I ignore the statement because they're right. "The hole in your people's security is how this person got into Helen's room in the first place. We'll take it from here."

"We're Athena's people, too."

"I know. I'm not saying any of your team is disloyal, but until we have more information, we assume worst-case scenario." I shrug. "Besides, your people are good, but we're still better."

Patroclus makes a choked sound. "He doesn't mean it like that."

"We both know he means it exactly like that." Bellerophon shakes their head. "If Helen agrees, that's fine. We're not in the business of policing what the champions do in between trials as long as no one's being threatened or made to be uncomfortable."

Helen finally stirs. "I'm fine staying here." She's still got her arms wrapped around herself too tightly, and I don't like the look in her eyes. She seems...cornered. Again, that ridiculous fucking impulse rises to tell her she has nothing to worry about, that we'll protect her. We already offered to play bodyguard, but not even a bodyguard can protect the precious princess from her own family.

I want to, though. I don't know what the fuck I'm supposed to do with *that*.

"Let me know if that changes. The second trial begins tomorrow. Try to stay out of trouble until then." Bellerophon turns and leaves the room at a pace just shy of running.

I turn and catch Patroclus's eye. He still looks confused, but I shake my head slightly to indicate that it's time to drop the topic. Helen's still bracing like she's going to be bashed over the head, and I highly doubt trying to figure out why her brother is being a dick is going to help her feel better.

I want her to feel better.

She's mine, after all.

I know better than to say as much, but sometimes in life, I come across a thing or goal and I know it's meant for me. It doesn't usually happen with people. In fact, it's only ever happened once. Patroclus. After our first week in Ares's boot camp, I knew he was meant for me and I was meant for him, that we'd be part of each other's lives in a permanent kind of way.

The feeling about Helen isn't identical, but it's similar. I didn't really understand until it was the three of us together, but she fits us in a way no one else has before. With her in the mix, it feels like it could make our pair even better, something I didn't think possible before this tournament.

I can be patient when the goal is worth it, and right now it's worth it. If I tell Helen she's meant for me, she'll take it as me talking about Ares and marrying her again, and it'll just piss her off.

Actually... That's a great fucking idea. Our princess works better when she's angry rather than sad. I just need to paint her a convenient target to aim all those messy emotions she's trying to bottle down at. She'll feel better once she exorcizes them.

"You know what Bellerophon was too cowardly to say? What your brother and Athena are thinking?" I give her my laziest, most arrogant grin. "You should quit."

Helen tenses right on cue. All the brittle, fragile bits of her disappear between one blink and the next, and the scared princess vanishes, replaced by the furious harpy. She narrows pretty amber eyes. "Excuse me?"

"Your brother is a dick, and there's only one reason he wouldn't come check on you." I cross my arms over my chest. "He thinks if you get scared enough, you'll quit."

"I won't."

"I know that. Patroclus knows that. You know that, too."

She glares. "You obviously have a brilliant point you're attempting to get to. Feel free to enlighten us."

I like her when she's prickly. It's loads better than when she appeared so fragile and out of sorts. Patroclus is looking between us like we've gone mad. When there's a problem to be solved, he's my man, but he lets logic get in the way of his instincts. Right now,

Helen's too emotional to sit still long enough for him to strategize our way out of this mess. She won't hear a damn thing he says, and she'll just keep sitting there, looking small and lost and sad the entire time. Once she snaps out of it, she'll feel better. *Then* she and Patroclus can bounce their brilliance off each other.

I can't say that, though. He won't understand. He drags his hands over his face. "We need to—"

"No, Patroclus. Achilles has something to say. Let him say it." Helen starts for me, lasers practically shooting from her eyes. She's beyond sexy when she's furious. No shit. I don't think it's possible for her to be anything less than gorgeous, no matter the circumstances. More importantly, though, is that the lost look on her face is gone.

She's not thinking about the attack or her messed-up family right now. The only thing Helen is focused on at the moment is cutting me down to size. I might not be a borderline genius like Patroclus, but I know how to maneuver around battlefields, and my interactions with Helen are exactly that.

I give a lazy smile designed to infuriate her further. "You're playing right into their hands, princess. This is just another kind of warfare. The second trial is tomorrow. Are you really going to spend the next twelve hours or so obsessing over your asshole brother?"

She opens her mouth and pauses. I can practically see her brain kicking into gear. It looks different on her than it does on Patroclus, but the vibe is very similar. Finally, Helen drags in a rough breath and slumps back into her chair. "You think this is all a mind game."

"I don't know what this is, but there's not a damn thing you can do about it until the tournament is over and we get out of this house." I hold her gaze. "You're smart. You know the trials are as much mental as they are physical. They can't make you quit, but they can undermine you until you fail."

She shakes her head slowly, almost wonderingly. "The gods really gave with both hands when they created you, didn't they?"

"That's what I've been trying to tell you, princess." Some of the tension bleeds out of me. She hasn't lost that haunted look in her eyes, but it seems the worst has passed. Damn woman bounces back fast, doesn't she? Or at least gives the appearance of it. Helen seems the type to stew—one way we differ—so she's not going to pour out her heart to us. Things would be simpler if it didn't feel like she was mine, which means I *want* her to fling open the doors barring us from her inner thoughts.

I drag my hand over my face. This shit is stressing me out. I preferred life simpler, when the most complicated thing I had to worry about was the next mission Athena sent us on and when Patroclus would be too distracted to remember to eat. I know him, so I never have to wonder what he's thinking or feeling. All the signs are right there, learned over more than a decade together. Things might have changed recently, but they haven't changed *that* much.

Like right now. He's thinking he doesn't understand what the fuck just happened. He glances between us and speaks slowly, cautiously. "Achilles...isn't wrong."

Helen smiles a little. "Why do you sound so shocked?"

"He's not usually subtle," Patroclus murmurs. He shakes his head. "How can we help, Helen?"

She picks up her coffee mug and stares down at it as if she can find answers in its depths. Patroclus and I share a look of perfect understanding. No matter how messy this situation is, we're going to give Helen what she needs. We can't control what the trial brings in the morning, but at least we can offer her a reprieve until then. It feels good to be on the same page with him after all the fighting and messy emotions. Things aren't resolved; they won't be resolved until the tournament is over and we've navigated the inevitable fallout.

In the meantime...

"Why?"

I look up to find Helen staring at me as if I'm a puzzle she can't quite figure out the shape of. It's tempting to offer her a charming smile or a bullshit answer, but if I want her to take this seriously—to take *me* seriously—the least I can do is explain myself. At least in this. "I don't like that lost look on your face."

She blinks those big eyes at me. "I... No, Achilles, I mean why try to make me feel better? Don't you want me to quit?"

A complicated question. I shrug. "I'm going to win this thing and become Ares." Her lips thin, but I keep going. She asked. I'm going to answer honestly. "But I don't like that shady bullshit. They're underestimating you, and it pisses me off."

"But... *Why?* Why does it piss you off? I don't understand why you're being so nice to me right now when it goes against your interests. It doesn't make any sense. You hate me."

"Helen." I wait for her to look at me fully. "I don't hate you. I like your contrary, difficult ass. You're strong and smart and ambitious as fuck. If I wasn't in this tournament, you could take Ares."

Patroclus snorts. "You just had to throw that in there, didn't you?" He turns to Helen. "What he means is—"

But she's not looking at Patroclus. For once, her attention is focused entirely on me. "You think I'm strong."

Her soft words aren't exactly a question, but I don't like how wonderingly she says it. Like no one has ever pointed it out before. "You *know* you're strong. You don't need me to confirm it."

Helen stares at me for a long moment and finally gives a faint smile. "Yeah. I guess I do." She stands slowly. "Let's go back to bed."

Patroclus looks like he wants to argue, but he just says, "Food first. Coffee isn't enough nutrition, not with the second trial tomorrow."

"I'll get it." I stand and stretch. "Any requests?"

She shrugs. "Whatever they have available."

Patroclus stands too. "I'll walk you out." He barely waits until we're out into the hall to turn on me. "What the fuck was that?"

"What the fuck was what?"

He gives me the look that question deserves. "You know what I'm talking about. She was reeling and you came at her like an opponent."

"Patroclus." I am suddenly tired. So fucking tired of him thinking the worst of me. I won't pretend that I don't deserve it, especially after the last couple days, but while I might be careless at times, I'm never cruel. Not intentionally, at least. "She was going to start spiraling and thinking too hard about what a dick her brother is." I have my own thoughts on Zeus, and that fucker will be lucky if I don't punch him in his perfect face the first chance I get.

My anger doesn't have a place in this fight, though. Helen might feel like mine, but she *isn't* mine. Her honor isn't mine to defend.

Good thing she's more than capable of defending herself when she gets out of her own way and forgets to think too much.

I hold Patroclus's gaze. "She's not fragile. She's not fucking breakable. Yeah, she's been knocked down more than a few times in the last week, but she just needed the right prodding to get back up and start swinging again."

"The right prodding." Patroclus narrows his eyes and gives a dry laugh. "Gods, you're a scary motherfucker sometimes. You know that, right?"

I shrug. "Keep her distracted while I get food. Then we'll fuck her until none of us have the energy to worry about shit outside our control." We need plenty of sleep, but the day is young and we're all in the best shape of our lives. No reason not to expel some pent-up energy in the most pleasurable way possible.

"Achilles."

I stop in the middle of turning away. "Yeah?"

"Sorry for thinking the worst." Patroclus runs his hand over his short dark hair. "This situation has my head all fucked up."

There's not much I can say to that. It stings that he thought the worst of me, but he's not entirely unjustified on making that jump. It's a fucked-up situation and it's not going to get less fucked up as time goes on. The only option is to keep pushing forward and then deal with the fallout after the tournament. "It's fine. Now, go take care of our princess while I get some breakfast."

PATROCLUS

WE SPEND THE REST OF THE DAY IN BED, BREAKING ONLY for meals. By unspoken agreement, none of us speak further about the assassin or Zeus or the tournament. Achilles and I do what we can to offer the comfort Helen will allow, which translates to orgasms.

That night, I take second shift. I sit in the chair next to the bed and watch them sleep. Helen didn't wake when we switched out, and Achilles passed out in the way he's always been able to—within seconds. He's got his arm slung over her waist and, a few seconds later, she snuggles back against his bigger body.

I press my hand to my chest. When he wins Ares, they'll sleep like this. They might snarl and snap at each other, but this morning Achilles demonstrated a deeper understanding of Helen than I have. He *gets* her, at least on some level.

No reason for that to make my chest ache. My foolish heart might care too deeply for her, might have given itself to Achilles long ago, but even if it breaks at the end of this, at least I have the bittersweet comfort of knowing they'll take care of each other.

If Achilles isn't the one to knock Helen out of the tournament. I don't like his odds of winning her forgiveness anytime soon if that happens. She as much as admitted that it would be impossible.

Maybe I should be the one to do it.

I rub my chest harder. Damn it, I can't. Even if it would help him, I can't do that to *her*. No matter how complicated the potential outcome, we can't go after her. She...trusts us. Maybe not entirely—Helen is no fool, after all—but she trusts us with her body, trusts us enough to at least share some small vulnerabilities. We can't turn around and crush her after the last couple of days.

By the time the alarm goes off, I still have no answers. We get ready in near silence. I dress in my workout gear; I have no one to impress, after all. Achilles dons another of the custom uniforms we commissioned for him. This one is inky black and clings to his body, showing off his impressive muscles and elevating his attractiveness to the point where it almost hurts to look at him.

And Helen?

She has on a skintight catsuit that looks like someone spilled oil down her body. With every move, different colors shine in the low light of the room. She's braided her hair and pinned it up around her head in an almost crown. Smart. The whole damn outfit is so *smart*. The fabric of the catsuit will make it challenging for anyone to keep hold of her, and her hair is no longer a liability to be grabbed in a fight. Every part of her...glitters. Her makeup is more stark than last time, too. She darkened from her eyes to nearly her temples, a dramatic look that, combined with her black lipstick, gives her the image of someone who should be on the front lines of some ancient army, leading her people into battle.

Helen looks like a warrior queen.

The crowd will be unable to take their eyes off her. More, they'll love her for the dramatics of it all, especially if she does well.

"Ready?" I finally manage.

"Doesn't matter if I am. It's time."

Achilles moves to the door. "Let's go."

Achilles and I share a look and keep Helen between us as we file out of the room and follow the rest of the champions out of the house. I don't like the way Paris watches her, like she's a prize that's his for the taking. It might be technically true, but it leaves a bad taste in my mouth all the same.

At the arena, I can't stop myself from grabbing Helen's hand and giving it a light squeeze. "It will be fine."

She spares me a faint smile. "I know." She squeezes my hand back before releasing it.

Then there's no more time for talking because we're being ushered through the concrete tunnel and out into the main area. I'm stunned by the transformation of the arena when the champions file through the entrance. Gone is the obstacle course, replaced by tall walls of varying heights. They look like concrete, but that's impossible. Concrete would be far too heavy to haul in here to form this...

It's a maze. It must be.

It's hard to focus with the ever-present cheering of the crowd. I think I'll hear that sound in my nightmares. It's a reminder that too many eyes are on me, that this trial will change things even more than the first. There are twelve champions left.

After this trial, that number will be more than halved.

I glance at Helen and, on the other side of her, Achilles. Both have their expressions locked down, but surely they feel the same tremor in their chests that I do. I have never once doubted that Achilles would win the title of Ares. I don't doubt it now.

But the cost...

The cost might be higher than I could have dreamed.

Directly in front of us and high above, the lights point at the box seat where Athena resides. She's wearing a cream suit and is furious. Oh, she has it locked down, but I've answered directly to her for too long not to know her moods. She's just as unhappy with the way things fell out with the would-be assassin as we are. More so since it happened on her watch.

She holds up a hand and the arena immediately falls to silence. Athena sweeps the champions with a single piercing look. "The second trial begins shortly. You will be positioned at different locations within the maze. There is one door leading to the exit, but it requires a key. There are five keys hidden within the maze. There is also a time limit. You may only take one key if and when you find them. If you have not found a key and the door exiting the maze within the time allotted, you will be eliminated."

This is where alliances begin to break down. Five keys means seven people eliminated. At least. We have to *find* the keys first, and there's no guarantee all will be discovered before the time limit is reached.

I take a slow breath and speak softly enough that only Helen and Achilles can hear me. "It's a good wager that the keys—or at least a few of them—will be in the center of the maze."

"Find your way in, find your way out," Achilles muses. "Seems simple enough."

Helen snorts. "Sure. Simple. Except for the other champions trying to do the same thing."

Down the line of champions, Bellerophon approaches with black hoods in their hands. Ah, that makes sense. They're not going to give us a chance to potentially memorize the way through the maze. If we're blindfolded and they take a strange route, it will be discombobulating enough that we should all start on even ground.

At least in theory.

Bellerophon eases the first hood over the Minotaur's head and tightens it a bit. Then they move to the next champion.

"There will be fighting and they're going to fight dirty." I'm not saying anything that they don't know, but I feel compelled all the same.

Helen shakes her head, her picture-perfect smile in place. "So will I." She looks between us. For the first time since we got into the vans this morning, some of the real woman shows beneath the mask. "Stay out of my way. I don't... Look, I like you two. In a perfect world, we wouldn't be competing against each other, but this isn't a perfect world and I'm not going to let my emotions compromise my goals. So no hard feelings, but I will go through you to get Ares if I have to."

My stomach twists at her words, even if they aren't surprising. The feeling only gets worse when Achilles booms out a laugh. "We'll see you on the other side, princess."

Her grin is downright feral. "Bet on it."

Then Bellerophon is in front of her, sliding the black hood over her head. They move to me next. Even knowing it's coming, it's still disorienting in the extreme to have all sight taken from me. The hood is perfectly blacked out, and the sound of the crowd feels particularly loud without my sight to distract me.

I jolt when hands touch my shoulders. They guide me forward, and even knowing we're maybe twenty feet from the maze, I still can't get my bearings. I try to keep track of the twists and turns, but it's a lost cause. And if *I'm* not able to, I highly doubt any of the others are having a more successful time of it.

Oh well. This isn't outside the expected parameters.

The hands on my shoulders tug me to a stop and a soft voice in my ear says, "Stay here with the hood on until Athena begins the trial."

I nod, and they release my shoulders. Without the touch to anchor me, I feel even more out of sorts. The sound is unrelenting, and with the darkness so complete, I have to fight against the urge to lift my hands defensively. Anyone could be standing just out of reach and...

The cheering goes quiet and Athena's familiar cool tone fills the empty space. "The second trial begins now. The trial will end in two hours or when five champions have escaped the maze. Good luck."

I drag the hood from my head and blink into the bright lights. The walls are just as high inside the maze as they were outside it, but I can still see the upper tiers of the arena and the several of the screens showing the various champions. It's impossible to gather enough info to be helpful, though. The maze walls seem to be uniformly gray. Even the differing heights of the walls—ranging anywhere from ten to fourteen feet, best I can tell—only add to the disorienting feeling of being unable to guess which direction to go. The other champions could be on the other side from me or the next path over, or they could be nowhere near me. Focusing on the screens will be more distraction than asset.

The path I'm on is relatively straight, one direction leading deeper into the maze and one appearing to lead toward the perimeter. When I was doing research on what the possible trials could be, mazes were on the list. The common advice to get out of a maze seems to be pick a direction and follow that wall to the exit.

Unfortunately, that won't help me now.

I need to find a key before I find the exit, and that means heading deeper into the maze rather than toward the perimeter. If I knew what style maze this was...

Oh well. There's only one way to find out. I take a deep breath and head in the approximate direction of the center in an easy jog. Fast enough to cover ground efficiently, but not so fast as to be caught unaware if I come upon another champion. The only champions that will be eliminated are the ones still in the maze when the time runs out, which means the smartest way to deal with anyone I come across is to incapacitate them in some way. Knocking someone unconscious isn't an easy feat, so that means going for the legs. Knees are the best bet.

Unfortunately, the other champions will be trying to do the same to me.

I wind my way through the maze, the paths leading me away

from and toward the center in turn. With the arena being the way it is, it's impossible to know if I'm making progress or just moving farther away from my goal.

The crowd screams and I stop short, gaze flying to the screens I can see from my current position. They all show Atalanta. She's flying through the maze, sprinting at a pace that has her locs streaming out in her wake. I see why a moment later when the Minotaur veers around the corner behind her.

"Oh fuck," I breathe. He looks like he wants to kill her.

He's almost on her when she turns on her heel, launching herself against the wall and spinning in the air to deliver a brutal punch to his square jaw. It knocks him back a step into the opposite wall. By the time he recovers, she's gone, disappeared around the nearest corner.

I watch for several more heartbeats before it's clear that she got away, and I feel a strange sort of relief. We'd be better served for Atalanta to be eliminated this trial, but that doesn't mean I want her hurt in the process. I exhale slowly and force myself to refocus. Now's not the time to get distracted. I need to keep my eye on the prize.

A flash of movement at the corner of my eye has me turning...

Right into Hector's fist.

HELEN

IT TAKES SEVERAL LONG, FRUSTRATING MINUTES OF weaving through this endless maze before my brain kicks into gear. Athena stated the rules at the beginning. Find the key. Get to the door out of the maze.

She didn't say anything about *how* we had to go through the maze.

I eye the walls. They're ten feet tall at their lowest point and mostly untextured, not leaving grooves or handholds to climb. But one of the potential obstacles I trained for was running up a wall. With enough lead-in, I might be able to make it. It's hard to tell how wide the walls themselves are, but I used to do the balance beam. They can't be much narrower than that.

It takes me a little longer to find a section of the maze with enough space to get a good takeoff. Overhead, the clock ticks down, but there's still plenty of time. I can't see all the screens from this position, but the ones I *can* see show the champions trying to work their way through the close paths.

If I do this, they'll video me.

The others will follow suit quickly. Or at least they'll try. They'd be fools not to. Whatever advantage being the first brings won't last for long if I don't hurry.

I take a deep breath and wipe my damp palms on my clothing. I haven't seen anything of Achilles or Patroclus yet, and I can't help worrying about them. My life would be easier if they were both eliminated in this round. I *should* be seeing this in black and white—what helps me become the next Ares and what stands in my way.

But if they're eliminated...this strange thing between the three of us ends.

They're the first people I've come across who seem to truly see *me*. Spoiled brat, yes. Pampered princess, mostly. But the strong, savvy woman beneath, too. Patroclus treats me like I'm something of true value. Achilles just takes my strength as fact. They both regard me as an equal.

It's a heady thing. Maybe I'm a fool, but I'm not ready to give it up yet.

There's no time to mull it over now. It doesn't matter what the clock overhead says; if I don't reach one of those keys first, I won't make it to the next round. I haven't come this far to fail.

I sprint at the wall. It feels a bit like running for the vault in gymnastics, except the vault is a ten-foot-tall wall and I get a quarter of the distance to pick up speed. I take one last step and launch myself at the wall. Up, up, up. My fingertips barely brush the top. I curse as I drop back to the ground and nearly land on my ass. "*Fuck.*"

The more times I attempt this, the more energy and time I'm wasting, neither of which I can afford. Maybe I should try something else... I shake my head hard. No. This is the best option. I've never let a little thing like failing once get in the way of my goals, and I'm not about to start now.

I retrace my steps back down the path and inhale slowly. I'll make it this time. I have to. My fingers hit the top of the wall and I concentrate on firming them up so I don't fall back to the ground. It hurts. Gods, it hurts. But I muscle past the pain and pull myself up until I can loop my leg over the top of the wall and drag my body the rest of the way up. At the top, it's about what I expected. Six inches. Plenty of space. If not for the differing wall heights, I wouldn't even bother taking off my shoes. As it is, it will be slow going, but I have the advantage of being able to see my path clearer than the other champions.

Around me, the sudden roar of the crowd feels like an almost physical thing pressing against my skin. It's hard to push it away, to not let it affect me. I force myself to take a moment and survey the maze. It's a twisty motherfucker, the pathways winding back and forth without any apparent rhyme or reason. I turn carefully and there it is.

The center.

I can follow the path with the foresight of seeing the way through...or I can take a shortcut.

The maze paths are about five feet apart. Not an insignificant distance but not so far that I can't easily jump it. The center is *right there*. Maybe fifty feet away. I can get there, get the key, and take the same path back to the perimeter to find the door. The walls might be different heights, but it looks like if I can get up to the higher section next to me, I have a clear shot to the center.

Against these competitors, I can't afford to be cautious.

More, I'm better suited than anyone to accomplish this with my gymnastics background. Five feet is *nothing* to cross, and the six-inch top of the walls might as well be flat ground. *I can do this.*

The screens shift above me and I take three seconds to watch one of the other champions try to run up the wall. He's quite a bit taller than me and manages to haul himself up, but when he tries to get his leg over, something goes wrong. I wince as he falls back to the ground with a dull thud I can almost feel, even if I can't hear it over the roar of the crowd. "Maybe I'm the *only one* who can do this," I murmur.

There's no more time to waste. I leap to the next wall and then use my momentum to leap to the third. Again and again, flying over the top of the maze. I vaguely register that many of the screens are showing me now, which means I have to hurry. Even if no one else can successfully scale the walls and use them the way I am—which is a big *if*—they will all know my location. I might as well have painted a target on my back.

The center of the maze isn't particularly large, maybe a twelve-by-twelve space. In the center is a steel beam crafted to look like a tree with five branches sticking out. On each dangles a skeleton key.

The center of the maze also contains another champion. Theseus.

He hasn't seen me yet, but he will as soon as he turns around. I don't need to take him out. I just need him to stay down long enough for me to get a key and flee. I can climb another wall further into the maze once I'm alone. I don't stop to think of all the ways this could go wrong. I throw myself at him, using my momentum and a healthy dose of gravity to drive him into the ground before he can reach the tree.

The impact jars me down to my bones. He's a big guy, but jumping down ten feet hardly makes for a soft landing. *Can't stop. Doesn't matter how much it hurts. Keep going.* I shove off his back and stagger to my feet. The tree is only a few feet away, but I barely make it a step before he grabs my ankle and yanks me down.

This time, when I hit the ground, it knocks the breath from my lungs. I don't let that stop me, though. Not with Theseus crawling up my body. If he pins me, he might actually kill me. He'll definitely incapacitate me to ensure I don't pass this trial.

Fuck that.

I bend at the waist, sitting up and putting as much strength as I can behind my fist when I punch him in his face. It's barely enough to stun him, but I manage to wiggle a few inches away before he recovers and tightens his grip on my leg. He drags me half under his body with a harsh yank. My bodysuit might have been designed to be hard to hold, but it doesn't matter when he can wrap most of his hand around my thigh.

Panic takes hold. I am so fucking *close* to what I want, and this man threatens to stand in my way. "Let go." I aim another punch at his face.

He just grunts in response and releases my thigh long enough to hammer a blow to my quad. Pain makes me light-headed, but I will not be stopped. Not now. Not by this man.

"You're fighting a losing battle." Theseus makes a sound perilously close to a snarl and rears back. "You're just a pampered little daddy's girl playing pretend warrior. You won't win."

I can't flip him. He's too damn big and I'm not in the right position for it. "*Watch me.*" I grab a fistful of his dark-red hair and jab my fingers into his eyes.

Theseus howls and flinches back. It's enough for me to scramble out from beneath him. My injured thigh threatens to buckle when I stand, but I grab a key and drape the lanyard over my neck. Each step hurts, but I don't have time to worry about that now.

I turn in time to see Theseus plant a hand on the ground and stagger to his feet. He teeters almost as if he'll fall but manages to stabilize. *Damn it.* His eyes are red and watering, but he must be able to see okay because he narrows them at me. He curses. "You'll pay for that."

"Get out of my way or I'll hurt you for real." There are two entrances to the center of the maze, but he's standing in front of the one that leads where I need to go. If I take the other, I'll have to work my way around the center again, and that's out of the question. I know my body well enough to know I'm on a timer with this thigh. I have to get out of here before adrenaline crashes and it gives out entirely.

Theseus shakes his head like a bull about to charge. "You Kasioses represent everything wrong with this viper's nest of a city. You're not making it past this trial."

The words send a shiver of true fear through me. I'd considered and discarded the notion that Theseus and his people might be here to attempt a coup on the Thirteen and, by extension,

Olympus. Apparently I was right the first time. They truly are here for Olympus. "You can't win. Even if you take Ares, you can't win."

"I'm not the one you have to worry about." He charges me.

I dodge at the last minute, ducking under his grasp and to the side. Theseus clangs into the tree and staggers back a step, but I'm already moving. I drive a kick into his knee at an angle, using all my strength. It gives with a stomach-turning pop and he lurches to the side, collapsing to the ground.

A dark, sickening desire rises inside me, an urge to stomp on that knee a few more times and ensure he's truly down. But I resist. It might protect me from *this* man, but it won't actually benefit me in the long run. The longer I stay here, the higher the chance of someone else coming in.

I curse and skirt around Theseus. He's moaning and cursing my name, but he makes no move to rise again. I don't think he can. *Good enough.*

My leg aches something fierce. It's now or never. I take a shuddering breath and break into a sprint. Each step threatens to buckle my injured thigh, but I manage to scramble up the wall on the first shot. It takes longer this time to haul my body up to the top, and by the time I find my balance, I'm panting.

Next is hauling myself up two more sections to the tallest bit I can easily access. I'll need the height to plot my way to the exit. This is easier, my balance surer, but I'm still overly cautious with my leg. A fall from ten feet would hurt like a motherfucker. A fall from fifteen?

Best not to risk it.

I look up at the screens in time to watch Atalanta nearly knock the Minotaur out with one well-placed punch. I manage a tired grin. "Nice." I don't look forward to facing her in the final challenge if it comes to that, but from our limited interactions, I like her quite a bit.

Then I refocus and survey the top of the maze. No one else has joined me up here yet, but I can't take for granted that there isn't someone else among the champions who's capable of it. I have to get moving. Unfortunately, I don't think I'm going to be able to jump from wall to wall the way I did before. If my leg gives out, a fall will do more damage than Theseus did.

I twist a little, searching for the door to the exit. It's near the archway we came in, which is in front of me and to the right. I try to control my rapid breathing as I map a path there. It will take more time, but I have a key and I just need to avoid the other champions. I should be able to do it.

The roar of the crowd changes. I thought it was intense before, but it's nothing compared to the sound that shakes the arena now. It's *bloodthirsty*. I turn in time to see the screens switch to Patroclus and Hector fighting.

I gasp as Hector delivers a devastating punch to Patroclus's stomach. From the look of them, they've been fighting for some time. Both sport bloodied knuckles and their handsome faces are broken and bruised, almost unrecognizable. Both weave on their feet as they circle each other.

They're in the best shape of their lives, but Hector moves more like Achilles...as if on instinct. I can practically *see* Patroclus's brain trying to map out his next strike, trying to anticipate his opponent. It would work on anyone else, but not Hector. He's too quick. I've never seen him fight, but he worked under Ares for years before transferring to Apollo. Apparently his time behind a desk haven't softened him at all.

Patroclus is going to lose.

My heart lodges itself in my throat. I scan the maze to try to figure out where they are. I don't know if I can help, but I have to try. I don't think Hector would permanently harm Patroclus; at least, he wouldn't do it on purpose. But accidents happen, especially in fights, *especially* when the stakes are so high.

There.

They aren't far. I could reach them in just a few minutes...but it means going in the opposite direction of the exit. If Patroclus is no match for Hector, I'm certainly not, either. Helping him might very well mean sacrificing my chance to pass the second trial.

Hector lands a punch that snaps Patroclus's head back. He barely stays on his feet. "No!"

A frustrated roar, heard even over the crowd, has me turning to find Achilles charging down the path. In the wrong direction.

I don't stop to think. I just scream. "*Achilles!*"

Somehow he hears me. He slams to a stop and looks up. I point in the opposite direction. "He's there!" A quick look is enough to map his course. "Two rights. Left. Right. Three lefts."

He nods and then he's off, flawlessly following my instructions. Within seconds, he careens around the corner nearest the fight and takes Hector down in a flying leap. *He* looks as fresh as when we entered the maze, and I exhale shakily. It will be fine. Achilles will take care of Patroclus. He won't let his lover be killed.

Thank the gods.

I force myself to tear my gaze from the fight. They will be okay. I have to worry about myself right now. There's nothing else I can do to help, nothing they *need* my help for. With one last glance at the screens, I leverage myself to my feet and start making my winding way toward the exit.

My leg holds, which is a bit of a miracle, but each step is agony. I catch sight of the Minotaur lumbering through the maze a few paths over. He looks up as I move past, narrowing his eyes. I tense, but he simply turns away, heading for the last few turns between him and the center of the maze.

I stop on the wall across from the door and ease down to drop to the floor. My leg finally buckles and I land on my ass. "Ouch."

"Impressive."

I look up to find Atalanta standing over me, a grin on her scarred face. In her hand, she holds a key. I offer back a tired grin of my own. "Right back at you."

She opens her mouth, but her eyes roll back in her head and she slumps to the ground. Behind her stands Paris. He shakes his head. "Poor thing. She never saw me coming."

I flinch, my body reacting before my mind fully processes that Paris has knocked *Atalanta* out. For a moment, something dark flickers across his face and I can practically see him weighing the chance to kick me while I'm down—maybe literally—and his desire to maintain his image as the charming playboy that Olympus believes him to be.

He shakes his head slowly and leans down to snag the key from Atalanta's limp hand. "Climbing the walls, huh? I knew you couldn't have gotten this far without cheating. You're taking that key from someone who truly deserves it. Pathetic." Paris turns and walks to the door. He inserts the key, opens it, and disappears through.

I stare for a beat, two, three. I *didn't* cheat. I went about solving the problem by nontraditional methods, but that doesn't make me weak. The irony of him accusing me of taking a key from someone who deserves it... I shake my head hard. Damn it, I'm letting him mess with my mind again. I scramble to Atalanta's side and ease her onto her back.

She's breathing evenly, and her dark eyes flutter open. "Motherfucker."

Relief makes me a little dizzy. She's okay. Or she will be. "I'm sorry." I can't stay here, can't risk suffering the same fate if someone decides to take a page out of Paris's handbook. I squeeze her shoulder and push away from her. "I'm so sorry, I have to go."

The only thing that matters is getting through that door and passing the second trial.

I use the wall to leverage myself to my feet and stagger to the door. It takes two tries to insert the key into the lock and twist. It swings soundlessly open and I step through and out of the maze.

Is the cheering of the crowd louder? I can't be sure, but I straighten my spine and work to keep the limp out of my walk as much as possible. Bellerophon stands just to the side of the door, an unreadable expression on their face. They motion to a bench that wasn't there when we started this trial. "Wait there, please."

I nod and walk to sit on the opposite side of the bench from Paris. I can feel his gaze on me, but I refuse to look over. Instead,

I pin my attention to the screens overhead. They show the various champions. Several of the others are on the ground, having suffered various bodily injuries. Theseus is still in the center of the maze, leaning against the wall and cradling his knee. I don't see Hector or the Minotaur.

Achilles is half carrying Patroclus, who looks wounded but—*thank the gods*—okay.

I fight not to react as I watch their slow progress, heart in my throat. We're over halfway through the time allotted. They have to hurry up if they want to pass the trial. I press my hands hard to my thighs, fighting to keep my expression even. Will Achilles leave Patroclus behind? Will either of them make it?

Come on. You can do it. Hurry.

ACHILLES

"LEAVE ME."

"Stop saying that," I growl. "We're getting out of this together." Earlier, I accidentally found the door out of the maze, so I've got the path back memorized. We just need to find the fucking center, get the keys, and get the fuck out of here. I gingerly adjust my grip around Patroclus's waist. "Did he get your ribs?"

"No." He's leaning too heavily on me, and I can't tell if he's lying or if Hector just knocked him for a loop to the point where he's woozy. He's got a split lip and I'm pretty sure his ankle is royally fucked. There's also a bruise darkening one of his cheekbones, and his glasses were shattered on the ground when I found him and Hector fighting.

Best not to think about that too closely.

I could tell at a glance that Patroclus would lose. And then Hector hit him with an uppercut that snapped his head back and he collapsed like a puppet with its strings cut. After that, I stopped thinking entirely. My only goal was to knock Hector the fuck out and protect the man I love. I don't give a fuck that Hector has his reasons for being here.

He doesn't want Ares. He just wants to pave the way for his shit stain of a little brother to be Ares, and he's willing to step on Patroclus to get there. If Helen hadn't been on the walls and able to guide me… I don't like to think what might have happened. "Fuck that."

Overhead, the screens change and the crowd goes wild. I look up in time to see Paris walk out of the maze. The asshole looks regal as fuck in royal blue. He doesn't appear to have even worked up a sweat. Bastard.

Right on his heels comes Helen.

She's limping and smiling, but I can tell she's furious. It's carefully hidden in her amber eyes as she turns and gives a wave to the crowd. Part of me had hoped she'd be eliminated in this trial for simplicity's sake, but I can't stop the flare of pure pride. She made it through, and she did it in a clever way, too. "That's our girl."

"Achilles." Patroclus's words are a little slurred, and I can't tell if it's because he hit his head or his busted lip. "I'm slowing you down. There are only three keys left. Leave me."

"Shut up." I haul him around another corner and another. We're close to the center. I'm sure of it. This maze isn't so bad when you're navigating from the entrance to the center. Sure enough, the next right turn opens up into the center of the maze. There's a weird metal tree-like structure in the middle of it and two keys hanging from branches. "Only two left."

The center also hold Theseus. I saw a glimpse of his fight with

Helen. She kicked his ass. Or, rather, his knee. He leans against a
wall with his eyes closed and his skin gone waxy with pain. Below
the bottom of his black shorts, his knee is grotesquely swollen
and turning an ugly shade of purple. At best, she dislocated it. At
worst, she shattered something important.

Good girl.

He's out of the tournament with an injury like that even if he'd
somehow managed to get a key. Still, I guide us away from him.
No reason to tempt the bastard into attempting to attack. I look
up. There's thirty minutes left in the trial. Plenty of time as long as
we don't run into trouble. But only if we don't linger. I grab one of
the keys and drape the lanyard over Patroclus's neck. The second
one goes around mine.

"Achilles." Patroclus grips my shirt and gives me a weak
shake. "Stop being stubborn."

"I'm not the one being stubborn. Stop telling me to leave you."

He glares, some of the strength coming back into his body.
"You're being ridiculous. I'm not going to be Ares. I was *never*
going to be Ares. I was only ever here for support, and you didn't
even need me." He shakes his head and winces. "Leave me behind.
It's what's best for you."

True fear flickers to life. I know he's talking about this trial
specifically, but I don't give a fuck. I can't shake the potential
future where he tells me that for real. He acts like I'm some shooting star and he's just along for the ride, that I'm the ambitious one
dragging him along at my side. As if he's not a full partner. As if
eventually I'll leave him behind for good. As if *choosing to stop
striving alongside me* isn't a fucking choice on its own.

I grab his shoulders. Too hard. I'm holding him too fucking harshly. "Listen to me, Patroclus. I am *never* leaving you behind. Not in this fucking trial. Not in life. Stop acting like a fucking martyr."

He flinches. "It's not being a martyr if it's the truth."

We're talking about the trial and not talking about the trial at the same time. I glare. "Are you done with me?"

"What?"

"You heard me. *Are you done with me?*" I can't help holding my breath, even as adrenaline floods my system.

He blinks and then blinks again. "No. I can't... I won't be the one to walk away."

Relief makes me a little light-headed, but we don't have time to get into it properly. Not here. Not like this. "Then shut the fuck up and hold on." I dip down and yank him over my shoulders in a fireman's carry. He curses and sputters, but it's more out of outrage than pain.

I keep an eye out as I retrace my path toward the entrance. Atalanta and the Minotaur are still in the maze somewhere. There are no keys left, which means one of them have the final key... assuming they can reach the exit.

Patroclus curses me the whole time, but at least he stops telling me to leave him. I'm breathing hard by the time I turn the corner and see the door. The clock overhead reads ten minutes. Cutting it too close, but we did it.

I carefully set Patroclus on his feet. "You go first."

He doesn't argue. He weaves his way to the door and inserts the key. The crowd goes wild as he stumbles through. I follow quickly. The moment I step out of the maze, it feels like setting down a massive weight I've been carrying for the last two hours. I knew we'd get through. I *knew* it.

But there were moments when I doubted.

Patroclus and I head for the bench and I see Helen. A furrow of concern appears between her brows as she watches Patroclus limp toward her. She tenses like she's going to leap to her feet, but I duck under Patroclus's arm and keep him moving. "I got it, princess."

"Are you okay?" she murmurs. For a second, I think she's talking to him, but when I look down, her amber eyes are on me. "I didn't see you on the screens most of the time I was in there."

"Just call it anticlimactic. I didn't see anyone until Hector." My stomach twists at the memory. I'm not one to linger on things, but I won't get the image of that last hit out of my head anytime soon. Even though I *knew* it would take more than a nasty upper-cut to take Patroclus out in any permanent way, seeing him fall to the ground was the stuff of nightmares. I swallow hard. "I'm...I'm good."

I guide Patroclus to the spot next to her, and my chest warms at the way she immediately takes his hand. Patroclus shakes his head. "Stop staring at me like that. I'm fine."

"Yeah, well, you look like shit." She says it almost fondly, though her expression is worried.

I sink onto the bench on the other side of Patroclus and he leans on me. Worry eats away at me. We can't get Patroclus looked at until the trial is over. The last minutes seem to take decades.

With five minutes to spare, the Minotaur comes around the

corner toward the exit. The last key is on its lanyard around his thick neck, and he's got his head down as he charges forward. It's the only reason he doesn't see Atalanta until she's on top of him.

I hold my breath as I watch her sweep his legs out from beneath him. She's good, really good, but she's not quite steady on her feet despite her obvious training. That has to be why she's not able to dance back fast enough when the Minotaur lashes out and yanks her off her feet.

"Paris knocked her out," Helen murmurs. She watches the screen with worried eyes. "If she gets hit in the head again..."

Nothing good.

On the screens, Atalanta perches on the Minotaur's broad chest and hammers him with elbow strikes. I wince. That shit has to hurt, but he's got his arms over his head and he seems to be waiting her out. His opportunity comes when she shifts to reach for the key.

The Minotaur slams his elbow into her side. The force of the blow knocks her off him and she lands against the far wall and clutches her stomach. He broke a rib there. Maybe more than one.

I tense as he climbs to his feet. If he goes after her now, there's not a damn thing I can do about it. For a long, pregnant pause, I can almost see him considering hurting her seriously. Then he turns and lumbers to the exit.

Seconds later, he throws open the door and stalks out. One of his eyes is almost entirely swollen shut from where Atalanta punched him, but he seems otherwise fine. I suppose it was too much to ask for him to have some more injuries to fuck him up for the next trial.

The crowd goes quiet as the spotlight aims at Athena. "The second trial is over." She gives a slow smile. "Congratulations to our champions who are moving on to the third and final trial. Achilles, Patroclus, the Minotaur, Helen, and Paris."

The arena goes wild. I can *feel* the cheering though the soles of my shoes, vibrating right down to my bones. Even though I want nothing more than to get the fuck out of here and get a doctor to look at Patroclus, I grin and wave. On the other side of him, Helen is doing the same.

I hate myself a little bit in that moment.

Why the fuck am I playing the game when one of the people I care most about in the world is so injured, he can't sit up entirely on his own? It says something about me and my goals, and it's a pretty shitty statement.

But with how far we've come, how hard we've fought to be here...

I can't give it up. It's not in my nature. I will fight to the bitter end, and the only thing I can do is hope that the cost isn't higher than I can pay. It never occurred to me that that was even an option before this point. Now? Now I'm not so sure.

Things move quickly after that.

Bellerophon and their people usher us out of the arena. There are few enough champions that we all fit in one van. I keep Patroclus between me and Helen. I don't like the way the other two men keep looking at him—at us.

Paris leans back against his seat and smirks. "Cute little thing you three have going. Don't you get tired, Achilles?" I stare stonily at him, but apparently he doesn't need a response. "You know, from carrying both Helen and Patroclus on your back?"

I sense Helen going tense, but I don't look over as I respond. "It must be exhausting for you, Paris."

He narrows his eyes. "What must be?"

"The mental gymnastics you go through to pretend like you're better than everyone." I shake my head. "You're a sneaky little shit and that's the only reason you made it through this trial. Don't think I didn't see the way you attacked Atalanta from behind. It's the only chance you had to beat her, because you sure as fuck wouldn't have done it in a fair fight. Anyone in this van could take you, including Patroclus with his current injuries. So shut the fuck up."

Paris's skin goes a mottled red but his tone is still full of that same infuriating charm when he speaks. "It's cute how you're sucking up to Helen like this." He leans forward a little, cruelty alighting in his eyes. "You don't have to work so hard. Just call her a dirty little slut and she'll be on her back with her legs spread for you."

Fury has me lurching forward, but Patroclus's hand on my chest stops me. His voice is low but vicious. "Spoken like a man who had something priceless and fucked it up."

I glance over at Helen, but she's staring out the window. I would have thought she'd go for Paris's throat for a comment like that. It's not as if she's subtle when she's furious, and she slapped me for less. Instead, her shoulders are curled in on herself and her body language is tense and brittle.

This isn't the first time he's said shit like this to her.

I don't really give a fuck what people think of me outside of a select few, but I've seen how Patroclus will sometimes let comments ping around inside his big brain until they muddle the truth and eat him up from the inside. It doesn't happen as often now as it did in our teens and early twenties, but this has the feel of that.

Helen loved Paris. I don't understand it, but I'm sure of it now. She loved him and let him in, and she might as well have cuddled up with a cobra, because he used that closeness against her.

I turn back to him. I'm no longer in danger of attacking him, but my anger is no less. I smile slowly. "I'm going to enjoy beating your face in during the next challenge. No Hector to protect you this time, Paris."

He shrugs. "We'll see, won't we?"

"Yes. We will."

The Minotaur snorts. "You four with your petty little squabbles. It exhausts me."

"Then stop listening," I snap. "No one was talking to you."

The van slows to a stop. Paris barely waits for the door to open before he's charging out of the vehicle. The Minotaur follows, but at a more reasonable pace. I half expect Helen to leave, too, but she turns to us. Her expression is locked down in a way I don't like. "I'll help you with Patroclus."

Neither of us comment that I can carry him without much trouble. She obviously needs something to occupy her after Paris being such a shit, and if Patroclus is fine with it, so am I. We carefully ease him out of the van, and Helen tucks herself under his arm. She's short enough that he doesn't have to raise his arm overmuch, and she doesn't so much as weave at his weight. She's deceptively strong for her size, but that's nothing new.

Bellerophon meets us there. They sweep a look over our trio. "The doctor will meet you in Patroclus's rooms."

"Perfect." Helen starts for the door.

Bellerophon and I watch for a moment. They speak softly. "He would have seen a doctor even if you didn't carry him out of the maze on your back. He probably would have seen one sooner."

"I know." I do. But I couldn't leave him behind, even if it means he's eliminated first in the next trial. I don't have it in me.

Bellerophon claps me on the shoulder. "Well, congrats on making it to the third trial. You all but have it in the bag."

I manage a slight smile, though I'm still tracking Helen and Patroclus as they reach the door. She's limping a little, and I don't think it's because he's leaning on her. Damn the woman. She should have said something if she was injured, too. I start for the front door. "Congratulate me when I'm named Ares."

"I never get over how confident you are. I'll do that." They chuckle. "Next trial is in two days. Be ready."

"I will," I call over my shoulder. I catch up to my pair quickly and duck under Patroclus's other arm. "I've got him."

"We were doing just fine without you." There's no snap to her tone. Helen just sounds exhausted.

"What happened to your leg, Helen?"

She sputters. "I'm fine."

"Bullshit. The doctor will look you over when we get to the room, too." She seems otherwise okay, but if she's anything like Patroclus, she wouldn't tell me even if she was bleeding out. The thought sends ice skittering down my spine.

These two might be some of the smartest people I've ever

encountered, but they don't have the self-preservation the gods give children. If left to their own devices, they will ignore their bodies and end up seriously hurt.

That's okay. If you won't look out for yourself, then I'll look out for you.

I spare a quick glance, taking in their profiles. Something soft and tender stirs in my chest. *Both of you.*

HELEN

NO MATTER WHAT I TELL ACHILLES AND PATROCLUS, MY thigh is one massive ache by the time we make it back to the room. I barely feel it. Between Paris's horrible words circling my head and Patroclus's obvious injuries, I have plenty beyond the physical to focus on.

That doesn't stop Achilles from bullying us to the couch and snarling when I try to stand. He points a blunt finger at me. "Sit the fuck down and wait for the doctor."

I should probably find his attitude aggravating, but... Much like when Patroclus stopped me on the treadmill, this is Achilles taking care of me. It's novel enough to be nice. Aggravating. But nice. People don't take care of me. Growing up in my father's house meant showing too much caring was just asking for Zeus to teach us a harsh lesson. We watched it happen again and again with Hercules, and we learned well. Too well, maybe.

I nudge Achilles's finger away from my face. "Theseus just got my thigh. It's a bruise."

"We'll see," he mutters. He eyes my catsuit. "That's going to be a bitch to get off. We'll cut you out."

"*Achilles.*"

He points at Patroclus. "Don't you start. You can barely lift your arms to your shoulders. I'm cutting you out of your shirt, too."

"Kinky," I murmur.

"You have no idea."

Patroclus and I share a look, and the exasperation I see mirrored in his dark eyes surprises a laugh out of me. It feels good, so I do it again. "Gods, Achilles, you're a delight."

"I know. It's good you're finally figuring it out." A knock on the door has him heading in that direction after one last severe look at us. "Behave, you two."

The doctor is a short, wizened woman with medium-brown skin, a tight bun of graying hair, and thick square glasses. She sweeps a look over us. "Injuries?"

"My thigh is bruised."

Patroclus hesitates but finally sighs. "Face. Ankle." He shoots a guilty look at Achilles. "Ribs."

"You motherfucker."

The doctor snaps her fingers at Achilles. "That's enough out of you. Either help them get out of their clothes without commentary or leave."

Instantly, he ducks his head. "Yes, ma'am."

"Better."

He grabs a pair of scissors from the kitchen. It feels far more intimate than it should for Achilles to sit so close, his handsome face a study in concentration as he carefully pulls the fabric away from my skin and cuts. The scissors are a cool slide with each snip, and a few minutes later, he peels the catsuit off.

He's just as careful with Patroclus, though he glares at the other man the entire time. "You should have said something."

"You would have worried." A thin thread of pain hints at exactly how hurt Patroclus is. Or maybe—hopefully—it's just adrenaline letdown. Bruises can hurt like motherfuckers. It doesn't mean he's seriously injured.

Worry curdles my stomach. "Look him over first."

"You have one injury. He has several." The doctor pokes and prods at my thigh and straightens. "A bruise. Ice it. If you weren't in the tournament, I would say take it easy for at least a week."

"That's not an option," I say quickly.

"I'm aware." Her tone is dry and unamused. "It might give out if you put too much stress on it, so keep that in mind during the next trial."

"Thank you."

She examines Patroclus next, asking a series of terse questions. I look over her head at Achilles. I've never seen him so sick with worry and guilt. He carried Patroclus out of the maze over his shoulders. If Patroclus has broken ribs...if that action made them worse... I can practically see those thoughts going through the big man's dark gaze.

Neither of us take a full breath until the doctor sits back. "You're lucky. I don't think anything's broken. I *would* like to get an X-ray of your ribs, though. To be sure."

"They're not broken." Patroclus touches his side gingerly. "I've had broken ribs before, and it was different."

She sighs. "Very well. Be stubborn. I can't force you to get care."

Achilles bristles. "Get the X-ray."

"I'm *fine*." Patroclus shakes his head. "I'm exhausted and filthy and want a shower, a meal, and bed. But I'm fine, Achilles. I swear it."

I don't know him well enough as an adult to know if he's lying. It's strange to realize that. It's been less than a week of being close to him, but it feels far longer. At least until moments like this when it's readily apparent that my knowledge is only skin deep.

But even Achilles looks at him like he's not sure what the truth is. Finally, he shakes his head. "If I find out you're lying, I'm going to kick your ass."

"I know."

Achilles turns to the doctor and gives her a polite smile. "Thank you so much for checking them out, ma'am."

"Ice and rest." She turns and walks out the door.

Achilles glares at us. "Can you be trusted to sit still and not fuck yourself up further while I go get some food for us? Or are you going to be vaulting out of windows and fighting the Minotaur?"

I roll my eyes. "It was a *trial*. I would say I got out pretty clean considering that I was facing down Theseus."

"Yeah, guess you did." He suddenly grins. "Saw his knee. Nice job, princess."

I flush in response to his praise. He offers it so freely, without a single string attached. I don't quite understand it, but I like it a lot. "Thanks."

"Go." Patroclus leverages himself slowly to his feet. It's painful to watch, but he's already moving better than he was earlier. He won't be in the morning, but that's a fight for tomorrow. "Get plenty of ice, too."

"Of course." Achilles gives him one last long look and leaves the room.

Patroclus shakes his head. "Come on. If we're not sitting docilely and waiting when he gets back, he's going to take it as evidence that we're in worse shape that we claim, and he'll be hollering for a second opinion from another doctor."

I smile a little despite myself. "Gods forbid."

"You joke, but Achilles goes into mother-hen mode the same way he goes into a fight. There's no winning."

"It's kind of cute, don't you think?" I lean carefully against him and prop my head on his shoulder. It's nice. Really nice.

He snorts. "'Cute' is one word for it, I guess."

Achilles comes back through the door less than ten minutes later. He rakes a gaze over us but seems satisfied. "Well, that's something." He sets a giant box on the table, filled with several ice packs and more food than I know what to do with. "Let's eat."

It's so *easy* to be with them. Even though I'm tired and I hurt and my heart is still aching from Paris's poisonous words, I'm more at ease here with these two men than I have been in longer than I can remember. I'm not worried about my lack of makeup or my relaxed appearance or about them trying to use my careless words as weapons to launch at me when I least expect it.

It's nice. More than nice. It's an indulgence I know better than to allow myself to enjoy. Yes, we all passed the second trial and granted our little trio a reprieve, but the end result is still the same.

One of us will be Ares. The others will lose out on a dream they've spent far too long chasing.

"Helen." Achilles's voice pulls me out of my head. He's watching me closely. "What Paris said in the van—"

Some of the warm feeling in my chest dissipates. "It's not important." I refuse to admit that Paris scares me. He pokes holes in my confidence, in my emotional security, and then stands there with that little smile on his lips when I lose control and rage. There was a time when I reassured myself that at least the damage was confined to the emotional, as if that makes it better. The truth is that he's done lasting damage to me, both mentally and emotionally. I take a deep breath. "*He* is not important."

Patroclus doesn't look like he believes me. "It's not right how he talks to you."

"No. It's not." I can see the question on their faces, and maybe that's why I answer without making them ask. *Why were you with a man like him?* "He wasn't like that when I first met him. He was...nice." Humiliation flames my face. I was raised in Olympus. I should have known better than to believe a nice facade, no matter how complete. But I was so starved for kindness that I'd fallen right into Paris's arms. "It was the whole frog-in-boiling-water thing. I didn't even notice he was cutting away at me until it was almost too late."

Achilles cracks his knuckles. "Want me to kick his ass for you?"

I smile despite everything. "That's not necessary. I can fight my own battles."

"Thank you for telling us, Helen." Patroclus considers me for a moment and finally says, "Paris won't win. He's the weakest contender, and with Hector eliminated, he doesn't stand a chance."

I wish I believed that. The problem is that Paris shouldn't have managed to get past the second trial. He works out enough to keep what he's decided is the ideal body type, but he's not an athlete or warrior like the other champions. There's absolutely no way he should have pulled off being the first through the door. When it comes to combat? He might not win in a fair fight, but Paris has never been in a fair fight even once in his life. How he ambushed Atalanta more than proves that.

"Underestimating him is a mistake." When they both look like they're going to argue, I wave it away. It's easier to focus on this—the tournament, the champions—than it is to think about what the *rest* of the future holds. Not to mention we have no answers about the assassin or why they were removed from Athena's jurisdiction. The only person who can give those answers is Zeus, but he won't hand them over without a fight, and I can't do *that* until after the tournament is over. I can't imagine I'm going to be happy with those answers. I rarely am when it comes to things my family would rather keep hidden.

And the rest? The future where this strange, tentative thing between me and Achilles and Patroclus crashes and burns away to ash? I can't stand the thought of it.

Easier, simpler to focus on the more immediate threats. "Besides, it's not as if he's the only one I have to worry about. Even if Paris isn't a true contender—and he is, or he wouldn't still be here—no one can argue that the Minotaur is anything less than dangerous."

"We'll deal with it." Patroclus speaks with such confidence, as if he's already planned for this. As if life doesn't have a habit of kicking you in the teeth when you least expect it. As if he's not halfway out of commission from being beaten by Hector. "You have nothing to worry about. Neither Paris nor the Minotaur will win."

"Yeah, that's what everyone keeps saying." I shake my head slowly. "Do you know what my brother said to comfort me when he sold me out to cement a potential future alliance? He said if the new Ares hurt me, he'd kill them."

Achilles narrows his eyes. "Seems forward of Zeus, but what's wrong with that?"

My laugh comes out ragged. "What's wrong is that he's making a whole lot of assumptions that aren't based in reality. Ares doesn't need *me* as their wife in order to hold the title. Somehow the so-called comfort of being avenged doesn't make me feel better. But then, he didn't say it to make me feel better. He said it to assuage whatever's left of his stunted conscience." Or, worse, to placate me into being a willing victim. I can't say that aloud, though. It's too much to share, even with these two.

Achilles lifts his brows. "I don't know what you're worried about, princess. I'm going to become the next Ares, and while I enjoy a bit of slap and tickle and fighting turning into fucking, I only enjoy it when everyone involved is having a good time. You're safe enough with me."

I stare up at him, temporarily dumbfounded. Does he think that's comforting? While I can admit that Achilles *is* the best candidate of the bunch, his winning means I've failed. It means I'll spend the rest of my life regulated to the supportive wife, the one always outside the inner circle, the *prize*.

I sink into the chair across from him, suddenly exhausted. I can't afford to forget that these men aren't my allies. Not really. They might be guarding my body and giving me more pleasure than I could have dreamed and... But it doesn't matter. We're at odds.

Gods, that shouldn't hurt so much. "That's not nearly as comforting as you'd like it to be."

"Achilles has his own way of doing things." Patroclus shrugs. "To be fair, he's the best option to win."

I bristle. It doesn't even occur to me to cover up my reaction. Not with these two. "*I* am the best option to win."

Achilles gives that arrogant grin like he's humoring me. "Really, princess? Have you dealt with a lot of soldiers and security efforts up in that gilded palace of a penthouse you live in?" The question might be barbed, but I can tell he's not trying to be cruel.

He's even right, at least in this. I don't have experience with soldiers. Not even a little bit. I've had security all my life, but they tend to either blend into the background or keep enough distance—at my insistence—that I forget they're there. I came into this tournament prepared to have to learn from the ground up when it comes to Ares's actual duties, but I'm smart, ambitious, and not afraid to play dirty. I can figure out the rest on my way down.

I lift my chin. "I'm a fast learner."

"Yeah, that's what I thought." He grins. "Look, Helen, you're a certified badass. No one is saying otherwise. You've kicked ass in both the challenges, and if I wasn't here, you'd have a better than decent chance of taking Ares. But the fact remains that you're not qualified for the title."

I am so fucking tired of being underestimated. Yes, I know only the basics of security from the client perspective, but that doesn't mean I'm ill-prepared for the title. These two men are both smart and ambitious and they actually take me seriously, but they *still* don't understand. There's absolutely no reason to feel stung by that. No one else sees the real me, understands what I'm actually capable of. Why would Achilles and Patroclus be the exception?

Honestly, it's an asset. No matter how it chafes, being underestimated has only benefited me. Right now is where I keep my mouth shut and let them believe they know something I don't.

I can't quite manage it, though. "Wrong. I'm not the one in over my head if I become Ares." I lean forward and tap Achilles on the chest with a single finger. "You are."

"You think so?" If anything, his grin widens. "Enlighten me."

You're showing your hand. I ignore the little voice inside me and answer him in kind. "I might not be out there playing soldier, but one thing I *do* know is politics. Can you say the same?"

"I'm a fast learner." He tosses my words back at me and jerks a thumb in Patroclus's direction. "And he's a fucking genius. We're fine."

"Cute." Even Patroclus looks convinced, though. How can *he* underestimate Olympus politics? Yes, he's never dabbled in them, but from what I understand, his mothers used to be particularly cutthroat in their twenties. Rumor has it that Sthenele was a top contender for the title of Aphrodite, but when Patroclus and I were eight, she and Polymele all but disappeared from Olympus politics, taking him with them. It's not a huge leap to assume they made that call to protect their family.

What must it be like to be loved that much?

I shove the thought away. "You can't just *learn* politics like you can with other skills. That's not how it works."

"If you say so."

Something like worry takes root inside me. I'm going to win. I have to believe I'm going to win. But if I don't? If Achilles does manage to secure Ares and steps into the viper's nest I grew up in... He's going to get hurt. He might get *dead*. "Because of the barrier, we haven't had to deal with an outside incursion in our lifetime."

"What's your point?"

"My point is that *no one* is qualified to defend the city properly, at least if we're talking about experience. The title of Ares is a glorified babysitter to ensure the petty squabbles between the rest of the Thirteen and their inner circles don't get out of hand. The responsibilities of the title matter less than the allies and enemies that you have to navigate."

Achilles shrugs. "I'm still more qualified than you are."

I raise my brows, trying not to let the strange worry inside me flourish. How can he be so determined not to see the pitfall right in front of him? Or, if not Achilles, how can *Patroclus* ignore the danger? I have to make them see, in the event that the worst comes to pass. I can't stand the thought of something happening to them. "Is that so? Then I'm sure you can tell me why the last Aphrodite took a hit out on Demeter's daughter."

Patroclus raises his brows. "Everyone knows she tried to kill Psyche. It was televised, Helen."

"Everyone knows it happened. Do you know *why*?"

"Because Psyche was fucking Eros, and Aphrodite doesn't share her toys," Achilles says lazily. "Next question."

"Wrong. She did it because Demeter had Psyche lined up to be the next Hera, and she went around Aphrodite to do it." Psyche would have been a good fit for the title, too, but I know better than to say as much to either my brother *or* Eros. I plant my hands on my hips. "Do you know who among the Thirteen Poseidon is sleeping with and how that influences where his alliances lie?"

"I didn't—"

I keep going. "How about what Hermes's endgame is—or are you naive enough to think she's merely stirring the pot to entertain herself? Can you trace all of Demeter's contacts across the rest of the Thirteen? Will you fall in with her or try to stand apart? Both decisions have consequences. Are you prepared to pay them?"

Achilles shrugs, but Patroclus is looking at me like he's never seen me before. *Finally*, he begins to understand. "All our strategy has been focused on the martial side of things," he says slowly.

"Exactly." A small voice whispers that the three of us as a team would be unstoppable, but I ignore it. Achilles has his sights set on Ares. So do I. That puts us on opposite sides, regardless of how he's taken care of me in that particular Achilles fashion, or how sweet Patroclus is, or how much I enjoy fucking them both. At the end of this tournament, it doesn't matter what he feels for me. He won't hold back in the final trial. The only thing that matters is his end goal. That's something of a compliment, I suppose. It makes my chest ache to think about facing him down in two days.

All this means I can't really trust either of these men. No matter how much I want to. "Even a *precious princess* isn't exempt from having to learn to swim in shark-infested waters. Information is just as dangerous as a gun, even more so in the right hands. The Thirteen will eat both of you alive."

PATROCLUS

I'VE UNDERESTIMATED HELEN. AGAIN. I STARE AT THE FIRE IN
her amber eyes and have to shift every path into the future I had
speculated on. Again. Our original plans didn't last past meeting
her, and now the pieces I'd slowly begun to put back together are
blown out of the water. Again.

We need her.

Not because we enjoy sex with her. Not because she's destined
to be Ares's wife, which means Achilles's wife. Not because we
both *like* her quite a bit in our own way.

We need her because she knows things that will make the
learning curve of entering into the Thirteen smoother and allow
Achilles to dodge potential pitfalls. No matter how smart I am, I
don't know what I don't know.

I don't know a single thing about what she just mentioned.

Oh, everyone knew that Aphrodite attempted to kill Psyche,
but it had appeared to be driven by jealousy and a desire to keep
the woman away from her son. I had no idea that Demeter was

involved at all. Or that I should be concerned about Poseidon's bedroom habits. Or that Hermes is more than just the creature of chaos she appears to be. Or any of the other shit.

"We'll figure it out," I finally say. My chest hurts, and I wish I could blame it on Hector's fists, but the feeling goes much deeper than the surface-level pain of my injuries.

"Not before you get yourself into trouble." Helen shakes her head slowly. "Learning the security stuff is a cakewalk compared to that viper's nest. Can you say the same if it's the other way around?"

No, we can't.

Achilles is brilliant when it comes to conflict, to anticipating an opponent's move and ensuring victory for him and his team. But this is a different kind of conflict that he's never had to deal with. That neither of us have, for all that my mothers are both from families that have a history of scheming for the available titles among the Thirteen. I think they used to indulge in more ambitious games before we moved away from the city center, but my life has been startlingly normal. Nothing like Achilles, with his ambition a hunger so large, I'm not sure Olympus itself can hold him. Certainly not like Helen, who is a warrior in her own right.

We need her.

Are you sure you're not just saying that?

I ignore the voice, just like I have been ignoring it since my talk with Helen the night of the nominations. It doesn't matter what I feel, because logic and facts reign supreme, and right now they're all pointing in one direction.

Fact: Achilles is going to win the tournament and become the next Ares.

Fact: Marrying Helen is an inevitable side effect to that conclusion.

Fact: Neither Achilles nor I have had to navigate the inner circles of the Thirteen before, aside from Athena, who is an outlier among the group in how she deals with her people.

Fact: Helen *has* navigated those circles and done it successfully since birth.

Conclusion: It's not enough for Achilles to marry her once he becomes Ares. We need her on our side and willing to lend us her expertise. When laid out like that, it seems simple enough. It seems *logical* and not at all an impulsive decision made because I can't stand the thought of this thing between the three of us ending within a few days. I can blame Achilles and his intense looks all I want, but my own feelings are no less complicated...or irrational. It's comforting to fall back on the strategy, to have it support the end result I selfishly want, but it *does* support that conclusion.

None of this is new information. Nothing we've talked about as we circled each other for the last few days is new information. It doesn't matter how much we argue, because it boils down to the facts, and *they* never change.

We can't argue or reason our way out of this situation.

I...don't know what the answer is.

"Patroclus." Achilles taps my forehead, bringing me back to the present. They're both staring at me, him with a bemused expression and Helen with a contemplative one. He lightly taps my forehead again. "I think that's enough for now."

Achilles always has a better head in situations where time is of the essence. He isn't weighed down by running scenarios and examining facts before choosing a route. He shoots from the hip, so to speak. I want to argue that right now, that isn't the approach we need, not when so much can go wrong, but Helen gives a small smile. "He's right. We've had a long day. Let's go to bed."

How seamlessly they move to guide me to the door, Helen tucking herself under my arm and Achilles falling a few steps behind to watch our backs. All without saying a single word. I shake my head. This is wrong. We are supposed to be looking after Helen, not coddling me because I was fool enough to get into a fight with Hector in the second trial.

Funny, but somewhere in the last day or so, I forgot I was jealous of the future bearing down on us. I glance down at Helen, waiting for the feeling to come roaring back, but there's just a strange sort of contentment twinning with my overall stress and the pain beating in time with my heart. I'm not sure how to process that.

Achilles barely waits for us to make it to the bedroom before he says, "Get naked."

Helen arches a perfect brow at him. "Someone's presumptuous."

He reaches overhead and lightly grips the doorframe, perfectly at ease, as if he's not putting on a show for an audience of two. "I'm all for tucking you two in and keeping watch if you can honestly tell me that you won't lie there in the dark and stare at the ceiling and stress yourself the fuck out." He transfers his attention to me. "Are you up for it, or were you lying to the good doctor?"

"I wasn't lying." Nothing's broken. I'm sure of it. I ache like a motherfucker and I'm going to be black and blue for a while, but I'm okay. I've had worse injuries in the past, even if I feel like I've been hit by a truck at the moment.

Helen crosses her arms over her chest and eyes Achilles. "There's nothing wrong with using our brains. You should try it sometime."

He grins. "Nah, I'll leave that to you two. I'll be here to help you check out when you start spiraling."

"You might have a point." A smile pulls at the edges of her lips but Helen shakes her head. "But we're on the opposite sides. Continuing to have sex at this point is—"

"A really great fucking idea. Pun intended." He sighs and drops his arms. "We were on opposite sides last night and again during the trial today. Nothing's changed. Are you going to treat me any differently in the final trial just because you've been bouncing on my cock?"

"Absolutely not."

"Good. I won't either. With that out of the way..." He leans down and lowers his voice, a rumble creeping into his words. "Take off your clothes, princess. I'm jealous as fuck that Patroclus got a taste of that pretty pussy. My turn."

She blinks. "Um."

"Achilles," I try again. "You're being pushy."

"Tell me you're too hurt to want her." He pins me with look. "Or, fuck, tell me you don't want her."

This is already complicated enough without tangling myself further up emotionally. Which is exactly what will happen. I've barely dealt with the implications of what comes next, of how it's shifted now that we've met Helen…slept with Helen. How am I supposed to make my peace with Achilles moving on without me if he keeps insisting on including me in this shit? "I'm not too injured, but I'm also not ruled by my wants."

"You should try it sometime. It's fun."

"How can you think of *fun* at a time like this?" Except he's told us what he's doing, hasn't he? This isn't Achilles being reckless; this is him taking care of us in that particular way of his. He's a man of action, and he's right that I'll spend the next few hours overthinking everything, going back over the events of the day and wondering what I could have done different, looking to the future and worrying about what comes next.

He's always used sex to help me stop spiraling mentally. It's always worked.

Now he's extending that to Helen as well.

As much as he was bothered by the idea of me and her before, he's totally set that aside now that he's involved in the picture, too. Now that he's got some future painted in his head with the three of us. If I were braver, I'd ask him what he intends, but I'm not sure I'm prepared for whatever the answer is.

Achilles shrugs. "Both of you need sleep. A few orgasms will help that along. I'm all too happy to provide them."

This whole situation would be aggravating if it wasn't so Achilles. He's more than capable of nuance, but he prefers to see the world in black and white. What serves his goals and can be acted on in this moment versus literally everything else. And he doesn't give a shit about the latter.

To him, there's nothing we can do until the next trial. We have Helen with us, so it's a given that we'll keep her safe until then. He'll fuck us to sleep and then take watch, probably until morning if I don't miss my guess. I sigh. "You competed today, too. You have to be exhausted."

"You know better. I have excellent stamina." He nods at Helen. "You're still dressed."

"It's really that easy for you, isn't it?" She sounds almost in awe. "I thought I compartmentalized well, but this is a whole different level."

"Aww, princess, are you falling for me?"

Her face goes a little red, but she shakes her head. "Absolutely not. I don't even like you."

"Liar. You like me a whole lot." Achilles strips quickly. I've been with this man for nearly half my life and yet my breath still catches at the sight of all that light-brown skin, of the promise that strong body holds. He's a study in perfection, has been as long as I can remember. At eighteen, I was awkward and unsure in my body. Achilles never seemed to have that problem. He's always known who he is and where he's headed.

The top.

He steps around us and walks into the shower to turn the water on. It takes only a few seconds before steam curls in our direction. I turn away. I have to because watching Achilles shower is one of my favorite vices. If I don't get control of myself right now, I'll be naked and with him beneath the water. Now is *not* the time for that. I have to remember that. I have to...

Helen presses her hands carefully to my upper chest. She looks a little fragile around the eyes but otherwise unbothered by Achilles being...Achilles. "He's always like this, isn't he?"

"Yes."

Her lips curve. "Your blood pressure must be through the roof. You're so logical and he's so...himself."

"You don't have to say yes," I blurt out. "With any of it. He's pushy, but he respects 'no.'" It's one of the many things I love about Achilles. In life, he might be willing to go through every obstacle in his path instead of finding a way around, but in the bedroom, he's very intent on making sure everyone involved is having a good time. The second they aren't, everything stops.

"I know." She smiles sweetly and goes up onto her toes to press an equally sweet kiss to my lips. "Like you said, he's taking care of both of us in his own way, though, isn't he?"

Achilles and Helen are so different from me. I don't see how fighting and fucking are more of a comfort than finding a solution. Don't get me wrong. I enjoy sparring with Achilles, especially when it gets him going and results in an especially rough fucking. And I can't deny that sex will always stop my mental spiraling in its tracks. Sex won't fix things or make them less complicated, though. It's only a stopgap, a bandage, a temporary detour.

Coming up with a solution, though? That will bring long-term relief.

Maybe there's room for both, for us each meeting a different need because of how different *we* are. Helen's already looking steadier on her feet and more like herself. I nod slowly. "Yeah, he's taking care of us in his own way." He's doing it right now.

Helen tugs on my shirt. "Come play with us, Patroclus. We'll be gentle. After we tire ourselves out, you can talk us through what's going on in your head."

I'm so tempted, but no matter what they both say, sex changes things. Has *already* changed things. I want to believe that we'll all land on our feet after this. I want to believe it so desperately, I'm tempted to ignore all the evidence pointing to the contrary. "This results in heartbreak. Either he ends up Ares, ruining your dreams, or you do, and it ruins his dreams. Or someone else entirely wins and that smashes both of you to bits." Doubly so because at least with Achilles or Helen winning, there's a small chance to fix things and reach the future I suddenly want more than anything. The three of us together.

That won't happen if Helen is married to another.

"Patroclus..." She leans up and kisses me again, lingering this time. "We can go round and round and round worrying about the future until we're ready to wring each other's necks. It won't change what happens in the next trial, and it won't change what happens after. Or...we can follow Achilles's lead and enjoy the time we have left together."

"But—"

"We can argue more about it later if you want." She speaks against my lips. "When life is just a series of bad scenarios, you learn to take your pleasure and joy where you can. I am tired and shaky and more than a little heartsore. I might be wrong, but I think you're feeling a bit of the same, if for different reasons."

I startle. "Why would you say that?"

"Call it an educated guess." She leans back and looks up at me. "I don't know what's going on with you and him, though if it has to do with me, I'm sorry." Helen worries her bottom lip. "Also, I realize that I'm being just as pushy as *he* is. So it's okay if you don't want to."

If I don't want to?

The thought almost makes me laugh. Of course I want to. It's not as simple as seeing something I desire and reaching out to acquire it. Except... Maybe it is? Maybe this once, I can throw the consequences to the wind and ride it out for a little while?

If we're all but destined to crash and burn, why not do as they suggest and take what little pleasure and joy I can where I can find it?

"Helen."

"Yes?"

"After this..." Why is it so hard to get the words out? I clear my throat and try again. "After this, I'll talk through what has me so tangled up, but only if you promise to do the same."

I half expect her to laugh it off or maybe agree easily with the intention never to follow through on it. We've known each other long enough that I understand Helen doesn't let people in. She's so different from the child I remember, different from the public persona she adapts with other people. Even so, I'm not naive enough to think she's giving us everything. She's too smart, and much too savvy, to expose herself like that.

Helen gives me a small smile that feels like a punch in the gut. "I'm not sure you really want that. I'm a mess."

"I like your mess." It's the truth. Too stark. Too honest.

She hesitates but finally nods. "If you show me yours, I'll show you mine."

"Deal." I offer her a smile of my own. "Now take off your clothes."

ACHILLES

BY THE TIME HELEN AND PATROCLUS JOIN ME IN THE shower, I've managed to get myself under control. I don't make a habit of lying to myself. There's no point. That shit just gets in the way of accomplishing what I want, so I accept new information as it comes and adapt accordingly.

The feeling that sprouted yesterday morning, the surety that Helen is meant to make our couple into a throuple, has solidified inside me with the completion of the second trial. She kicked ass in that trial, and I don't give a fuck that the three of us making it to the final one continues to complicate things. It means more time together before we have to deal with Ares.

I like having her around. I like *her*. Yeah, she's got a point about the politics and shit, but that just reinforces my belief that the three of us were meant to be working as a team instead of at odds with each other. Helen will make a stellar ally. She's smart and she's experienced, and she knows the ins and outs of this new battlefield better than we do. More, I enjoyed the fuck out of watching her shove that knowledge down our throats. There's nothing sexier than competence, and the woman has it in spades.

I can clearly see a future where I'm married to Helen. The long, lazy evenings where she and Patroclus strategize until I get tired of all the talking and drag them to the bedroom. The irritating parties made much less so by watching Helen work the room, dressed to the nines in gold and diamonds, a warrior of words and thinly veiled politics. The early mornings where Patroclus and I are up and going through our normal workout routine and Helen wakes up in time to share a cup of coffee and a quick breakfast before we all go about our days.

It feels real. It's just a matter of getting us there.

There's the issue of her wanting to be Ares, but she'll get over it. She doesn't seem one to linger on things as they should be when she can adapt to things as they are. It might take some time to earn her forgiveness, but I already know her weakness.

All I have to do is provoke her enough, and we'll start fighting and end up fucking. Do it enough times and eventually we'll skip over the fighting and get right to the fucking. I don't see how that's a bad thing by any definition of the word. Besides, I don't have to be Patroclus to understand that Helen's grasp of the politics of the Thirteen is an asset we don't want to lose.

Helen ducks underneath the showerhead next to me. When I first saw the showers in these suites, I thought they were ridiculous. I'm a big guy, but even I don't need four showerheads and this much room. I get it now.

I watch her wash her hair out of the corner of my eye while

Patroclus comes up on my other side. He's still got that sexy little furrow between his brows that makes me want to kiss it away. He always worries too much. We have this in the bag, and now that I don't have to be worried about him running off into the sunset with the precious princess, everything is coming up aces.

There is the final trial to consider, but none of the remaining contenders are enough to worry me. None of that matters for the next two days, though, so I hook Helen around the hips and pull her against my chest. She resists the tiniest bit, but not like she really wants to go anywhere else.

"How's the leg?" She's sporting a nasty bruise from where Theseus hit her. Looking at it now, I kind of wished I'd kicked the fucker while he was down.

"It looks worse than it is." Her nails prick my chest, and my cock hardens even more in response. I like this about her, too. She's not afraid to play rough and doesn't seem to pull her punches. Does she understand the depth of the compliment she's giving me as a result? Maybe. Maybe not. It's hard to tell with her.

I grin down at her. "Shower or bed?"

Helen reaches up and slicks back her hair, pressing her breasts against my chest. "Why not dream a little bigger, Achilles? Let's do both."

"In that case..." I don't hesitate. I spin her around, grab her wrists, and lift them up to pin against my chest on either side of her head. "A little help here, Patroclus."

I take the opportunity to get a good look at his injuries, too. He's moving okay, so he's likely telling the truth about it just being bruising. Thank fuck. I don't know what I'd do if something happened to him. His body will be a spectacular array of purple, blue, and green tomorrow, but he's okay.

He watches us as he soaps up his body, his hands moving unhurriedly over muscles I want to sink my teeth into. He always was a fucking tease when given half the chance. Usually, I'm impatient so I get things rolling, but I don't have that option right now. Not unless I want to release Helen, and I'm never letting her go. She just doesn't know it yet.

Patroclus drinks in the sight of her, of us, as he finishes washing himself slowly. I don't think he realizes his heart is in his eyes. Gods, the way this man *wants*. He makes me strive to be better, to be worthy of it. Knowing he feels that way toward Helen only ramps up my determination to make us work. I don't waste time with bullshit about this happening too fast. If you know what you want, why dick around about going for it?

I want Patroclus.

I want Helen.

I mean to have them. Permanently.

"Tease," Helen murmurs. She leans her head against my chest and arches her back, putting her tits on display. "Let go of my hand, Achilles. I'll do this myself."

"No." Patroclus shakes his head sharply. "Both of you need to learn some godsdamned patience." He steps beneath the spray and makes quick work of washing himself off.

I watch the water course over his body and my mouth waters. Yesterday was barely enough to take the edge off wanting these two. Today worrying about them in the trial has only heightened my need. We're not doing this in the shower, though. It's hardly the safest way to fuck even if everyone was fully healthy. With Patroclus's injuries and Helen's leg in danger of buckling, it's out of the question. I want them, but I don't want either of them harmed in the process.

Gods, I'm a fucking sap.

Finally Patroclus turns to face us fully and takes a step to close the distance. He plants his hands on her hips and leans forward... bypassing Helen's face to kiss me. Patroclus always had the tiniest of sadistic streaks when we entertain others in our bed, but it feels different with Helen. Neither of us gave a fuck about those other people, aside from getting them off as hard as we could. With Helen, there's...more. Jealousy or possession or something else altogether. I don't know, but I fucking like it.

Patroclus kisses me like it's just us, like it will always just be us. A reminder. A promise. Who the fuck knows? I kiss him back just as intensely.

And then he moves to Helen, taking her mouth with the same command he took mine. My breath comes faster as Patroclus presses her back against me even harder with the force of his mouth. She tries to reach for him, but I tighten my grip on her wrists. Helen's strong, but I'm stronger, and I think she likes that because she moans. Or maybe what she likes is that I don't treat her like she's made of spun glass.

Patroclus eases down her body, finally kneeling before us. He kisses her lower stomach, just above her pussy. "Her legs, Achilles. Hold her for me."

"I'm...standing right here." Her breath is coming even harsher, faster than ours. "Stop talking about me like I'm a toy."

"Don't you want to be our toy, princess? The perks are pretty great."

She sputters a little and rolls her hips, rubbing her ass against my cock. "Anything resembling submission is *strictly* confined to sex and only sex. Don't get any funny ideas."

Patroclus's eyes go hot. "Noted."

"Wouldn't dream of expecting you to kneel unless it's to suck my cock." I grin against her hair. "Now be a good girl and loop your arms around my neck. You won't be able to stand for long once Patroclus gets going."

"Cocky."

"Accurate." I release her wrists and wait for her to do what I command. She doesn't make me wait long. I like this about her, too. How sometimes she fights and sometimes she submits, and the sharp is just as sexy as the sweet. She's a perfectly curated greenhouse rose, too gorgeous to be real and with curves that create the temptation to hold her in my hands. So tempting, it's easy to miss the thorns until one bites deep.

Or maybe it's easy for others to ignore the thorns, seeing only what they want to see. Not me. I like the thorns. What use is a defenseless flower except to shove in a vase and let wither until its once-beautiful petals fall off?

They want to do that to Helen.

Fuck, *we* want to do that to Helen.

The realization makes me shift, not liking the direction of my thoughts. Patroclus and I aren't the same as the other champions, the rest of the Thirteen. Yes, I plan to squash Helen's dream with my own, but that doesn't mean I want to watch her wither away.

She doesn't have to be Ares to get what she wants. She'll figure that out as soon as this whole tournament is over.

That's fine. I don't have to see every step of the journey to know my destination. That's what Patroclus is for. I have no doubt that he wants Helen, too. He'll find us a way forward.

I grab Helen's thighs, careful to avoid the bruise, and spread her wide for Patroclus. He makes a deep appreciative noise, and I laugh. "Somehow, you get her pussy first again and I'm stuck here doing all the work."

"It's good for you not to get everything you want right when you want it." He doesn't wait for a response before he dips down and drags his tongue over her exposed center. I'm tall enough that I get a great view of him eating her out. She's as perfect there as she is everywhere else. I'm not sure I believe in the gods, but if they exist, they really spent the extra time forming this woman.

She squirms in my arms, but even slippery from being in the shower, I hold her immobile as Patroclus works her clit with the flat of his tongue. He goes about it like he goes about everything in life: with utter precision and a determination to be the best. Helen's breasts heave with every breath, and impatience flickers. "Hurry up and make her come. It's my turn next."

Helen turns her head and I take the unspoken offer, kissing her mouth even as Patroclus kisses her pussy. She tastes a little like him, and the realization has my cock hardening to an almost painful level. She's not one to take her pleasure, this kiss, passively. It's a battle the same way everything between us is a battle.

And then she's coming, moaning against my tongue and trying to thrash. I tighten my grip on her thighs, enjoying the way her muscles flex and fight against my hands. She's athletic as fuck. Both trials have more than proven what she's capable of. I bet we could get into some crazy creative positions between the three of us.

Later. After the tournament is over and everyone is healthy and healed.

I break the kiss as Patroclus pushes to his feet and reaches behind us to turn off the water. "Bed. Now."

"Don't have to tell me twice." I carefully set Helen down…but only long enough to grab her hips and toss her over my shoulder. Her screech is music to my ears, and I can't help laughing and giving her ass a light smack. "Quiet. You're going to have the guards busting down the door."

"I'm going to kick your ass!"

"Nah, but if you ask nicely, I'll let you kiss it." I grin when she gives another screech. Patroclus and I get rough sometimes, but we don't play like this, this fighting that turns hot and charged and morphs into fucking. I've never had this with anyone but Helen.

Patroclus follows me out of the bathroom, a strange look on his face as I carefully toss Helen onto the bed. She bounces, but she's fast, already rolling before she hits the mattress a second time. I snag her calf and flip her onto her back. "Don't tell me one orgasm was enough for you." I dodge a kick aimed at my face. "Be a good girl and spread your legs."

"Fuck you!" Her words are harsh, but her eyes dance and she's obviously fighting down a smile.

I laugh. Gods, this is *fun*. "If you don't play nice, I'm going to tell Patroclus to hold you down."

Her amber gaze flicks to him, and I see the exact moment she realizes that will get her off even harder. "Oh no," she drawls. "Not that." When I don't immediately move, she curses and tries to kick me in the face again.

Brat.

"Patroclus." I don't have to lift my voice because he's only a few feet away. "Hold her down."

I watch him closely as he moves onto the bed. If either of them show the first sign of their injuries being more serious than they and the doctor claim, I'm shutting this whole thing down.

Patroclus kneels on the mattress above Helen's head and catches her wrists, pressing them to the bed. She struggles, but I can tell she's not fighting as hard as she could. I catch her eyeing his ribs, and my chest goes warm at how she's taking care of him without being overt about it. Good girl. I move up between her thighs and press them wide and up, spreading her obscenely.

What a picture we make.

Patroclus is breathing harder than the effort to hold our princess down requires, and his cock is so stiff, it'll be a fucking miracle if he doesn't come just from the foreplay. It's fine if he does. We have all of tonight and tomorrow. I plan on tucking these two in for some rest after I fuck the worry right out of their heads, but that doesn't mean it has to be rushed.

Every muscle in Helen's body quivers as she tries to fight our superior strength. Her pussy, though? She's so wet, she's practically dripping. I lick my lips and she makes a little whimpering sound that goes straight to my balls. Yeah, I can't wait to get my mouth all over Helen Kasios again. I glance at Patroclus. He looks turned on and conflicted about it.

First, though, a few ground rules.

"You want to stop, tell us."

Helen blinks at me, a little frown pulling at the corners of her lips. "But saying stop can be sexy."

"Say 'wait' instead," Patroclus says slowly. "We'll check in."

She considers this and finally nods. "Okay, that's fair. Same goes for you two, though."

I don't bother to tell them that it won't be an issue with me. I appreciate the thought. There's a level of caring that I've only experienced with Patroclus, and I'm too turned on to think too hard about it. Maybe later, when I'm not looking at the perfection that is Helen's naked body, her pussy an invitation I have no intention of declining. "Sure."

"Yeah." Patroclus's voice has gone hoarse.

I don't give her a warning before I move, quickly sliding down and releasing her thighs. She only has a second to tense before I band my forearm across the back of her thighs and press them up. I can't spread her as wide like this, but it's fine. I don't need to in order to accomplish what I want. I drag the tip of my finger over her slit. "I've changed my mind about you."

"Ask me if I care." The sharp words don't match her breathy tone.

"You care." I hold her gaze as I press a single finger into her. Not enough to do more than tease her, though *fuck* she feels good. "Do you want to know why?"

"Enlighten me."

"Because I only play with people I like." I press a second finger into her.

It's entertaining as fuck to watch her expressions flicker. Desire and confusion and need. "What are you talking about?"

"I'm going to play with *you*, princess." I nod at Patroclus even as I twist my wrist, exploring her until I find the spot that makes her give another of those delicious whimpers. "How many times do you think we can make her come before we crash, Patroclus?"

He blinks. "You mean before her body gives out."

"Oh my *gods*."

I keep stroking her G-spot with my fingertips and pretend to consider. "Sure. Before her body gives out or before we crash. Whichever comes first."

"*Helen* comes first." He shifts, pressing her wrists harder into the mattress. "I think you can beat our record."

"Game on."

HELEN

I'M STILL HAVING A HARD TIME PROCESSING THAT I'M HERE, in between these two men, when Achilles starts eating me out. When Patroclus is between my thighs, he's methodical. Achilles goes after me like he can't get enough, like he's less worried about getting me off than he is about tasting every inch of me. It's sexier than I could have dreamed, and all the while he keeps up that steady rhythm with his fingertips inside me.

I don't remember closing my eyes, but when I open them, Patroclus is staring down at me. He studies my face as if determined to memorize every piece of me. As if he can see beneath my skin to the selfish, petty, ambitious woman beneath. He shifts back, still maintaining his grip on my wrists, and eases down onto his stomach on the bed.

Patroclus's lips brush the shell of my ear. "You fight so fucking hard, Helen. To be taken seriously. To be seen as a person. To forget how often neither of those things happen." He speaks in a soft murmur completely at odds with the way Achilles is sucking on my clit.

I tense. I didn't ask for this. I'm already held down and spread open. Being stripped bare, too? It's too much. "Stop."

Between my thighs, Achilles pauses, but stop isn't *wait*. After the barest of hesitations, he resumes, settling into a rhythm of rubbing the flat of his tongue against my clit. My whole body goes tight in response. "Please." I don't know what I'm asking for. Patroclus to stop before he says something I can't take. Achilles to make me come so hard, I stop thinking entirely. Both. Neither.

Patroclus, devil on my shoulder, just keeps spilling words directly into my ear. "Has anyone ever taken care of you, Helen? Not as a prize to be shown off but as a *woman*?"

He might as well have split open my rib cage and ripped my heart right out of my chest. This is only supposed to be sex, to be a convenient escape from how ugly the inside of my head is right now. It's no supposed to be Patroclus or Achilles—or both—*seeing* me. "Stop," I whisper.

"Do you really want me to stop?" He kisses my neck and then nips my earlobe. "It could be like this. You don't have to pretend with me—with us. We don't expect perfection. We just want you."

My eyes burn and I blink rapidly, hating the tears that slip free. I can't concentrate, can't even *think*. "You don't..." Whatever protest I'm trying to make disappears as Achilles sucks hard enough on my clit to bow my back.

He shifts to nip first one thigh and then the other. "You're making her cry." I can't tell if he's pleased or bothered by it.

"I'm just telling the truth." Patroclus kisses my neck and moves to my shoulder. "You want to keep her." Patroclus pauses as if waiting for Achilles to deny it. When he stays silent, Patroclus continues. "*We* want to keep her."

Keep me.

The very idea should infuriate me. I am not someone to be *kept*. The whole reason I'm here in the first place is to avoid that fate...

Except when Patroclus says they want to keep me, it doesn't feel like he's saying they want to keep me in a gilded cage, a trophy wife to bring out for parties and events to prove what badass guys they are. Taming Helen Kasios and all that bullshit.

No, when he says *keep*, it sounds a whole lot like...

"You're thinking too hard. Stop making her think too hard."

Achilles sounds so irritated, I smile despite myself. "Maybe you're just not doing a good enough job."

He lifts a brow, a devastatingly cocky expression on his face. "Hmmm. Guess I need to up my game, then." He glances at Patroclus, and they share one of those silent conversations I envy so much. This time, I get flashes of intent. Achilles is asking a question. Patroclus grunts in response. I don't know the nature of the question, but I'm ridiculously pleased to have picked up even that much.

So pleased that I don't have time to tense before they move as a unit. Patroclus grabs me under the arms and lifts me as he rises. He eases onto his back on the bed with me straddling him facing Achilles. "What..." My voice trails off as Achilles wraps a fist around Patroclus's big cock.

He gives me that wicked grin that promises all sorts of fun and pleasure. "Up."

No mistaking his intent. I rise slowly and bite my bottom lip as he drags Patroclus's cock through my folds. Back and forth. Back and forth. He catches against my entrance, and I start to sink down, but Patroclus grabs my hips, holding me in position. "Not yet."

"But I *want* it."

"Not even a princess always gets what she wants." Achilles stops any argument by dipping down and sucking Patroclus's cock into his mouth. His cheeks hollow beneath his beard and he hums with obvious pleasure.

I go still as I realize what's happening. He's tasting *me* on his boyfriend's cock. He's obviously a fan because he gives Patroclus one last rough suck and then his mouth is on my pussy again. This time, the sight is even better than before.

Patroclus's hands denting the skin at my hips as he fights both me and gravity to keep my body aloft. His hard cock practically throbbing with need and wet from Achilles's mouth. Achilles's eyes holding my gaze as he works my clit exactly how I need to get off.

For as long as I live, I'm never going to forget my time sharing a bed with these men.

Never forget? I might laugh if I could breathe though the orgasm barreling down upon me. More like I'll be scandalizing my grandchildren someday recounting the time I allowed myself to be seduced by two warrior men.

Patroclus's hands tighten on my hips, and it's the only warning I get before he slams me down on his thick cock. I didn't even realize Achilles had positioned him at my entrance.

I come so hard I scream, but Achilles doesn't stop that decadent motion with his tongue against my clit. Patroclus starts rocking me on his cock, the tiniest movement that has my toes curling. "Gods!"

"Nah." Achilles leans back and licks his lips. His beard is soaked from me, and a dark, possessive part of me loves the sight. He kisses his way up my stomach, pausing to lavish my breasts with attention before kneeling before us. Through it all, Patroclus keeps me rocking on him, keeps me on edge. Achilles frames my face with his big hands. For once, he looks devastatingly serious. "Let us keep you, Helen."

The shock of my actual name on his lips nearly sucks me under. I can't submit, not to this. Not here, not now, not when so much is at stake. It should have been an easy thing to deny. One little word, two tiny letters. *No.*

I...can't say it.

I can't agree, but I can't push them away, either.

Instead, I do the only thing I can think of. I hook Achilles's thick neck and yank him down to claim his mouth. I pour everything into the kiss, all my doubts and fears and sorrow. Because this can't last. It doesn't matter what these two men think, how right the words they say, how safe they make me feel. It simply cannot last.

But we have tonight.

Achilles growls against my mouth. "Fine, then." He breaks the kiss long enough to grab a pillow. "Lift."

Patroclus almost unseats me when he obeys. I catch myself on Achilles's shoulders and for a moment he looks at me like...well, like he wants to keep me. Then he plants those massive hands on my hips, lifting me and turning me around to face Patroclus. "I want to watch," I protest.

"Another time." His casual assurance that there *will* be another time should irritate me, but it makes me all melty inside instead. He works me down on Patroclus's cock, and that draws my attention to our third.

Gods, he has his heart in his eyes.

I rock my hips, fucking him slowly as Achilles climbs off the bed long enough to grab lube from the nightstand. Patroclus looks at me like I'm a puzzle, a marvel, a gift. Like he's in full agreement with Achilles about keeping me. That should piss me off. It really should.

But then, nothing is like it *should* be with these two. They defy expectation.

Patroclus slides his hands up to cup my breasts. "One day."

I can't quite catch my breath. "One day?"

"One day you'll say yes." He pulls me down into a kiss. I expect something soft and sweet and maybe a little polite. Joke's on me. Patroclus kisses me like he needs the air in my lungs to breathe. Like if he just claims my mouth effectively enough, he'll claim my words, my future, my everything. I can't think past the rushing in my head, past the pleasure pulsing inside me, so close to completion.

The bed gives beneath Achilles as he crawls to take position between Patroclus's spread thighs. He shoves them wide and up and makes a really sexy pleased sound. "I like you two like this." He drags a big finger down the center of my ass. Patroclus jolts, so he must be getting the same treatment. "I could have either one of you," Achilles muses. "Yeah, I like this a lot."

I break the kiss long enough to say, "You're talking too much."

"Nah, you like it when I talk."

Patroclus goes tense, and I know without a shadow of a doubt that Achilles is feeding him his cock. With the flick of a switch, this became more about Patroclus's pleasure than it became about mine. I press back a little so I can move more effectively...and so I can give him a show. The way he watches my body, it's like he's still not quite sure this is real, but he really, really wants it to be.

I'm not sure it's real, either.

I lift my arms over my head as I roll my hips, and it's the most natural thing in the world to twine them around Achilles's neck. He's tall enough that I have to stretch, but the way Patroclus curses at the sight, it's more than worth it.

Patroclus moves one hand from my hips to press his thumb against my clit, and then he holds perfectly still so I can rub against him how I need. "I want to feel you come on my cock again, Helen."

"Keep it up and I will," I gasp.

Achilles palms my breasts as he picks up his pace, fucking Patroclus so roughly, I can feel every stroke. So roughly, it's as if he wants to reassure himself that Patroclus is okay, and this is the only way to do it. It's almost like the thrust starts with him and cascades in a wave through Patroclus to me, where I rise and sink back down, sending it back to Achilles. It's surreal and sexy, and I never, ever want it to stop.

I never want any of this to stop.

It feels too good, though. The pressure builds and builds, and I want to fight it but not enough to stop or slow down. Achilles plucks at my nipples, little pinpricks of pain that only add to Patroclus's thumb against my clit, his cock filling me entirely. I open my mouth to demand more and then it's too late. I'm coming.

I start to slump forward, but they hold me up between them. Achilles picks up his pace, and I dazedly realize he was holding back until now. He's not holding back any longer. His thrusts have Patroclus's cock moving inside me and my orgasm just keeps coming. Wave after wave, until it feels like my very bones have turned liquid. Achilles holds me surprisingly gently considering how he's fucking Patroclus, and I swear I feel him kiss my temple.

Patroclus curses. "Fuck, I'm—" His grip on my hips turns punishing and then he's driving up into me, yanking me down onto him as he comes so hard, I feel it.

Achilles presses me gently down against Patroclus's chest. Patroclus wastes no time in claiming my mouth again, but I barely have time to sink into it before I feel something wet lash my ass. I pull back. "Achilles."

"Mmm."

"Did you just come all over my ass?"

He chuckles. "Yeah."

I wait for irritation, but all I feel is a ridiculous sort of amusement. I grin down at Patroclus. "He really likes to mark his territory, doesn't he? Like a dog."

"Nah." Achilles slaps my ass lightly. "Just marking my *intent*."

Patroclus gives a choked laugh. "Stop. You're making her clench around me and it's too good."

"Shower. Then bed."

"We just had a shower, Achilles."

"And I just got you all kinds of filthy. Come on. It will be fun." Achilles slides off the bed, hooks me around the waist, and lifts me into his arms. I don't screech this time. I'm still too boneless from the orgasm and... Maybe I don't totally hate being hauled around by Achilles. I like the possessive way Patroclus watches us even more as he gingerly hauls himself off the bed and follows us into the shower.

We barely last five minutes in the shower before Achilles is on his knees, Patroclus's cock in his mouth and his fingers buried in my pussy. At some point, we tumble back into the bed, wet and slippery and intent on our pleasure. Over and over again, as if we're racing the clock to pack as many orgasms in before we have to return to reality.

Eventually, though, reality intercedes. It always does.

Achilles stretches, looks at the clock, and sighs. "Bedtime." He rolls over and grabs the phone. I can't help appreciating the way his muscles move. He really does have the body of a warrior. On my other side, Patroclus shifts so he can coast his hand down my side to my hip. Not a sexual touch, but it feels so good, I nearly moan. The casual intimacy is something I'm going to miss almost as much as the sex. Both he and Achilles are so free with their touch, with their words. I'm going to...miss them.

"You just tensed up. What are you thinking?"

I want to lie or do something to turn away the question, but maybe I'm more fucked up than I thought, because I answer honestly. "I'm going to miss you. Not just the sex, though that's fun, but..." I try for a shrug, but it's rather challenging to shrug while flat on your back. "It's nothing."

"It's not nothing." He brushes my hair back from my face. I try very hard not to think of how much a mess I must look right now. I *hate* that Paris's poison still occupies space in my head despite my best efforts. I know he was using criticism to manipulate and control me, but that doesn't stop insecurity from lashing me at the most inconvenient times.

Patroclus hesitates, his dark gaze flicking to Achilles, who's gone silent and still on my other side. "You don't have to pretend with us."

"I know." It's even the truth. That's not the problem, though. Pretending and putting on a mask are second nature, and even if I feel safe enough with these two men to be my true self, that doesn't change how fucked up our circumstances are. "But—"

"Do you always borrow trouble?" Achilles sits up and stretches his arms over his head. "The third trial will decide the future. No point in worrying about it until then."

"Achilles."

I glance between the men, but this time, I have no idea what they're conveying back and forth. What must it be like to trust someone that much, to have that level of history, that you can speak without words? I can do it with Eris a bit, but that's more shared trauma than anything else. And my silent conversations with Hermes and Dionysus basically consist of "*Can you believe this bitch?*" while at Dodona Tower parties. What Achilles and Patroclus have is something else altogether.

Finally Achilles looks down at me. "I wasn't talking out of my ass earlier. We mean to keep you."

"You can't keep a person."

"All the same."

I can't have this conversation again while flat on my back. Why are we retreading this ground? Nothing's changed, no matter how many orgasms we've exchanged. We've gone beyond beating a dead horse with this situation. I sit up and scoot back to press against the headboard. "You want to be Ares. I want to be Ares, too. We are diametrically opposed."

"Only in that."

As if it's that easy. "When I win, you'll have to go back to being Athena's second-in-command. You'll never forgive me."

"Maybe." He shrugs those wide shoulders. "And when I win, you'll lose out on Ares but become my wife."

The thought isn't as unattractive as it was the first time I thought it. If I were a different person, maybe tonight would be enough to make me change my mind, doubt my goals. It wouldn't be so bad to be kept by this man and Patroclus.

Except being *kept* is the thing that's slowly choking the life out of me. No matter how nice the cage, the bird inside is still trapped. Being married to one of the Thirteen is not the same thing as being one of the Thirteen. If I fail, I will spend the rest of my life on the outside looking in. "You honestly expect me to accept that."

"I honestly expect you to accept the results of the tournament, yeah." Another of those shrugs. What must it be like to be Achilles, totally and completely sure of his place in the world and the path laid out before him? I envy him, even as I just don't fucking understand how easy it seems to be.

My stomach twists a little, but I force myself to stare him down. "So *you'll* accept the results of the tournament, too?"

Maybe I should leave it alone, but I can't quite make myself. "You say you want to keep me, both of you. So that extends to my potentially winning Ares. If—*when*—I win, you'll still want... What? A relationship? Is that what you're saying?"

Achilles smiles. "Yeah, princess. Exactly." He answers too easily, as if indulging me. As if he doesn't believe for a second that it's really a possibility. "That's usually what 'keeping' means."

It's too good to be true. No matter the strength of the connection, I've only known these men for a few days. Relationships that last years couldn't weather what we're about to. What are the odds *we* will?

I push the thought away. I can't afford to let myself get derailed worrying about things that might or might not happen. Either it will or it won't. Ruining things with Achilles and Patroclus based on theories... Maybe it would be smarter, but I don't want to do it.

Instead, I stretch. "I'm tired. Let's brush our teeth, change the sheets, and go to bed." I ignore the little voice inside me whispering that we're only playing house and this will end in tears.

Everything in Olympus ends in tears.

You have to take your joy where you can find it.

PATROCLUS

FOR BETTER OR WORSE, WE'RE HEADED FOR A SINGLE DESTI-nation. There are no exits, no diverging paths, no way to change what will come. Within a few days, the title for Ares will be awarded to the winner of this tournament. Reality will invade this safe space we've created. There's no avoiding it.

But not yet.

"I'm surprised you convinced Bellerophon to have breakfast delivered." The layout isn't fancy—eggs, hash browns, fruit, and pancakes—but it's more than I expected.

Achilles pulls out a chair for Helen, ignoring her suspicious look, and grins. "Bellerophon is being overly cautious leading up to the third trial. Add in the assassination attempt, and they'd rather keep us as separate as possible for the next twenty-four hours."

"I don't need special treatment," Helen says. She examines the food available and finally adds a bit of each to her plate. "I don't like the idea of hiding in the room. It looks like I'm scared."

"No one will see it. It's not like they televise what goes on in this house." Achilles pauses, expression going thoughtful. "Though Bellerophon did say they are canceling the interviews that were supposed to happen today. It's a security risk, though they're spinning it as something else for the public."

"Gods forbid we provide a less than perfect image for the public," I murmur. I sink into the empty chair and start filling a plate. I'm starving. Spending the night exerting the kind of energy we did wasn't wise, but I don't regret it. I'm not prepared to say that sometimes plans should be thrown out, but I can't deny that I didn't plan on Helen. It doesn't matter. I'm still 100 percent with Achilles on finding a way to make this work.

She's still right, though. There isn't a single scenario that is perfect. The odds aren't in our favor, but—

"Patroclus." From the patient way Helen says my name, it's not the first time. She's got that little indulgent smile on her face, and my whole body goes warm in response. Gods, this woman does something to me. I don't fully understand it, but I'm beyond questioning it.

"Yeah?"

"Your mom Sthenele. She was almost Aphrodite, right? It was when we were kids, but my dad used to talk about her a lot before you moved away." Helen glances away, a shadow flickering over her face before she seems to put it away. "Why did she withdraw her name?"

It's an old story, but I don't mind retelling it. I give the untouched plate in front of her a pointed look. "Eat while I tell you."

"Bossy."

"You need the calories."

She gives me a stubborn look, but her amber eyes dance. "You aren't telling Achilles to eat."

I tilt my head in his direction. He's created a mounding plate of food and is already halfway through devouring it. When he catches us looking, he shrugs. "I'm hungry."

Helen shakes her head. "Okay, you have a point." She holds my gaze and takes a dainty bite of the omelet.

Satisfied she'll continue eating, I pour three mugs of coffee and start at the beginning. "My moms—Sthenele and Polymele—have been together since they were teenagers."

"Like someone else we know," Achilles mutters.

I ignore him. He's heard this story a thousand times, and as a result, I can predict his interruptions the same way he can predict how it unfolds. "They're both from families that have had members in the Thirteen in past generations, and with several of the titles primed to switch over, they had a good chance at claiming one for themselves. Sthenele worked under the last Aphrodite, and she was a top contender for the position." The last Aphrodite liked her quite a bit, I think, and since the current holder of that title is the one who names their heir, it made my mother a front-runner.

"What happened?"

I wait until she takes another bite to look away. "They wanted more kids. Polymele was pregnant." The details are a little hazy for me after all this time, but the thing I *do* remember is how excited I was at the thought of a sibling...and how quickly joy turned to fear. "There was an, ah, attack."

"What he means is that the bitch Peitho orchestrated an attack on Polymele as a way to put pressure on Sthenele." Achilles raises his brows when I sigh. "What? It's the truth. She did it, even if they never proved it. And she *is* a bitch. The years haven't changed that, or she wouldn't be exiled right now."

"Peitho…" Helen's eyes go wide. "That's Eros's mom's name. I kind of forgot she had one before becoming Aphrodite."

"Yeah, well, she's not Aphrodite anymore, is she?" Achilles takes a massive bite of sandwich.

"I guess she's not," Helen says faintly.

I lean back in my chair. "Polymele miscarried." My moms still get kind of sad when that subject comes up. It wasn't the only miscarriage she suffered in the years after that. They used to call me their miracle baby with a smile, but I know the fact I'm an only child is a bittersweet thing for both of them. "Sthenele made the decision to resign her position and put as much distance between our family and Olympian politics as possible."

Helen studies the plate in front of her. "Why didn't they strike back? Removing Peitho would have removed the threat."

"You know better." Even existing mostly on the outskirts of the Thirteen, I understand how things work. There's always another threat, another enemy. The people who stay and thrive in that atmosphere are willing to pay the price—or allow those closest to them to pay the price. My moms decided the cost was too high.

She sighs. "Yeah. I guess I do know better." Helen picks up her fork and puts it down again. "That's all very romantic. Do they regret it?"

I shrug. "They wanted our family to be safe more than they wanted power. They seem happy enough with the results." I grew up in a household filled with love and safety. I don't know that the latter would be true if my moms had chased their ambition. I still remember the tension and fights they had when I was small. So much is indistinct, but *that* isn't. They relaxed once we moved, fought less.

She nods slowly. "And what do they think of you being in the tournament?"

"They know the score." Achilles snorts. "Patroclus and I have been on this path a long time. They knew we were headed for glory and everything that entails."

Despite myself, I smile. Achilles often exasperates my moms, but they love him nearly as much as I do. "Yeah, you've had your eye on the top for a long time. It's one of the first things you ever said to me in boot camp. You looked around and said, 'Someday, everyone in Olympus is going to know my name.'"

Achilles doesn't bother to blush. "I know what I want."

Helen's shoulders go tense, a sure sign we're about to reenter our argument about Ares and what it means and what the future will hold. We'll end up going in circles again and again, because there's no solution. We only have theories right now.

I cut in before we can go off the rails. "I've shown you mine. Now show me yours."

Her smile is half-hearted at best. "You had a happy childhood, didn't you? Even before you moved?"

"Yeah." It's the truth. I never went without. I knew my moms loved me. There was the normal kid shit, especially being a person who needs a lot of time to think, but nothing worth commenting on.

"I didn't." She flicks her hair over her shoulder. "All my physical needs were taken care of. I know, I know, Achilles, poor little rich girl, but..."

He looks a little guilty. "But Zeus."

"Yeah, but Zeus." She sighs and pushes her plate away. She's eaten half the omelet and a few bites of fruit, which isn't enough, but I don't want to press her right now, not when she's lowering her walls just a few inches, letting us see part of her she's kept back until now. "He killed my mom. I know that's the rumor and everyone kind of takes it as something like an urban legend, but it's the truth. They were fighting and he shoved her down the stairs. She snapped her neck."

Achilles tenses and looks to me. I don't know what I'm supposed to say to that. Saying "I'm sorry" sounds like the biggest bullshit. I'm still waffling over responses when Helen continues.

"I don't say that so you'll feel sorry for me. It's just one of the many sins to lay at my father's feet. He was a monster, and he raised me, which makes me at least a little bit monstrous." She finally lifts her gaze, and the determination shining from her face is staggering. "So, yeah, I am a spoiled princess, but that's not all I am. I survived him. I'll survive whatever my siblings are planning, too. Maybe there was a time when I might have gone along with their plans, at least in part, in order to keep the peace, but that's not who I am anymore. I deserve to be more than a prize."

My chest twinges with a strength I'm not prepared for. "Helen..."

"I need a little space. I'm going to try to take a nap." She pushes up from the table and walks down the hall to the bedroom. The door closing sounds unnaturally loud in the suite.

I turn to Achilles and sigh. "This is a mess."

"She'll get over her disappointment once this all shakes out." He's frowning, though, and he pushes his plate away without finishing the food he'd been working his way through. "It might take time to earn her forgiveness, but we will." He doesn't sound as confident as normal. "She *has* to forgive us."

I don't think Helen has to do a single thing, up to and including forgive us. Not for this. It makes me a little sick to my stomach. Obviously, everyone who knew Zeus's reputation knew that he wasn't a good guy. Three dead wives, more than a handful of whispered allegations of assault, and a son he ran out of town when he wouldn't fall in line. It all adds up to an unsavory picture. I don't know how I didn't consider what it would be like growing up in that household. If I remember correctly, Helen's mother died when she was a teenager. Her stepmom didn't last more than a handful of years after Zeus remarried.

My skin prickles. "What if this breaks her?"

"Breaks her?" Achilles shakes his head. "Have you met the woman? She's too strong, too fucking stubborn. She might doubt herself sometimes, but like she said, she's a survivor. It will take more than a little disappointment to break her."

I want to believe that. I do. But people are more than just a problem to be solved. Emotions often have nothing to do with logic. If they did, we wouldn't be in this situation to begin with. "I hope so."

Achilles flinches, the tiniest reaction. He slumps back in his chair. "I don't want to break her, but I..."

"You've wanted this for a long time." His reasons for striving to claim the Ares title are just as valid as Helen's, just as rooted in past pain and uncertainty. He's no longer the powerless child who grew up in one of Hera's orphanages and was palmed off to be a soldier for Ares. It's completely understandable that he's seeking to cement his place of power and ambition. Failing to claim it probably won't break him, either, but Achilles has never suffered a true setback once he's decided on an outcome. I don't know how losing would affect him. "I don't know what the answer is."

"That's a first." He gives a tired smile and pushes to his feet. Achilles claps me on the shoulder. "Let's clean this up, toss a snack for Helen into the mini fridge in case she gets hungry later, and do some restorative yoga. You're doing a shitty job of covering up how stiff you are, and it will probably help." He gives a tight smile. "Whatever comes, we'll figure it out."

"No matter what?" It's a child's plea, with no basis in logic, but I can't help making it all the same. I want them both happy. I want this not to be the end. Foolish. So fucking foolish.

"Yeah, Patroclus. No matter what."

We put together some leftovers to store in the mini fridge and snag one of Bellerophon's people to dispose of the rest. Achilles locks the door, and I take one last pass around the suite. With the interviews canceled, we don't have anywhere we have to be today, but there's still the chance of another assassination attempt on Helen. Whoever was pissed she passed the first trial has to be *furious* that she's moving on to the final.

The only light fighting back the darkness of the bedroom is from a crack between the curtains. Helen's huddled in the middle of the bed, the covers pulled up around her head. She looks smaller like this, and my chest gives another uncomfortable lurch. No, not my chest. My fucking heart. Achilles is always going on about how soft I am, but it's not the truth. I can be plenty cold when the situation requires it. Except this one. Helen's planted her roots in my center over the course of a few days. It shouldn't be possible for it to happen this quickly, but my mom always talks about how she looked across the room, saw my other mom, and just *knew*.

I *knew* when I saw Achilles. Maybe not that I'd be in love with him within a week and we'd spend the next twelve years together, but I knew he'd be important to me. That he already *was* important to me.

It didn't hit like a lightning bolt with Helen. Not when we were kids, and certainly not when we collided again as adults. It was more like the tide coming in, each interaction with her a wave that brought me closer to her until this moment. I'm drowning but I don't even miss the taste of air. I want this new reality. I want to be as sure as Achilles that it's possible even if I can't see how in this moment.

I return to find Achilles has pushed the couch back to create room. He watches me closely as I ease onto the ground, eyes narrowed. "We were too rough with you last night?"

"If you were too rough with me, I would have said something." Last night, the pleasure had overcome my aches and bruises, but Achilles was right when he said my body had stiffened up overnight. I hold his gaze. "Just bruises and achy muscles. I'll bitch and moan about it, but I'll be fine."

"I'll hold you to that." He grabs a pillow and helps me get into the first position. Restorative yoga is basically just holding a single position that's fully supported for several long minutes. It's about all I'm capable of right now, which irks me.

I'll recover. I know that. But in time for the third trial?

"I know you're worried about shit. We'll figure it out." Achilles props his elbows on his knees and leans against the couch. "Trust me."

"I do." It's even the truth. If anyone can see us through out of sheer stubbornness, it's this man. We fall into a comfortable silence as I move into the next position. By the time I finish up, I'm still sore as fuck, but my mind feels calmer. I allow Achilles to pull me to my feet and hook the back of his neck to pull him down into a quick kiss. "I love you. Always."

"I love you, too." He smacks my ass. "Now let's go cuddle our princess. She needs the grounding."

"Okay." He's been right about so much, sensing what Helen needs before I can reason through it. They're similar enough in a lot of ways, so that might play into it. I'm not sure. I'm hardly going to complain about the three of us sharing a bed. "I'll take first watch."

"In the bedroom."

I hesitate, but I don't want to argue. Fighting this because I *should* is silly. "Sure."

"Let's go." I follow him into the bedroom, pausing only long enough to shut off the hallway light. He slides beneath the blankets on one side of the bed, and I crawl up to sit against the headboard on her other side. Helen tenses. "Did I invite you?"

"Aw, princess." Achilles drops an arm over her waist and drags her back against him. "You won't make us take naps on the couch, will you? Especially since you're one-third responsible for all the lost sleep last night. You already said how uncomfortable the couch is."

She sighs. "You're trying to provoke me."

"Nah, I just want to cuddle you while Patroclus keeps watch." He brushes a kiss against her temple. "Close your eyes. We'll keep you safe."

She shifts and I nearly startle when her fingers brush my elbow. She follows my arm down to my hand and laces her fingers through mine. My heart twists and surges, and I don't know what the fuck is happening, but I think I might be falling in love with Helen Kasios.

ACHILLES

THE MOMENT WE WALK THROUGH THE TUNNEL AND INTO the arena, it's like entering a different world. I think it's the sheer noise the people in the stands make. It reverberates through my body right down to my bones. The maze is gone as if it'd never been here to begin with. Instead, the oval is sand like it was during the opening ceremony. They're really leaning into the gladiator shit, which is about what I expected since the final trial is combat.

Last person standing becomes the next Ares.

I glance at Patroclus. He's got his game face on, every expression locked down and nothing slipping through. He's wearing his normal gym clothes, and he's limping a bit, but he's moving better than he was yesterday. That's fine. He doesn't have to be in top form for this trial. He's here to watch my back, which means there's no reason for him to be sticking his neck out.

I'll make sure he doesn't feel like he has to, even if I have to eliminate him myself.

I have on clothes similar to the last two trials, gold and black that give me a dark prince kind of vibe. Or that's what Athena's designer informed me when he put together the clothing I was to wear for each event and trial.

Helen is in her warrior queen getup. I watched her put on the golden one-piece earlier, and it had been entertaining and sexy to hear her swear as she wrestled it up her body, but I can't deny that the overall effect is stunning. It's a body suit that leaves her arms bare and stops a few inches above her knees. There's plenty of give so she can move, but the slick surface is similar to the one she wore in the second trial. It will make it damn near impossible to grab her or pin her. She's pulled her hair back into a braid thing that's pinned up around her head—another potential handhold gone— and there's the ever-present gold glitter dusting her skin.

She catches me watching her, and her gaze skates away from me. She's been like this all morning. Skittish. I can't blame her, but part of me wants to comfort her when I should be focused on my end goal within sight. Pass this trial, win the next. Ares is so close, I can taste it.

The camaraderie from the second challenge is gone. We don't have that padding between us any longer. At the end of this trial, one of us will have our dreams crushed, and the others will be left to pick up the pieces.

A shiver of foreboding goes through me. We *will* pick up the pieces. The three of us together work, and that's rare enough that I'm not willing to give it up without a fight. I *like* Helen a whole fucking lot. She'll forgive me eventually. She has to.

The crowd quiets as the spotlights make their way to Athena. She's in another suit, a deep amber one this time that is about as fancy as she gets. She looks good, though. She always looks good. She lifts her hands, instantly commanding the attention of everyone in the space. When they're quiet enough, she speaks. "The final trial is the trial of combat." A pause while people lose their shit. They quiet down faster this time. "The champions will fight until only one remains. Elimination is by tapping out or first blood." She waves a graceful hand to encompass the oval of sand we stand on the edge of. "Choose your weapons, champions. The trial begins in three...two..."

Patroclus tenses. "Batons." He jerks his chin to the right, and I see exactly what he means. There are a trio of expandable batons hanging on a rack halfway around the arena on the right. It means running past several options, but he's right. We should stick to what we know.

"Yeah, okay."

"Don't wait for me. I'll be right behind you."

He turns to Helen, but it's too late. Athena's voice says, "One. Begin." The crowd's screaming drowns out everything else.

I don't hesitate. I sprint across the sand toward the batons. They might not be flashy, but they can break bone easily enough and have a decent reach on them. More importantly, we use them regularly during our tasks for Athena. The heavy handle is comfortable and familiar against my palm.

The feeling of someone behind me surprises me. Surely Patroclus didn't keep up with that sprint? I turn, expecting to see him beside me, but Patroclus is nowhere in sight. Instead, it's Paris bearing down on me, a dagger in his hand. The fucker is aiming it right between my shoulder blades. I dodge back, the sand giving beneath my feet and threatening my balance. Fuck, we should have thought to practice sparring in a sand ring. It's a complication I hadn't anticipated.

Paris strikes again, his face a mask of fury. "I know you're fucking Helen!"

I get my baton up in time, and the knife slides along its edge. The guy isn't going for first blood. He wants me dead. The feeling is entirely mutual. I stagger back another step, allowing him to think he's got me on the ropes. "Did you send the assassin?"

He pauses. "What?"

His confusion seems genuine, but what do I know? I didn't realize Paris was a potential threat until I saw him through Helen's eyes. He could be lying. Ultimately, it doesn't matter. I would have enjoyed eliminating him personally even before I knew that he hurt her, scared her, made her doubt herself. Now, it's personal.

I step to the side to avoid his next attack. He's good, but he's not better than I am. I whip out the baton, so fast it makes a whistling noise. Paris tries to dodge, but I catch the tip of the knife and send it spinning though the air away from us.

He flinches and backs away, his hands outstretched. "Achilles, wait."

"You hurt her." I attack again. Again, he barely avoids the strike. "She trusted you, and you *hurt* her."

"I never touched her! She's lying." He scrambles away, barely staying ahead of me. "It's all bullshit."

His ankle rolls and I'm on him, shoving him off his feet and into the sand. "The baton isn't the best option to draw blood." I kick him, flipping him onto his back. "Guess I'll have to hit you a few times to make sure you're eliminated."

"Achilles!"

I lift the baton over my head. "Stop talking, Paris. You're just going to make me angrier."

"Patroclus!" He points a shaking finger behind me.

I know better. Truly, I do. But I still twist to look behind me.

I find Patroclus instantly. I'm sure I'll always find him, regardless of how many people stand between us. In an arena of only five, there's nothing to distract from the scene playing out before me.

The Minotaur stalks him across the sand, light on his feet despite his big body. Patroclus has found a small knife somewhere, but it looks like a toy in his hand. The Minotaur has a *fucking sword*. It's one of the big ones, big enough that he has to hold it with two hands. Big enough to cut Patroclus in fucking half. I glance up at Athena, but she hasn't moved from the spot where she stood when she announced the start of the trial. There's going to be no last-minute save for any of us.

Patroclus could take the Minotaur in a fair fight. Probably. But right now, when he's favoring his ankle and has bruised ribs limiting his range of motion? It's going to be a fucking bloodbath. The way the Minotaur swings that sword, he doesn't care if he removes limbs to get to Patroclus's blood.

He'll kill him.

Even as the thought crosses my mind, Helen appears like an avenging goddess behind the Minotaur. She raises a pair of daggers and holds his death in her gorgeous face. Our woman doesn't hesitate, striking at his exposed back.

The Minotaur must sense her, because he spins easily out of the way and cuts back at her with a stroke that would take her head if it landed. She ducks easily beneath it, but that doesn't stop my lungs from turning to stone in my chest. Both of them. Both of them are in fucking danger, and they're outmatched.

If the Minotaur lands a blow...

Even as the thought crosses my mind, I'm moving, leaving Paris behind and heading for them. I don't give a fuck if the rules don't encourage murder. Someone tried to kill Helen in the house, and Patroclus is injured right now. The way the Minotaur swings that sword has every alarm bell in my head blaring. He's swiping it at them like he wants to hurt them. Helen is fierce and quick on her feet, but she's too small. She can't take even one hit from that thing. She'll lose a limb, and that's the *best*-case scenario.

And Patroclus? He'll sacrifice himself for her, the fool. I already know it.

I pick up my pace, the sand churning beneath my feet as I pelt across the space. If I can just *get there*, I can stop him. I'm better than this fucker. I know I am.

Helen shifts her grip on the knife like she might throw it but seems to think better of it. Good girl. Never toss a weapon that's still useful. I should have told her that. Fuck, I should have told her a lot of things.

I'm too fucking far away. I'll never make it in time.

The Minotaur picks up momentum, spinning the sword with a comfort that seems like he's done it before. Helen and Patroclus circle him, but they're too aware of each other, too determined to save each other. It's a glaring fault line to exploit, and the Minotaur is smart enough to do exactly that.

He seems to focus on Helen, pressing her hard. She scrambles away from the spinning blade, but the sand is too unsteady beneath her feet. Patroclus lunges to shove her out of the way, hand outstretched and chest wide open.

The Minotaur doesn't miss a beat. He shifts his stance, reversing his cut.

"No!"

It happens so fast. Too fast.

The sword descends. Patroclus's blood sprays, turning his white shirt red. He sinks to his knees almost in slow motion, shock written over his handsome face, and topples to the sand.

"*No!*"

Above us, his face flashes with *Eliminated* written over it. I don't give a shit. I fly across the sand, moving faster than I ever have before. Too slow. All this training, *years* of training, and when it counts, I'm too damn slow. I skid to a stop in front of Patroclus, but there's no time. I can't go to my knees with the enemy standing over us.

"There you are." The Minotaur swings the sword again. He doesn't look happy with the damage he's caused. He doesn't look like anything at all, his expression curiously blank. "Took you long enough to get here." He steps forward, his sword picking up speed again. "Figured you'd both come running when your little boyfriend was threatened."

How could I do anything else? Patroclus is only in this arena right now because I wanted him here. He never would have chosen it on his own. I lift my baton. It seems a pathetic defense against his sword. "Let's do this."

"Gladly."

He comes at me like a tornado, too quick, the sword seeming to be everywhere at once. I land a strike on his thigh, but it barely slows him down. Holy fuck, the man is a monster.

I...don't know if I can beat him.

The thought staggers me. I've never doubted until now, when it matters the most. If I can't do this... I dodge a nasty backswing. He should be slowing down by now. Those swords aren't light, and he hasn't been conserving energy and movement since this started. Except he's *not* slowing down.

I am.

Where the fuck did Helen go?

As if the thought summons her, I catch sight of movement behind him, a flash of gold in the bright stadium lights. It's the only warning we have before Helen launches herself onto his back. She has her knife in a death grip, and for one endless beat of my heart, I think she means to slit his throat. Instead, she drags the tip down the side of his face, spilling his blood to mix with Patroclus's at his feet. "You're done, asshole."

He shakes her off without the slightest bit of effort. She lands on her feet, but only barely. That hesitation costs her. The Minotaur spins on her and brings the sword over his head. Shock nearly roots my feet to the ground. What the fuck is he *doing*? Being eliminated means stopping right fucking now. Why the fuck is he still fighting?

Instinct takes over before my brain has a chance to catch up. I throw myself at his back, taking him down in a messy flying tackle. We hit the sand hard, but he's already swinging those meaty fists, pummeling my sides.

I should disentangle from him, should let the refs take over and handle this because that's their fucking job. I don't. All I can see is him swinging on Helen, cutting Patroclus down. He meant to *kill* them.

I won't let him have another chance at it.

Each punch I land on his face is one less chance he'll have to hurt those I love again. One strike closer to removing him as a threat entirely. He won't touch them again. I'll make fucking sure of it.

Hands grab my arms and I'm hauled off the Minotaur by two refs. He starts to sit up but a third ref grabs him and shoves him back to the sand. I start to struggle, but the ref on my right gets in my face. "You're eliminated. Stand down."

"*What?*"

"Blood was drawn." The ref points at my calf.

I follow their motion and go still. There's an arrow sticking out of my calf. I didn't even feel it. I look up slowly to see Paris standing a good distance away, a bow in his hands and a smirk on his face. "Fuck."

My knees hit the sand, and I have no fucking memory of deciding to kneel. I can't... I can't think about being eliminated right now. I crawl to Patroclus. He has his hands pressed to his stomach, but there's so much fucking blood. I glare at the referee. "We need a medic!"

The woman flinches but shakes her head. "No one enters the arena until the trial is over."

I bend over Patroclus and cover his hands with mine. "I'm so godsdamned sorry."

"My fault. Too...slow." He turns his head to me, too slow, too much effort behind the small move. "Achilles..."

"This isn't how it happens." I can't seem to process that I've been eliminated. It wasn't supposed to happen like this. We had a plan. Fuck, *I* had a plan. The Minotaur. Then Paris. "*Helen.*"

I lost sight of her when I tackled the Minotaur, but surely she isn't eliminated. If Paris wins... We promised her. We fucking *promised* her, and I lost sight of everything in the last few minutes.

I twist to look for her. *There*. Helen stalks Paris, fury written over her perfect face. She's still only got those fucking daggers, and he's got an honest-to-gods bow drawn and pointed in her direction.

He could shoot her. He could fucking *kill* her.

Paris lets loose an arrow and Helen dances to the side, dodging it at the last moment. She narrows her eyes and picks up her pace, sprinting toward him. Paris flinches and scrambles for another arrow. He's got them embedded in the sand at his feet like he's some old-time warrior instead of a cowardly little prick who sat back and let everyone fight it out so he could pick off the winner. He strings another arrow and fires, but Helen drops to the sand and it flies over her head.

I chance a glance at Patroclus. He's still breathing and he wraps his hands around my wrists. The strength of his grip reassures me. "She'll do it."

I follow his gaze to Helen again. I want her to win. Of course I do. It's not even a contest between her and Paris. But I can't *think* properly right now. Not with her and Patroclus still in danger. Not with my entire plan upended.

A third arrow flies. She spins out of the way like a dancer, light on her feet and using the turn to pick up momentum until she's flying over the sand.

She's so close now. Less than ten feet from him. Paris grabs another arrow, but he's panicking, his movements clumsy. He nearly drops it. That's all the opening she needs. The little fool flings one of her knives at him. Fifty percent chance it hits, and even that's optimistic.

Except it does.

It takes him in the shoulder, spinning Paris away from his fucking arrows and into the wall surrounding the main arena. He slides to the ground, clutching his shoulder and screaming something I can't hear over the cheers of thousands of people around us.

Helen takes one more step before she seems to remember herself. She straightens and turns to face Athena. From this angle, I can't see her expression, but there's a fury in the set of her shoulders that practically dares Athena to do anything but declare her the winner.

Athena stares down at her for a long time, long enough for the cheers to die down and the silence to gain an eerie quality. Finally she lifts her hands. "We have a winner. Congratulations...Ares."

The arena goes wild.

On the sand, medics rush out from one of the arches, teams splitting up to take each of the injured champions. I wave mine off. I'm barely injured. A fucking *scratch*. That's all it took to snatch my dreams from me. I was so close. So fucking close.

It's...over.

I've lost.

My dreams are dead and gone, and it's my own damn fault.

HELEN

I CAN'T STOP SHAKING. I NEED TO SEE PATROCLUS, TO MAKE sure he's okay. The medics have him on a stretcher, and they move past me as they carry him out of the arena. I barely get a glimpse of his pale face before he's gone.

The referees march the Minotaur out behind him. They keep looking at the big man as if they're not sure whether he'll leave peacefully. His words still ring in my ears. *Figured you'd both come running when your little boyfriend was threatened.* He *used* Patroclus to draw Achilles and me to him. Guilt has me in a choke hold.

If I'd been stronger...

If I'd eliminated the Minotaur before he had a chance to nearly kill Patroclus...

If...

Achilles limps toward the exit. He barely looks at me as he passes. I should give him space, should let him process what the fuck just happened. *I* haven't processed what happened, so I can't imagine he has.

But I can't. Fear swamps me, stronger than I could have anticipated. "Achilles."

He doesn't look at me, doesn't stop, doesn't so much as slow down.

The feeling gets worse. "Achilles, *talk to me*."

He barely hesitates. "You got what you wanted, Helen. Get that sad look off your face." He's still not looking at me, instead offering me his perfect profile. "Celebrate."

The bottom of my stomach drops out. "Was it all bullshit? The talk of the future and keeping me?"

He shakes his head. "I have to go with Patroclus to the hospital. I'll talk to you later."

It doesn't sound like a promise. He tosses out the words as if he'll say whatever it takes to end this conversation. To end...this.

I don't call his name again. I stand there and watch him walk away, taking a chunk of my heart with him. When did *that* happen? I've said from the beginning that we didn't have a future. Not me and him. Not me and Patroclus. Certainly not the three of us. It doesn't matter how well we meshed during the trials or the way they seemed to see me or...

A sob catches in my chest, but I refuse to release it. This is what I wanted, what I've fought so hard to accomplish. I'm realizing my dreams and ensuring all of Olympus is forced to take me seriously.

Achilles is right. I should be celebrating and doing a victory lap. I shouldn't be standing here and trying not to cry.

Bellerophon appears at my side as if by magic, their expression carefully blank. "I need you to come with me, Ares."

Ares.

I did it. I fucking *won*. No one can look at me and believe I'm just a pretty face, a pawn to be moved about the chessboard at the whim of those more powerful than I am. I should be elated and celebrating and riding a high unlike any other.

Instead, I just want to make sure Patroclus is okay, to talk to Achilles properly and have him reassure me that everything he said yesterday wasn't just bullshit. That he really meant it now that we're staring the future right in the face.

"*Ares.*"

I take a breath and try to calm my racing heart, to *think*. My actions have consequences: both entering the tournament and winning it. As much as I want to chase after Achilles and Patroclus until this awful gaping wound in my chest is healed, becoming Ares means I have responsibilities beyond my own personal needs.

My men will have to wait. Hopefully they'll still be there for me after everything that's happened.

I've barely let myself consider that they might actually be mine, and now it may very well be over. I close my eyes, take another breath, and when I open them, I have my game face on. *I am Ares and I will not be underestimated.*

I smile up at Bellerophon. "Lead the way."

They don't speak until we've entered one of the arches—a different one than we've been entering and exiting for the trials—and head up a flight of stairs. "There will be a formal event introducing you as Ares tonight, but the title was officially yours the moment you won the third trial."

I can't read anything in their tone about their thoughts on

my winning. That's just as well. Plenty of people will be pissed about it, and I need to get used to it. That doesn't mean I can't be gracious in this moment. "Thank you for hosting the champions. I know it wasn't an easy duty."

Bellerophon doesn't comment on that. We take another set of stairs up. My adrenaline is still going strong, but I can already sense the crash coming. Too much, too quickly. This is exactly what I wanted, so I should be happy, right? I don't understand this strange sense of loss that feels like someone wrapped me in a lead blanket and tossed me off a pier.

They open the door at the top of this flight of stairs and step back. "They're waiting."

I don't know why I'm surprised to see my brother standing next to Athena. He might not have been visible in the box seat when she made the announcements, but he's not the type to let something this important pass without witnessing it.

Perseus has on a charcoal-gray suit with a cream shirt underneath it. The only sign that he's less than perfectly put together are the faint creases in his slacks that almost look like he was gripping the fabric in his fists like he used to when he was a child and trying not to react. But that's ridiculous. Perseus hasn't shown that kind of loss of control since our mother died. Longer, even.

Athena waits for the door to shut behind me to sigh. "Well, you fucked that right up, didn't you?"

"Excuse me?"

"It's too late to worry about it now. You're Ares, for better or worse." She checks her phone. "I need to go check on my men."

"Wait." The word is out before I can call it back. "Is Patroclus going to be okay?"

Athena's dark eyes flash, the only outward sign that she's furious right now. "He's on his way to the hospital now. The damage was too much for the medics to handle, so it'll be up to the surgeon. They had *damn well* better save him."

Save him. Because he might die.

"No." Panic flares, strong enough to rock me back on my heels. I turn for the door. "I'm coming too."

"Plant your feet, Ares," she snaps. She waits for me to look at her again to continue. "You're new to the Thirteen, so I'll let that insult slide despite the fact that you should know better, being a Kasios. You are Ares now." She speaks slowly, but it's not patronizing. "I am Athena. Those men, Achilles and Patroclus? They're *my* people, which means they're *my* responsibility. Do not spend your first day as Ares stepping on my toes, or I'll make you regret it."

I open my mouth to argue but manage to hold the words back at the last minute. She's right. It doesn't matter what promises the men and I made... Except *were* they promises? They certainly sounded like it when Achilles spoke with such confidence, but that was before he brushed me off just now, before he walked away without looking back.

He's never going to forgive you. It was a nice dream while it lasted, but it's over now.

I inhale slowly. If I ignore Athena's warning and show up at the hospital, there's a decent chance neither of the men will want to see me. I don't think they lied, exactly, but I know how quickly people stop saying what you want to hear when you stop giving them what *they* want.

Achilles thought he'd become Ares. When he made those promises, it was with the intent of *me* bending when all the chips were down. He never actually thought I had a chance of winning, and his confidence reflected that. Now that he's lost his dream?

He won't forgive me.

He certainly won't play second fiddle to *me* being Ares.

I swallow hard. Would I feel differently if our positions were reversed? It's easy to pretend I would have gotten over it and we'd dance our way to some happy little triad, but the loss of something I've wanted with every fiber of my being? I can't say I'd be able to look him in the face, married or no.

When I speak, my tone is perfectly cordial, doing nothing to reflect the loss driving its roots deep into me. "Of course, Athena. My apologies."

"Better." She sweeps past me and out of the room.

I can see the storm brewing in Perseus's blue eyes, and I want nothing more than to follow Athena out the door to avoid it, but I didn't come this far to be cowardly when it counted. I got what I wanted, and that means facing down the consequences of my actions.

I'm one of the Thirteen now, after all. I lift my chin. "Zeus."

"No. You don't get to call me Zeus right now." He drags his hands through his hair. "What the fuck, Helen? Do you know the trouble you've caused? I've been putting out fucking fires for the last week while you gallivanted around—"

"I'm going to stop you there." I start to wrap my arms around myself but stop and straighten. "You don't get to take the high road with me, Perseus. Yeah, I became a champion without talking to you first, but after I was *fucking attacked*, *you* didn't even come by to see if I was okay."

Immediately, he goes cold. Covering up messier emotions. We're all such liars in my family, myself included. My brother finally says, "I had my reasons."

"Do tell." I wait, but he doesn't seem inclined to share. Fine. I draw myself up. "As the new Ares, I *will* be taking that prisoner back. They're key to discovering the responsible parties and ensuring no other attacks are leveled against other members of the Thirteen and their families. As Ares, that's *my* specialty, and not even you can stop me."

"They claimed diplomatic immunity."

That pulls me up short. "Excuse me?"

"The attacker. They were one of Minos's people." He says it so casually, his tone belying the careful way he watches me as if I might spring into violence at any moment. "They weren't a citizen of the city, and as such, Minos requested leave to be the one to exact punishment. He removed them from Olympus."

I force myself not to react, to slow down long enough to piece out what he's saying...and what he isn't. "You can't seriously believe that Minos had no knowledge of the attack. That doesn't even make sense. What are the odds that one of his carefully selected people randomly decided to sneak into my room and try to kill me?"

"My hands are tied."

"*Why?*" When he doesn't immediately answer, I press. "You're

Zeus. You get to make the executive call when it comes to strangers in Olympus. There's no reason they need to be here now that the title of Ares is filled. You don't have to let them stay. Send them home."

For a moment, Perseus looks so fucking tired that if we were a hugging family, I might try to hug him. It doesn't last. His moments of weakness never do. He shakes his head and straightens his shoulders. "There are extenuating circumstances." For a moment, I think he won't continue, but he sighs. "I suppose you'll be briefed on it officially tomorrow with the rest of the Thirteen. Minos brought news of a credible threat against Olympus. He wants to cut a deal in return for sharing that information."

I snort. "Sounds like bullshit to me."

"Yeah." Perseus gives a ghost of a smile. "But because of the situation, I can't make the call by myself. It will come to a vote on how to deal with him. If he's telling the truth and does have details about this threat that are valuable... We can't afford to turn it away."

"But *why*? We're separate from the rest of the world. What could he possibly offer that makes it worth the risk of allowing him to stay within the city limits?"

He looks out over the arena and then back to me. "The barrier is failing."

I go still. "You're shitting me." I shake my head, stunned. "How? Why?"

"If I knew that, I could fix it. Or at least try." He gives a ghost of a smile, but it fades quickly. "It's easier to slip in and out than it was a generation ago, even a decade ago. We've worked hard to keep it quiet, so only the Thirteen and a few of Poseidon's people know, but that won't last for long. We can no longer guarantee that we're protected from outside assault."

True fear slices through me. This is big. Really big. If we have to go to war, a huge portion of the responsibility for soldiers and combat will rest on *my* shoulders, and as Achilles was quick to point out before, I have a steep learning curve ahead of me before I'm ready for something like that. "Perseus, surely there's information in the archives about the barrier." I've looked myself, but there are sections that only Apollo has access to, and he's not the sharing type. He'd answer Zeus's questions, though. He wouldn't have a choice. "There's—"

"We've been looking." My brother shakes his head. "The records were destroyed at some point, and if there are backups, we can't find them. It's the first thing I tasked Apollo with when I took over." His mouth twists. "Our father didn't feel it was a high enough priority to investigate."

"I had no idea," I say faintly.

"We aren't exactly advertising it." He runs his hands through his hair. "I don't know how long the barrier will last or if it will survive a full-on assault. No matter how distasteful the transaction, we can't afford to refuse any potential information Minos has." He meets my gaze. "Not even if I suspect him of being responsible for the attack on you."

I want to be mad about that, but I can't. I might not like being left in the dark, but I can't deny that my brother is doing his best for Olympus. I swallow hard. "I see."

"Like I said, we'll discuss options in full in a few days when the entire Thirteen meets."

It strikes me then, why this feels so different. "Dad never had the whole Thirteen meet. He just made executive decisions and expected everyone to fall in line."

"I know." Perseus looks away. "I'm not him, Helen. I might be a monster, but I'm Olympus's monster. Everything I do, I do for this city and the people in it. We need the entire Thirteen unified if there's an outside threat." He pauses. "Will you stand with me?"

What kind of question is that? Except as I consider it, consider him, I realize I'm not a sure thing from Perseus's view. He's treated me like a piece to be moved about the board, has used and misused me. Our father preached loyalty to family above all else, but we both know it's bullshit. Gods, Perseus hasn't even given a proper apology, and as much as I love him, I know better than to hold my breath and wait for one. I could—should—hate my brother for what he's done.

But this is Olympus.

We're all monsters here.

Even monsters have to work together when threatened by an outside force. I'm sure Achilles... I stop the thought before it can reach completion. It doesn't matter what Achilles would or wouldn't do. I can't make decisions based on his and Patroclus's theoretical position in my life when it's all but guaranteed they'll never want to see me again.

Helen Kasios may have had time and space to mourn something like the loss currently residing deep inside me. Ares doesn't. With the safety of Olympus in the balance, I will do my duty. "Yes," I finally say. "I'll stand with you."

He nods and walks past me to the door, only to pause with his hand on the knob. "Helen."

"Yes?"

"You being Ares fucks things up. It will make it harder to get some members of the Thirteen on our side. It makes our family look power-hungry and greedy, which complicates everyone's life."

The words sting, but I manage to keep a sarcastic reply internal. Mostly. "And?"

He glances over his shoulder. For a moment, the briefest blink, his eyes warm up and his smile is bright and sharp just like it used to be before our father beat every soft emotion out of him. "I'm proud of you. You were amazing out there." He opens the door and walks out of the room before I can work though my shock to come up with an answer.

My brother is proud of me.

Maybe pigs will fly next.

Still not an apology. I shake my head. Apparently I can't help wishing for the moon even when I'm getting everything I ever wanted. It's exceedingly frustrating to have to keep reminding myself of that fact.

"I am Ares. I did it." Even speaking it aloud does nothing to dispel the cloud of loss around me. The feeling in my throat gets worse. I press my hand there, as if the physical touch can do anything to alleviate the emotional. "Damn it." I understand that Achilles was worried about Patroclus. *I'm* worried about Patroclus. But...couldn't he have thrown me a single sentence of comfort? Something to convey that we *would* talk later rather than brushing me off?

I can't go to him. Not without pissing off Athena, but even without her in play, it feels wrong to show up uninvited. If they don't want to see me, it's cruel to force them to.

Before I can take a step, the door flies open and Eris, Hermes, and Dionysus pour into the room, towing Eros and Psyche behind them. Dionysus sweeps me up into a hug and spins me around until I feel sick. "Ares! Look at you, little warrior!"

"Put her down before she barfs on you." Eris barely lets my feet touch the ground before she takes my shoulders. "You are the biggest pain in the ass a big sister could be, but you were wonderful out there. The way you handled the maze! Eliminating the Minotaur!" She shakes her head. "Always an agent of chaos."

"Always," I say faintly.

I should be happy to see my friends. This is what I wanted, after all. We stand on the same level now. I'm no longer being left behind. I just...I didn't expect the win to feel so hollow.

As Dionysus and Eris cut to the bar at the back of the box seat, Hermes and Psyche chat easily like old friends. *This is what I wanted. This is everything I wanted. I'm Ares.* Too bad it feels like I'm missing a limb.

"Hey." Eros nudges me with his shoulder. He looks as good as always, for all that he's dressed down in a pair of jeans and a knit sweater. His wife's influence, no doubt. The obvious way they love each other makes my chest ache.

"Hey." I try for a smile, but it wobbles around the edges.

He watches Psyche laugh at something Hermes says while Dionysus pours out six drinks. "Hermes told me a wild rumor a few days ago." He says it so casually, voice pitched low to only carry to me. "She claims you're hooking up with both Achilles and Patroclus."

The wobble in my bottom lip gets worse despite myself. "I like them. For real. Maybe more than like." I don't know why I'm confessing to him. We're friends, but some wounds are best kept hidden. I can't quite seem to manage it in the face of his presence.

"Sometimes love comes at you fast." His blue eyes warm when Psyche laughs again. She's a pretty plus-sized white woman with excellent style and one of the savviest minds I've ever encountered. She plays it down and pretends she's just a social-media influencer—all beauty and no brains—but she's equally as dangerous as her mother, Demeter. I like her quite a bit. She makes my friend happy, and she's given him a chance for real love for the first time in his life.

"You've got rose-tinted glasses on, Eros. What you have is rarer than red diamonds. Not everyone gets that."

"Maybe." He shrugs. "You won't know until you try."

You won't know until you try.

Becoming Ares has complicated that. I can't get to Patroclus and Achilles without stepping on Athena's toes, and that isn't an option. Not when it might mean a split Thirteen. My brother's right; if there's an outside threat, our petty rivalries shouldn't stand in the way of an allied Thirteen. Unfortunately, I know too well how *should* doesn't mean shit. I can't threaten that. I *can't*.

But Eros isn't one of the Thirteen.

"Remember that time I banked a favor from you?" I wait for him to nod to continue. "I'd like to call it in now, please."

"I'm listening."

I shift closer and lower my voice. "Would you check on Patroclus? He was injured and I want to make sure he's okay. I can't do it without stepping on Athena's toes, and she'll never forgive me for starting out my time as Ares by fucking with her."

Eros lifts his brows. "That all?"

Was that all? The cowardly part of me wants to leave it at that, but I've come this far. Maybe my feelings for my men will blow up in my face, but if I don't *try*, then it definitely will. I drag in a breath. "And tell them..." Gods, why is it so hard to get this out? "Tell them that I still want that pretty future they painted. If they do, that is."

He waits, but what else is there to say? That I think I might have gone straight past falling in love and into love itself? That I want Achilles's wonderful and aggravating assurance at my back for whatever comes next, no matter how large or small? That I want Patroclus's brilliant mind and stern determination to take care of us? Eros wouldn't understand, and laying myself bare even this much is almost more than I can handle. "That's all."

He nods. "Do you want me to go now?"

The longer I have to wait for an answer, the worse it will be. Not just for what happens next. Patroclus has to be okay. He *has* to be. "Please."

"Consider it done." Eros slings an arm around my shoulders and pulls me into a brief hug. He kisses the top of my head. "You did well out there. Kicked a lot of ass."

"Thanks." I manage a smile this time, but barely. No matter what we said yesterday, there is no happily-ever-after guaranteed. Achilles believed with his whole heart that he would become Ares.

How can he stand next to me when it will feel like he's standing in my shadow? And Patroclus? No matter how strong our connection and history, he has a foundation-deep love with Achilles. If it becomes a choice between the two of us, it's no choice at all. I would never ask that of him, either.

I inhale slowly and exhale just as slowly. I'm dirty and sweaty and exhausted, and all I want to do is go home and sleep for three days until this new world settles around me. That might have been an option for Helen, but it's not an option for Ares.

I square my shoulders, paste a smile on my face, and head to join my sister and friends at the box-seat bar.

ACHILLES

I GO STRAIGHT FROM THE ARENA TO THE HOSPITAL, following the ambulance they stuffed Patroclus into. He needs surgery, though the nurses keep telling me it isn't serious, that the doctor is optimistic, that he'll be just fine. *Optimistic.* That shit isn't a sure thing. I pace around the waiting room until they find an empty room to stash me in.

I wait and wait and wait. I'm practically climbing the walls as the minutes tick by without news, two thoughts rolling through my head at regular intervals.

I need him to be okay.

Helen should be here.

Except she's not Helen anymore, is she? She's Ares. She got what she always wanted, snatched that shit right out of my hands even if she wasn't the one to eliminate me. Why would she be worried about me, about Patroclus now? It's not a fair thought, but it's clear she has no intention of coming. She would have shown up by now if she wanted to be here.

More than that... I don't know if I'm ready to see her. The future I had in my head, the one I'd been working toward for years, is gone. No matter what else is true, I will never be Ares now. Without that title...

I drag my hands over my face. I don't know what the fuck I'm doing. I can't find my feet, can't figure out next steps, until I know Patroclus is okay. He'll figure out the future for both of us.

Unless he doesn't want me anymore. I'm not the winner he fell in love with. It's my fault he got hurt. He wouldn't even have been in the tournament if not for me. He begged me to leave him behind in the second trial and I ignored him.

I curse. Patroclus wouldn't dump me for not securing the title. That's not how he operates, no matter what my sudden insecurity is sure of. No, it's far more likely that things with Patroclus will fall apart if we can't find a way forward with Helen. He got a taste of how well she balanced the two of us. How can he be satisfied with only me now that he's had her, too?

A knock on the door has me spinning on my heel, but the person who steps inside isn't a nurse and it's sure as fuck not Helen. It's Eros. I know who he is, know who his mother was to Patroclus's moms. Enemy. Rival. Danger. Eros and I have never had reason to cross paths. He plays the part of the golden fuckboy, and I'm the soldier. Or at least both those things used to be true. Now Eros has, by all appearances, settled down into domestic life with Psyche Dimitriou.

And me? I don't know who I am anymore. "What are you doing here?"

"Giving Hermes a respite from playing messenger." He leans

against the door. He might look like a playboy, but everyone knows the rumor about him. When his mother was still Aphrodite, he was her fixer. She pointed him at the people she wanted taken out and pulled the trigger. What the fuck is he doing *here*?

I cross my arms over my chest. "I'm listening."

"Helen can't come. You're Athena's people, and she doesn't want the new Ares anywhere near you." He narrows his eyes. "I also get the feeling that she's not sure of her welcome."

"Sounds like excuses to me." If I were in Helen's place, I would have told Athena to fuck off, no matter how much I admire her. Patroclus matters more than anything.

"Spoken like a man with more brawn than brain."

I start to snarl back, but I can't help thinking about the conversation we had with Helen after the second trial. She might not have any experience leading soldiers, but her brain is more than twisty enough to be at home steeped in the Thirteen's fucked-up politics. I have a prior relationship with Athena, which might have smoothed the way when I became Ares, but I know better than most that she bends for no one.

Would she truly have kept me from Patroclus?

The thought leaves me cold.

"Ah. Maybe there is a brain in there after all." Eros shrugs. "It's not my business. I'm only here to deliver Helen's message. She said, and I quote, 'Tell them that I still want that pretty future they painted. If they do, that is.'"

She wants a future with us. I don't know whether to laugh or curse. This is probably some fucked-up version of karma for being so sure that she'd forgive me if I took Ares from her, but it's not the same. *It's not the same.* Without Ares, Helen is still a Kasios. She might be a pawn moved about by her brother, but she has power. Only a fool would say she doesn't. People will remember her forever, would have even before she entered her name as a contender for Ares.

Even before she won.

I know who I am as Athena's second-in-command. It's not the role I wanted to play forever, but I understand the parameters. I'm good at it, too. The best.

If I gamble it all on Helen, that means sacrificing my place beneath Athena. She's not one to allow her people to serve two masters, and starting a romantic relationship with Ares is exactly that. Leaving her command means there's no going back. If things fall apart with Helen, I'll truly be left with nothing. "She's asking too much."

"If you say so." Eros sighs like I've disappointed him. I don't get how. I barely know the guy. "Look, Helen is a friend, so I'm going to be uncharacteristically straight with you. Her charging to your side and defying Athena on her first day as Ares might sound romantic as fuck, but every action she makes now has consequences. There's something happening in Olympus, something beyond the petty politics, and she can't afford to make enemies right now. Not for anyone. It's not just your lover's life on the line." He pulls open the door. "I'll be in the waiting room until Patroclus gets out of surgery because she wants an update on him. If you decide you want to send a message back, that's where you can find me." He leaves without another word.

"Dick," I mutter.

I can't settle down, though. Helen's words from yesterday come back to haunt me. How she said I wasn't prepared for what it really means to be one of the Thirteen. I thought she was full of shit at the time, but who the fuck cares about someone and lets politics get in the way of making sure they're okay?

I know what I would have done in her position.

Even knowing there might be far-reaching complications, I can't say I'd do anything differently if I had won the title of Ares. Patroclus is mine. Olympus can burn if it means making sure he's okay.

Rationally, I see why Helen made the choice she did, but I don't know if it matters. The risk is too high with so little guaranteed payoff. For the first time in my life, I can't see a way forward. I don't have my internal assurance that I'll realize the future I want.

I...failed.

I'll come to terms with that—I know myself well enough to understand that—but I can't think of anything at all until I'm assured Patroclus made it through surgery and I see him with my own eyes. Everything else can wait until then.

The door opens again, and this time it's Athena who appears. She looks as perfectly put together as she appeared on the screen in the arena, only a faint tightness around her eyes giving lie to the image. "Patroclus is out of surgery and in recovery." She holds up a hand when I start forward. "They need time to get him settled, but as soon as it's possible, you'll get access to his room."

Not soon enough, but I trust Athena. If she says he made it through surgery, then he did. I exhale in a rush. Relief makes me a little dizzy, but I can barely believe it for truth. I need to see him.

I need him to anchor me in the middle of this storm. I can't see a path, but surely Patroclus will be able to. "This is so fucked."

"Without a doubt." She shakes her head slowly. "I'm going to be frank with you."

I stop short. Athena doesn't usually couch her criticism by easing people into it. She's frank and to the point, and that's one of the many reasons we are so loyal to her. "When are you anything but blunt with me?"

She smiles a little, but it doesn't reach her eyes. "We're in trouble. Olympus. I don't know all the details yet, but Minos brought in information when he brought his people. There's a threat on the horizon, and I don't know that the barrier will protect us from it." She hesitates but finally says, "We needed you as Ares."

Bitterness claws up my throat at the reminder of my failure. Athena never mentioned that there might be the potential for an attempted invasion, but it just reinforces that with me as Ares, there would be no unknowns. Even though I'm conflicted as fuck right now, I still find myself saying, "Helen will surprise you."

"Maybe. I still would rather it have been you."

I shrug, but I'm unable to keep the tension out of my voice. "Take that up with Paris." Easier to blame him than to admit I fucked up. The moment Helen and Patroclus were in danger, I forgot about eliminating Paris and ran for them. I kept fighting the Minotaur even after he was eliminated because I wanted to remove him as a threat—and *that* had nothing to do with the tournament.

Helen was the one who eliminated the Minotaur and didn't

stick around to beat him to a pulp. She immediately went for Paris. That's why she won and I didn't. If I'd been paying attention, I could have dodged Paris's arrows, too.

I lost sight of my goal.

Helen didn't.

"Mmm." Athena moves to the single window in the room and stares out. "He's still in surgery. It will be a while before we know for sure, but it's looking like Helen did permanent damage to his shoulder. He won't ever draw a bow again."

"Considering how often people use *bows*, I doubt that will slow him up any." Which is a damn shame. That asshole better crawl back into whatever glittering hole he left when he entered the tournament, because if I see him on the street, I'm not certain I'll be able to control the impulse to beat his handsome face in.

"All the same." She shrugs. "Either way, we don't deal with things as we wish they were; we deal with them as reality deals us the cards. Helen Kasios just became Ares in a moment when we need someone with military experience. It's not ideal."

She's not wrong, but it still pricks at me to hear her talk about Helen that way. "She might not have the combat experience, but she's got politics down to a science. She's not a bad fit. Like I said, I think she'll surprise you."

"Maybe." Athena studies me for a long moment. "Bellerophon says you and Patroclus got rather...close...with her."

"Bellerophon should know better than to gossip like a teenager," I snap.

"You know better." She's being careful, but Athena doesn't have much patience for dancing around a topic. "You're the best damn second-in-command I've ever had, and I'm going to need your skill set in the coming confrontation." She hesitates. "But I will respect whatever decision you make in regard to the future."

"Athena." I wait for her to look at me. "If I resign and end up changing my mind..."

Her smile is bittersweet. "You're smarter than that, Achilles. That decision is one that will stick. For better or worse, the fact is appearances matter in this city. I can't have my position undermined by welcoming back Ares's cast-offs." She moves to the door. "Whatever your decision ends up being, be sure it's what you want, because you'll have to live with it." Then she's gone, closing the door softly behind her.

Everyone's making a dramatic exit today.

It's another hour before a nurse comes and collects me, herding me down the hall and up an elevator and through another series of halls to the room where Patroclus lies in a hospital bed. He looks too pale, too thin. It has the fear from before rushing back, amplifying. "He's going to be okay?"

"The doctor will explain everything." The nurse hesitates, but she must read the panic on my face because she leans closer and lowers her voice. "He'll make a full recovery. There might be some hiccups along the way, but he'll be fine."

I don't know if I believe her. I *have* to believe her. "Thanks."

"He'll wake up when he's ready. Please be patient." With one last significant look at me, she slips out of the room.

He looks...small. Patroclus lies on the bed, hooked up to several machines, his skin even paler than normal. Guilt pricks me, digging deep. The only reason he was in the tournament in the first place was to watch my back. I should have let him be eliminated in the second trial like he wanted, should have listened to him every time he warned me of the danger of pushing forward stubbornly. I bullied him into entering, and then I bullied him into continuing even when he was injured. I wanted him with me, and that selfish desire is the reason he's in this bed now, still and drained.

I might not have wielded the sword that cut him, but this is my fault.

There's not as much space here as there was downstairs, and I'm afraid if I start pacing again, I'll knock into his bed and cause him pain on accident or something. So I don't. I force my restless energy down deep and drop into the chair next to his bed.

It's like the bastard was waiting for me to stop moving, because he opens his eyes almost immediately. "Achilles?" Even his voice is fucked up, raspy and too quiet.

I drag the chair forward and take his hand. "I'm here." Touching him calms me a little, though it does nothing to remove the guilt plaguing me. My chest goes tight and awful. *He's okay. That's the only thing that matters. He's okay.*

"I fucked up."

"I think it's more than safe to say the only one who really fucked up is me." The horrible feeling in my chest shows up in my voice, making the words thick. "I got you into this mess because I couldn't bear the thought of not having you at my side. You got hurt—twice—because I didn't give a fuck about anything but *my* needs. I'm sorry. I know that's not enough, but I'm fucking sorry, Patroclus."

"Achilles..." Patroclus grips my hand hard. It's much weaker than he's normally capable of, but he gets his point across. "*Did Paris win Ares?*"

"No."

He exhales and goes limp. "Thank the gods. If after everything, Helen was married to that bastard… We promised her that it wouldn't happen." His eyes fly open. "Wait, that means Helen is Ares."

"Yes." The bitterness is back in my tone, but even I don't know if I'm bitter at Helen or the entire situation. I shake my head slowly. "You should have seen her. She dodged three arrows and threw one of her knives at him."

"Risky," he murmurs.

"She pulled it off." I find myself smiling despite everything. "Hit him right in the shoulder joint and knocked his ass to the ground."

Patroclus squeezes my hand. "I'm sorry."

"What do *you* have to be sorry for?" I'm speaking too harshly, but there's only one person in this room that fucked up spectacularly, and it's me.

He smiles faintly. "I know you wanted Ares. I'm sorry you didn't get to live out your dream."

I hesitate, but Patroclus is in this with me, too, and I can't hold back information from him, no matter how Athena's words still churn away in the back of my mind. "Athena came by the hospital." He doesn't speak, so I force myself to continue. "She says she wants me to stay on as her second-in-command. I guess Bellerophon reported about how *close* we got with Helen, and she wanted to let me know that in order to pursue things with the new Ares, it means resigning with Athena. Do that, and there's no going back."

"Ah."

I wait, but Patroclus doesn't offer any brilliant insight. "Well?"

"Well, what?" He leans back and gives my hand another squeeze. "I can't tell you what the right call is, Achilles. It's a big decision, and you're the only one who can make it."

"What the fuck are you talking about?"

He shakes his head. "It's up to you to decide if the cost is too high."

I consider his words, what he did and didn't say. "You're going to Helen."

"I'm not choosing," Patroclus says firmly. "I love you. I will always love you. But I can't ignore what I feel for her, either."

"Athena won't be happy if you try to straddle that line."

He shrugs. "Then I'll resign and see if Apollo's willing to hire me. He's one who sees value in information, so he won't balk if I pursue a relationship with the new Ares and also with Athena's second-in-command."

"You've thought about this." I can't tell if I'm accusing him or not.

"I thought you'd become Ares." He finally looks away. "I honestly hadn't thought about contingency plans leading into the third trial. But, Achilles..." He meets my gaze. "I know you. You weren't talking out your ass about keeping Helen. If you weren't serious, you never would have brought it up. Did things really change that quickly just because you didn't become Ares?"

I don't have an easy answer. I don't know if an easy answer

exists. Finally, I say, "If I try with Helen and it blows up in my face, I'll actually have lost everything. It's not an easy choice for me."

"Isn't it?"

I open my mouth but stop before I keep arguing. Is Patroclus right? Yeah, it's a risk to resign and go to Helen. She might have been playing a deeper game during the tournament, manipulating us into being allies who will watch her back, but...

I don't believe it. Not for a second.

The connection between the three of us was real. More than that, I *get* Helen. I don't have to be brilliant like Patroclus to understand the woman. She felt safe with us. She showed us vulnerability. That was real. I'm sure of it.

I sit back in the uncomfortable hospital chair but maintain my grip on Patroclus's hand. As usual, he's right. If what we shared was real, then there's no choice at all. I expected Helen to get over her loss of dreams when I won. It's hypocritical in the extreme to not be willing to do the same, even if I'm afraid. I shake my head, a reluctant smile pulling at my lips. "You really are a smart motherfucker."

He smiles in return. "You would have figured it out eventually. I just helped things along." He squeezes my hand, already feeling stronger. "You've always had enough faith for both of us. It's my turn now. It will work out with Helen. I'm sure of it."

"I believe you." The door opens and a tall white man in surgical scrubs walks in. The doctor. I glance at Patroclus. "Let's figure out what the damage is so we can get you checked out of this place and go get our girl."

HELEN

ATTENDING A MEETING WITH ALL THE MEMBERS OF THE Thirteen is one of the most surreal experiences of my life. My father made it a habit of keeping them as separate as possible, aside from his endless parties, but even if he hadn't, *I* would not have had a place at the massive oblong table we occupy now.

I study them each in turn, all too aware of the way they study me right back. There are my brother and Eris, of course, him at the head of the table and her across from me. Hermes and Dionysus sit close with their heads together, whispering and pretending they don't see the way Poseidon glares in disapproval. He's a giant white man with short red hair and an even redder beard, and he looks like he can haul shipping containers around with his bare hands.

Then there's Demeter sitting passively with her hands folded on the table. She's a white woman in her fifties with a distinct earth-mother vibe that almost manages to hide the sharp ambition in her hazel eyes.

Next is Apollo. I haven't interacted with him a ton, but I'm a big fan of Cassandra, who works for him. He's an East Asian man who's about my age and who doesn't often contribute to the political backbiting so common with this group. He catches my eye and gives me something resembling a reassuring smile. I smile back, even though I don't trust him as far as I can throw him.

Hades and Callisto—Hera—sit together at the end of the table across from my brother. Callisto is Hades's sister-in-law, so their easy way with each other make sense, but it still weirds me out. I notice a vein in my brother's temple throbbing as he looks at them, but he glances away and smooths out his expression.

Hephaestus and Artemis are cousins, both sharing the same light-brown skin and glossy dark hair. They're also wearing identical expressions of distrust as they watch me. I won't find allies in that corner, but hopefully they'll be willing to work together to protect Olympus.

The door opens and our final member arrives. Athena is wearing a cream suit and walks with purpose as she moves to my brother's right hand. She catches my eye, but I can't decipher her expression. It's not warm, but it's not icy, either.

My brother clears his throat. "It's time to have a frank discussion."

The next two hours are a study in frustration. I knew the Thirteen were fractured, but seeing it firsthand has me digging my nails into my palm to keep from yelling at them. My brother lays out the information he has, but Hephaestus, Artemis, and Poseidon argue that he's exaggerating the threat to consolidate power for himself. Dionysus and Hermes make quips at everyone, though they watch the proceedings with sharp eyes. My sister has plenty of opinions, but even I'm not sure if she's supporting our brother or not. I swear she's simply playing coy to infuriate everyone and confuse the situation.

Hades and Demeter, surprisingly, don't say much at all. From the way they watch the arguments that spring up and get diverted, I expect there will be a secondary meeting with them and perhaps Hera where they discuss their position.

Athena staunchly supports my brother, but she's quick to say it's *Olympus* she's supporting. Not Zeus.

In short, it's a fucking mess.

We adjourn without any sort of a plan or even an agreement. I pause next to my brother. "I understand now."

He gives me a brief smile. "Come around tomorrow and we'll talk."

More back-office meetings. I expect there will be a lot of that going around in the near future, the segments of the Thirteen breaking off to converse with like-minded people. I don't know how we can get them all on the same page. I don't know if it's even possible.

The only other option is for Olympus to risk falling to the enemies we can barely see yet.

I head to my new office. It's only been a few days since I was named Ares, but my crash course in the job has spotlighted how lazy the last Ares was. Nothing is filed properly. His second-in-command thought he could talk over me because of my gender. I fired him, but not before I nearly put his head through a wall when he tried to punch me. It's a mess.

Maybe I'd be more optimistic if I wasn't nursing a broken heart.

Three days, and not a single word from Achilles or Patroclus. Eros returned late that first night to let me know that Patroclus came through surgery just fine and is expected to make a full recovery. He's out of danger, but Achilles still hasn't reached out.

Hard to misinterpret that.

Maybe they meant what they said during the trials. Even if it was true then, their feelings didn't hold up to my ruining their plans. And fuck if that doesn't hurt more every time I think about it.

So I don't think about it.

I have plenty of work to keep me busy. If sometimes I hide in my office and cry when the emotions get too tangled in my chest, I'm only human.

A knock on my door has me biting back a curse. "I swear to the gods, Diomedes, if you're here to bitch about the schedule again, I'm going to fire you, too."

"Rough start to the job?"

I freeze, my gaze pinned on my desk. Surely I'm hallucinating. I *must* be, because there's no way Achilles is here after three days of silence. When I look up, it's going to hurt all over again, and then I'm going to have to do something about this heartache, because I need all my facilities for this job.

But when I look up, he's actually here. More, he's not alone. He looks every inch the golden god he always does while standing behind a wheelchair containing Patroclus. *He* looks good, considering the last time I saw him, he was being rushed to the emergency room. He's paler than normal and there's a bandage peeking out from the collar of his shirt, but he's here and smiling.

They're both here and smiling.

I can't move. I don't have any frame of reference for them to show up like this. Are they here to let me down gently? Or...

"Can we come in?" Patroclus's voice is a little raspy.

"Um. Right. Yes." I start to stand but stop myself. "Shut the door behind you." If this goes bad, the last thing I need is the old Ares's people hearing me be officially dumped. It will undermine my authority even more. Achilles and Patroclus were soldiers beneath the last Ares before they went to Athena. I haven't missed the whispers saying Achilles should have won, that's he's one of them and a known quantity. I'd just resigned myself to having to add my soldiers to the list of motherfuckers I'm going to prove wrong.

Achilles wheels Patroclus into the office and pauses to softly shut the door behind him. I open my mouth but force myself to hold my silence. *They* came to *me*. Achilles pushes Patroclus closer and drops into the empty chair next to him. He sighs. "Sorry it took us so long. The doctor was being stubborn—"

"If by stubborn, you mean doing his job," Patroclus cuts in.

"Yeah. That." Achilles waves the statement away. "How's it being Ares?"

I plant my hands on the desk, mostly to hide the way I'm shaking. "I'm not saying I'm not happy to see you, but I would like to know why you're here. Did you really come all this way to make small talk?"

"Right. That." Achilles gives me a faintly guilty look. "You reached out for reassurance at the end of the last trial, and I kind of brushed you off. I'm sorry about that. It was a lot all at once, and I wasn't thinking clearly. Still, that doesn't excuse leaving you in the wind, and I'm sorry."

An...apology.

Hope flares, so sharp that I flinch. "It's nothing. Forget about it."

Patroclus shakes his head. "It's not nothing, or you wouldn't be looking at us like that." He hesitates. "Unless you've changed your mind about the future we talked about."

The hope inside me gets stronger. I could shut this down and keep from putting myself out there only to be let down devastatingly gently. I can't. If there's even a chance to be with these men, to realize the future they spun out for me, I have to try. I lick my lips. "No. I didn't change my mind about it or about you."

"Thank fuck." Achilles slumps back in his chair. He grins, looking like his old self for the first time since he walked into my office. "We resigned from Athena's leadership. We're free agents right now. Let's make it official." He leans forward. "Make us yours."

"Just like that," I say faintly. This is happening so quickly, it's making my head spin. "I don't understand. You wanted Ares more than anything. You're really going to set aside your ambition just like that?"

"No, of course not." He hesitates, a strange look passing over his face. "When it came right down to it, you wanted Ares more than I did. I faltered. You didn't. You deserved the win, princess. You earned it."

"I..." I swallow hard. "But—"

"But that doesn't mean I'm going to kick back and ride on your coattails for the rest of our lives." Achilles grins. "Sometimes plans change. Make me your second-in-command. We'll kick these fuckers into shape, and I'll make a name for myself helping you keep Olympus safe. Really, it's better this way. Instead of just another Ares, I'll always be Achilles."

There he is. Relief makes me a little weak. I should have known that nothing sets Achilles back on his heels for long. "Ambitious, aren't you?"

"That's not going to change."

Thank the gods.

Patroclus clears his throat. "We...we make a really good team, Helen. I think we'd make an even better one with you involved."

My disappointment is even stronger than my fledgling hope. "A...team."

Achilles nudges Patroclus's shoulder. "You're being too careful. She thinks we're offering a business partnership." His grin widens. "Team in public. True triad in private. Patroclus has to take it easy for a few weeks, but there's no reason we can't tease him a bit in the meantime."

"*Achilles.*" The exasperation in Patroclus's tone is tempered by fondness. He turns back to me. "We want you, Helen. All of you. Will you have us?"

I'm already nodding. "Yes. How is that even a question? *Yes*, I'll have you."

"Good." Achilles pushes to his feet. "Let's get married."

My jaw drops. "*What?*"

"Kidding!" He booms out a laugh but then goes serious. "At least for now. That can come later."

Patroclus and I share a look, and this time, I don't have to decipher the meaning. We're both so hopeful for the future, so happy to have years ahead of us with this man at our sides. I don't know if I believe in happily-ever-afters, but these two men are going to do their damnedest to convince me.

I wouldn't have it any other way.

RADIANT SIN

CASSANDRA

I HATE PARTIES, OLYMPUS, AND POLITICS...BUT NOT NECESsarily in that order. I can avoid two out of the three on good days, but today is promising to be a bad one. It started this morning when I spilled my coffee all over Apollo's shirt. A rookie mistake, and one that might get me fired if my boss was anyone other than *Apollo*. He just gave a small smile, assured me it was his fault when it was clearly mine, and changed into the spare suit he kept in his office.

He should have yelled at me.

I've worked for the man for five years now, and even that isn't enough time to stop expecting the other shoe to drop. He's hardly perfect—he's one of the Thirteen who rule Olympus, after all, and there are no saints among them—but he's the best of the bunch. He's never abused his power over me, never turned his position as my boss into an excuse to be a petty tyrant, has never even raised his voice no matter how thoroughly I've fucked up from time to time.

I shove my hair back, hating that I can feel sweat slicking down my back as I climb the last flight of stairs. Something is wrong with the elevator in Dodona Tower and for reasons that seem suspect, it only goes halfway up the tower. I glare down at the file in my hand. I *should* have just left it alone when I realized Apollo forgot it when he rushed out the door for his meeting with Zeus. He's an adult and is more than capable of dealing with the consequences of forgetting an important file for an important meeting.

But...he didn't yell at me. And so I'm here.

No one who knows me would call me a bleeding heart—more like a cold-hearted bitch—so I have absolutely no reason to have caught a cab to the center of the upper city, taken the elevator halfway up, and then proceeded to climb the rest of the thirty floors on foot.

In six-inch heels, no less.

There's something wrong with me. There must be. Maybe I have a fever.

I press the back of my hand to my forehead, and then feel extra foolish because of *course* I feel overheated. I just did more exercise than I would ever intentionally commit to unless running for my life. And even then, I'd fight before I ran.

I curse myself for the millionth time as I push through the stairwell door and out into the hallway where Zeus's office is located. Then I get a look at my reflection in the massive mirror next to the elevator. "Oh no."

My red hair has gone flat, there's a *sweat stain* darkening the line under my breasts—which means there's an answering one down my spine—and I'm shiny. In a city obsessed with appearances, I can't let anyone see me like this.

"Fuck this, he doesn't need the file that bad." I turn for the elevator...and then remember that to flee, I have to make the return trip down fifteen flights of stairs. My thighs shake at the thought. Or maybe they're shaking from the climb.

Does it count as a workplace accident if I fall down the stairs on an errand I technically wasn't asked to do? Apollo would probably find some way to blame himself and pay for my medical bills, but getting hurt like that means no paycheck and no paycheck means Alexandra might not have the money she needs to buy books or school supplies or all the other random shit being at university requires. I can't risk an injury, even if it means I'm humiliated in the process.

"Cassandra?"

I curse myself yet again and turn to face the gorgeous white woman with light brown hair walking down the hallway. Ares is her name now, but it used to be Helen Kasios. I wouldn't call us friends, but I've attended the parties she used to throw from time to time before she became one of the Thirteen. It always felt a bit like watching animals in a zoo as I witnessed the powerful people from Olympus's legacy families poke and snap at each other. I've learned a lot from playing the sidelines; nearly enough to protect me and my sister from the circling wolves.

Helen isn't too bad, honestly. She's never cruel when kindness will further her goals, and she's perfected a glittery exterior that everyone seems to think means she's empty-headed, but I've always interpreted as a warning not to get too close. No one surfs the political currents as adeptly as she does if they're not smarter than most of the people in the room.

But that was before she became Ares. Now I can't take

anything for granted when it comes to her. We aren't on the same level—two women from legacy families, even if mine is disgraced and hers rules Olympus. She's one of them, now, and I'm still me.

"Helen." I strive to keep my tone even, but her name still comes out too sharp. "What are you doing here?"

"Meeting with my lovely brother." She shrugs. She's built slim the way her mother was, though there's clear muscle definition in the arms left bare by her black sheath dress. She looks cool and professional and untouchable.

I feel grimy standing next to her. I haven't wanted a thin body in over a decade—I love my curves out of sheer defiance of everyone who acts like they should be part of a *before* picture—but it's hard not to compare us when we stand like this.

She gives me a long look. "Apollo's in with him now. I don't think he knew you were coming or he would have waited for you."

Without a doubt. Apollo is courteous like that. When I first met him, I thought it was an act, but he's never once faltered in five years. Even as jaded as I am, I have to admit it's just who he is. Either that or he's a better liar than anyone else in Olympus, a city filled to the brim with liars and cheats.

There's no getting out of this. I'm here. I might as well see it through. I hold up the file between us like a shield. "He forgot this."

"Ah." She glances back down the hallway. "Well, I'll walk you there."

"That's really not necessary."

"It really is." She spins on a heel and faces the same direction as me. "With things in a bit of upheaval right now, the security is ramped up. Honestly, I'm not sure how you got up here at all. My people are supposed to have the upper floors locked down."

Ah. That explains the elevator "malfunction" and why the guy downstairs was such an asshole. I shrug a single shoulder. "I'm persuasive."

"More like you're terrifying." She laughs, a sound so happy it makes my chest pang in envy. I don't want what Ares has—the title, the power, the responsibility—but it must be nice to be so comfortable in how she moves through the world, sure that it will bend to her impressive will.

I have to take stronger measures.

"Your people are specially trained," I snap. "If they can't take me, that sounds like a *you* problem."

"Absolutely." She agrees so damn easily. "By the way, is Orpheus still bothering you?"

Mention of Apollo's brother makes me frown. What does Orpheus have to do with anything? It takes several steps for understanding to settle over me. She's talking about that single party where he was being an arrogant little prick, but that was months ago. I'm honestly surprised she remembered at all. "I can handle Orpheus." He might be bigger than me, but he's brittle. I could break him without lifting a finger.

"If you're sure...I know it's a touchy subject because he's Apollo's little brother."

I snort. I can't help it. "Apollo has more or less washed his hands of Orpheus." As much as Apollo can wash his hands of anyone in his family. What it really translates to is that he's stopped smoothing over Orpheus's messes and cut off his money.

With how their mother babies the spoiled brat, it never would have worked if Apollo wasn't, well, Apollo. "When he shapes up, he can play prodigal son and get all the attention he's deprived of right now. He has bigger things to worry about than chasing some woman who doesn't want him."

"If that ever changes, don't hesitate to call me."

"Sure," I lie. I know better than to trust anyone in this gods forsaken city. Ares might be better than most, but that doesn't change that she's part of this place. When push comes to shove, she will look out for herself and her interests before helping someone else. Expecting anything else is like expecting a fish to sprout wings and fly. "I'll do that."

"No, you won't." Ares smiles. "But the offer still stands. Here we are." She stops in front of a large dark door with Zeus's name stamped in gold on it. The current Zeus is Ares's brother. The last one was her father. I'd rather chew off my own arm than deal with either of the men who have held the title during my lifetime, but I'm here. It's too late to go back now.

I do my best not to hold my breath—not with Ares watching— and knock.

Apollo's the one who opens it, and I refuse to hold my breath at the sight of him, either. I hate looking at Apollo. He's too fucking perfect, a product of his Swedish father and his Korean model of a mother. Tall, broad shoulders, perfectly trimmed black hair and kind dark eyes. It's the latter that always hits me like a blow to the chest.

I should have quit a long time ago.

Better to work in an office job I loathe than to have…feelings…

about my boss. Even if the feelings in question are something as simple as lust. It complicates things, though I'd throw myself out the window before I let him know.

Which I why my instincts kick in and I shove the file at him. "You forgot this." My voice is too sharp, too bitchy. He didn't ask me to do this, but I'm embarrassed and it's so much easier to snarl and snap than admit it. "I'm not your errand girl, and now I'm in overtime for the week."

Apollo raises a single dark brow. "You didn't have to come all this way, Cassandra. I could have done without."

Without a doubt. He's capable on a truly terrifying level and has nearly perfect recall of anything he's ever read. He would have been fine relaying the contents of the file without having it on hand. He probably only put it together to hand it off to Zeus at the end of the meeting.

But he was nice to me this morning.

I am a *fool*.

"You're welcome." I turn on my heel. "See you tomorrow."

"Cassandra."

I ignore him and keep going. If security is the reason the elevators won't go above floor fifteen, then I bet they'll descend from here. They're keeping people out, not in. My exit won't be marred by having to take a breather on the stairwell and praying to gods I don't believe exist that no one stumbles on me. My pride won't be able to handle it.

"Cassandra." He's closer. Damn it, I should have known he wouldn't let this go.

I sigh and stop. It's beneath both our dignity to have him chase me down the hall in front of Helen. Apollo stops next to me, his longer legs having covered the distance easily. He pauses. "Thank you for bringing this. If you'll hold on for a few minutes, I'm just wrapping up. I'll give you a ride home."

The temptation to say yes nearly makes my knees buckle. I've shared enough rides with him over the years on the way from one meeting to another. I know exactly how it will go. He'll slump back against the seat and loosen his perfect black tie. Not a lot. Just enough to drive me to distraction. Then he'll pull out his phone and leave me to my thoughts.

Apollo never prattles on the way some people do. He's not one of those strong silent types, but he doesn't feel the need to fill quiet moments with inane chatter. The car ride will be comfortable and lovely and I absolutely cannot say yes to it. It's one thing to have those moments during the work day when I can excuse them. After hours?

No. Absolutely not.

"I'm fine."

He searches my face like he knows I'm being stubborn for the sake of being stubborn, but Apollo is a man who respects boundaries and so he just nods. "Keep the cab fare receipt and expense it."

I hate how weak I get at the simple thoughtfulness he continually demonstrates. Apollo is too savvy not to know how tight money is for me—his entire job is information, after all—and he also knows me well enough to know I won't take charity. Not from him. Not from anyone. Not when it's never really charity and always comes with strings attached.

But a business expense?

My pride can handle that.

"Fine."

"See you tomorrow, Cassandra." Maybe I'm imagining the warmth lingering in his tone as I turn away and march to the elevators. I must be. I am no slouch in the looks department, but I've seen the people who populate Zeus's parties. They might not all be on Helen's level, but they're closer to hers than mine. Apollo's mother is a *model*, and both Apollo and Orpheus really got her looks. Orpheus might be the only one who plays them up, but I've seen Apollo literally leave a wake of people staring after him when we walked down the sidewalk. Not that he noticed.

No, this unfortunate attraction is one-sided and that's just fine with me.

It's only a matter of time before I get out of this cursed city once and for all. The last thing I need is to get entangled with one of the Thirteen—*another* one of the Thirteen—before I do.

ACKNOWLEDGMENTS

This series wouldn't have gotten off the ground without the support of so many people. First and foremost, always thank you to my readers. Thank you for rolling with my chaos and trusting me to play fast and loose with your favorite Greek myths. Thank you to all the indie bookstore sellers, reviewers, influencers, and readers who have shoved this series into people's hands and championed it from the beginning.

All my gratitude to Mary Altman for telling me yes when I randomly sent an email that was like "Hey, I know we planned on Achilles and Helen for this one, but I'd like Patroclus to be in there, too." I couldn't ask for a better editor willing to roll with my personal brand of chaos and give me enough leeway to make the magic happen. This book is a thousand times better because of your support and input.

Much thanks to Christa Désir for telling me the thing I didn't want to hear but desperately needed to hear. Thank you for helping me find the plot and pull it out so this wasn't just three people being angsty and talking in circles.

Endless appreciation to Stefani Sloma for holding my hand through promo and marketing. This series has legs because of your support and enthusiasm, and I couldn't ask for a better publicist!

Thanks to the rest of the Sourcebooks team, including Jessica Smith, Dawn Adams, Rachel Gilmer, Jocelyn Travis, Katie Stutz, and Susie Benton.

Big thanks to Piper J. Drake, Asa Maria Bradley, Jenny Nordbak, Nisha Sharma, and Andie J. Christopher for being there through the ups and downs and hard right turns. Big thanks to K Sterling, Reese Ryan, Fortune Whelan, Ali Williams, Amanda Cinelli, and Brina Starler for keeping me company during early morning writing sprints.

Last, but never least, thank you to Tim. Yeah, I know you were skimming looking for your name. Thank you for being my biggest cheerleader, the kick in the ass when I need it, and never hesitating to remind me that you're proud of me. Love you!

ABOUT THE AUTHOR

Katee Robert is a *New York Times* and *USA Today* bestselling author of contemporary romance and romantic suspense. *Entertainment Weekly* calls her writing "unspeakably hot." Her books have sold over a million copies. She lives in the Pacific Northwest with her husband, children, a cat who thinks he's a dog, and two Great Danes who think they're lap dogs. You can visit her at kateerobert.com or on Twitter @katee_robert.

ALSO BY
KATEE ROBERT

Dark Olympus
Neon Gods
Electric Idol